Advance Praise for *Race to Judgment*

"Reads with the pace of a whip crack. Judge Block knows this world cold. Take the plunge."

—**David Baldacci**, *#1 New York Times* best-selling author

"With heroes and villains as boldly drawn as the tabloid headlines, *Race to Judgment* provides a thrill ride through the bad not-so-old days of the Brooklyn justice system. This first novel by Judge Frederic Block brings a federal jurist's keen eye to detail as the story powers through grimy holding cells, law offices where the real deal goes down, and courtrooms both ornate and gritty."

—**Ron Kuby**, criminal defense and civil rights lawyer

"An impactful crime drama. And the music is a joy. Hearing Judge Block sing his songs had me smiling all the way through!"

—**James Barbour**, Broadway star, *The Phantom of the Opera*

"Block's *Race to Judgment* is the inside skinny on the justice system from a man who lives it every day, but it's the story that shines. Read and enjoy."

—**Reed Farrel Coleman**, *New York Times* best-selling author of *What You Break*

"Only an author with a finely tuned sense of drama and an exhaustive knowledge of the legal system could have written this brilliant crime novel. Judge Frederic Block is that man."

—**Daniel Klein**, *New York Times* best-selling author of *Travels with Epicurus* and *Plato and a Platypus Walk into a Bar* (coauthored with Thomas Cathcart)

"*Race to Judgment* is a riveting thriller about truth and justice from a courtroom pro who has viewed the bench from both sides. Block's narrative is taut and compelling, and a wonderful addition to the crime genre."

—**Linda Fairstein**, *New York Times* best-selling author

"Judge Block's *Race to Judgment* is a gripping page-turner with the added virtue of realism, thanks to the author's decades of experience as a lawyer and federal judge. I devoured it in a weekend, and I suspect you will do the same."

—**David Lat**, founder of AboveTheLaw.com and author of *Supreme Ambitions*

"In his courtroom in Brooklyn, Judge Block has seen it all. It's those experiences that shape this book, a fascinating kind of companion novel to his memoir *Disrobed*."

—**Ryan Holiday,** best-selling author of *The Obstacle Is the Way* and *Trust Me, I'm Lying*

Race
to
Judgment

Race
to
Judgment

Frederic Block

SelectBooks, Inc.
New York

This edition published by SelectBooks, Inc.
For information address SelectBooks, Inc., New York, New York.

First Edition

ISBN 978-1-59079-438-8

Library of Congress Cataloging-in-Publication Data

Names: Block, Frederic, 1934- author.
Title: Race to judgment / Judge Frederic Block.
Description: First edition. | New York : SelectBooks, Inc., [2017]
Identifiers: LCCN 2017012067 | ISBN 9781590794388 (hardcover : acid-free paper)
Subjects: LCSH: African American lawyers--Fiction. | Public prosecutors--Fiction. | GSAFD: Legal stories.
Classification: LCC PS3602.L6427 R33 2017 | DDC 813/.6--dc23 LC record available at https://lccn.loc.gov/2017012067

Book design by Janice Benight

Manufactured in the United States of America
10 9 8 7 6 5 4 3 2 1

Dedicated to the memory of Ken Thompson

OTHER WORKS BY THIS AUTHOR

*Disrobed: An Inside Look at the Life and Work
of a Federal Trial Judge*
(2012)

Coauthor of the musical *Professionally Speaking*
(music and lyrics)
(1985)

PREFACE

The idea for this novel came to me while I was reading some historical fiction a few years ago. Two works in particular captured my interest: Robert Harris's *An Officer and a Spy* and Ken Follett's *Fall of Giants,* the first of his Century Trilogy. I was intrigued by how the authors based their novels on true events but took literary license with the characters and events to create great stories. A friend of mine suggested that I might think about using a similar format based upon real cases I have handled over the years as a federal trial judge, and events that flowed from them. I was taken by the idea and started to believe that I had a good story to tell by taking literary license with these real-life experiences to develop the plot lines of my novel. I call it reality-fiction.

Thus, the storyline flows from my Crown Heights race riot case in the 1990s; the trial of Lemrick Nelson for stabbing Yankel Rosenbaum to death during the riots; the trial of an African-American, law-abiding twenty-two-year-old young man who was charged with murdering a sixteen-year-old boy six years after the murder; the case of Jabbar Collins, who spent sixteen years in jail on a trumped-up charge of the murder of a Hasidic rabbi before he was exonerated and set free; and the recent defeat of the Irish Brooklyn District Attorney by an African American who campaigned in large part against what he believed was a corrupt DA's office because in addition to the Collins conviction, the former DA's office had obtained a startling number of other unlawful convictions against other blacks.

In the epilogue I explain what is reality and what is fiction. But resist the temptation to look at it now, since it might spoil what I think is a good read.

A Note to the Reader
About the Music in *Race to Judgment*

The protagonist in this book has a hobby as a jazz pianist and a song-writer. Eight of his songs are scattered throughout the book, inspired by events and comments by some of the characters. He has a particular love for country music that "tells a good story," and six of the songs are "good, old-fashioned country songs." The others are a tear-jerker, wedding love song and a whoop-it-up party song.

The musical charts for the songs are in the songbook at the end of the book. But if you are curious and want to hear them sung by the characters in the book, there is an album of music that accompanies this novel titled *Race to Judgment* by Frederic Block containing all original music composed by the author. The album is available for download or streaming on all digital music services worldwide and at the author's website, www.fredericblock.com.

"Good Instead of Bad"
"Look What She's Costing Me Now"
"Lonesome Together with You"
"Everybody Wants to Go to Heaven"
"Like Father Like Son"
"High and Dry"
"How I'll Always Love You"
"Se Agapame"

Three of the songs, "Good Instead of Bad," "How I'll Always Love You," and "Se Agapame" are sung by the author/composer.

1

Ken didn't arrive home from his gig at Arturo's until well past midnight when he received the phone call that would forever change his life.

"Who in God's name is waking me up at this hour?" he grumbled as he picked up the phone at the side of his bed.

"Is this Mr. Williams?" came the frightened voice.

He felt foolish.

"I'm sorry. It was a long day. Who's been arrested?"

"How do you know that?"

"No one calls me at this hour to wish me happy birthday."

She started to cry. He backed off.

"Alright. What precinct is he at?"

"They took him to the 70th."

"They'll keep him overnight. He'll be arraigned in the criminal courts building tomorrow morning. I'll arrange to have someone meet you there."

"Mr. Williams, I'm sitting in the waiting room of the precinct right now. My husband has been arrested for murder."

"What's his name?"

"Troy. Troy Jackson."

"I'll be right there."

As soon as he jumped out of bed, he called the precinct.

"Sergeant Markham here."

"This is Ken Williams. You got a Troy Jackson there. I'm recording this call. He's not to be questioned. Play it straight. Mug shots and prints—and nothing else."

"Fuck you, Williams."

"Watch your language, Markham, or you'll be on night desk duty for the rest of your life. I'm coming right down."

Ken hated the 70th. It's where wacko cops had shoved a broomstick up Abner Louima's ass. The 1997 case had become a national symbol of police brutality and reinforced beliefs that New York City police officers were harassing and abusing young black men as part of a city-wide crackdown on crime.

Ken was in his last year at New York University Law School when it happened. It outraged him, but in a way, as shocking as it was, it didn't surprise him. He was one of the lucky ones who had escaped from the projects unscathed, but he had seen the cops rough up a lot of kids there. He swore that one day he would do something about it.

He donned a pair of black trousers and a gray turtleneck. No need to wear his lawyer uniform. He was not going to court. He quickly brushed his teeth, tossed some water on his face, and ran his fingers through his short-cropped hair.

He liked what he saw in the mirror.

"Not bad for a guy a little over forty," he mumbled. "Not exactly Denzel Washington, but close. A little gray at the temples. Makes me look distinguished."

It was cold. He grabbed his three-quarter-length black leather jacket. In minutes he was parking his yellow MINI Cooper in front of the precinct. Trish Jackson was waiting. Her head was buried in trembling hands as she sat in the gray metal chair nearest the entrance. But her petite good looks and well-cropped Afro stood out. So did the bulge in her belly.

"How much longer do you have?" Ken asked.

She slowly lifted her head before she answered.

"About three months. What is going to happen to my husband?"

"We'll talk later. Try to compose yourself, if you can. Let me try to find him."

❦

Sergeant Markham was sitting behind the glass wall. He glared at Ken.

"You can't see him yet, big shot. They haven't finished with the intake."

"Don't jerk me around, Markham. You don't need any more problems."

Ken knew that Markham was up on charges for beating up a black kid whom he had stopped and frisked for no legitimate reason.

The cop begrudgingly got up from behind his desk and led Ken into a small room with a few metal chairs around a metal table. Within minutes, the door opened and a scared-looking, well-built, tall young man with curly black hair was led in by two shorter burly police officers.

"You've got ten minutes," the taller one said.

"Leave us alone, Hurley."

They sat across the table from each other. As soon as the officers left, the frightened young man sobbed.

"Mr. Williams, please get me out of here. They tell me I've been arrested for murder. It can't be. It can't be—It just can't be!"

"Try to stay calm, Troy. We'll get to the bottom of this soon enough. Right now, try to get some sleep. I told them not to ask you any questions. Don't talk to anyone. You'll be arraigned tomorrow morning. I'll see you there. You'll say 'not guilty' when the judge asks you how you plead. Not another word."

"Will I be able to go home?"

"No. I'll ask for a bail hearing, which probably won't happen for a day or two, but the chances of getting bail are zero. I've never seen it granted yet for a black dude charged with murder. Nonetheless, it will give me an opportunity to put some wheels in motion. They'll send you to Rikers. Be careful who you talk to there. Don't say anything to anyone about what's happened. I'll get there tomorrow afternoon."

"I can't believe this is happening to me, Mr. Williams."

"I know it's terrible, Troy, but for the sake of Trish and your soon-to-be new baby you've got to hang in and tough it out. I'll get my investigator on it as soon as I can, and we'll find out what's going on."

"I remember when you came to my school and spoke at the assembly, Mr. Williams. The kids idolized you. I know your reputation for taking on the police in racially tense situations. And I know from the press that you are representing a brother who's been sitting in jail sixteen years after he was convicted on what you claim was a trumped-up phony charge by the Brooklyn DA."

"Do you have any idea why this has happened to you?" asked Ken. "None."

❧

Ken drove Trish home. Her hands were still trembling as she fastened her seat belt.

"We live at 293 Hooper Street in Williamsburg," she told him, her eyes still brimming with tears. His GPS took him there in about ten minutes. He wondered how they were able to afford the new condo in that happening part of town. After they had driven for a few minutes, Ken broke the silence.

"Trish, we don't have to talk tonight if you're not up to it. Come to court for the arraignment tomorrow morning. We'll be able to talk more then."

"Will I be able to talk to Troy?"

"No, but I'm sure he would like to see you there. They'll be taking him to Rikers Island after. I'll make sure you can visit him the next day."

As tears trickled down her cheeks, she haltingly told Ken what had happened that night.

"We moved here just last summer and were planning to spend our first Christmas in our new home this month. We both teach.

I teach science at Corpus Christi Junior High. Ken is a high school guidance counselor for troubled African-American kids at Bushwick. We were able to get a jumbo mortgage. It was our dream come true. We were sound asleep. It was a school night. We had to be up by 7:00. Suddenly, there was loud knocking on the front door and a shout I'll never forget: 'Open up! Police!' We jumped out of bed. I had my nightgown on. Troy was sleeping in boxer shorts. We ran through the living room into the hallway, looked through the peephole, and saw the heads and torsos of four policemen. They threatened to break the door down if we didn't open it right away."

"I'm sure they didn't have to break in," said Ken.

"I hid behind my husband as he unbolted the latch and started to slowly open the door. The first officer shoved it hard. We almost fell. I wrapped my arms around Troy's waist and screamed. The police all jumped in. Two of them jerked Troy loose from me, grabbed his arms, and pulled them behind his back. One of them put handcuffs on Troy. The third one stood at the entrance with his gun drawn and asked the officer who had cuffed Troy if they were sure they had the right guy."

"What exactly did the guy with the gun say?"

"'Are you sure this isn't one big fuckup, Sarge? This whole thing just doesn't seem to add up. Nice apartment, good-looking, clean-cut couple, a pregnant wife. I don't get it.'"

"Well, Trish, obviously it didn't stop them from arresting Troy."

"No. They told us he was being arrested for murder and read Troy his rights. They wouldn't give us any more information. Troy said there must be a terrible mistake. My knees just crumbled as I tried to hang onto him. I thought I was going to faint and I started to cry. The police officer who had handcuffed Troy said I looked like I was in shock. He grabbed a chair and had me sit. He got a glass of water from the kitchen and made me drink it. I couldn't understand why they did this in the middle of the night."

"They knew what they were doing, Trish. If they arrested him during the day they would have to arraign him right away. At night, they can keep him until the morning. He's tired and more vulnerable to questioning. Most confessions happen under those circumstances, but don't worry, I told the police not to question him and I told Troy not to talk—to them or anybody. What happened next?"

"Somehow I got myself together. The officer who gave me the water walked me into our bedroom, and I got Troy a clean white shirt, a light gray sweater, and charcoal pants. And I took out his black leather dress boots and a smart-looking leather winter jacket. I didn't want my husband to look like a criminal."

"What about you?" Ken asked.

"I was only thinking about Troy and never thought about getting dressed. I didn't even realize I was still walking around in a flimsy, pink nightgown. Troy was still in the hallway when I got back. They took the handcuffs off him so he could get dressed. After he put on his clothes they put the handcuffs on him again. They pushed Troy toward the door and told me they were taking him to the 70th Precinct. Troy tried to turn and yelled over his shoulder, 'Call Ken Williams and tell him to come get me!'"

"I'm glad you did, Trish. I can appreciate how traumatic all this must be."

As her tears started again, she cried out. "Mr. Williams, our dream has turned into a nightmare."

Ken parked his car in front of the No Parking sign at the glass entrance to the building and walked Trish to the lobby.

"I can get my fiancée to stay with you tonight," he said.

"Thank you, but I think I can manage. I'll call my mother. She lives near here. She'll come and stay with me. Anyway, if you leave that car there you'll get a ticket."

"Won't be the first time, Trish."

She smiled, and her hands finally stopped trembling.

Seconds after Ken left, Trish was on the phone.

"Why are you sobbing, my baby?"

"Mama, Troy's been arrested for murder."

"Lord Jesus," her mother said. "What did he do? Where is he?"

"Nothing, Mama. He's in jail like an animal."

"I'll be right there, dear."

2

Ken was only able to get a few hours of sleep. Before he left for court in the morning, he made two phone calls. The first was to Betsy.

"How's my favorite prosecutor doing?"

"Working like a dog. Had to prep witnesses for the big trial next week."

"That's the price you gotta pay, baby, if you want to try cases for that lousy DA. I wish you'd quit and come work with me. I'm getting a ton of new business lately, and I could use more help."

"Someday, Ken, but not right now. Since I'm no longer in General Crimes, soon they are going to have me trying real heavy-duty felony cases. I want that, Ken. I'll be getting great experience. A couple more years as an ADA in Brooklyn and I'll be ready to join you— as long as the letterhead reads Brown and Williams."

He laughed. "Maybe by that time it might even be Williams and Williams. Gotta run. Can't talk longer. Got an arraignment to handle on a new case. See you tonight. Remember, it's Queen's night out. Love you."

The other call was to his investigator.

"Get your ass down to the arraignment part, Mickey. We got work to do."

❧

The massive Criminal Courts building swooped over downtown Brooklyn like a giant vulture. Perched on the southwest corner of Adams and Schermerhorn Streets, it had seen better days. In 2012 it was the last of the great Renaissance Revival edifices in the borough, but now—almost one hundred years old—its once luminous granite base and limestone clad exterior walls had turned a sullen gray. Pigeons were lined up like toy soldiers at the tops of its ten Corinthian columns. The early morning lines of people waiting to pass through the ominous triple-arched entryway and the metal detectors inside often snaked around the corner. They were helpless targets for the birds' droppings.

Although lawyers did not have to wait in the long lines, once inside Ken would be stuffed into one of the antiquated, cramped, and smelly elevators. Since he suffered from a touch of claustrophobia, he frequently climbed the six floors to courtroom AP1. He decided to do this on the day of Troy's arraignment.

Once out of the stairwell, Ken had to weave his way through the packed corridor leading to the courtroom past the old wooden benches along the walls. He was always amused by the range of carvings embedded in them—from every initial to all sorts of "I love you's." As he approached the courtroom, he wondered why the janitors had still not sanded off the "fuck you" carving on the top of the bench next to its entrance.

Inside the courtroom Ken spotted Trish sitting in the last of the seven wooden rows of public benches. A well-groomed and slender gray-haired woman was sitting next to her. They both stood as Ken came toward them. Trish was quick to introduce her.

"Mr. Williams, this is my mother."

"Glad to meet you, ma'am," Ken said softly. "Trish certainly needs your support. Troy will be coming into the courtroom soon. He'll be with other detainees, and they'll be seated in the jurors' box just to the right side of the judge's bench. We won't be here long. While Trish can't speak to Troy now, when I'm at Rikers this afternoon I'll arrange for her to visit him tomorrow morning. I'm glad you both came. Troy needs to know his family will be there with him all the way, especially his wife."

It was as Ken said it would be. After about fifteen minutes, the prisoners were brought into the courtroom and placed in the front row of the jury box. There were seven of them. Troy was in the second seat. He immediately spotted Trish and his mother-in-law and meekly waved. He looked as if he hadn't slept, but he stood out from the others. The clothes that Trish had insisted he change into before the police took him away were a little wrinkled, but he looked well-dressed compared to the other prisoners. He didn't look like he belonged in their company.

Soon there was a knocking on the other side of a door next to the judge's bench and the familiar cry "Oyez! Oyez! Oyez! All Rise!" rang through the courtroom as the door opened and the bailiff and judge entered. Ken recognized Judge Archibald Spatt. He was new to the bench, and as a rookie judge had been assigned for six months to the mundane job of handling *pro forma* criminal complaint arraignments. He would not be the trial judge.

When the bailiff shouted, "People of the State of New York versus LaTroy Jackson," Troy was taken from his seat by a court officer and brought in front of Judge Spatt. Seeing how well-dressed he looked, the judge was surprised to read that he was being charged with murder. He then handed the criminal complaint to Ken.

Ken couldn't believe what he read.

"Troy, according to this, you killed someone named Menachem Mendel Bernstein seven years ago on Chess Street."

"It's crazy, Mr. Williams. I was only seventeen then, and I haven't lived on that street since I was fourteen. I've never even heard of a Menachem Mendel Bernstein."

"Do you wish to have the charges publicly read, Mr. Williams?" asked Judge Spatt.

"That won't be necessary," said Ken.

"How does your client plead?"

"Not guilty," shouted Troy.

Although his lawyer had told him not to say anything else, Troy Jackson could not contain himself: "I'm innocent," he screamed. "Why is this happening?"

"Calm yourself," answered the startled judge.

"I don't mean to be disrespectful, Your Honor, but I have a pregnant wife and a full schedule of kids back at school waiting to see their guidance counselor today. If they find out I'm locked up in jail, all the work I've put in to keep them off the streets and winding up in Rikers will be a complete waste. Please let me go home. I promise I'll be back here whenever I'm needed."

Although he was new to the bench, Judge Spatt had quickly developed a reputation for being a strong but sensitive and caring jurist. He took his owlish glasses off his benign, rotund face, placed them down, leaned forward, and spoke softly:

"Young man, I know nothing about your case. You may well be innocent and this may all be a travesty. But given the fact that you are charged with murder, and if convicted could be sentenced to jail for the rest of your life, I just can't let you go now. However, you have an excellent lawyer, and he knows what to do to properly represent you."

Judge Spatt then turned to Ken. "Mr. Williams, do you have an application?"

"Yes, Your Honor, I would like the case to be set down promptly for a bail hearing."

"How about two days from now?" asked the judge.

"Fine, Your Honor," answered Ken. "One more thing. My client intends to testify before the grand jury."

Ken knew the rules. In the absence of a waiver, the DA had five days after an arrest to hand up an indictment. This would require his office to present its case to a grand jury; only it had the power to indict. If it did not happen by that time, the accused had to be let out of jail; however, the charges would not be dismissed unless an indictment was not rendered within 180 days from the date of the arrest. The grand jurors were drawn from the same random pool as regular jurors, and twenty-three was empaneled to sit for a month. Rarely did they all show up every day. Only a majority of twelve was needed to indict.

There was an ongoing debate in the criminal justice community about the value of the grand jury. It was a one-way street. The assistant district attorney handling the case before the grand jury was the only lawyer involved, and all the ADA had to do was present enough evidence to convince the grand jurors that there was probable cause to warrant an indictment. It was not a trial. The defendant's lawyer was not allowed to participate or cross-examine the witnesses. And, with one exception, the defense attorney was not even allowed to be present. The exception was that the defendant had a right to testify, and his lawyer could sit next to him and listen—that was all. He could not ask his client any questions or present any evidence on his behalf. In fact, he could not talk at all. The common saying among defense lawyers was that "the DA could get a grand jury to indict a ham sandwich."

When an indictment did not occur, it was usually when the defendant did choose to testify. But it was the extraordinary case when a lawyer would allow his client to do that. Testifying was fraught with peril. The ADA could cross-examine the defendant, attack his credibility, and bring out any prior convictions. And if the defendant chose to testify at the trial, his grand jury testimony could be used against him. Since many defendants have checkered pasts, going before the grand jury could only make matters worse, and a good criminal defense lawyer would rarely let his client "be fed to the wolves."

Nonetheless, a good attorney would want to keep his options open and would routinely give notice that his client wished to testify. This is exactly what Ken had done when he appeared before Judge Spatt. The ADA was now required to fix a date and time for Troy to "put up or shut up." Unless the prosecutor obtained an extension from the judge, this had to happen before the five-day period ended. Ken would then have to decide whether he would really permit Troy to testify.

As soon as Ken told Judge Spatt that his client would go before the grand jury, the ADA snapped: "The day after the bail hearing at 2:00 p.m."

The ball was now in Ken's court.

As Troy was being taken out of the courtroom by the court officers, Ken spotted Mickey sitting close to Trish.

"Trish, you go home with your mom. I'll catch up with you after I see Troy at Rikers. Mickey, let's grab some lunch at Junior's after I swing by the office, and we'll talk this over before I go."

"You're the boss," said Mickey.

❧

Ken loved Mickey Zissou, although he was a little rough around the edges. He was a certifiable character, but a crackerjack "private eye." Mickey had a knack for gaining the trust of lots of bad folks; he looked and spoke like he could be one of them. Mickey's mother was a dark-skinned beauty from Jamaica. She came to the U.S. on a work visa when she was nineteen and landed a job as a waitress at a Greek diner in Brooklyn Heights. Mickey's father owned the place and, even though Greek men usually do not marry outside their own kind—let alone a black woman—he was smitten by her.

Mickey's dad, Costantino Zissou, didn't exactly look like Apollo. He was short and fat with black curly hair and a scrunched-up face. But he was rich and charming, and Mickey's mother was poor and desperate. She liked Costantino in spite of his funny looks. She often told him that if they got married, they would have great kids. "They could have my great looks and your great brains," she would say. And he would tease: "What if they had my looks and your brains?"

"I was the second born," Mickey would explain. "They gave me a Greek name, Mikali, but I wanted an American name so I said I was

Mickey. My younger sister came out tall, fair, and good-looking, but a little on the dumb side. I came out short, dark, and ugly, but smart."

Mickey was raised in Astoria's large Greek community across the Queens Midtown Bridge from Manhattan. College was not his thing, and he dropped out after two years. Costantino Zissou was disappointed when his son told him that "the restaurant business is not my thing either." Mikali wanted more action in the real world and because of his natural smarts got a job as an investigator for the New York City Housing Department. It didn't pay much, but he liked the work. He made some good contacts, and soon he was picking up some PI jobs on the side for a few criminal defense lawyers.

Mickey decided to live in the crime-infested Armstrong low-income housing project on Clifton Place in the middle of Bed-Stuy. It was cheap and, more importantly, he got to blend in with the druggies and gangs, which would prove to be invaluable for his burgeoning clientele. After a few years with the Housing Department, he had enough new business to become a full-time criminal investigator. As part of his networking, he had joined the Chisholm Democratic Club where he met Ken. They hit it off immediately. Soon Mickey Zissou became Ken Williams' chief investigator.

It was a twenty-minute walk down Fulton Street—a few blocks from the Criminal Courts building—to Ken's law office on Flatbush Avenue. In the early '80s that seven-block stretch of Fulton was transformed into a pedestrian mall. Over the years, the Fulton Mall became a shopping mecca for downtown Brooklyn. It was home to more than 230 stores. As Ken and Mickey walked down the mall, it was apparent that the retail catered to African Americans. It was representative of the demographic changes sweeping through Brooklyn's roughly 2.75 million population—the largest of New York City's five boroughs. In fact, recent statistics revealed that Brooklyn's Caucasian population had dipped below fifty percent; "white" was the new minority. Ken Williams believed that Brooklyn's extraordinary diversity—African Americans, Hispanics, Jews,

Italians, Russians, Chinese, Arabs, and just about every other ethnic stripe—was truly reflective of the dynamic melting pot that helped make Brooklyn great.

In the middle of the first block, Mickey stopped and stared at the large Lane Bryant billboard draping the building across the street.

"Hey, Ken, look at that bitch's big ass in that bikini. She's fire. What a difference between a black woman and those scrawny Victoria's Secret white girls. Maybe I'll luck out and find me one like her."

"You're going to have to find one that's a lot shorter," quipped Ken, "let alone one that doesn't mind hanging with an ugly dude like you."

"Go fuck yourself, big shot. Just because you've got a hottie doesn't mean I can't have one, too."

As they walked along Fulton Street, Mickey stopped in front of Spike's Tattoo. A short, thin white guy who didn't look old enough to buy booze was standing outside. The mosaic of multicolored tattoos rimming his neck and cascading down each arm looked like a work of modern art that belonged in the new Whitney Museum in the Meatpacking District in Manhattan.

"Hey, Mickey, how's that evil eye I did for you last month?" Spike asked. "Bet you're getting lots of looks. Why don't you do one on the other arm? I'll give you a discount."

"You charged me too fucking much, Spike. I could have gotten it cheaper down the street."

"Yeah, but it wouldn't be as good as the one by the master. Just ask your buddy. How cool does that look?" he asked, looking at Ken.

Spike was right. Ken had been impressed when Mickey first showed it to him the week before. It covered his whole left upper arm, from the shoulder to the elbow. You could tell it was meant to be an eye. There was a black dot in the middle surrounded by a small yellow circle and then a larger light blue one. A circular strip of white rimmed it. Dangling from the eye was a brown twisted rope holding a dazzling array of multi-colored beads. The last one, which touched the tip of Mickey's elbow, was a tiny teardrop replica of the big eye.

"What do you think, Ken?" Mickey asked. "Should I do another one on the other arm? It's kind of cool. The evil eye is called a *matiasma* in Greek. Every Greek household has one to ward off the evil spirits. And in my business there's lots of them around all the time."

"Well, for you it serves a double purpose, Mickey," was Ken's response. "It sure is fitting for a private eye, but I think one's enough."

Mickey told Spike he would think about it. The lawyer and his favorite investigator crossed Duffield Street, also called Abolitionist Place, dating back to the days of the Civil War. Mickey stopped by an outdoor blackboard on the sidewalk in the middle of the street. It was leaning up against the entrance to a two-story walk-up. He gazed at the chalk hand-written message scratched on it: "Dentist Upstairs (718) 555-3200 The Best Down Town."

"I can't believe I let that quack pull my rotten molar," Mickey mumbled. "It hurt like hell. The guy should be in jail."

Ken didn't hesitate to respond. "If you weren't such a cheap son-of-a-bitch you would have gone to a real dentist."

Finally they reached Albee Square, where Fulton Street turned into DeKalb Avenue. They stopped and stared at the gleaming mammoth white stone granite building looming ahead of them. A replica of an alien culture of a bygone era with different aesthetic values, it would not look out of place if it sat next to the Acropolis or the Roman Colosseum.

"Look at that sucker," exclaimed Mickey. "It never ceases to amaze me. It looks so strange in the midst of all these tattoo parlors, pawn shops, and pizza joints."

Ken agreed: "The world's just not what it used to be, Mickey. Not all progress is linear. I sometimes think we've lost our way."

"Just look at that marble exterior and all those colonnades, and that soaring dome, Ken. I'd put my money in that place if it were still open."

The old Dime Savings Bank of Brooklyn built the building in the neoclassical style at the turn of the last century. Its big daddy successor, the Dime Savings Bank of New York, ran the third-largest savings bank in the country there until it closed its doors in 2002, the victim of an acquisition that ultimately failed in the next financial crisis. The building had lain fallow ever since. The facade at the top of the twin-columned bronze door entrance still bore the original name, "Dime Savings Bank of Brooklyn," chiseled indelibly into the stone. Its remarkable exterior was matched by its equally remarkable interior, boasting large gilded Mercury-head dimes and twelve red marble columns supporting the rotunda.

"It's a landmark building, Ken, but I read that some money-hungry vultures bought it and plan to incorporate it into a new super-tall skyscraper. Fucking Trump's probably behind it."

"It's a shame, Mickey. It's just the way our corrupt political system seems to work. We do the best we can in our own way to try to make a difference, but it'll probably take a revolution."

Next to the Dime Savings Bank, on the corner of DeKalb and Flatbush Avenues, was another Brooklyn landmark. Junior's Restaurant had been serving "The World's Most Fabulous Cheesecake" there since 1950. With its red- and white-striped menus, flashbulb-adorned signs, rust-colored booths, and wooden bar, it was a shrine to the Brooklyn of old, but its neon exterior looked strangely out of place next to the elegant old bank.

"Get a table, Mickey, and order me a brisket sandwich and a diet cream soda. I'm just going to drop by the office for a second."

Ken crossed Flatbush Avenue and walked past the entrance to the DeKalb Avenue Subway Station to the wood-framed storefront building next to it. For good luck, he always touched the gold-leafed sign, "Law Offices of Kenneth Evers Williams," every time he opened the faux mahogany door.

A young, attractive, African-American woman, who Ken thought looked a little like Betsy, was there to greet him.

"How'd things go in court today, Ken?"

"New case, I'll tell you all about it later. Mickey's waiting for me at Junior's. Here's the criminal complaint. Open a file. People v.

Jackson. I'm going to Rikers after. Probably be back late afternoon. You can make appointments for after four."

As he was walking out the door, Ashanti told him, "Zeke dropped by and told me to tell you he has two tickets for the Islanders hockey game tonight at the Barclays Center. 'They're playing their nemesis, the New Jersey Devils.' That's what he said."

Ken had been hesitant to hire Ashanti as his secretary and gal Friday. She had no real legal experience, but he couldn't say no to her uncle, the boss of the Brooklyn Democratic Party. Ken would need Ezekial "Zeke" Thomas's support if he ever decided to run for public office.

"Tell him I'd love to go," said a disappointed Ken, "but I'm too tied up with the new Jackson case."

Hockey was Ken's favorite sport, and the New York Islanders were his favorite team. He was the only African-American player on his college team, but he was happy to see that professional hockey was gradually shedding its reputation as purely a white man's sport. His favorite black player, Kyle Okposo, was a star for the Islanders. Ken was at the game against the hated Devils several years ago and saw Okposo net his first goal as an Islander on a game-winning power play.

The Islanders were playing then in the Nassau Coliseum on Long Island. But a few years ago they moved into the new Barclays Center, just a short walk from Ken's office, where Flatbush Avenue crosses Atlantic Avenue. The new sports complex was the centerpiece of a major commercial and residential development project that was in the throes of transforming that blighted part of Brooklyn into a modern, urban center.

～

The brisket sandwich was waiting for Ken at Junior's, and Mickey's remaining molars were chomping away at a big, gooey hoagie.

"Don't tell me you're eating another one of those brisket melts, Mickey. The cheese is dripping down your chin."

"You know it's my favorite," mumbled Mickey. "The plain brisket is fucking boring. Anyway, what's up?"

"They've arrested this clean-cut black kid for a murder committed seven years ago on Chess Street. It makes no sense. Neary must be out of his mind again. Find out what this is all about. There were probably newspaper accounts you can get at the big library, and check out that neighborhood. See who knew what was happening back then. This smells worse than that sandwich you're eating. And try to tone down that cursing. It's not becoming. You sound worse than Officer Markham."

"Look, Ken. Get off my case. I'll swear all I want. There ain't no fun I ever had when I was good instead of bad."

"Alright. I know I've got to put up with it because there's no one better than you at your job. But at least try not to be so vulgar when you're around Jackson's wife. She's a classy woman. And by the way, Mickey, you just gave me a good hook for another country song."

"What the fuck. Anyway, I'll try to be a good boy when I'm with her."

"Talking about women," continued Ken. "How's your love life these days?"

"None of your business. But I'm a lot happier ever since I left that bitch of an ex-wife. Thought I'd be living happily with Loralee, but little did I know she was cheating on me."

Ken did a double take, "Not only did you give me the hook, you also gave me the first line. Anyway, well, knowing you, you'll be hitched again in no time."

"I doubt it. All they're after is your money," Mickey snarled, as he sunk the rest of his teeth into the brisket melt.

Ken couldn't resist. "Well, it certainly won't be for your good looks."

"Fuck you, man," snapped Mickey as Ken paid the check.

3

As he had done many times before, Ken drove his MINI Cooper across the Triborough Bridge and got off at the large white and blue sign proclaiming Rikers Island as the "Home of New York's Boldest." He always wondered how the prisoners must have felt in the drab green and white prison buses taking them there as the road toward the island swept across the East River and gave them—for many, the last time—a sweeping view of the majestic New York City skyline and a good look at LaGuardia Airport.

Ken certainly knew the routine. He would have to park his car in a parking lot patrolled by drug-sniffing dogs, far removed from the entrance to the prison grounds, and board a Corrections Department bus that took lawyers, family members, and others to the jail they were visiting. There were ten jails, each in a desultory, industrial-style, red brick building surrounded by a concrete parking lot.

He remembered the last time he was at Rikers. It was just a few days ago, when he visited an eighteen-year-old kid from his old neighborhood doing a year there after he was caught with a few grams of cocaine on a stop-and-frisk coming home from a friend's house late one night. He was being housed in Jail Number One, where they put the least violent serving a small amount of time for minor crimes. It was the so-called "model prison." Many of the inmates were teenagers, and it housed the school that gave these kids a chance to get a high school diploma—none had graduated—called a GED.

The warden prided himself on showing off the school, and on that day Ken was able to visit his client in one of the classrooms.

After class, it was time for the inmates' lunch and Ken saw maybe thirty kids line up in the hall to go to the lunchroom. They were all black. "Where are the white drug pushers?" he wondered.

Ken was not surprised. Rikers reform was on his short list of causes he wanted to champion. He had done his homework and was tooling up for bringing a civil rights lawsuit to call attention to the prison's overcrowded, inhumane conditions, and especially the predominantly black and Latino population. Rikers was the largest municipal jail complex in the country. The city's Department of Correction, charged with running the facility, was spending more than a billion dollars a year to house about 14,000 inmates. Most, like Troy, were pretrial detainees; one of the ten jails housed sentenced inmates serving terms of one year or less. The majority of blacks were either convicted of or facing drug charges. Ken had recently finished reading Michelle Alexander's book, *The New Jim Crow*, and became a believer that the War on Drugs was responsible for the racist mass incarceration of black people. Something had to be done about that.

"Which jail today, honey?" Ken heard as he jumped on the bus, clinging to his scuffed-up, black, leather-like briefcase.

He recognized the bus driver's voice. "Ten, Mabel."

He got a big kick out of her. But he had a hard time understanding how she could be so fat and cheerful at the same time—and how she managed to stuff herself into the driver's seat. He shifted his mind to his future wife's dynamite body.

"I guess you got another murderer, honey," Mabel said. "Ten's the pits. They treat them like crap there."

It took Mabel just five minutes to pull her bus up to the security checkpoint at the fence surrounding Parking Lot 10. There were a few others on the bus, but Ken was the only one who got off. He walked through the opaque metal door at the entrance, emptied his pockets into a small white basket, placed it and his briefcase onto the conveyer belt feeding the X-ray machine, walked through the screening device, and got patted down by a portly, bald corrections officer.

"So, you got the Jackson kid, Williams. Saw it on TV this morning. Good-looking wife. Give them credit. How'd they find a sexy looking picture of her before she was pregnant? Cute little thing."

"How long before they bring him down, Curley?"

"Chill, man. I'll see what I can do. Since he's in for murder, you'll only be able to see him through the grate."

"I know. Just make sure that no one can listen and no tapes are running. It's lawyer-client stuff."

A few minutes later, Troy Jackson entered the little cubicle separated by a three-by-five-foot cutout of metal bars from the small room where Ken was sitting at a small metal table. There was a similar table and metal chair on Troy's side.

"Sit down, Troy, and let's talk." Ken pulled a blank yellow legal pad out of his briefcase and placed it on the table. He took out a silver Cross rollerball pen from his inside jacket pocket and with his left hand printed at the top of the page: JACKSON CASE: FIRST INTERVIEW. He dated it at the upper right, placed the pen down on the paper, looked Troy square in the eyes, and spoke to him for the first time since their brief meetings at the precinct and the arraignment.

"How are they treating you?"

It was always the way he broke the ice. It was not going to be an interrogation. Ken was his lawyer, not a cop. He had to first gain his client's trust before he got down to business. And he was never going to ask him the sixty-four-dollar question—whether he committed the crime. Most criminal defense lawyers never did that.

"It's a nightmare, Mr. Williams. I've never been in jail before."

"I'll try to get you out as soon as I can."

"I'm scared, Mr. Williams. They put me in a cell with a guy who is a lot bigger than I am. Tells me he was a bouncer before he shot his boss. He says he can't understand why a good-looking, clean-cut brother is his cell mate and asks me whether I ever did it with another guy."

"Just try to stay cool. Try to fit in if you can, and keep your faith."

"I'll try for the sake of Trish, but I would be lying if I didn't tell you I'm not sure I can make it here."

"Stay strong, Troy. Let's get started and see if we can quickly get to the bottom of this."

Ken picked up his pen and scribbled his first note: "Worried! Hope it doesn't end like the Dickens kid."

He remembered just a few days ago being struck by the front page *New York Post* headline: INMATE, 18, HANGS HIMSELF IN RIKERS ISLAND CELL, and the full-page story on page three, with a bigger-than-life picture of the sheet with which the young man hung himself in his jail cell in a general-population housing unit for young adults after he had been in solitary confinement for a month. He was found by a correction officer. City officials vowed to reform the "troubled" ten-jail facility, especially the treatment of teenage and young adult inmates. The Associated Press had reported a few months ago—based on city and state investigative documents of Rikers Island—that in nine of eleven inmate suicides since 2009, established protocols designed to prevent vulnerable inmates from hurting themselves weren't followed.

Worse yet, a scandal was in full swing about the suicide the previous summer of a twenty-two-year-old young black man who had spent three years at Rikers before being released. He had never been convicted of any crime. Like Troy, James Brooks was good-looking and clean-cut and was easy pickings for the hardened criminals he had to live with every day. Shocking Rikers security footage had surfaced showing a correction officer slamming Brooks to a cellblock floor and pummeling him. Other footage showed him being beaten by ten tough-looking young inmate thugs.

"When you go over the three years that he spent at Rikers and all the horrific things he endured, it's unbelievable that this could happen to a young man in New York City," his lawyer said. "He didn't get tortured in some prison camp in another country. It was right here!"

The cops had arrested Brooks on Arthur Avenue in the Bronx after a teen accused him of stealing his backpack. His family was unable to raise his $3,000 bail, so he remained locked up in Rikers awaiting trial. He was offered a plea deal after thirty-three months, which he refused. As the months had turned into years, the stress got to him and he attempted suicide in jail several times.

Brooks spent more than four hundred days in solitary confinement for twenty-three hours a day until the flimsy charges were dropped and he was released. The warden told the press that "it was for his own safety so he wouldn't get beat up anymore." After getting out of jail, Brooks enrolled in Bronx Community College. But haunted by his experience at Rikers—and especially by being confined like an animal in solitary for more than a year—he suffered bouts of depression that triggered more suicide attempts before he finally succeeded in ending his life.

Ken knew about solitary confinement. Its formal name was the Special Housing Unit, but everyone referred to it simply as the SHU. Other clients of his had been locked up in the SHU. It was mostly used to punish violent or disruptive inmates but was also used to protect vulnerable prisoners—like James Brooks—from getting beaten up. Remarkably, life in the SHU was the same for both. The cells were just a little larger than Ken's six-by-nine kitchen, with a metal cot covered by a razor-thin mattress, a toilet and tiny sink stuck in the far left corner, and a small opening in the metal door for food to be slipped in. One small bulb hung from the cement ceiling. There was one small wooden chair, but no windows. The inmates were let out for one hour each day to walk around in a small courtyard, take a shower, and make one phone call. They could have reading material—it was all they could do—and were allowed out to see visitors for fifteen minutes one day a week if anyone came to see them.

～

"So what's your take on this, Troy?"

"I don't have a clue, Mr. Williams. I haven't lived on Chess Street for the last ten years. We had lived there with my grandmother after I was born, but my mom took me out of there when I was going to start high school. The new neighborhood was a new beginning for me. It was a nice, middle-class mix of hard-working whites and blacks, away from the projects, and I could walk down the street without being picked on by a bunch of drugged-up bullies."

"So you were in your senior year in high school, miles away, when he was killed?"

"Yes. I was in school, and I would meet Trish after class most every day to walk her home."

"Why do you say you were picked on all the time?"

"It was like this. The Chess Street gang was selling weed and coke every day. It seemed like everyone on the block was doing it. They were organized, like a club. The leader was the King; the others were either Rooks, Bishops, or Pawns. I never wanted to be part of that. I had good grades at school and liked it. They wanted me to be a Pawn like the rest of the kids my age, but I told them it wasn't my thing. They would make fun of me, push me around, call me a pussy. I was miserable. Once my mom got me out of there, I only went back to visit my grandmother."

"Ok, Troy, enough for now. I'll see you in court in two days when I'll make a pitch for bail. Like I told Trish, it won't be granted, but it will give me a chance to learn a little bit of the state's case. Also, the press will be there, and it will be important to start getting your story out. I'll have to think about whether I'll let you testify before the grand jury. But we'll talk about that later. I arranged for Trish to visit you tomorrow morning."

Ken picked up his pen and wrote two words in bold print: PATSY. RAILROADED.

～

On the way back to his office, Ken called his young associate from his cell phone. "It's been a long day, Gary. I'm heading home to unwind for a little while before meeting Betsy. Remember, it's Queen's night out. I'll see you first thing tomorrow morning. We got work to do on the Jackson case. Get hold of Mickey and get him there, too. The first thing we have to do is decide whether Troy should go before the grand jury."

Ken loved Gary Ricco. He had been an intern for famous civil rights litigator Ron Kuby for years while going to Brooklyn Law School at night. Gary graduated number two in his class, and Ken hired him right away. Gary started to polish his adversarial skills by handling lots of routine court appearances for Ken and doing the legal research and paperwork on all of his cases. He assisted Ken during trials, helped prepare witnesses, and had become Ken's indispensable second chair, but he had yet to try his first case.

At 6′1″ Gary was an imposing physical presence. He had been a gym rat since his high school football days and a decade and a half later was still proud of his chiseled body—the product of working out on an almost daily basis. He tipped the scales at 210 and boasted of bench-pressing his weight.

Since Ken's practice was really taking off now, he was thinking of bringing on board another bright young African American who, like Gary and himself, had escaped the projects and worked through law school. He had interviewed a bunch and narrowed his choice to two. Betsy was pushing for the woman.

～

Franco nodded to Faherty, the bartender, as he led Ken and Betsy to their favorite seat at Queen Restaurant, the intimate, small, round table near the kitchen. As Queen's maître d' for the past thirty-two years, Francesco Bertini was an institution. And the Queen was also an institution. There was nothing fancy about the place, but three generations of the same family were preserving its reputation as one of the best—if not the best—Italian restaurants in Brooklyn.

Age was beginning to take its toll on Franco as he wobbled around the table. Short and stocky, with remnants of curly gray hair, his rather benign looks betrayed the personal attention he bestowed on his regulars. After seating the couple, he turned and took two drinks from the waiter's tray that had suddenly appeared, seemingly unbidden, but Ken knew better. Franco placed the glass of Chianti next to Ken and the straight-up martini next to Betsy.

"Haven't seen you in a coupla weeks. How are the Williamses doin'?"

"Franco, how many times have I told you we're not married yet? When we get hitched, we'll be here to celebrate first thing."

"It's a shame, Mr. Williams. Rosa and me fifty-two years. It's beautiful. You should have kids like my Bruno and Sophia. I'll tell the chef to make the Chicken Fontina for Mr. Williams and a special pasta for the missis."

When Ken did not respond, Betsy asked, "What's wrong, honey? You seem really down."

"The Jackson kid is being set up. He's a perfect foil for a lot of bad guys who probably have cut cooperation deals to save their own necks."

"You're probably right, Ken. I know what a hard fight this will be. But let's not ruin our evening."

❧

After dinner they went to Ken's apartment. Betsy playfully pushed Ken onto his bed, stripped off his pants, pulled down his black jockey shorts, and stroked his penis until it got semi-hard. She unbuttoned her pink blouse, dropped her charcoal-black skirt and white satin panties to the floor, and jumped on top of him. She bucked up and down, using her best cowgirl moves, but couldn't make him come.

"I guess I can't compete with Troy tonight. You feel bad and should."

She got up, took off her blouse and bra, and snuggled up to Ken, who was still lying flat on his back. Within minutes they were both sound asleep.

～

Ken got to work a little late in the morning. Gary and Mickey were waiting in Gary's office, down the hall from Ken's. Gary thought that Ken got a great deal on the place. The long hallway ran from the front waiting room, where their secretary sat, to a good-sized room at the end that they used for storage. They also put a couple of cots in it in case anyone who was working late was too tired to go home. The two big rooms off the hall were converted into their spacious offices.

"Mickey, what have you come up with so far?" Ken asked.

"Not much. The street's quiet. Haven't had a chance to run down the old papers. Do you know anything yet?"

"No, but I'll try to find out something tomorrow at the bail hearing."

"I did run a rap sheet on him, Ken. He's clean except for a marijuana possession arrest when he was thirteen. The charges were dropped."

Ken wasn't too concerned.

"I'll talk to him about it. Every kid in that neighborhood smokes the stuff. He should make a good impression before the grand jurors. Maybe this is the exceptional case where we should do it. Let's think about it."

Suddenly Ashanti burst into the room. Ken had never seen his secretary so agitated. "Mrs. Jackson's on the phone and she's hysterical."

Before Ken could say one word after he picked up the phone, Trish Jackson screamed: "They put Troy in solitary confinement. Someone tried to rape him!"

"Be in court with me tomorrow morning, Trish. I'll try to get the judge to do something about this. It's an outrage."

☙

As soon as Trish hung up, her stomach cramps returned. She had been getting them intermittently ever since Troy was arrested and had taken an early maternity leave from school. But this one was the worst. She staggered into the bathroom and threw up. There was a phone on the bathroom wall next to the toilet. She picked it up and called her mother at work.

"Mama, Troy's been put in solitary confinement because someone tried to rape him. They let him call me. The stomach pains are worse than ever and I just threw up. I'm going to lose the baby."

"Calm yourself, child. I'll be right there. I'll call the doctor. I'm sure everything will be alright. You're in your last trimester and you and Troy Junior have been healthy. These things do happen. It doesn't mean that there are any real problems. The same things happened to me when I had you."

While Trish was waiting for her mother to arrive she was able to make her way into the bedroom to change her clothes. There were blood stains on her white panties.

☙

For being so short and thin, Dr. Gold had a large presence. His demeanor was perfect for a gynecologist and he always wore a kindly, avuncular look. After examining Trish, he spoke to her and her mother in his office in a gentle but reassuring voice.

"The baby is fine, so far. The spotting is not unusual and is not a matter of concern."

But before he could say another word, Trish interrupted.

"What do you mean, so far?"

"I don't want you to be alarmed, but I'm concerned about something called preeclampsia, which is a condition of pregnancy characterized by high blood pressure, and your blood pressure, which I just took, is very high. It's always been normal before."

Trish sank in her chair on the other side of Dr. Gold's ornate, gold-leafed oriental desk and looked like she might cry.

He nudged toward her a box of tissues in a beautiful black leather box adorned with painted white lilies and tenderly asked, "Trish, is there any reason that you can think of that would cause your blood pressure to suddenly spike?"

"My husband has been arrested for murder. He's in jail. He called me a few hours ago and told me they put him in solitary confinement because someone tried to rape him. I can't take it anymore."

"This is terrible news. I am so sorry."

Within moments, the tissue box was half empty, and Trish's mother helped her daughter compose herself before Dr. Gold explained that when preeclampsia occurs it is, as in Trish's case, usually after the twentieth week of a first pregnancy. The two women sat silently as he continued to explain.

"If not properly managed, preeclampsia can progress to eclampsia, which entails seizures."

Trish was speechless, but her mother was able to compose herself and ask questions.

"Just how serious is that, Dr. Gold?"

"Well, the good news is that only one out of about two hundred cases of preeclampsia leads to eclampsia."

She then asked the obvious follow-up question.

"But what if that were to happen, doctor?"

After an awkward pause, Dr. Gold solemnly answered.

"I'm afraid it could be fatal to the mother or the baby, or both."

With tears rolling down her cheeks, Trish could barely be heard when she plaintively asked, "What do I do?"

Dr. Gold gently held her hands as he spoke. "We'll get through this together, Trish. You and the baby are healthy now, and if you do as I tell you, everything should be fine."

"I'll try, Dr. Gold."

"First, you are going to take blood pressure pills and monitor your pressure every day. There are good machines at every drug store or you can buy a cuff that does it automatically at home. Next, you're going to try to be supportive of your husband without letting it affect your health."

"How can I do that, Doctor, knowing that he's rotting away in jail? My poor husband. How can this be happening to us?"

Trish's mom shot her daughter a stern look as she spoke. "I raised you to be strong. We pulled ourselves out of the crime-infested slums. We know that Troy is a victim of some horrible mistake and that Mr. Williams is going to make everything turn out right, and Troy will be home to see his baby son when he is born. Just do as the doctor says."

"I will, Mama."

Dr. Gold was quick to join in. "Your mother is giving you good advice, Trish. I'm going to also give you a prescription for a corticosteroid to help the baby's lungs and magnesium sulfate to prevent seizures. There are other things we can do if you can't manage your stress and your blood pressure doesn't go down. But let's not worry about that now. I want to see you every week. And if you experience any more extreme stress and those severe cramps return, you are to call me immediately."

The tissue box was now empty.

4

Ken needed to get his mind off the case, so he took Gary and Mickey with him that night to Arturo's. It was the first night he'd been there since Troy Jackson was arrested. Ken was one of the regulars who played the piano at the unique pizza joint at the northeast corner of Thompson and Houston Streets in Greenwich Village where jazz pianists could try out new stuff they were working on. Though Ken didn't think he was as good as most of them, he could play pretty well. His mother had a love for music and had an upright in their home. It was now in Ken's apartment.

Ken took to the piano easily. Before he was nine he could play boogie-woogie just like his idols, Jelly Roll Morton and Meade Lux Lewis. Soon he was playing all of Scott Joplin's rags. He also liked to compose. Nothing great, but he got a kick out of putting things people would say to music and was a big fan of country. He and his best friend got the country music bug when they met as undergraduates at Vanderbilt in Nashville and heard the first black country star, Charlie Pride, sing *Kiss An Angel Good Morning* at the Grand Ole Opry. The country songs Ken liked to write were the old-fashioned kind because "they always told a good story."

Dante "Dusty" Daniels stayed behind in Nashville after they graduated and became a successful promoter of up-and-coming black country musicians. He was close to Darius Rucker, who had left Hootie and the Blowfish to become the latest black country music sensation.

Ken and Dusty stayed in touch through the years. They would periodically visit each other and often spoke on the phone.

Arturo Junior was tending bar that night as Ken, Gary, and Mickey walked past a crowd of NYU students standing under the red awning entrance in the chill of the night. The family still ran the place after its founder, Junior's father, had passed away a few years earlier. It was only a couple of blocks from Vanderbilt Hall, the classical red-brick building housing NYU Law School—across from Washington Park—that was part of the eclectic mix of buildings on the NYU campus surrounding the park. Ken discovered Arturo's during his first semester of law school.

"I see you brought your rooting section, Kenny," said Arturo, as the three of them bellied up to the old wooden bar. "But why are you guys so dressed up tonight?"

"We just came from a meeting of the Chisholm Democratic Club," said Gary. "The pretzels and chips didn't do it for us, so we thought we'd eat here while Ken did his thing."

"Well, you know you came to the right place," smiled Arturo, as he proudly displayed the red t-shirt he was wearing with white letters across the front: BEST PIZZA IN NYC SINCE 1956.

Ken was always fascinated by Arturo's upswept, bushy, handlebar mustache. It compensated for the swept-over strands of dyed black hair plastered over his head. His mustache came to sharp waxed points at the ends. Ken always had the urge to one day take two thimbles from Betsy's sewing kit and place them on top of the points to see if they would move.

After Mickey and Gary downed a couple of beers, they sat across from the bar in one of the four red leatherette booths in the crowded front dining room. It was the one closest to the piano at the far end of the room where Ken removed his suit jacket, took off his tie, rolled up the sleeves of his white shirt, sat down on the piano stool, and started to play a Scott Joplin rag.

He was not alone. On the drums to his right was Frankie "Sticks" Levitano, and cradling the bass to his left, like it was one of his young boyfriends, was "Flaming" Jimmy Steve Edwards. They were fixtures who were there every night to accompany the piano players. Because Ken would try out his new country songs there, Flaming Jimmy kept a steel guitar and fiddle handy, which he learned to play as well as the bass.

When Ken played Fats Waller's *Your Feet's Too Big* and *Honeysuckle Rose* he got the attention of the raucous crowd at the bar. They knew he was a big-shot lawyer and thought it was cool for him to play there.

After he finished his set, Ken sat down with Mickey and Gary who had saved a couple of slices for him. The drummer joined them and sat next to Ken.

"That was cool tonight, Kenny," he said. "But how come you didn't do any of your country songs?"

"I'm actually working on a new one. Mickey here is a constant source of inspiration. He unwittingly keeps giving me great hooks. Maybe it'll be finished by the time I'm here again. What's cooking with you these days?"

"I hit seven-o last week and still love playing the sticks every day, ever since I got out of the used car business last year."

"Still married?" asked Ken.

"Free as a bird, at last," he shot back. "No more work, no more wives, no more worries. Got me an Asian. Gives the best massages in town, know what I mean?"

Mickey was taking it all in. "Do they do blacks, too, Frankie, or just guineas?"

"Probably, but maybe not short, fat, ugly ones like you."

"You never would know these guys were buddies, Gary," chimed in Ken.

"Why not," said Gary. "Make them both black or white and they could pass as brothers, if Frankie had hair."

While the banter continued, Ken spotted the sexy-looking thirtyish blonde slither her way across the room. With her tight-knit, short white skirt and dark tanned body—except for the ample white skin on the top of the ample breasts bulging out of her strapless halter—she got most of the guys at the bar to stop drinking and take in the sight.

She made her way to their table and squeezed in next to Ken.

"Did I ever tell you I'm turned on by tall, good-looking black guys, Kenny boy? Too bad you're so damn loyal to Miss DA."

"How about me, Wendy?" asked Mickey.

Gary couldn't resist: "She said tall and good-looking, Mickey."

"Fuck you, Gary," shot back Mickey.

"Mickey, watch your tongue. You're in the company of a classy woman," said Frankie, chuckling.

Wendy Baker was the main female singer by night and a hot-shot real estate agent during the day. She used to be Wendy Butcher before changing her name when she went to work for the Downtown Real Estate Group. Once she became a Baker—and started to dress like a sex bomb—she quickly developed a niche clientele of divorced middle-aged Wall Street types and sold lots of multimillion-dollar condo conversions in Tribeca within walking distance of the World Financial Center. The male brokers couldn't compete. She had a way of closing a deal that raised eyebrows, but she made lots of money for her and her bosses.

"Kenny," began Wendy in her sultry voice, "I've got a real big fish on the line who is coming tonight. I'll be singing during your next set. We'll do the song as soon as I see him."

"You should give me a commission, Wendy."

"As soon as you get rid of Miss DA."

She could really sing. And Ken really enjoyed accompanying her. And the bar got really quiet as they did a couple of standards. The glass jar at the end of the piano filled up with lots of dollars.

Suddenly her client appeared and stood in the middle of the bar staring at her as she finished singing an up-tempo version of *Blue Skies*. She nodded to Ken, and looking at the man squarely in his eyes, she started to sing *I'm in the Mood for Love*.

It was the last song she sang that night before Ken watched her walking out with him arm in arm to his double-parked Rolls Royce.

❧

When he returned to Brooklyn late that night, Ken found a parking space for his little MINI Cooper down the street from his two-story walk-up brownstone in Carroll Gardens. He liked the neighborhood and its tree-lined streets. He hoped that some day when he and Betsy were married and could afford it, they would buy a place here.

Ken was tired, but he took his diary out of the top drawer of his whistle-clean mahogany desk, opened it to the first blank page, and started to write:

> Got interesting new case. Unlike other crimes, no statute of limitations for murder. But they just don't happen seven years later. And not against a clean-cut guy like Jackson. Feel terrible for him. Shades of JoJo."

He hadn't read his diary in a while, but he started to get agitated as he thought about the hell that Troy was going through at Rikers. He'd had some interesting cases since he left the U.S. Attorney's office, but this one might take the cake. He had written about all of them, as well as his days as a federal prosecutor. Ken started to thumb through the pages. He stopped when he came to where he wrote about first meeting Betsy.

> January 17, 2010
>
> What a way to start the year. Lost the Rodriguez case today. Can't get every drug pusher off. ADA did great job. Smart to have a black prosecutor try

a case against a black defendant. Smooth as silk.
Jury loved her. Also, cute as hell. Couldn't keep my
eyes off her. Wasn't total loss. Called her after to
congratulate her. Told her like to do it in person over
dinner. She laughed. Said OK because we have no
pending cases with each other. Went to Queen on
Church Street. One of best Italian restaurants in
Brooklyn. Tried the Chicken Fontina. Wow, was
it good. She ate like a bird, but drank like a fish.
Talked small talk. Said we'll do it again soon. Love
the Queen, especially its name. Who knows? Might
be prophetic.

Ever since then, it would be Queen's night out at least once a
month. He would always order the Chicken Fontina and wash it
down with a glass of Chianti. Betsy would eat a little pasta, but
always started with a dry martini straight up. Marriage was on hold.
Their careers took center stage, but they were now talking about fixing a wedding date in the not-too-distant future.

It was past midnight and Ken had a busy day ahead of him. But
he was hooked on the diary and read what he wrote about the career-
making things that had happened to him since he graduated from
law school.

June 6, 1998

Got offered job as AUSA in Brooklyn. Guess
my district court clerkship this year with Judge
Melancon paid off. Got to thank the judge for going
to bat for me. Not keen on being prosecutor but can't
turn it down. Great prestige and experience.

Ken rummaged through the next several months of diary
entries, describing how he broke in as an Assistant U.S. Attorney,

the training he got, the investigators he met, and the colleagues he worked with. But he stopped and read what he wrote one night in February 1999.

February 4, 1999

Been in General Crimes since being sworn in last September. Have second-seated a couple of times and assigned last week to first solo trial. Felon-in-possession case. Upset today about Amadou Diallo. Granny Effie called and chewed me out for prosecuting black kids.

Amadou Diallo was a 23-year-old immigrant from Guinea when he was shot to death by four New York City Police Department plain-clothes officers. They had fired a combined total of forty-one shots, nineteen of which struck Diallo when he was outside his apartment in the Soundview section of the Bronx. Diallo was unarmed and his death triggered a huge outcry both within and outside New York. There were protests all over the city. Al Sharpton led the charge. But he wasn't alone. Sharpton was joined by many civil rights leaders and clergy of all persuasions who demanded accountability. Issues such as police brutality, racial profiling, and contagious shooting—where one officer shooting prompts others to shoot as well—took center stage.

Next, Ken read what he wrote about his first "felon-in-posses-sion" trial a little more than a month later.

March 15, 1999

Won my first felon-in-possession case. Defendant pled guilty after losing suppression motion. Bothers me. Was thin stuff. Cops may have been lying. Probably will get two years. Granny Effie got on my case again. "How can you turn against your own kind? You should be helping them, not hurting *them." Glad to see that the four cops who slaughtered Diallo were indicted today for murder.*

Felon-in-possession cases were simple. Under federal law, if someone had a prior felony conviction and was caught with a gun, he faced years in jail. The young defendant had been picked up late at night in one of the tough black neighborhoods that the police had on their radar screen. He was smoking a cigarette but was stopped by two rookie cops on the pretense that it was a joint. They searched him, found a loaded pistol in the right pocket of his baggy pants, and arrested him on the spot.

If the case went to trial before a jury and the gun was placed in evidence, the defendant would surely be convicted. However, before this could happen, the lawyer had the right to bring a motion for a suppression hearing before a judge on the ground that the gun was the product of an illegal search. If the judge granted the motion, the gun could not, therefore, be placed in evidence at trial, so a jury would never know about it. But it would never get that far. Without the gun, the government would be ethically obliged to ask the court to dismiss the case for lack of admissible evidence.

Ken had to oppose the lawyer's motion. The hearing took place before Judge Leslie Chosed, the federal district judge who had randomly drawn the case. At the hearing, the two officers testified that it was a hot summer night, and as they drove by in their unmarked car with the windows wide open they smelled marijuana.

If it was decided there was probable cause to stop and frisk someone who the police believed was violating the law, the search and seizure would be legal. Judge Chosed, a tough law-and-order guy and former prosecutor, accepted the cops' testimony and denied the motion. Ken had won, but it bugged the hell out of him. It was common knowledge that the black kids in the projects carried guns for their own safety. And there was a growing suspicion by the civil liberties lawyers that the police had adopted a tough stop-and-frisk policy targeting blacks as part of the mayor's campaign to get the guns off the streets.

Since the gun could then be introduced into evidence, the trial would be open and shut. Wisely, the defendant pled guilty in the hope that he would get less jail time. Judge Chosed sentenced him to two years.

Ken was given a few more felon-in-possession cases against black defendants. He did his job well and won them all. But it was bothering him more and more. He also started to distrust his witnesses, but if the judge didn't think the cops lied, there was nothing he could do. He began to believe the word on the street that blacks were indeed being targeted. One of his African-American friends told him that he was stopped and frisked for no reason whatsoever when he was coming home late one night from a party. The cop who patted him down didn't even apologize when he found nothing.

And then the jury returned its verdict in the Diallo case. He read what his diary said about his reaction.

February 25, 2000

Disgusted. Diallo's murderers were acquitted. Sick and tired of putting black kids in jail for carrying guns to protect themselves. Don't like all the stop and frisk crap going on. Can't do it anymore. Not cut out to be prosecutor. Saved up a few bucks. Made some good contacts with some of the African-American leaders. Have no wife or kids to support. Will give solo practice a shot. What the hell!

After a year and a half in the U.S. Attorney's Office, Ken quit and hung out a shingle in a storefront on Brooklyn's bustling Fulton Avenue. He joined the Chisholm Democratic Club, the local political African-American club named after Shirley Chisholm, the first black congresswoman. With his great legal background, and his commitment to "the cause," he was assured by the big shots in the club that he would be fed all the business he could handle. Given the nature of his prospective clientele, he wasn't planning on becoming rich, but he was single, with no financial ties, and would somehow manage.

Soon he was marching with Sharpton and his cronies whenever there was a white-on-black shooting. He began to speak at rallies, and as a former AUSA and gifted public speaker, he got a lot of TV exposure. Soon he was a regular on CNN's late news hour, articulating the angst of the African-American community and debating various spokesmen from the law enforcement establishment, including the Director of Public Relations for the Brooklyn DA's Office.

Ken had some high-profile cases over the next several years. As he rummaged through his diary, two stood out.

June 28, 2008

> Retained by Dunne's parents today to sue police for gunning down their unarmed son. Was 18. Just graduated from high school. Honor student. Starting Columbia in September. Had misfortune of resembling another young black kid wanted by the cops for a string of robberies in Brooklyn Heights. Was walking on Montague Street. Had just left girlfriend's apt in Heights. Cops told him he was under arrest. Panicked and ran when they started to cuff. Had eighteen bullets in him.

The murder of Zachariah Dunne was all over the news for days. Ken Williams appeared on every national TV channel to demand that District Attorney James Neary prosecute officers Bart Pohorelsky, Scott Fink, Ciarán O'Reilly, and Joey Bianco for Dunne's murder.

It never happened. The four cops were brought up only on disciplinary charges. Although they were reduced in rank and assigned to permanent desk duty, they were not held criminally responsible for what DA Neary described as "an unfortunate honest case of mistaken identity."

Ken was livid. He accused the DA of being in Police Commissioner Brown's pocket and sued the cops, as well as the City of New York for its police department's negligence in failing to properly train them. About a year later, Ken took the cops' depositions. He read what he wrote about them in his diary.

June 16, 2009

> Four tough white cops. One was Polish, one Jewish, one Irish, one Italian. Were pissed that I was grilling them. Asked why they had to plug the kid 18 times. No rational answer. No bullets left in guns. Trigger happy cops. Poor kid. Cops angry that they were on permanent desk duty. Careers shot. Good for them. Couldn't care less.

After the devastating depositions, the city's Corporation Counsel, whose office was required to represent the cops and pay any judgments, offered Zach's grief-stricken parents twelve million dollars to settle the case. The police commissioner then caved in to the relentless public pressure and fired the four cops.

The money would not bring Zachariah Dunne back to life, but it brought some closure to what Ken described in his news conference as "another pathetic case of racially motivated police brutality." With the family's blessings Ken took a two-million-dollar fee. It was a ton of money, but it was half the customary one-third retainer for these types of high-risk cases. He told the Dunne family that he would put the money to good use. He only had a secretary, and he now would be able to hire more help and take on worthy cases without worrying about getting paid.

There was one more diary entry Ken read before turning in. It was one of his most recent high-profile cases.

May 14, 2011

Dominican maid for Plaza Hotel said raped by
Italian diplomat in suite. Told cops he came out of
bathroom naked. Started to leave. Would not let her.
Threw down on bed. Ripped off clothes.

Vito Scanlonetti planned to catch an afternoon plane back to Rome, but he was arrested at JFK as he was waiting to board and put in jail. It made big news, but soon the battle lines were drawn. The Italian embassy hired one of the city's top legal guns to represent Scanlonetti. Roberto Anello would be able to speak to his client in his native tongue. The black waiters at the hotel told the maid to call Ken.

There was no escaping the media. Pretty soon Anello and Ken were going head-to-head on just about every TV news channel. Anello was famous for his scorched-earth tactics and launched a personal attack. He portrayed Imelda Gomez as a greedy immigrant who would "undoubtedly be suing Scanlonetti for tons of money." Ken fought back. He defended the honor of "the poor, hard-working helpless victim of a powerful Italian big shot with close ties to Prime Minister Berlusconi" and who, like the Prime Minister, "had a richly deserved reputation in Italy as a womanizer."

Eventually, it all fizzled out. It was a "he said, she said" situation, and there was not a lot of evidence to back up Imelda's story, especially since she refused to be medically examined. Anello convinced the Manhattan DA that he should drop the case and let Scanlonetti go home. Ken had gotten a lot of media mileage for his reputation as a defender of the downtrodden, but he thought better about suing. It was, as a practical matter, a sure loser. However, he did help raise about $10,000 for Imelda from his contacts at the Chisholm Democratic Club. She was grateful and publicly praised Ken for his willingness "to come to the aid of defenseless minorities."

With all this notoriety, Ken started to get a lot of letters from African-American inmates. They all seemed to have a common theme: They were doing big time for crimes they swore they never committed, and many claimed that they were prosecuted on trumped-up evidence by Anthony Racanelli, the chief prosecutor for the Brooklyn District Attorney. But one letter immediately caught his attention. It was short and to the point. It was in the file he had on his desk, next to the diary, and the last thing he looked at before he went to sleep.

August 10, 2012

Dear Mr. Williams:

I have been locked up for going on 16 years on a life sentence for a crime I never committed. The only real evidence against me at my trial was from three cooperators with criminal records who had cut a deal with the DA's office to finger me. One of them, Solomon Butler, came to visit me. He said he was dying from cancer and wanted to make things right before he met his maker. He told me that Assistant District Attorney Racanelli pressured him to testify that he saw me kill the rabbi and told him he would never see the light of day if he didn't do that. But he also told me that he had written a letter to the prosecutor right after saying that it ain't the truth. And he said that the other guys also lied, and told the cops that I had put them up to it. None of them said any of that at the trial cause they were scared. Can you help me?

JoJo Jones
No. 386574820 - Green Haven Correctional Facility

5

The next morning, the Brooklyn DA held a press conference at his office to announce that the murder of the son of Rabbi Israel Bernstein had been finally solved. James Neary had a big smile on his face when he stepped up to the mics.

"About sixteen years ago we put away for life the killer of Rabbi Bernstein. We solved the shooting death of the father right away. Unfortunately, it took us a little longer to find out who killed his son. But justice must be served. Our office never rests until murderers are caught, no matter how long it takes."

"But this one took seven years. That's more than a little longer, Mr. DA."

Neary recognized the surly, confrontational voice of Jimmy Margiotta right away. Over the years he had written a number of articles for the *Daily News* critical of Neary. The first was back in 1992, during Neary's first term, when a jury acquitted Lemrick Nelson in Brooklyn state court of the murder of Yankel Rosenbaum during the infamous Crown Heights riots.

The case had received national media coverage, and the "not guilty" verdict mystified the public since Nelson admitted to the police that he was the one who stabbed Rosenbaum. Moreover, the police found in Nelson's possession a bloody knife; blotches of blood with the same type as Rosenbaum's were on Nelson's pants; and before Rosenbaum died, he identified Nelson as the one who had stabbed him.

An official investigation concluded that the jury had little choice but to acquit in view of the bungling of the case by the new Brooklyn DA. One of the jurors who agreed to talk to the press said that there were "inconsistencies in the police officers' testimony," and "it didn't seem like they got their act together and were properly prepared." Another said that the young prosecutors who tried the case "seemed inexperienced" and "kind of cavalier; they had a hard time asking simple, direct questions. They confused me."

Margiotta was scathing in his criticism of Neary. He would never let him forget it, and he wrote years later that "the jury's verdict kept the riots on center stage and caused unprecedented divisiveness between Jews and blacks which took years to heal." More than any other member of the press, Margiotta had become Neary's most virulent critic.

Jimmy Margiotta was a tough, no-holds-barred reporter. His face looked like it had taken one too many punches when he tried to make it in the ring while growing up in the toughest area of the Bronx. But his brains remained intact, and while he slugged his way through the ring he also excelled in journalism school. Because of his smarts, he landed a job as a beat reporter for the *News* soon after he graduated.

Surprisingly, Margiotta's hawk-like nose was never broken, which contributed to his nickname as "the Predator." It was befitting of both his animal looks as well as the way he would pursue his prey once he got hold of a nationally newsworthy story. And the Crown Heights riots—among the worst in the city's history—certainly was one of them.

The riots were triggered by an unfortunate series of events when, during the early evening of August 19, 1991, a station wagon driven by a Hasidic Jew collided with another vehicle at the intersection of President Street and Utica Avenue in the Crown Heights section of Brooklyn. It veered out of control, and struck two black children— seven-year-old Gavin Cato and his nine-year-old cousin, Angela.

The station wagon was part of a police-led motorcade accompanying Grand Rebbe Menachem Mendel Schneerson, the spiritual leader of the Hasidic community.

Within minutes, an ambulance from a private Jewish organization arrived. Soon a New York City ambulance also appeared. A group of African Americans had gathered at the site of the accident, and several physically assaulted the driver of the station wagon and his two passengers. A police officer directed the Jewish ambulance to take them to the hospital, while the city ambulance took the two black children to the hospital, where Gavin Cato was pronounced dead.

The accident sparked an immediate and violent reaction among members of the African-American community. Angry crowds of blacks beat up more than one hundred Jews, broke the windows of their homes, shouted "Heil Hitler," and burnt the Israeli flag—shocking the country. The riots were fueled by the perception among African Americans that the Hasidic community received preferential treatment from the city because of police escorts routinely given to the Rebbe and the rumor that the Jewish ambulance had failed to render aid to the seriously injured black children, favoring the less-injured Hasidic driver and passengers.

The most violent aspect of the riots occurred just hours after the accident when a group of African-American men accosted Yankel Rosenbaum, a rabbinical student, who was stabbed to death. The next day Nelson was arrested and charged with killing Rosenbaum.

The jury's acquittal of Nelson sent shockwaves throughout the city. Margiotta accused Neary of "taking the case for granted, and stupidly putting it in the hands of inexperienced rookie prosecutors."

An outraged public of all racial persuasions would not let the matter rest with the acquittal, and pressure was placed upon the federal government to act. The groundswell for federal intervention culminated in a unanimous United States Senate resolution calling for the Justice Department to launch a full-scale investigation into whether civil rights violations occurred during the riots and Yankel

Rosenbaum's murder. This led to the impaneling of a federal grand jury in Brooklyn, which indicted Nelson for violating Rosenbaum's civil rights.

In one of his many articles about the riots, Margiotta explained why someone who had been acquitted of murder in a state court could nonetheless be prosecuted again in a federal court:

> Against the backdrop of severe race riots in several major cities during the '50s and '60s, Congress, in 1968, enacted a statute making it a crime to willfully injure or interfere with "any person because of his race, color, religion, or national origin and because he is or has been participating in or enjoying any benefit, service, privilege, program, facility, or activity provided or administered by any State or subdivision thereof." Under the statute a "facility" would include using the public streets, and Jews were considered a race.
>
> Killing Yankel Rosenbaum as he was walking on Prospect Street because he was a Jew would therefore be a federal crime. This was the criminal civil rights statute that the government invoked to try Lemrick Nelson in federal court after he had been acquitted of murder in the state court.

So Nelson was retried in the Brooklyn federal court. It was not double jeopardy because the federal charge was considered a separate crime; therefore, even though Nelson was acquitted of murder in the state court, he could still be tried in the federal court for causing Rosenbaum's death by violating his civil rights.

Not surprisingly, the federal prosecutors did a better job than Neary's incompetent ones, and Nelson was convicted by a jury for violating Rosenbaum's civil rights and causing his death. The judge sentenced Nelson to twenty years. However, the conviction was overturned by the Circuit Court of Appeals because it disapproved of the manner by which the judge selected the jury; instead of providing for random selection, as the law required, the judge, in order to select a jury with "moral validity," tried to balance the jury's racial composition, which the appellate court struck down as impermissible "jurymandering." The case had to be retried before a new judge. It was reassigned to District Judge Felix Black.

Judge Black's last name came from his great-grandfather, who had changed his Lithuanian name after landing on Ellis Island; he thought Biabalablacksi would not play well in the New World. The judge's parents chose Felix as his first name after Felix Frankfurter—the trusted Jewish adviser to the second President Roosevelt—who would later become a Supreme Court Justice.

Because of all the time the first two trials took and the time that elapsed between the trials and the appellate court's decision to allow yet another trial, several years had gone by before Lemrick Nelson was tried for a third time. The third trial only lasted six days, but there were dramatic moments. The government produced witnesses who testified that Nelson attacked Rosenbaum after people had shouted: "There's a Jew. Get the Jew!" Others who had witnessed the attack heard Rosenbaum ask Nelson, "Why did you stab me?" And the prosecutors also elicited testimony from the detective who spoke to Nelson after he was arrested, saying Nelson told him that "I stabbed him because I was excited."

Surprisingly, although the jury again convicted Nelson of violating Rosenbaum's civil rights, this time it did not find that Nelson's actions resulted in Rosenbaum's death.

Margiotta reported in the *Daily News*' lead story the next day that as soon as the jury had announced its verdict, "Nelson slumped in his chair in apparent relief that the split verdict would spare him from being sentenced for murdering Rosenbaum—and then flashed a broad smile. But the outcome—and Nelson's joyful reaction—brought tears to Norman Rosenbaum, Yankel's brother. The mixed verdict did not bring peace to the Rosenbaum family."

Living up to his nickname, the predator reporter tracked down the jury foreperson, who told him that the jurors cleared Nelson of causing Rosenbaum's death not because of anything that came up at trial, but because they knew from old news accounts that Rosenbaum's family had a pending negligence lawsuit against the hospital where he died.

"Everybody knew that," she told Margiotta, and asked rhetorically, "How can you sue the hospital for negligence and at the same time tell people this guy stabbed him to death?"

Judge Black was furious to learn that the jurors considered facts not in evidence. Under the law, what happened at the hospital was irrelevant—all that mattered was whether death was foreseeable. The judge could have set aside the verdict for juror misconduct and ordered yet another trial. However, he decided to let the verdict stand, simply stating that "it was time to put the Crown Heights riots to rest."

The judge sentenced Lemrick Nelson to ten years. Given that he was not held responsible for the death of Yankel Rosenbaum, it was the maximum allowable under the law. Finally, years after Nelson had stabbed Rosenbaum, the criminal prosecutions were over. But it would take many years before the racial flames that had flared between the Hasidic and black communities would die out, and in another scathing article, Margiotta placed the blame squarely on the DA:

"If DA James Neary didn't butcher the state court trial, this whole tortured ordeal would never have been."

To his credit, Neary did try to make amends by appointing a committee of Jewish and African-American leaders to try to bring the communities together and made Lillian Bloom its chairperson. Bloom was a well-respected civic activist and, although a secular Jew, had many friends in both the Hasidic and African-American communities. She was largely credited with the committee's success in quelling the aftermath of the riots.

Throughout the years, in an apparent effort to appease the Hasidim, Neary also vigorously prosecuted a number of black youths for committing crimes against Hasidic shopkeepers and landlords.

The most significant crime happened in the beginning of 1997. The Hasidic community was enraged when Rabbi Israel Bernstein was killed in the middle of the day on Chess Street near a building he owned, and they demanded that Neary quickly find and convict his killer.

Chief Rabbi Mordecai Horowitz warned that "this better not be another Lemrick Nelson fiasco."

Within days an arrest was made. This time, the DA assigned Anthony Racanelli to handle the case. He didn't disappoint. Six months later, JoJo Jones was convicted of murdering Rabbi Bernstein and sentenced to life.

~

After the press conference, Racanelli followed his furious boss into his office, watched Neary slam the door and listened to him curse Margiotta for what must have been the hundredth time:

"That son of a bitch. Ever since Nelson he won't let go. He's always doing a number on me. And that trouble-making, race-baiting lawyer, Williams, is feeding him shit all the time."

"Big Jim" was a hulk of a man, and he seemed even taller than his six-foot frame as he paced up and down, his eyes bulging and his face redder than it looked after downing his customary two martinis at lunch every day at Armando's. He was a burly, tough-looking, tough-talking career prosecutor who hadn't lost an election for DA since he was first elected twenty-four years ago. Then again, he never had any serious opponents. He was the darling of the Brooklyn Democratic political bosses, and in Brooklyn being on the Democratic line was tantamount to election. While the Republicans put up some token opposition in the general elections, Neary had amassed a sizeable war chest that discouraged anyone from ever challenging him in a primary for his party's nod. He was still vigorous at the age of sixty-two and had no intention of stepping down. His next election the following November would be his seventh four-year term.

"I don't know why the hell it took you so goddamn long to find the Rabbi's son's killer," he barked.

"Lay off me," snapped Racanelli. "We had people from the projects turn on JoJo right away, but not this time."

"Yeah, but Jones has been bitching for years that he was framed, and now that headline-seeking, so-called civil rights crusader has taken his case and brought a habeas proceeding in federal court claiming you framed him."

"So what else is new? JoJo's not the only black guy who has bitched that he was wrongly convicted. They all do. They have nothing better to do while they're rotting in jail than to file habeas papers all the time. It's a great country, and the judges have to process all of them, but the courts are swamped with them. Once in a blue moon there may be some merit to them, but certainly not in JoJo Jones' case."

Big Jim slumped into his maroon leather, high-back chair behind his imposing walnut desk. Papers were scattered all over. He knew there was a lot of truth to what Racanelli said about habeas cases. Under the law, once someone is convicted of a crime—even if his conviction is upheld on appeal—he could still come back to court and ask for a "writ of habeas corpus," in the form of a written petition. Literally, the writ means "produce the body." It is a court order to a person or agency holding someone in custody—such as a warden—to deliver the imprisoned individual to the court issuing the order and to show a valid reason for that person's detention. If the court grants the writ, the prisoner goes free. The writ of habeas corpus has a rich history, dating back to the enactment of the Habeas Corpus Act in the seventeenth century by the Brits to give a remedy for those claiming they were being illegally imprisoned by the king.

Convicted defendants commonly paper the courts with habeas petitions to complain about their lousy lawyers, or to claim that new evidence would prove that they were innocent, or that the prosecutor's misconduct deprived them of a fair trial. And since all these types of claims implicate the Due Process Clause of the federal Constitution, they could be brought into the federal courts. If the judge thought there was real merit to the petition and it was backed by sworn affidavits, he or she could order a hearing to flush out the facts. It was not like a criminal trial before a jury. The judge would listen to the evidence, size up the credibility of the witnesses, and decide the case. And unlike a jury trial, the defendant would have the burden of proof.

Racanelli sat down across from his boss. He was wearing a neat charcoal gray, pinstriped suit that clung to his muscular body and a white button-down shirt with a red, white, and blue striped tie. "Tough Tony," as the chief prosecutor was deferentially referred to by his colleagues, was a few inches taller than Neary and still looked like the Marine he was thirty-five years ago, although the temples of his crew cut were starting to turn gray. He went to Fordham Law after the service, and with his army background and classic prosecutor's looks he had no trouble getting hired by the DA's office. He quickly worked his way up the ladder until he became James Neary's go-to guy. During the twenty years that he had worked for Neary, he was credited with cracking just about every tough murder case.

He told Neary, "Williams is going no place with his habeas case, and he must know it. Everyone complains of being wrongly convicted, but we haven't seen a successful case in years. We all know the conservatives on the Supreme Court have made it almost impossible for a defendant to have a chance at getting habeas. This is about Williams showing his political ambitions. He's just another Sharpton. He wants to rile up the blacks who think you have it in for them because you are beholden to those Hasidic Jews who've been your deep pockets all these years."

Neary shifted uneasily as the chair seemed to swallow him up. Tony's cocky air of confidence wasn't reassuring him that there was no merit to JoJo's case.

He pulled open his top desk drawer, opened a fresh pack of Marlboro Lights and was soon puffing away. Although he tried to quit many times, he was never able to kick the habit, but now he smoked mostly when he was worried.

"Tony, have you even read the habeas petition Williams filed with the federal court? He claims that you got the witnesses who testified against Jones at the trial to lie."

"He can say whatever he wants, but that's a lot different than proving it," shot back Racanelli.

"But he submitted sworn affidavits from them claiming that you threatened to prosecute them for a bunch of crimes if they didn't nail Jones."

"Sixteen years later? Give me a break. Who's going to believe them? They have zero credibility. They're all ex-cons. Do you really think I would stoop so low? C'mon Jim."

"But Williams is not stopping with Jones. He's telling the press that he is not the only black you've railroaded, and he's planning on bringing more habeas cases. I guess I'm just pissed that he's using the race card against me. And after all the things I've done since the riots to bring peace in Crown Heights between the blacks and Jews."

"You have nothing to be ashamed of. Just look at all the plaques on the wall. Kudos from the Baptist churches, Anti-Defamation League, NAACP, Temple Israel, Brooklyn Bar Association. This is nothing more than a lousy racist attack against the great reputation you've earned over the years. Williams and his cronies should rot in hell. The nerve of them. And don't let the Hasids jerk your chain, either, after all you've done for them. Every time the black-hats get on your case, you bend over backwards to accommodate them."

Neary put out his cigarette and leaned forward, folding his hands on the top of the desk. "I'm not in their pocket, Tony. I'm not in anyone's pocket. But realistically I don't want to alienate the Hasidim. They've been good to me throughout the years. They were upset that if it were not for the feds Nelson would have gotten off completely. I can't blame them. How the hell did we blow that case?"

"Yeah, there's no doubt we fucked up," mumbled Racanelli. "The head of general crimes didn't bother to put our best prosecutors on the case. It was so open and shut they must have taken it for granted. And the police investigation on the night of the murder was a fiasco. They didn't bother to record the suspects they interviewed and didn't properly handle the physical evidence. Shit happens."

"That's why I assigned you afterward to take charge of all the big cases, especially those involving crimes by blacks against Jews—so we don't have another Crown Heights."

Racanelli stood and straightened his tie.

"And I haven't disappointed you. Jones is still in for killing the Rabbi, and he's not getting out. And now we got the rabbi's son's killer."

"It's about time. You know the heat I've been getting from the Chief Rabbi for letting the murder go unsolved for all these years? 'No more campaign money from us,' he threatened. Hopefully, he's satisfied now. I told him better late than never. But he warned that we better not lose this one, like we did with Nelson. They still can't understand why he was never convicted for murder and is out of jail now for only violating Rosenbaum's so-called civil rights. It sticks in their craw to this day. Whatever you do, don't blow the Jackson trial."

"Not a chance, Chief. We have him dead to rights."

"Are you sure? Seven years later we're prosecuting a clean-cut kid with a pregnant wife for murdering Rabbi Bernstein's son."

Big Jim lit up another cigarette.

6

Ken was livid as he and Gary walked into the courtroom. He had called the warden to try to find out what had happened to Troy, but was told he was not in. He never got a call back. The two lawyers sat down at the defense counsel's wood table, just a few feet in front of the judge's bench and the witness stand. Ken was always amused that they called them a "bench" and "stand"—both the judges and the witnesses sat on black vinyl chairs.

The courtroom door swung open as Anthony Racanelli swaggered in with an entourage and sat at the front of the prosecutor's table. About ten feet separated the warring sides. Tough Tony didn't come to the *pro forma* arraignment, but now that the bell was about to ring he was center stage. Ken recognized Racanelli's female paralegal and the handsome young ADA who sat down next to him. Betsy had told him that Tyrus Cohen was a rising star. Ken thought it was clever of Racanelli to have a smart Jew as part of his team.

Soon Troy was brought in from a side door escorted by two uniformed court officers. As a defendant, he was entitled to be at all court proceedings, and he had been taken out of the SHU and brought over from Rikers on the early prison bus. The officers sat him down next to Ken. He looked terrible, but Ken had to talk to him about his marijuana arrest.

"I know it was over ten years ago. You were just a kid, but what was that all about?"

"Mr. Williams, everybody on the block smoked joints. It was no big deal. I didn't want to look like a total misfit. But I stopped smoking as soon as I got out of there and met Trish. I was getting something late that night at the bodega for my grandmother when the cop stopped and frisked me. I had a few joints in my pocket. He busted me and took me to the local precinct. But when I got there, the desk sergeant told the officer it wasn't serious enough to book me. I was only thirteen. They gave me a lecture to stay out of trouble and let me go."

Suddenly, Trish came in and sat in the first row of the public benches. She blew her husband a kiss and gave him a thumbs-up.

Troy sat slumped in his seat, weakly waived, and mumbled to Ken, "I'm so ashamed and embarrassed."

A moment later the judge's door opened. The bailiff did his star turn and called the case. Reginald Cogan limped into the courtroom. The bailiff helped him climb the two steps to the bench. The judge carefully lowered his corpulent body into the chair, cleared his raspy throat, ran his hands through his flowing grayish hair, stroked his horseshoe mustache, and sternly spoke.

"Mr. Williams, you have a bail application. Proceed."

Ken rose quickly: "Your Honor, my client, looking like death warmed over, is a twenty-four-year-old, well-loved, high school guidance counselor. He is accused of committing a murder that happened seven years ago, when he was seventeen. He is married to a wonderful young woman who teaches science at Corpus Christi Junior High. They own their own condo in Williamsburg and in a few months their first child will be born. He says he's innocent and has been set-up. And I believe him. There is no reason to keep him in jail pending the trial."

"Well, Mr. Williams, you know it's unethical to vouch for your client. You do not know of your own knowledge that he did not do it."

"You're right, Your Honor. I guess I got carried away because I sense a travesty has been committed by my distinguished adversary, who is developing a bit of a reputation for putting innocent people behind bars."

Racanelli could not control himself. He jumped to his feet and shouted: "That's an outrage. My less-than-distinguished adversary should be sanctioned for impugning my character. I won't stand for it."

"How about the JoJo Jones case, Mr. Prosecutor?"

Racanelli shot back: "You filed a bunch of habeas papers complete with affidavits from a bunch of criminals. Nothing has happened since, and I doubt it will go anywhere."

Sitting in the seats reserved for the press, Jimmy Margiotta was taking notes. He was not the only reporter there. The Jackson case was starting to receive a lot of newspaper ink and local TV play.

"Sit down, and listen to me," snapped the judge. "There's going to be decorum in my courtroom. I don't want to hold either of you in contempt of court, but if we have any more outbursts, I will."

Ken knew he meant it. He had great respect for Judge Cogan. He was fair but stern, befitting his Scottish roots. Cogan returned to his birthplace every year and loved to hike. His limp was the by-product of a bad fall he had taken the past summer while trekking through the rugged Highlands, and the surgery on his knees had only been partially successful. The judge's wife had warned him that a roly-poly man in his mid-sixties was no longer fit for such vigorous exercise. He didn't listen.

But the judge would always listen carefully to counsel and called the shots down the middle. He had been on the bench for more than two decades and was a no-nonsense, seasoned jurist. The administrative judge often assigned him to preside over high-profile cases.

Ken cautiously rose to speak.

"May I continue, Your Honor?"

Judge Cogan nodded.

"It's obviously tough on this young man to be locked up at Rikers, but it's even worse than it looks. Two nights ago, Mr. Jackson was asleep and his cellmate tried to rape him. The assailant flipped Mr. Jackson over and warned him not to speak or he would kill him. Mr. Jackson screamed for help. Fortunately, a correction officer was close, but by the time he got to the cell the assailant was back in his bunk. Mr. Jackson was traumatized, as you would expect. He told the guard what had happened and was put in the SHU for his own safety."

"Do you know anything about this, Mr. Racanelli?"

"No, Your Honor. But I'll check with the warden."

"Your Honor," continued Ken, "a recent report by the United States Attorney's Office for the Southern District here in Manhattan describes Rikers Island as 'engaging in a pattern or practice of conduct that violates the constitutional rights of its inmates.' And, specifically, it concludes that the correction officers and their supervisors do not protect vulnerable teenagers and young adults from violence by other inmates. Moreover, as documented in the report, the jail's extensive reliance on punitive segregation subjects these kids to an excessive risk of harm. We know about the recent Dickens and Brooks suicides. I don't want Troy Jackson to become another statistic."

Margiotta's eyes were riveted on Ken as he continued: "What's bizarre about all this, Judge, is that they put inmates in the SHU for their own protection, and they are treated just the same as those bad apples who arguably deserve to be there. They in effect are being punished for having the misfortune of being preyed on by violent prisoners. It's absurd and cruel, and something has to be done about it. But in the meantime, my client must be let out of there. And he's got to be protected against the animal who threatened to kill him. That's even more reason for bail to be granted."

Judge Cogan sat upright and turned to Racanelli. "What do the People have to say about that?"

Tough Tony didn't hesitate: "He's being charged with murder, and all they're trying to do is to keep him alive until the trial, when we will have three witnesses testify that they saw this supposed boy scout shoot the late Rabbi's son point blank. That's three. Not one, not two, but three, and—"

Ken interrupted: "Seven years later, three witnesses come out of the woodwork? I'd like to know who they are, and why it's taken all these years for them to suddenly appear. It's fishy as hell. My client is being set up."

There was a smirk on Racanelli's face as he shot back, "You know that under the rules I don't have to tell you who they are until the day before they testify, unless the judge tells me otherwise. And I intend to play by the rules."

Ken was not deterred and continued arguing to Judge Cogan: "Be that as it may, you can't put in solitary confinement a pretrial detainee who has done nothing wrong in jail. It's just plain inhumane. And it's against the Constitution to boot. The Supreme Court made that clear long ago in *Bell v. Wolfish*, when it held that administrative detention is punitive when it is not rationally connected to the government's reason for holding the defendant in a place like the SHU, and to place my client there for his safety is totally off the wall. We have to put an end to that, and there ought to be a full-scale investigation by Washington. Surely, there must be a better way. And if there is no better way, he should be let out on bail."

The judge was quick to respond.

"I've never given bail in a murder case in all my years on the bench, but what Mr. Williams says troubles me. In light of the rash of suicides we've had lately by young adults in custody in Rikers and the report that Mr. Williams referred to, which I read yesterday, which also condemns the use of excessive force by the correction officers there, this might be the first time. I want to talk to the warden. Get him here tomorrow morning, 10:00 a.m."

Before Racanelli could say anything, the judge pivoted out of his chair and abruptly left the courtroom. Tough Tony shot Ken a dirty look, picked up his papers, and hurried out. Ken smiled.

"Back to the office, Gary. We got lots to think about."

As Troy was led away by the court officers, Ken said: "Stay strong, you'll be back tomorrow to watch more fireworks. At least it will give you some time out of the SHU. I'm sure Trish will be here again, though they won't let you speak to her."

~

Mickey was talking to Ashanti as Ken and Gary walked past their secretary into Ken's office. Soon Mickey joined them.

"Sit down, everyone," Ken said. "First thing, do we put Troy in front of the grand jury tomorrow afternoon?"

Gary spoke first: "Well, you told us to think about it, and I don't think we should. Racanelli is going to be there, and if Troy tells his story Racanelli has the right to cross-examine him. Tony obviously has the rap sheet and knows about the marijuana arrest. He'll rip into him. He'll ask him how often he smoked weed, who gave it to him, what was he doing when the cops stopped him, and on and on. No good can come of it."

"Gary's right," chimed in Mickey.

"I was thinking of taking a chance and letting Troy do it," Ken said, "but I agree. Now we know Racanelli will have his three witnesses testify, and unlike the trial, there's no one there to cross-examine them. The chances are nil that Racanelli will be unsuccessful at getting them to indict. Whatever Troy says under Racanelli's questioning, while I'm sitting there with my thumb up my ass because I can't object, will come back to haunt Troy if we decide to let him testify at trial. So now on to the most important thing. How do we find out who the witnesses are?"

Mickey was quick to respond: "How's this for a start?"

He pulled his iPhone from the left pocket of his rumpled blue jeans and scrolled to the photos. "Look at this, guys. I figured the DA has been calling witnesses to testify before the grand jury ever since Jackson was arrested, so I sat outside the grand jury room yesterday and watched the passing scene. There were a few grand jury proceedings going on at the same time. There must have been a dozen people sitting there just waiting. Suddenly I saw Ty Cohen come out of the third grand jury room and take a short scrawny black dude in. He was sitting a few rows in front of me. I figured it might be the Jackson case, so I got his picture. They don't take your cell phones away in that building."

"Mickey, you're a genius," said Ken.

～

Ken picked up the *Daily News* first thing in the morning on his way to court. He was amused and thrilled by the half-page headline: ONE SHU FITS ALL.

"Hats off to the headline writer," Ken mused.

In the exclusive inside story on page three, Margiotta lambasted Rikers for putting people like Troy Jackson into solitary confinement, and quoted Ken's comment that "there should be a full-scale investigation by Washington."

Before Judge Cogan took the bench, Ken showed Troy the picture Mickey had taken.

"Do you recognize this guy, Troy?"

"He's Wee Willie, Mr. Williams. I knew him from the old days. We used to be friends."

"Well, he's no friend of yours anymore."

Judge Cogan, Anthony Racanelli, and Warden A. Cecil Leonard all came into the courtroom at the same time. Ken wondered why a prison full of black kids couldn't have a black warden.

"Warden, what's going on at that jail of yours? Is it true that pretrial detainees are really being put in solitary confinement for their so-called 'own protection'?"

"Yes, Your Honor. It's for their own good. It's the safest way to protect them."

"Well, you can't do that. Think of a different way."

"Your Honor, I guess we can put him into our model jail where we house the young, nonviolent kids on drug charges going to school there, though I don't like to do that for anyone charged with murder."

"Well, Warden Leonard, I don't think from everything I've seen that you need be concerned about this young man. Why don't we do that?"

"Alright, Your Honor. Under the circumstances we'll make an exception in this case. But if anything happens, it's not my neck."

"That's enough, Warden, but that being the case, I won't release him. Regardless of what you tell me, Mr. Williams, your client is, after all, being charged with murder. And Mr. Racanelli has told the court that he has three eyewitnesses. I'll give you the first open trial date I have, but it probably won't be until sometime in April."

Ken was happy that he got Troy out of the SHU, and that the press was into it, but he was hoping for an earlier trial date. He was clearly annoyed, but spoke deferentially. "Your Honor, that's about four months from now. The baby is expected in March. I'm confident Troy's not going to be convicted and I'd like to have him home for that blessed event."

"I'd like to accommodate you, Mr. Williams," Judge Cogan responded, "but I just can't. I have a complex multiple defendant murder case that I scheduled a long time ago to start after the first of the new year that's estimated to last a good three months."

Ken was not pleased, but his spirits picked up as soon as he returned to his office and read the decision that Ashanti had placed on his desk from federal District Judge Dolores Gonzalez. He scanned the thirteen pages, but quickly read what the judge had concluded on the last page:

> In light of the fact that embedded in the DA's file was a copy of a letter of recantation addressed to ADA Racanelli by the prosecutor's key witness, the day after the start of Mr. Jones' trial, and the fact that neither the original—if it was not destroyed—nor the copy, were ever disclosed to defense counsel, this is one of those rare habeas cases which requires a factual hearing.

～

That night he was back at Arturo's. He had called his buddy Dusty to tell him that he had just finished the new country song for which Mickey unknowingly had given him the hook and the idea. Ken put his cell phone on the top of the piano so Dusty could hear it.

This time he wasn't wearing his suit. He was in his country digs, complete with a ten-gallon cowboy hat and boots. He also decided to wear his shades to not be readily recognized in case anyone he knew happened to be there.

Frankie did a double-take: "You look like a cross between Hank Williams and Stevie Wonder," he howled.

The joint was hopping, and started to whoop it up as Ken played and sang.

> When I was hitched to Loralee
> I thought I'd be livin' happily
> She was young and sexy and perty as can be
> But little did I know she was cheatin' on me
>
> Couldn't believe she gave me the gate
> Never came late, was the perfect mate
> But when she left me it opened my eyes
> And I began to realize
>
> That there ain't no fun I ever had
> When I was good instead of bad
>
> I gave her rings and fancy things
> And all the while she was having her flings
> Did whatever she said I should
> Became the joke of the neighborhood
>
> To drown my sorrows I took to drink
> But when I sobered up I started to think
> I'm big and strong and now that I'm free
> There's lots of other fish in that deep blue sea
>
> And there ain't no fun I ever had
> When I was good instead of bad

No, there ain't no fun I ever had
When I was good instead of bad

Then just like that she called one day
I picked up the phone to hear her say
Let's try again, big boy, let's give it a whirl
I'll no longer be a cheatin' girl

I couldn't believe what I just heard
But dug down deep to find the right words
It's too late baby, and gave her the news
I no longer am a goody two shoes

And there ain't no fun I ever had
When I was good instead of bad
No, there ain't no fun I ever had
When I was good instead of bad

⌁

Aside from unwittingly giving Ken material for his country songs, Mickey was also at work trying to unravel the Jackson case. He took up Ken's suggestion to check the back papers and knew that the estimable Brooklyn Public Library would surely have them. He loved the library and was as comfortable among the stacks as he was among the streets of his beloved Brooklyn. He learned everything about the borough's rich history from the millions of books housed there—making it the fifth-largest public library in the country—and the old newspaper stories in the local *Brooklyn Eagle*. Mickey particularly found it fascinating to read the *Eagle*'s accounts of the debates among the councilmen in the 1890s as to whether, after the Brooklyn Bridge was opened in 1883, Brooklyn—which was the third largest city in the country at the time—should become a borough of New York City as Kings County.

The current library building itself was part of that rich history, dating back to 1912, when ground was broken at its present location at the intersection of Flatbush Avenue and the beginning of Eastern Parkway, two of the avenues intersecting the circular Grand Army Plaza. Today, the library is considered one of America's greatest Art Deco buildings.

Mickey knew where the periodical reading room was, but he stopped on his way there to say hello to his favorite reference librarian.

"Got to check out some old papers, Miss Lindsay. Any new Brooklyn books lately?"

She sat straight up at her desk and peered out from behind the tiny rimless glasses roped around her elongated neck, and spoke in an appropriately hushed voice: "There's one that you would like a lot, Mr. Zissou. I'll check it out for you. Goes all the way back to the 17th century Dutch settlers from Breukelen, Holland."

"So I guess if the Brits would have kept the original name, they would have been called the Breukelen Dodgers," quipped Mickey.

It didn't take him long to find what he was looking for. Margiotta had covered the story for the *Daily News*. The day after the murder the paper had a half-page photo of Menachem Mendel Bernstein lying dead on the floor of the neighborhood bodega. Lying next to him was a black book with gold-colored Hebrew lettering on the cover. He was dressed like a Hasid, but the front of his black coat had a bullet hole in the middle. Surprisingly, his black hat was still on his head. Margiotta's story was relatively short. He just wrote that the Hasidic community was up in arms that the son of Rabbi Bernstein was shot on the same street as his father years before, and that the police were conducting their investigation and looking for suspects. But the following week he ripped into the DA for not solving the crime:

> The Hasidic community cannot understand why Rabbi
> Bernstein's son's killer has not been found. One Hasidic

leader said this "has all the earmarks of another bungled case by DA Neary, just like Lemrick Nelson."

Neary did not take it lying down. The next day, the *Daily News*
printed his op-ed in response:

> Years ago we found Rabbi Bernstein's killer right away
> and he is doing 25 to life in an upstate maximum secu-
> rity prison. We are conducting a full investigation to
> find his son's killer, and I am confident that this will
> happen. But, unfortunately, unlike the JoJo Jones case,
> this one is tougher to crack because we have no cooper-
> ators—yet. The street is quiet and nobody is talking—
> yet. We suspect that this may be drug-related. The
> Hebrew book we found had a false bottom and tested
> positive for traces of cocaine. We know who the lead-
> ers of the Chess Street gang are but they have all dis-
> appeared. I've assigned my chief prosecutor, Anthony
> Racanelli, to find them and get to the bottom of this.

But the years went by and it became a "cold case." Margiotta
never let up. On each anniversary of the unsolved crime he would
remind his readers in a bylined column that "because of the DA's
ineptitude, Menachem Mendel Bernstein's killer is still at large."

7

Lillian Bloom sat down across from Jim Neary in the booth at the back of Armando's.

"Long time no see, Lil. It's like old times."

They used to meet frequently at Neary's favorite watering hole and would sit next to each other in the booth. But their get-togethers started to cool when rumors began to spread that there might be more to their relationship than their mutual concern about bringing peace to the Crown Heights community after the riots. They were both committed to the cause, and after Neary had appointed Lillian to head up his special committee to help bridge the tensions and get the black and Hasidic leaders in a constructive dialogue, she had become a highly regarded reform leader. There was even talk of her entering the political fray and possibly putting her hat in the ring for Public Advocate. She was articulate and attractive. Some of her friends thought she looked a little like her idol, Gloria Steinem.

"Lil, you know, Mary never recovered from her stroke so many years ago, and she's been gone for three years now. And you've been divorced from Myron for even longer. We don't have to worry anymore, and being celibate isn't good for either of us. Why don't we give it another chance?"

"I miss our tender times together, too, Jim," she said, breezing past his invitation. "But right now I want to talk to you about Rebecca Hyman."

"Who the hell is Rebecca Hyman?"

"She came to see me a few days ago. The poor thing was shaking like a leaf. It took me a long time to get her to calm down and tell me what was wrong. Finally, she was able to compose herself a little bit and blurt it all out."

"Why did she come to see you?"

"Lately I've been actively trying to get the Hasidic leaders to seriously address all the stories out there about the abuse of Hasidic women and children by their husbands and fathers. Even though I'm a secular Jew, I've built up some good relationships in the community since Crown Heights, and the time has come to do something about this. They live in their own world and they have a mortal fear of reporting deviant sexual behavior to the police. I presume you read that exposé in *The New Yorker* about the Hasidic man who found himself the target of a criminal investigation by your office after he reported that his teenage son had told him he had been molested by a man who had prayed at their synagogue. And it wasn't written by Margiotta."

"Yeah, I was told about it, but I'm not going to read that crap."

"Well, they really took a shot at you. I brought a copy in case you're interested. Here's what they said."

Lillian pulled the article out of her Tod's pocketbook, put on her reading glasses, flipped to page nine, cleared her throat, and started to read:

> Neary had been supported by the Hasidic bloc for nearly two decades and worked diligently to maintain an amicable relationship with leading rabbis in the community. He had a history of offering unusually light plea deals to Hasidic offenders, whose names his office kept confidential—a practice uniquely enjoyed by the Hasidic community. *Der Yid,* the influential Yiddish newspaper, ran a full-page notice explaining that community leaders had benefitted from an "open door with James Neary for the past 24 years" and "know firsthand what happens when they get themselves

entangled with the law, how District Attorney Neary *found ways* to avoid sending them to jail."

She took off her glasses, took a sip of water, and explained: "As you've probably been told, the article tells the pathetic story of the plight of Sam Kellner, how he claims his son was 'molested by Baruch Lebovits, a prominent cantor with twenty-four grandchildren and a descendant of a rabbinic dynasty,' and how Kellner was ostracized by the Hasidic community for reporting it to your office. And, ironically, how Kellner wound up in jail, while Lebovits went free."

Neary was getting agitated. "Lillian, I know all about it. You may remember that I held a press conference after Kellner was indicted but cautioned that we have to be very careful about false complaints. I was convinced that Kellner was simply making up stories to gain money for his own benefit."

"But the article documents how all that was a bunch of garbage, James. There was real merit to Kellner's claim, and it details how influential members of the Hasidic community turned the tables on Kellner and got their revenge on him for going to the police. It's typical of how they handle these so-called internal affairs, but the upshot is that sexual predators in their secret world are getting away with murder."

"Let's not be so dramatic, Lillian. We will prosecute legitimate cases but we have to have credible evidence, and witnesses are tough to come by from that community. Without them, it's difficult to get convictions."

Lillian knew that he had a point. Hasidism emerged in the eighteenth century as a mystical, populist alternative to traditional Judaism. Its men dress in black frock coats, wear black broad-brimmed hats, and have long strands of twirled hair called *peas* running down the sides of their faces. Married women wear long skirts and hide their hair under shawls or wigs. All Hasidic people speak Yiddish and resist television, the Internet, and other secular forms of entertainment. Moreover, Hasidic parents take literally the Lord's order to "be fruitful and multiply." There are large Hasidic communities in London and Montreal, but New York's is the largest. With a current population of 165,000, they are the fastest-growing segment of the Jewish population in the city. Almost all live in the Crown Heights, Borough Park, and South Williamsburg parts of Brooklyn.

The Hasidim pride themselves on their insularity from the secular world. They have their own court, called the *beth din,* and their own methods for dealing with problems among their members short of going to the police. Before a Hasid could do that he would need a rabbi's permission, lest he be ostracized from the community. It would truly be an exception to the Talmudic prohibition against *mesirah,* the act of turning over another Jew to civil authorities. According to some interpretations of Talmudic law, a Jew who informs on another Jew has committed a capital crime. And no one dares to defy the Talmud. As the twelfth-century scholar Maimonides wrote, such an informer would be considered a "wicked man," who has "blasphemed and rebelled against the law of Moses."

Hasidic men practice and adhere to a strict form of sexual discrimination and view any contact with the opposite sex, other than with their wives and daughters, as something that must be avoided at all costs, lest they be tempted to have sexual thoughts. They are allowed to have sex with their wives only for procreation. Their sons and daughters are not allowed to attend secular schools and are married in their late teens, through arranged marriages, so they can get an early opportunity to raise a large family. Most women do not work. Those who do are often under economic pressure from their husbands to contribute to the family's support. The married woman's primary job is to keep a good home and make sure that their many children do not stray from the straight and narrow Hasidic world.

Lillian wasn't finished talking about the Hasidim.

"While I respect religious diversity, Jim, and certainly recognize the rights of anyone to practice their own beliefs, the men are plain horny and go to extreme lengths to suppress their sexuality. When they fly to Israel, they won't sit next to a woman on the plane, and they have their own buses where the women are required to sit in the back, just like blacks during the Jim Crow era. They won't dance with women or engage them in conversation. They make them sit in the balconies at their synagogues. Just last week, the mayor ordered the Parks Department to take down large signs on the streets warning women in the Hasidic neighborhoods to step aside for men."

"I know that, Lil. I was the one who spoke to the mayor about that."

"Do you know, James, there's actually a prayer the men say every day, 'Thank you, God for not making me a woman'?"

"No kidding? But there's only so much I can do, Lil. I can't make them come to me with their problems. They just don't trust us, and they are terrified that if they become a *mesirah* they will disgrace their families and won't be able to arrange good marriages for their children."

"I'm impressed with your knowledge of Yiddish, but how did you learn their word for an informer? Anyway, I'm hearing more and more frightening stories like the Kellner case about Hasidic men sexually abusing children. If their parents find out, instead of coming to you, they go to a modesty committee, called *vaad hatznius,* which internally enforces standards of sexual propriety. While it disciplines those who express their sexuality or behave lewdly, in a community where all non-marital sex is considered shameful, molestation tends to be regarded as roughly the same as having an affair. When children complain about being molested, the council doesn't notify the police. Instead, it devises its own punishments for offenders: Sometimes they are compelled to apologize, pay restitution, or move to Israel. Nobody goes to jail."

"So what do you want me to do?"

"You've got to speak out and do whatever it takes to help these abused women and children to break out of that trap."

"Lillian, I have to use some good common sense. While I'll certainly bring charges against sexual predators, of whatever religious or ethnic stripe, the Kellner case taught me that I have to be very cautious in taking the word of those folks. Their credibility leaves a lot to be desired when they're dealing with the outside world."

Lillian did all she could to contain herself. "I guess you still believe that Kellner was lying. And I guess there may be some truth to the rumors that you're afraid to alienate the Hasidim because they have always voted for you. There's noise in the black community about putting up someone to challenge you in the next primary because of all the blacks like JoJo Jones who claim they were railroaded. And since the Hasidic people vote as a bloc, whoever the rabbis support gets all their tens of thousands of votes."

"It's not so simple, Lillian," Neary snapped. "I will never compromise my oath and fail to prosecute when warranted. Enough for one night. It's getting late. I've got a lot to do tomorrow. I'll drive you home."

"That won't be necessary. Good night, Mr. DA."

She never told him about Rebecca Hyman.

8

It was the second time Ken had met JoJo. The first was several months ago when he visited him at Green Haven—the State's upstate maximum security prison in Stormville—where convicted murderers were stowed away. Now he would be meeting him at the Metropolitan Detention Center in Brooklyn.

The MDC was a relatively short ride from the Theodore Roosevelt Federal Courthouse, where the habeas corpus hearing would be held, and prisoners who had to be in court there were temporarily brought to the local jail so the marshals could readily bus them in for their court appearances. Ken had made the necessary arrangements to have JoJo "writted down" from Green Haven for the habeas hearing.

Talking to the prisoners at the MDC was not much different than other jails. There was a pretense of privacy for lawyer-client conferences, but there were eyes and ears all over the place and plenty of desperate criminals who were champing at the bit to snitch on a fellow prisoner so they could cut a cooperation deal with the government. Time and again the feds would march inmates into court to testify about incriminating statements a fellow jailbird had told them about the crime for which they were being tried. The cooperation deals were referred to by the defense bar as "get out of jail cards." If the federal prosecutors were satisfied with the inmate's testimony—especially if it resulted in a conviction—they would report that to the judge who had the authority to cut the snitch's jail time or even let him go free. The judge would invariably oblige; otherwise the pool of cooperators would run dry. It was estimated that about one-third of the convictions in the Brooklyn federal courthouse were because of cooperation agreements with inmates who had either been convicted and sentenced or whose trials were pending.

"Thanks for coming, Mr. Williams," began an appreciative JoJo. "Good to see you again. And, man, thank the Lord for Judge Gonzales. Finally, after all these years, someone has paid attention."

"She's a good judge, JoJo, and tomorrow will be the big day. Just make sure you don't talk to anyone. There are more bugs around here than an ant colony, and everyone is trying to suck up to the feds to save their ass."

"Don't I know it. That's why before I got here, I've spent the last sixteen years of my life in Green Haven—since I was twenty-two, man—rotting away in a maximum security prison."

Green Haven was notorious. It used to house "Old Sparky"—the electric chair once thought to administer "humane" executions—in the old days before the state's high court struck down New York's death penalty as unconstitutional. Various efforts to dust off the chair throughout the years were not successful, and today New York is one of twenty states that do not put people to death. But some say that being in Green Haven is worse than death.

JoJo Jones was hardly the jail's most famous inmate. He was just another number. But it had been the home of some of the country's most celebrated gangsters. Lucky Luciano, who founded the modern Cosa Nostra, was there in 1936 before being deported to Italy. Ronald DeFeo Jr., who was convicted of killing his parents and four siblings at their home in Long Island—inspiring the best-selling *Amityville Horror* book and movie—is an inmate there now. And Nicky Barnes, the brutal drug lord; Joey Gallo, the number one enforcer for the Profaci crime family; and John Gotti, the infamous "Teflon Don," all spent time there.

"Let's not talk about it now, JoJo. I have all our ducks lined up for the hearing. I'll have Butler, Jordan, and possibly Shillique there to testify. And Judge Gonzales, of course, has the copy of Butler's letter to Racanelli recanting his testimony. And my investigator Mickey has done his thing. Let's all say a prayer tonight and keep our fingers crossed. If all goes right, and the judge gives me a little play in the joints to let me do my thing, the day in court tomorrow will end in a huge surprise."

"Well, you're my lawyer—just what kind of surprise do you have up your sleeve?"

"Now, JoJo, it won't be much of a surprise if I tell you now."

"In any event, I want to testify too, Mr. Williams. I want to tell my story. How I've had to live like an animal for the best years of my life; how I lost my wife and children; how I've had to try to sleep each night knowing that I was framed by that jackass DA and his hatchet man. It's been tough."

"You'll finally have your chance. Try to get some rest. I brought you a nice dark suit, white shirt, and red power tie. The prison orderly will bring it to you tomorrow morning before you're taken to court. Make sure you're clean-shaven, and trim that little black goatee. And put a little shine on that bald scalp of yours. The press will try to get a shot of you being led into the courthouse."

"Brother Williams, you are my last hope. God bless you."

~

As he was getting up to leave, Ken recalled the first time he spoke to JoJo at Green Haven and was struck by his strong, firm voice. Immediately, Ken had realized that JoJo was on a mission. He was a man possessed. Ken had been mesmerized as JoJo had told him how he had been spending his time behind bars. Each morning, for more than 6,000 days, he knew exactly what he would wear when he woke up: a dark green shirt with matching dark green pants.

He told Ken that the prison greenies of a convicted murderer "were overly starched in the beginning, but as time wore on, and after repeated washes, they were worn and dull, like so many other things on the inside."

For all those years—until Ken took on his case—JoJo knew the only way his wardrobe would change was if he did something that's rare. He'd have to lawyer his way out of jail. There was no crusading journalist, no nonprofit group taking his cause, just Inmate 386574820, a tall, slim, high-school dropout from Brooklyn, alone in a computer-less prison law library. He didn't blame his assigned trial counsel. He had tried his best but the cards were stacked against him.

Three witnesses had implicated JoJo in the shooting of Rabbi Bernstein. JoJo knew he was at home getting a haircut at the time and wanted to testify on his own behalf. But his well-intentioned lawyer told him it would only make matters worse. He told JoJo that the jury would never believe it, especially since he couldn't find his so-called personal barber to back up his testimony.

And his credibility would be destroyed once the prosecutor brought out under cross-examination that JoJo had spent a year in jail after he was convicted of robbing a bodega when he was an aimless sixteen-year-old. It would also open the door to the government dredging up his wayward past. Up to that point, he had been drifting. His father died when he was twelve years old, and his mother worked two jobs while also studying nursing. Under-supervised, he skipped school often, smoked a lot of dope, and fathered the first of his three children, with three different women, when he was fifteen.

But to his credit, although he dropped out of school when he was seventeen, JoJo had turned his life around. He had obtained a GED, gotten a steady daytime job in the maintenance department of Home Depot, taken some evening classes at Long Island University, and was trying to transfer to night school at John Jay College of Criminal Justice when he was arrested for Rabbi Bernstein's murder. He was living in a small, two-bedroom, rented apartment in one of the buildings that Rabbi Bernstein owned with the "baby mama" of his latest child and his two children from the other women.

JoJo told Ken that during his trial, "I felt like a school kid. Everyone talking over my head. But when I heard my mother wailing as I was taken away, I realized that I had a life of misery ahead of me, and the only way I was going to ever get out was to become my own lawyer."

While at Green Haven he had become a model prisoner and was rewarded by being permitted to spend many hours in the prison's law library, where he poured himself into legal books: *Federal Rules of Criminal Procedure, McKinney's Consolidated Laws of New York, The Legal Research Manual.* A thick text for paralegals called *Case Analysis and Fundamentals of Legal Writing* became his bible. And he spent months mastering the intricacies of state law on access to public records, especially New York's Freedom of Information Act, commonly known as FOIA.

Using his new-found knowledge, in July 2004 he requested from the DA's FOIA officer access to all his trial records. He received a stamped, three-word response: "PRIVILEGED and UNAVAILABLE." Over the years he filed six more requests. Each time he got the same cryptic response. Handwritten appeals to DA Neary were ignored. Finally, he brought a lawsuit, and a judge ordered the FOIA officer to comply with JoJo's requests.

Soon JoJo was in possession of a bunch of audio tapes and 239 pages of documents. It was such a mass of material that the FOIA officer, who was charged with copying the tapes and papers and delivering them to the prison, did not realize that included in the file was a copy of the letter that Butler had told JoJo he sent to Anthony Racanelli. It was addressed to him and "cc'ed" the "office of the DA."

JoJo had written to a few lawyers over the years to help him, but each time he was told that without hard evidence there was no way a judge was going to do anything just based upon his own, uncorroborated story. Once he found the copy of the letter JoJo called Ken. He had been reading about all the big cases Ken had handled for black clients. Ken, too, had been the most sought-after lawyer by the inmates, who would be begging him to help them. Ken thought a number of their cases might have some merit, and he was considering hiring someone full time to dig into those voluminous files.

But this one jumped out of the pages. After JoJo had written to him about the dying man's letter recanting his testimony, Ken decided to visit JoJo at Green Haven. There, JoJo gave him the letter to read. Ken couldn't believe it.

"How could the DA deep-six it?" he muttered. "It's totally exculpatory," he told JoJo, "and under the Constitution it had to be turned over to your trial attorney."

JoJo, finally, had gotten a new lawyer.

~

Just moments after he returned to his office, Ashanti buzzed Ken on the intercom: "Uncle Zeke is here, Ken."

He didn't have an appointment, but Ken would not turn the Brooklyn Democratic leader away. In addition to being his secretary's uncle, Ezekial Thomas was the most influential black leader in New York City.

He was talking to his niece as Ken rushed outside to greet him. "You dropped by at the right time, Zeke. I could use a little break from JoJo's case."

As Ken ushered Thomas into his office and motioned him to sit in one of the two dark green, cushiony club chairs across from his desk, he could not help but notice how svelte Zeke looked for a large, heavy-set man. The Democratic boss lit up a cigar without asking Ken's permission, leaned back, and spoke in his deep, resonant voice.

"Ken, I've been reading all about it in the papers. Margiotta's been all over it. Just wanted to wish you good luck tomorrow."

Ken responded courteously as he sat down in the other chair. "Thanks. I'm hopeful."

Thomas continued: "Ken, with all the bad press that Neary's been getting lately about the way he's been treating our black brothers, some of the boys at the Chisholm Club are telling me that maybe we need a new DA. The primary's coming next September. They think you might be the right man to take him on. I'm not at all sure, however, that a primary is a good thing for the party."

"I'm flattered, Zeke, but right now my head is buzzing with JoJo's case, and then I have to concentrate on Jackson. I've also got a bunch of new clients, and I doubt that I would have the time to do right by them."

"Think about it, Ken. No need to decide right now. We'll talk again soon. But in the meantime I would like you to head up the march we're planning next week over the Brooklyn Bridge to protest the rise of police misconduct and the killings of innocent blacks. Sharpton will be leading a march in Washington the same day. I'm sure he would like you to be his surrogate."

"I guess I can do that, Zeke. I'll arrange to meet with the organizers."

⌐

Ken didn't much care for the Reverend Al Sharpton. While he believed in appropriate peaceful protests to help focus the nation's attention on racial injustices, he was dismayed—given Sharpton's checkered past and lifestyle—that President Obama could make him his White House advisor on race relations and describe him as "the voice of the voiceless and a champion of the downtrodden." He was more inclined to agree with Sharpton's critics, such as the African-American City College Professor Clarence Taylor, who described him in his book *Black Religious Intellectuals* as "a political radical who is to blame, in part, for the deterioration of race relations," and the sociologist Orlando Patterson, who referred to him as a "racial arsonist."

Ken could not get out of his craw the notorious way Sharpton began to get national attention. It was back in 1987 when he championed the cause of fifteen-year-old African-American teenager Tawana Brawley. She had been missing for four days from her home

in upstate New York before she had been found, seemingly uncon-
scious and unresponsive, near an apartment where she had once
lived. Brawley was lying in a garbage bag, her clothing torn and
burned, and her body smothered with feces. The words "KKK," "nigger," and "bitch" were written on her torso.

After Brawley was taken to the emergency room, a white detective from the Sheriff's Juvenile Aid Bureau was summoned to interview her, but she remained unresponsive. Finally, the police sent
a black officer, at the family's request, to meet with her. Brawley
communicated with the officer with nods of the head, shrugs of the
shoulder, and written notes. The interview lasted twenty minutes,
during which she uttered one word: "neon." Through gestures and
writing, however, she indicated she had been raped repeatedly in a
wooded area by three white men, at least one of whom, she claimed,
was a police officer.

A sexual assault kit was administered, and the police began
building a case. But forensic tests found no evidence that a sexual
assault of any kind had occurred. And there was no evidence of
hypothermia from exposure to the elements, which would have
been expected in a victim held for several days in the woods at a time
when the temperature dropped below freezing at night. Further sus-
picions were aroused when Brawley initially was unable to provide
any names or descriptions of her assailants.

Nonetheless, public response to Brawley's story was sympathetic
at first. Actor Bill Cosby—later held in disrepute for his own sexual misadventures—pledged support and helped raise money for a
legal fund, and 1,000 people, including Nation of Islam leader Louis
Farrakhan, marched through the streets of Newburgh, New York, in
her support.

Brawley's claims captured headlines across the country. More
public rallies were held denouncing the incident, and racial tensions
climbed. Soon Sharpton, a relatively unheralded, self-proclaimed
civil rights activist, jumped on the bandwagon, and together with

two lawyers—Alton H. Maddox and C. Vernon Mason—began handling Brawley's publicity. The case quickly took on an explosive edge. At the height of the controversy in June 1988, a poll showed a gap of 34 percentage points between whites and blacks when asked whether she was lying—85 percent for whites and 51 percent for blacks.

Sharpton, Maddox, and Mason, as they hoped and planned, generated a national media sensation. They claimed officials all the way up to the state government were engaged in a cover up because the accused alleged assailants were white. Specifically, they singled out Steven Pagones, an Assistant District Attorney in Dutchess County, as one of the rapists, and called him a racist as well.

A grand jury was convened to hear evidence. On October 6, 1988, it released a 170-page report concluding that Brawley had not been abducted, assaulted, raped, and sodomized, as had been claimed by Brawley and Sharpton. The report further concluded that the "unsworn public allegations" against Pagones were false. Before issuing its report, the grand jury heard from 180 witnesses, saw 250 exhibits, and recorded more than 6,000 pages of testimony.

In its report, the grand jury noted many problems with Brawley's story. In addition to the negative results from the rape kit, and that she had not suffered from hypothermia, there were a number of other indications that she was flat out lying: Despite her clothing being charred, there were no burns on her body; although a shoe she was wearing was cut through, she had no injuries to her foot; the racial epithets written on her were upside down, which led to suspicion that Brawley had written the words herself; testimony from her schoolmates revealed that she had attended a local party during the time of her supposed abduction; one witness claimed to have observed Brawley climb into the garbage bag, and the feces on her body was identified as coming from her neighbor's dog. Moreover, Brawley refused to testify.

Much of the grand jury evidence pointed to a possible motive for Brawley's falsifying the incident: trying to avoid violent punishment from her mother and her stepfather, Ralph King. Witnesses testified that Glenda Brawley had previously beaten her daughter for running away and for spending the night with boys. King had a history of violence that included stabbing his first wife fourteen times and shooting her. There was considerable evidence that King would violently attack Brawley. When Brawley had been arrested on a shoplifting charge the previous May, he attempted to beat her for the offense while at the police station.

Finally, in April 1989, *Newsday* published claims by a boyfriend of Brawley's, Daryl Rodriguez, that she had told him the story was fabricated, with help from her mother, in order to avert the wrath of her stepfather.

Regrettably, the Tawana Brawley case exposed deep mistrust in the black community about winning justice from legal institutions, and Ken placed the blame plainly on Sharpton's incendiary and irresponsible behavior. There certainly were legitimate causes to champion about racial injustice, but Tawana Brawley was not one of them. Ken believed that the Brawley fiasco gave a black eye to legitimate complaints about the justice system, and could never forgive Sharpton for inappropriately fanning the racial fires for his own self-interest. He also felt sorry for the innocent Assistant DA, whom Sharpton vilified, and was pleased that Paganes subsequently obtained a substantial monetary judgment against Sharpton after a jury found that he had made seven defamatory statements about him. Sharpton never personally paid the judgment.

Ken had other misgivings about Sharpton. In 1993 he pleaded guilty to a misdemeanor for failing to file a state income tax return. More damning was that on May 9, 2008, the Associated Press reported that Sharpton personally owed $931,000 in federal income taxes and $366,000 in New York State taxes, and that his for-profit company, Rev. Al Communications, owed another $176,000 to the state. Ken thought Sharpton's personal life also left something to be desired. While still married to his second wife, he was reported by the *Daily News* to have a thirty-five-year-old "girlfriend," Aisha McShaw, who was twenty-five years younger, that the couple had been an item for months, and had been photographed at elegant bashes all over the country. And although he had no discernable employment until he had fairly recently landed his own TV show, Sharpton somehow had always lived a life of a multimillionaire while running around the country leading racial protests.

But most troubling to Ken were the inflammatory racist comments Sharpton would venomously spew out, which caused Ken to tend to agree with Professor Taylor's and Sociologist Patterson's less than charitable view of him. A number of them really troubled Ken.

It started more than twenty years ago, when Sharpton stood before a crowd at Kean College in New Jersey and told the student audience: "White folks was in the caves while we was building empires. We built pyramids before Donald Trump even knew what architecture was. We taught philosophy and astrology and mathematics before Socrates and them Greek homos ever got around to it. Do some cracker come and tell you, 'Well my mother and father blood go back to the Mayflower,' you better hold your pocket. That ain't nothing to be proud of; that means their forefathers was crooks."

In addition to alienating the gay community, he inflamed more racial tensions in 1995 when a black Pentecostal Church, which owned a retail property on 125th Street, asked a Jewish tenant who operated Freddie's Fashion Mart to evict his longtime black subtenant who owned a record store called The Record Shack. Sharpton led a protest in Harlem against the planned eviction and told reporters, "We will not stand by and allow them to move this brother so that some white interloper can expand his business." At another time, he called Attorney General Robert Abrams, who was Jewish, "Mr. Hitler." And during the Crown Heights riots, he arranged a rally after Gavin Cato's death and was seen inflaming tensions by making remarks that included, "If the Jews want to get it on, tell them to pin their yarmulkes back and come over to my house."

Perhaps most offensive to Ken were Sharpton's attacks against moderate black politicians close to the Democratic Party, just like Ken, deriding them as "cocktail-sip negroes" or "yellow niggers." Ken just could not fathom how the president, a moderate black Democrat himself, could embrace this type of person. Perhaps it was pure politics: A 2013 Zogby Analytics poll found that one-quarter of African-Americans said that Sharpton speaks for them. Ken couldn't imagine that they would have said that if they knew the real Al Sharpton.

Nonetheless, Sharpton had become a powerful political force, and Ken saw no profit in publicly alienating him. He also recognized that Sharpton had made enormous efforts to distance himself from his ugly past and was in the eyes of many a "new man who had found redemption." They point out that subsequent to the Tawana Brawley fiasco, he founded the National Action Network, a civil rights organization committed to exposing the evils of racial profiling and police brutality. Sharpton also took several credible stabs at running for public office—coming in second in 1997 in New York City's mayoral primary—and addressed the Democratic National Convention in July 2004. Also on the 50th anniversary of the 1954 Supreme Court's historic decision in *Brown v. Board of Education*, he joined with House Speaker Newt Gingrich to announce that they would be working together to explore how the educational gap between races and classes can be fixed. His show on MSNBC, *PoliticsNation with Al Sharpton* is watched by thousands of his devoted followers.

While Ken thought that Sharpton would use any opportunity to mount a demonstration that would get national exposure in order to keep his name in the news, Ken did support selective peaceful marches to bring public attention to major race-relation issues, just like his idol Dr. Martin Luther King, Jr.

Ken also thought that Sharpton should be marching down Chess Street and demanding that the black community take responsibility for cleaning up its own drug-infested projects. He thought it was a distortion to only focus attention on the horrendous behavior of white police officers shooting unarmed blacks—which would be the focus of Sharpton's march. He suspected that Sharpton saw no personal political profit in addressing the rampant black-on-black killings, and Ken's real heroes were the unsung, young, educated black men like Troy Jackson who were committing their lives to dealing with the inner-city problems in the African-American communities, like those where he and Troy had been raised.

Thus, Ken had on his private agenda that one day he would organize a march through places like Chess Street. In the meantime, he thought that it certainly was important to protest the recent wave of police misconduct to bring about needed nationwide changes, especially to better train the police to avoid, rather than inflame, racial tensions. Martin Luther King would approve. Ken would therefore support the planned march that Sharpton would be leading in the nation's capital while he would lead the march in New York City that same day. Ken was worried, however, that Sharpton's march would be unfocused and could potentially cause a backlash that would foment rather than heal the country's racial divide. His, by contrast, would be in support of a specific, constructive list of proposals for the city and state to implement, which his media team would distribute to the press. The list would include taking police misconduct cases out of the hands of district attorneys and into the purview of a new special prosecutor, the prompt release of the identities of police involved in fatal shootings, and a law preventing officers fired in one jurisdiction from being hired in another.

〰

When Ken arrived home that night, he was tired. But he never forgot to write in his diary and made the following entry:

February 7, 2013

Met with JoJo this morning. Spent rest of day preparing for hearing. Got interrupted by Zeke.

Threw out overture for DA run. Too busy to think
about it now. Got to get good night's sleep for the big
day tomorrow.

Even though he was exhausted, he tossed and turned all night.
He knew that winning a habeas corpus case in federal court after a
state court murder conviction almost sixteen years ago was something that rarely, if ever, happened.

9

It was just like coming home when he went the next day for the start of JoJo's habeas hearing. Every time Ken had walked into the Theodore Roosevelt Brooklyn federal courthouse in the old days when he was an AUSA, he was impressed. "What a contrast to the state criminal court building," Ken would tell his friends. He was particularly inspired by the beautiful five-story atrium linking the north and south wings, and the sweeping white marble staircase leading from the ground floor to the central jury room on the second floor. He was also captivated by the color of the marble stones throughout the halls. Unlike the sterile Manhattan federal courthouse across the Brooklyn Bridge with its monolithic white walls, Cesar Pelli, the acclaimed Argentine architect, created a less austere environment for the Brooklyn courthouse by using a beautiful burnt-orange marble on the lower half of the walls.

Ken never could understand why Congress named the building after the first President Roosevelt, who had no particular roots in Brooklyn or connection to the federal judiciary. He thought Ruth Bader Ginsburg, "a Brooklyn gal through and through," would have been a better choice, but he knew that the right wing of the Republican-controlled Congress would never agree to naming it after a Jewish, liberal Supreme Court Justice.

It was a cold but sunny winter day, and he was wearing his pinstriped, dark-blue lawyer suit under his equally dark-blue top coat as he passed through the security checkpoint.

"Haven't seen you in a while, Ken."

Ken knew all the court security officers, and he could never forget the booming voice of the friendly CSO checking out all the people passing through the booth.

"Thanks, Jefferson. Been mostly tied up in state court lately."

"Well, good luck today, Ken. I've been reading about it in all the papers. Get that poor brother out of jail. Man, can you imagine, sixteen years?"

"Keep your fingers crossed, big guy."

Before he stepped into the elevator, Ken stopped at the art gallery at the back of the lobby. Every few months the courthouse featured a new exhibit by a local artist. He thought it was a great idea. The courthouse was a public place, and an art display added a human touch to the seriousness of the legal business that brought everyone into the building. He was captivated by the current exhibit, a display of large, brightly colored, abstract paintings that he thought were creative and original. Ken took a bio of the artist, Bernard Aptekar, from the table at the entrance to the gallery, and thought that one day he would like to meet him and tell him how much he liked his work.

When Ken stepped out of the elevator on the tenth floor, Gary was waiting for him in the hallway. Ken had told Mickey to stay away, but to be within shouting distance in case he needed him. Ken and Gary walked into Judge Gonzales's courtroom and took their places at the large, rectangular, mahogany table closest to the wall where the defense counsel sat. Across the way, at a similar table closer to the jury box, sat Ty Cohen and a few others he did not recognize. Ken assumed they were either young Assistant DAs or paralegals. He also assumed that Racanelli had decided it would be best for him to stay away and let his legal beagles convince the judge that this was nothing more than another desperate habeas case by a murderer who had been convicted years ago in state court after "a full and fair trial before a tried and true jury"—as Cohen would undoubtedly tell the judge. Ken surmised that Racanelli apparently didn't want to dignify the event or appear terribly concerned about it.

Within minutes, the door behind Ken swung open, and two marshals brought JoJo into the courtroom. Behind the door were two holding cells. There were many more in the basement. The prisoners who had to be in court were brought there in the morning from the MDC by marshals, and a secured elevator carried them to the holding cells next to the courtrooms when they were needed in court.

Two marshals uncuffed JoJo and stood watch a few feet behind him as he sat down next to Ken.

"Well, JoJo, you're looking good in the clothes I got for you."

"Thanks, Mr. Williams, but I'm nervous as hell."

"All rise," shouted Judge Gonzales' courtroom deputy as the door at the left side of the bench slowly opened and the judge gingerly mounted the steps leading to her high-backed, swivel, black leather chair.

"Everyone, please sit. Mr. Innelli, call the case."

The short, wafer-thin, long-haired deputy stepped up from his workstation at the foot of the judges' bench and authoritatively announced: "Joaquin Jones versus the People of the State of New York. Counsel, state your appearances for the record."

"Kenneth Williams for the habeas petitioner."

"Tyrus Cohen for the district attorney."

"Very well," responded the judge. "As you gentlemen know, this is a habeas corpus hearing and not a criminal trial. Therefore, there is no jury and I am the sole judge of the facts. The defendant was convicted by a jury many years ago at his trial. Nonetheless, I have determined, as you know from the decision I wrote, that this is the unusual case which warrants a factual habeas corpus hearing. Now, Mr. Williams, since you brought this petition in behalf of your client, you have the burden of going forward. How do you plan to proceed today?"

"A brief opening statement, Your Honor, and then I have a number of witnesses whose testimony will probably take up the rest of the day."

"Well, I've ordered the hearing, so I'm anxious to listen to what they will be saying under oath."

Ty Cohen jumped up: "Your Honor, before we do that, I would respectfully ask you to reconsider your decision. Having a habeas hearing sixteen years after a jury has convicted a murderer is unprecedented."

"That may well be, Mr. Cohen, but this may be the exception. I ordered the hearing principally because of the copy of the letter from Butler that was in the case file. Jones' trial lawyer has sworn in an affidavit submitted in support of the habeas petition that it was never turned over to him. You don't contend otherwise, do you?"

"The copy, no, Your Honor. The original, I have no personal knowledge of that one way or the other. But in light of the overwhelming evidence against the defendant, it really didn't matter. Moreover, the fact that the copy was in the file shows that, at best, it was an inadvertent oversight. If it were otherwise, and the prosecutor was acting unscrupulously, which can't possibly be the case; it would have been destroyed."

"It didn't matter, Mr. Cohen? Really? Let's read it together. It's handwritten and not exactly the King's English, but it's legible enough, even with all the misspellings."

Judge Gonzales had it right on top of her file. She put on her reading glasses, leaned forward, and slowly started to read. "It's dated April 25, 1997," she began. "That's about sixteen years ago, and it's addressed to 'Mr. Racanelli.'"

Jimmy Margiotta and a host of other reporters sitting in the rows reserved for the press took out their pens.

Mr. Racanelli,

I testified in court yesterday just like you told me I had to. But you know it ain't the truth. You made me do it and threatened me with all sorts of shit. I've

done bad things in my life, but never radded out a
bro before. You may not beleave this, but I DO have a
conshens. I never saw JoJo shoot nobody.

Solomon Butler

Judge Gonzales handed the letter to her courtroom deputy and instructed: "Let's mark this as Exhibit A, Mr. Innelli." She then swiveled around to face Cohen. "It has a 'cc' to the DA. This is the letter that Butler was apparently able to copy and send to the DA. Where is the original, Mr. Cohen?"

"As I said, I don't know, Your Honor," he replied sheepishly as he slowly stood up.

"Well, did you ever ask Mr. Racanelli if he received it, and if so, what he did with it?"

"I did, Your Honor. He told me he doesn't remember."

The judge was quick to respond: "But at the very least, we all know that the copy buried in the DA's file never saw the light of day until the Freedom of Information Officer was ordered to turn over the file to Mr. Jones."

Cohen did not say anything. The judge was making a statement, and there was no question to which he had to respond. He politely nodded, and quietly sat down.

Judge Gonzales turned to Ken. "Mr. Williams, let's hear your opening statement."

Ken slowly walked to the lectern, a few feet in front of the first row of the public seats, tapped the microphone to make sure it was on, and with a measured cadence, began to speak.

"Your Honor, I'll be brief, and let the witnesses do the talking. You have obviously carefully read the habeas petition that I drafted and the supporting affidavits. The crux of this case, and what makes it different than the run-of-the mill federal habeas petitions that flood the courts from justly convicted, desperate criminals, is the blatant disregard from the likes of Anthony Racanelli, with the apparent blessing from the DA himself, of the basic constitutional obligation of the prosecutor to turn over to the defendant's lawyer, prior to the trial, all exculpatory information in his possession. And here, the exculpatory evidence is not just verbal statements, though there's plenty of that, but an actual, written letter, hand-delivered by Solomon Butler to Racanelli the day after Butler told the grand jury that he saw JoJo Jones shoot Rabbi Bernstein.

"That letter of recantation was classic *Brady* material, and every prosecutor, defense attorney, and judge knows that. Like it or not, that letter had to be disclosed. Not to do that was a clear violation of the Due Process Clause of the United States Constitution. And while the original, addressed to Racanelli, never has surfaced, we know it was written because, thank God, JoJo made a copy of it and sent it off to the DA. It was perhaps fortuitous that it made its way into the file."

"Let me interrupt you, Mr. Williams," said the judge. "Of course I'm familiar with the Supreme Court's decision in *Brady v. Maryland*—it was a landmark ruling when made in 1963—and I also know that the federal district court in Washington, DC, recently vacated the conviction of the late United States Senator Ted Stevens because the federal prosecutors intentionally withheld and concealed *Brady* material from Stevens's defense lawyers that included witness statements and key details that could have undermined the prosecutors' star witnesses. They allowed false testimony to be presented to the jury. It was a huge scandal, Mr. Cohen, and remains to this day a black mark on the criminal justice system. A prosecutor's responsibility is to seek justice, and not to secure a conviction at any cost. What do you say about all this, Mr. Cohen?"

Tyrus Cohen got up and was quick to respond.

"Your Honor, I agree with what you say, but it's not so black and white in this case. Are we to take the word of a criminal convicted of murder who has an incentive to say just about anything to wiggle his way out of jail? After all, how do we really know the so-called original was really written by Butler and given to Mr. Racanelli? And even if the copy somehow made its way into the file, how do we know that either Mr. Racanelli or the DA ever saw it? It might have simply been put into the file by a secretary who never read it. There is simply no showing that anyone acted in bad faith."

Judge Gonzales was perturbed: "I'm afraid you have not read the *Brady* case carefully enough, Mr. Cohen. It's such a landmark constitutional case that I always keep a copy of it nearby. Just let me find it."

Cohen started to perspire as the judge opened her desk drawer, thumbed through some papers, and pulled out what appeared to be a copy of a judicial opinion. "Here's what the United States Supreme Court wrote in *Brady*, Mr. Cohen":

> We now hold that the suppression by the prosecution
> of evidence favorable to an accused upon request vio-
> lates due process where the evidence is material either
> to guilt or punishment, irrespective of the good faith
> or bad faith of the prosecution.

Judge Gonzales's voice had gotten louder as she read "irrespective of the good faith or bad faith of the prosecution." She slowly put the opinion back into the drawer, and triumphantly spoke. "What do you have to say about that, Mr. Cohen?"

To his credit, Cohen—ever quick on his feet—shot back. "Well, I may have inadvertently misspoken, Your Honor, but it says two other things that deserve consideration. First, the accused must request the so-called evidence, and second it must be material."

Ken could not contain himself. "With all due respect, Your Honor, you will find in the file the standard written request by trial counsel 'to turn over all *Brady* material.' So much for Mr. Cohen's first contention. And as for the issue of materiality, what can be more material than a written recantation by the prosecution's star witness?"

Cohen was not finished. "But even if the so-called copy was inadvertently not turned over, there is another principle of law that comes into play. It could simply be viewed as harmless error if there was other overwhelming evidence of guilt, and in Jones' case there were two other witnesses. One saw JoJo pull the trigger, and the other saw him running from the scene."

"But they also told Racanelli that they lied," shouted Ken.

"Did they really?" Cohen flared. "Let them say it under oath and perjure themselves. All we have is their phony affidavits. There's nothing in writing from anyone else, and even if they say that now, for whatever reason, I'm sure Mr. Racanelli knows nothing about that, and if need be would so testify."

Pacing in front of the bench, Cohen continued.

"Surely, Judge Gonzales, you would not take the word of convicted criminals over the word of the DA's highly respected chief prosecutor, who has put more murderers behind bars than anyone else in the entire city?"

"Enough of this, gentlemen," fumed a clearly agitated judge. "Call your first witness, Mr. Williams."

"Solomon Butler, Your Honor. He's waiting outside in the hallway."

Gary Rico got up, went to the back of the courtroom, and opened the solid wood double door. In walked a feeble-looking black man who appeared twenty years older than he probably was. Solomon Butler was escorted by two matronly African-American women in nurses' uniforms who were propping him up as he walked between the prosecutor and defense counsels' tables to the front of the courtroom. He was drawn and sallow-looking, and Ken had to help him into the witness chair.

Obviously concerned, Innelli said: "You don't have to stand, sir, but you'll have to raise your right hand, and tell the court if you solemnly swear to tell the truth, the whole truth, and nothing but the truth, so help you God?"

"I do," he whispered.

"Try to speak up," ordered the judge delicately. "I suggest that you use the microphone."

The deputy clerk continued. "Please state and spell your name for the record."

With the help of the mic, he complied: "Solomon Butler, S-O-L-O-M-O-N B-U-T-L-E-R."

Ken returned to the podium and, as was the protocol, politely addressed the court: "May I inquire, Your Honor?"

"You may," responded Judge Gonzales, almost by rote.

"Will the clerk please hand me what has been marked in evidence as Exhibit A?"

Innelli, the keeper of the exhibits, quickly complied.

Placing it in front of the witness, Ken asked, "Is this the copy of the letter you sent to the DA, and is that your signature at the bottom?"

"Yessir, yessir."

Without pausing, Ken continued: "Alright, Solomon. I know it's hard, but try to keep your voice up. Before we talk more about the letter, let's first start with this 911 call a few hours after Rabbi Bernstein was shot." Turning to Judge Gonzales, Ken asked, "Can we have it marked as Exhibit B, Your Honor? This is one of the audio tapes that was in the DA's file."

Ty Cohen did not object, and Ken played it on the tape recorder that was at the far end of defense counsel's table. It was short. "I call youse to tell youse dat JoJo Jones shot the Jew, and Solomon Butler knows it."

"Do you recognize the voice, Solomon?"

"No sir. There's lots of black folks in the hood that sounds like that and just wants to make trouble."

"Tell us what happened then."

"The police come and arrest me for a stickup I did that day. I needed the bread to get some heroin. I was on withdrawal and was getting terrible shakes. I had to have a fix fast. I never was able to get

it before I got nailed. Two cops grilled me all night and wouldn't let
me take my methadone. They ask me if I knew JoJo Jones. I told them
I sees him around, but that's all. I couldn't stop shaking and needed
shut-eye. They asked me if I seen him shoot the Jew. I said I didn't,
but they kept grillin' me. One of the cops, who was called Tony, did
most of it. I couldn't take it anymore. The shakes was making me
nuts. I caved and told the cops I would say whatever they wanted if
they would give me my meth and let me cop some zees. They wrote
something down and told me to sign it. They gave me the meth for
the shakes as soon as I did, and put me in a cell so I could sleep."

"Your Honor, the paper that Mr. Butler just referred to also was
in the DA's file. I assume Mr. Cohen would have no objection to it
being placed in evidence as Exhibit C?"

"Of course not," answered Cohen. "It's what he told Mr.
Racanelli and the other detective who was there that night."

Ken placed it in front of the witness. "Is this what you signed,
Solomon?"

He didn't hesitate to answer: "Looks like it."

"Tell us what happened next," asked Ken.

Solomon Butler wiggled his decrepit body closer to the microphone and tried to speak louder. "Well, they told me I would have
to tell it to a grand jury, and if I told it just like what they wrote, they
would drops the robbery charge and lets me go free. If I didn't says
it like that, they would nail me for the robbery and send me up the
river for ten years. Coupla days later I did what they tells me, and
they lets me go home."

"Tell the judge what happened then," Ken asked.

"When I got home I was mad. I was not shakin' no more, feeling better. And I was mad they made me do that to an innocent
brother. So I finds out that the Tony who was grillin' me the most
was Racanelli, so I wrote him that letter. And since I don't trust him,
I made a copy, puts it in an envelope, address it to the Brooklyn DA,
goes to the Post Office and mails it with a good stamp on it."

Ken was leading him on step by step. "Tell us what you did with the original?"

"The next day, I goes to Racanelli's office and gives it to him."

"What did he do?"

Solomon Butler moved even closer to the microphone. "He rips it up and tells me that if I don't stick to what they wrote and what I told the grand jury when I testifies at Jones' trial, they would arrest me for lying under oath, arrest me again for the robbery, and throw the book at me. I didn't wants to go back to jail. They says it might be for twenty years now. At the trial, I did what they told me."

"What you said wasn't true, was it, Solomon?"

"No it wasn't," he sheepishly responded.

"No further questions at this time, Your Honor."

Cohen shot back, "What do you mean, 'at this time?' Before I start my cross examination, either you're finished questioning him or you're not."

"Your Honor," responded Ken, "with the court's indulgence I would like to ask Mr. Butler one more question later on. There's a reason for it."

"Well, it's an unusual request, but there's no jury here, and I assume you are acting in good faith, so I'll let you do it. Go ahead, Mr. Cohen."

"I just have one question to ask the witness, Your Honor."

Cohen approached the witness stand, stood just a few feet in front of Solomon Butler, stared at him, and snarled, "Mr. Butler, why did you wait sixteen years before you decided to come out of the woodwork and change your grand jury and trial testimony? You know all too well that you can be prosecuted now for lying."

"I ain't lying no more, I'm dying. I can't see the Lord without making things right. My mama read the Bible and done give me the name Solomon and tells me that someday you will do right just like him before you meets yo' maker."

"And you want this court to believe that you got religion sixteen years later?"

Without waiting for an answer, Cohen turned to Judge Gonzales: "No other questions, Your Honor."

"Very well then," responded the judge. "We've been going for some time. Let's have another witness before lunch and see if we can wrap this up by the end of the day. Who do you have now, Mr. Williams?"

"Dr. Martin Post, Your Honor."

As she walked out of the courtroom, the judge told Ken: "Have him here when we return in fifteen minutes."

Solomon Butler was still on the witness stand. He looked drained. Ken helped him down and walked him over to defense counsel's table. Butler slumped into the first chair he reached. His breathing was labored and he looked pale. Ken poured him a glass of water and had to hold the glass as Solomon drank slowly.

10

Gary ushered a slender, well-groomed, middle-aged man into the courtroom and led him to the witness stand. In contrast to Solomon Butler, he appeared in robust health. As he sat, he tapped the microphone to make sure it was on. He had a manila folder with him and placed it next to the mic. Soon, Judge Gonzales came back into the courtroom and nodded to her courtroom deputy. After Innelli gave the witness the oath and had him state and spell his name, Ken—with the court's blessing—began his direct examination.

"Dr. Post, what is the nature of your medical practice?"

"I am a board-certified oncologist. I'm affiliated with Mount Sinai and my practice is limited to treating cancer patients."

"Did you bring your vitae with you?"

The doctor reached into his file. "I have one right here, counselor. It runs several pages. It sets forth my education, the titles of many articles that I authored that have been published in recognized medical journals about various aspects of oncology, and also references a handbook that I also authored that was recently published by the American Medical Association on the medical and spiritual management of terminal cancer patients."

Looking at Cohen, Ken asked: "Do the People have any objection to this being placed in evidence?"

Tyrus Cohen was a pro and Ken knew he would not run the risk of annoying the judge by challenging Dr. Post's obviously stellar credentials. "No, Your Honor," he quickly answered. "The doctor is obviously a qualified oncologist."

"Very well," responded Judge Gonzales. "Let's have it marked Exhibit D. Next question, Mr. Williams."

"Do you know Solomon Butler?"

"I do. I see him sitting over there. He's been my patient for several months. He's had extensive chemotherapy and radiation for stage four lung cancer. I told Solomon about a month ago that there was nothing more we could do for him and to get his affairs in order. He knows he's dying. It could be any time now."

"When did you last see him, doctor?"

"Just last week when we arranged to put him in Good Samaritan Hospice. He said he was ready to meet his maker, but asked me if he could come to court today. He said he wanted to clear his conscience and make things right. It was his dying wish. I arranged to have two hospice care attendants bring him here today."

"Thank you, Dr. Post. That will be all, unless Mr. Cohen wishes to inquire."

Cohen did not look happy but tried his best to put on his game face. "No questions, Your Honor."

As Dr. Post stepped down, he walked over to Solomon Butler before leaving the courtroom, patted him on his slumped shoulders, and whispered: "Bless you, son. May God be with you."

JoJo Jones, who was sitting close by, gently touched Solomon's right arm and added: "Amen, brother. I forgive you."

Even the hardened press corps seemed to be moved, and Judge Gonzales dabbed her eyes as she spoke: "We'll take an hour for lunch. Mr. Williams, have your next witnesses ready when we resume."

⌇

Solomon was not in any condition to go out to eat. Ken had arranged for the attendants to have some food for him. He was given a little soup, while Ken and Gary ate sandwiches. Defense counsel's table became a lunch counter.

After Butler slurped down the soup, Ken wiped his chin and spoke to him: "Solomon, you don't have to stay if you're not up to it.

You don't have to do it. I set it up so you could think about it as long as possible."

"I thought about it all morning, Mr. Williams. JoJo telling me he forgives me. I wants to do it."

Ken said, "Okay, Solomon, I'll get you back on the stand right after we have Lamar testify."

~

When everyone was back in the courtroom, Ken called Lamar Jordan as his next witness. He went right to the heart of Lamar's testimony at JoJo's trial as soon as the swearing-in formalities were completed.

"Mr. Jordan, you testified before the grand jury and again at the trial that you saw my client, JoJo Jones, pull the trigger, correct?"

Lamar was casually dressed. He was wearing neatly pressed long blue jeans, which just about covered his gangling legs. A white cut-off t-shirt revealed a road map of tattoos on his muscular arms. He had another one on the back of his shaved head—a red and black dagger.

"I done say that, Mr. Lawyer."

"Was it true?" came Ken's next question.

Ken was taken by surprise by the answer: "I wouldn't have said it if it wasn't, would I?"

"Mr. Jordan," snapped Ken, "were you talking to anybody from the DA's office during our lunch break?"

"Objection," shouted Cohen.

"He's now a hostile witness, Your Honor," shot back Ken.

"Objection overruled. The witness will answer the question."

His answer was barely audible: "Well, Mr. Racanelli was outside and just told me to tell the truth just like I did before."

Ken knew that Jordan had been gotten to and was scared off from testifying the way he had told Ken he would. He was furious that Racanelli would stoop so low, but he didn't lose his cool.

"One moment, Your Honor," he said calmly. "I need to get something out of my file."

A moment later, Ken slowly approached the witness, and as he waved a paper in front of him, asked, "Lamar, isn't this the affidavit you signed some time ago saying that your testimony at JoJo Jones' trial was a pack of lies?"

Lamar squirmed, and meekly responded, "I dunno. They asked me to sign that thing but it wasn't the truth. I was scared, so I did what they said."

Ken went right after him. "Who asked you to do that?"

His hands were shaking as he answered haltingly, "Some big guys on the street, I think. Don't remember."

Ken was confident that Judge Gonzales would know that Lamar was lying and that Racanelli had done a number on him again, but Ken had left nothing to chance and was prepared.

Ken turned to the judge, and asked, "Your Honor, may I have just a moment? I have a brief tape, which I would like to play. While my associate sets up the recorder, can I have it marked for identification, subject to connection?"

"Mark it Exhibit E for ID, Mr. Innelli," ordered Judge Gonzales.

"Listen to the beginning, Lamar, do you recognize the four voices?"

"Yeah, it's me and Shillique talkin' to our friend Kelvin last week on the street. I don't know the other voice. Kelvin say it's a friend of his. Funny-looking, short guy. How did you get that? Was that brother wearing a wire?"

"Never mind, Lamar. Let's listen to the rest of what you said to Kelvin."

"Do we really have to, Your Honor?" Lamar asked, almost pleading, as he swiveled in his chair toward Judge Gonzales.

Before the judge could answer, Cohen jumped to his feet.

"Your Honor, we have never been given a copy of this tape. It's a cheap trick and in violation of the disclosure requirements of the Rules of Criminal Procedure."

Ken was livid. "We never would have introduced this if the witness didn't turn on us. Under the circumstances, the normal rules don't apply."

Judge Gonzales spoke two words. "Play it."

Gary pressed the play button again. He had revved up the volume. It was loud enough for the last person in the last row of the packed courtroom to hear clearly.

"I hear you and Shillique gonna have your big day in court, Lamar."

Ken told Gary to stop playing it, and asked Jordan, "Who is that speaking?"

"That's Kelvin," he answered. Jordan turned to Judge Gonzales. "Judge, do I really have to answer these questions?"

"Yes, you do," she answered tersely.

Ken motioned to Gary to start it again, and said to no one in particular, "Alright. Let's hear the rest of what went on."

"Yeah," came Jordan's voice, after Gary pressed the play button again. "It's payback time for that son-of-a-bitch, Racanelli. Solomon's gonna come clean, and I'm gonna cover his ass. I told Racanelli after he talked me into saying that I saw JoJo do it, that it ain't true. I'm gonna tell the truth now when I go to court next week."

"What are you going to say?" Kelvin asked.

"I'm gonna tell it like it was. I was on probation for three years for ripping off the shoe store around the corner. One of the things I had to do was to get permission from the probation officer before if I had to go out of the city. I was in my last month of probation. Soon I wouldn't have nobody on my ass no more, and I don't have to report to nobody no more. Then I get a call from Jamaica that my mama is dying. I go to see her, but forget to tell probation. It was no big deal, but I gets arrested and flown back to Brooklyn."

Lamar paused for a breath on the tape. "So they take me to an office with a big sign that says DA. Racanelli comes in and asks me if I knows JoJo from the hood. I says I do, but he's a clean dude. Never cause any trouble. He tells me that JoJo's in trouble now cause he was fingered as the guy who shot the rabbi. I says I don't know anything about that. He tells me that if I just say I saw JoJo pull the trigger, they ain't gonna charge me with violating my probation, and I could go back to be with my mama. Otherwise, I goes back to jail."

Ken signaled Gary to stop the tape, and asked Jordan, "Lamar, was Shillique standing near you when you were telling this to Kelvin?"

"He was right next to me, listening to what I was saying."

Ken nodded to Gary, and he pressed the play button. "Is that Shillique talking now, Lamar?"

"Yeah, that's him," he mumbled.

Gary pressed the stop button.

"Let's hear what he says now." Gary pressed the play button again.

"So I'm mad. Racanelli knew I was big in the hood. They picked me up and said they was holding me as a material witness. I didn't know what they was talking about, but they locked me up at Rikers for two weeks and lets me go only after I agree to say I saw JoJo run away. But I ain't gonna testify. Don't want no more trouble."

"That's it, Your Honor," said Ken. "There's no more tape and no more questions of this witness. I would just like to recall Solomon Butler now."

Ken lifted Butler out of his chair and held his left arm as he slowly walked him back into the witness chair.

"You are still under oath, Mr. Witness," reminded the court clerk.

Ken stood just a few feet in front of Butler, and wasted no time. He asked, "Solomon, do you know who killed Rabbi Bernstein?"

Solomon looked to the ceiling and clasped his hands before he answered. His body was weak, but his voice was strong.

"I did."

There were murmurs throughout the courtroom as Ken quickly said, "Tell us why."

Solomon exhaled, took a deep breath, and answered, "He may have been a rabbi, but we all knows him as a Jew landlord who come every month to collect the rents. He comes that day to get the rents from the apartment I'm living in with my baby mama. She tells him she just got a new job taking care of a rich, old lady in the neighborhood and asks him if she could pay next month. He says she done this before, and if she don't pays up by tomorrow, he will go to the judge. He tells us we better start looking for another place to live."

Ken interrupted, "Slow down, Solomon, and tell us what happened next."

Butler took a sip of water, and continued. "I follows him down Chess Street. He goes into another building of his and comes out soon counting the money he got there. I stop him and tells him not to kick us out. He says I'm a no-good shvartzah. I know he's calling me a nigger. He turns his back and starts to walk away. I turn him around and take the money from him. He starts fighting me. I take out the gun and shoot him."

"That's all I have of this witness, Your Honor."

"I think we've had enough drama for the day," quipped Judge Gonzales. "Do you have any other witnesses, Mr. Williams, or do you rest your case?"

"That's it, Your Honor," Ken replied, "except for Anthony Racanelli and the district attorney. And JoJo also wants to testify."

"Do we really need him?" asked Judge Gonzales. "As you know, Mr. Williams, this is a habeas case and I am the trier of the facts. In the handful of habeas hearings I have had throughout the years, I never found any of the petitioner's witnesses believable. They usually have a criminal record a mile long and an incentive to lie. But there's always an exception, and that's what we have today. I believe that Mr. Butler has told the truth. So I'm making that credibility finding."

Ken was thrilled, but nonetheless told Gonzales, "Your Honor, JoJo wants to tell his story, how he's been locked up like a dog for sixteen years for a crime he never committed, and how Anthony Racanelli and James Neary railroaded him."

"You don't have to put him on the stand, Mr. Williams, unless you really want to, but given the serious nature of the accusations, which go right to the core of the integrity of the criminal justice system in our country, I'll let you call Racanelli and the DA. I'm anxious to get to the bottom of all of this."

The judge banged her gavel for the first time as she rose, and said to Tyrus Cohen, "Make sure you have them here tomorrow morning, 10:00 a.m. sharp."

11

After he followed Racanelli and Cohen to his office, Neary slammed the door and shouted into his office intercom: "No calls or interruptions, Naomi, until I say so."

Naomi Moskowitz had been Neary's loyal secretary from the beginning, but she'd never heard that voice before. Soon she smelled cigarette smoke.

Big Jim was puffing away. His chief prosecutor and his trial attorney stood next to the club chairs. They were not going to sit while their boss was pacing up and down. They knew what was coming.

"How the fuck did this happen?" he fumed. "Tony, you've got a lot of explaining to do."

They finally all sat down. Racanelli took a deep breath and began to talk. Like his boss, his speech was often full of profanity when challenged.

"That no-good, motherfucker, son-of-a-bitch, lying bastard. Dying, my ass! You would think it was some kind of Italian opera. What was in that confession came right from his mouth. We didn't lean on him that much. We picked him and Jones up right after that 911 call. If you think JoJo was home getting a haircut from his mysterious personal barber, then you believe in Santa Claus. Butler didn't know about the 911, and he validated it by acknowledging that he did indeed know what happened, just like the caller said. There was no reason not to believe him when he fingered Jones."

But Neary looked puzzled. "How about the letter, Tony?"

"Well, I don't remember any letter, and I don't remember that lying piece of shit changing his story. But while we're on the subject, how about the so-called copy that was in your file?"

"Well, I don't look at every piece of mail that comes into my office. That's Moskowitz's job. She must have put it into the file. I never saw it."

Up to this time, Cohen was silent, but he thought he now had to speak.

"I don't mean to be the bearer of bad news, but I feel obligated to say it straight. The judge has made it pretty clear by ruling that she finds Butler's testimony to be credible, that she's going in all likelihood to grant habeas relief. But she's clearly upset that the copy of the letter in the file, not to mention the alleged missing original, was never given to Jones' trial counsel. And, as I learned the hard way this morning, when Gonzales took me to the woodshed, it doesn't matter if it was an innocent oversight or whatnot. Under *Brady*, it was clearly exculpatory and the lawyer had a right to see it."

"So what's the downside?" asked the DA.

Cohen went on: "Well, she apparently believes she has some overriding responsibility to dig further. She's offended at what happened with the Stevens case and seems to be on some sort of mission to make sure the government has learned its lesson and doesn't play fast and loose with the rules."

Racanelli couldn't resist chiming in. "That's pretty much typical of one of those knee-jerk liberal, minority judges that Obama appointed to the federal bench."

"Be that as it may," continued Cohen, "but the reality is that she wants to hear what each of you is going to say under oath in court tomorrow. And, after Williams does his best to make you both look foolish with his questions, she's likely to also question you. She has the right to do that."

Just then, Naomi's voice came over the intercom. "I'm sorry, boss, I know you didn't want to be disturbed, but I thought you would want to see the late afternoon news stories that just came over the Internet about the Jones case. I just printed them out."

Curiosity got the best of Big Jim. "I assume they are all from Margiotta. Let's see what the son-of-a-bitch wrote. Bring them in."

"Right away, but I'm afraid there's a lot more than just Margiotta's."

Naomi Moskowitz came into the office with a pile of news clippings and put them on the corner of Neary's desk. She was always impeccably dressed—usually in a black pantsuit—and didn't look much different than when she started working for Neary as soon as she had graduated from business school fifteen years ago. Neary often thought that Gene Austin must have had someone like her in mind when he wrote his signature song nine decades ago, "Five Foot Two, Eyes of Blue."

After Naomi left, Neary picked up the papers. The *Daily News* was the first.

"Holy shit," he exclaimed. "Front page! And there's my picture under that fucking headline, making me look like I just came from a funeral."

He slammed it down and Racanelli picked it up and looked at it.

"Typical, wiseass headline writer," he gasped. "Don't let it get to you."

Cohen's curiosity got the best of him. When he looked, he tried hard not to react as he read it: NEARY NOT SO CHEERY.

It wasn't only the *News*. The front page of the *Post* had a picture of Neary at a fund-raising barbeque the previous summer with the headline: DA TO BE GRILLED. But Cohen thought to himself that the cleverest of all was the picture of "Old Sparky" on the front page of *Newsday* with the banner DISTRICT ATTORNEY IN HOT SEAT.

Most disturbing, however, was the lead article of the Metro Section of the *New York Times* reporting on the entire history of the Jones case. A whole column was devoted to Jones' exculpatory letter and recounting the suppression of evidence during Senator Stevens's trial. And it didn't stop there. The *Times*'s lead editorial called for an investigation by an independent special prosecutor. The Jones case and the conduct of the DA's office had gone viral.

"Well, Tony," said a startled district attorney, "it looks like the shit has hit the fan. And you're the fucking cause of it."

Racanelli's face reddened. "Don't put all the blame on me. Remember, that letter was found in your file, not mine. And you told me that I better get the rabbi's killer fast because you were getting a lot of heat from the Grand Rebbe."

Neary lit up another cigarette.

"Alright, alright, let's try to calm down and think this through. I'll get our PR people on it right away. In the meantime, no fuckin' way we're going to expose ourselves to being questioned by that shithead Williams and that commie judge. Cohen, you go tell her that we won't oppose the habeas petition, but without prejudice."

"That means that Jones will stay in jail while we decide whether to retry him."

"That's right. Ask her for thirty days for us to decide. Maybe Butler will be dead by then, and he won't be able to testify if we decide to try the case again."

⌁

The courtroom was overflowing the next morning, and the hallway was packed with journalists and supporters who could not get in. Outside on the sidewalk, a host of newspaper photographers and TV crews from CBS, NBC, ABC, CNN, and local affiliates were lined up, hoping for the shot that would lead the paper or six o'clock news. They would get their wish.

"May it please the court," Cohen obsequiously began, "the People will no longer oppose the habeas corpus petition, and consent to the granting of the writ."

There was stunned silence as Judge Gonzales inched forward and stated, "Mr. Cohen, that means that Mr. Jones can now walk out of this courtroom a free man."

"No, Your Honor. We request that the dismissal be without prejudice, and that he be kept in jail for another month while the People decide whether it can gather enough credible evidence to warrant a retrial."

"Even in light of Solomon Butler's confession?"

"Yes, Your Honor," Cohen meekly responded.

"It's not going to happen, Mr. Cohen. You call your boss, who apparently has decided not to show his face today, and tell him that unless it's with prejudice—meaning the People dismiss the underlying indictment, and drop all charges against Mr. Jones so that he cannot be tried again—the hearing will continue and he and Mr. Racanelli will have to testify."

"Yes, Your Honor," said Cohen, even more meekly. "May I have a few minutes to try to reach him?"

"We'll wait," snapped the judge.

Cohen went into the men's room down the hall. He checked the stalls to make sure that no one else was there and took out his cell phone. Within a matter of minutes, he returned to the courtroom and reported, "Your Honor, the People consent to a dismissal with prejudice."

Judge Gonzales slowly rose, straightened out her robe, and announced, "Mr. Jones, you are a free man. I apologize to you on behalf of our criminal justice system for this horrendous miscarriage of justice. You are free to leave. I hope you will not lead the rest of your life a bitter man, and can, with God's help, put this terrible chapter behind you."

12

As soon as the judge left for her chambers, the courtroom was in a frenzy. With Jimmy Margiotta leading the charge, a scrum of reporters rushed to speak to JoJo, who was sitting next to Ken. JoJo had his hands prayerfully clasped, and his face was looking straight up. They heard him murmur: "Thank you, Lord."

"Not now, guys," said Ken. "Give him some space. We'll talk to everyone in a few minutes outside the building."

Ken asked the court security officers to lead them past the crowd in the hallway and to the privacy of the lawyers' lounge at the end of the corridor. After Judge Gonzales had said the day before that she believed Solomon Butler was telling the truth, Ken had prepared himself for this moment. And JoJo was also prepared. Together, they walked side by side out of the courthouse and into the bright sunlight that greeted them on the cold day. It was like a war zone. Five marshals kept the crowd at a reasonable distance as flashbulbs popped like firecrackers and dozens of TV cameras began to whirl.

"Ladies and gentlemen," began Ken. "After sixteen years the face of justice has risen over the rotten body of a corrupt DA and his number one henchman. But I have good reason to believe that JoJo Jones is not the only one who has been railroaded and been the victim of a phony prosecution. And I will not rest until we get to the bottom of all this. JoJo is now a free man, but there are other innocent victims he tells me who are still sitting in jail. I will not rest until all of them are standing beside me as free human beings outside of this courthouse. JoJo wants to say a few words now, and then please let him have some peace so he can start adjusting to his new life."

JoJo was not dressed for the cold temperature. Ken forgot to bring him an overcoat. But it didn't seem to matter; he never felt the cold. He stood erect and proud of what he had accomplished, his jailhouse lawyering having worked a seeming miracle. His voice resonated.

"Ladies and gentlemen, I want to first thank Ken Williams, his associate Gary Ricco, and not to be forgotten, his investigator Mickey Zissou. They had faith in me. Without them I would not be standing before you today. I've had lots of time to think about life during the many years I've been in jail. I have read lots of books and have tried to become a literate, intelligent human being under the most adverse conditions. And my faith in the Lord has been key. Without the Bible I could have become a revengeful man. But that will not be. I have love and compassion for all of us. And I have a mission I must complete. Mr. Williams alluded to others who have not been as fortunate as I am to taste freedom again. I will devote my life to working on their cases, just like I worked on mine, and see to it that someday we will have a justice system in Brooklyn that we can all be proud of.

"And I look forward to working with people of all religions, including the unfortunate Hasidim who have suffered at the hands of some of my wrong-headed brothers, to bring peace and goodwill to our communities. But right now, I'm going with Mr. Williams to have a little private celebration and then try to get some rest for the beginning of a new dawn. God bless all of you."

JoJo put his arms around Ken as the TV cameras continued whirling and the press photographers kept shooting away. Mickey was waiting at the wheel of Ken's MINI Cooper on Tillary Street, just a few hundred feet from the entrance to the courthouse. JoJo and Ken squeezed into the back seat. Gary sat next to Mickey in the front.

"Haven't seen you for a while," Ken said to Mickey. "Gary tells me you got yourself a new woman."

"So far, so good. I kind of like her, boss. She sure likes to party. Cost me a fortune to take her to Vegas last week. She was a cheap date when I first met her, but you should see what she's costing me now."

Ken's eyes lit up. "That's another country hook if I ever heard one. Does she have a name, Mickey?"

"I'll tell you but you better not make any wiseass comments."

"C'mon Mickey, you know I'm not that type of guy."

"Well, her real name is Maureen, but she's so short they call her Mouse."

"Seems like you two should have gone to Disneyland instead of Las Vegas."

"Fuck you, boss."

Ken noticed that even JoJo was laughing.

"Say hello to JoJo Jones," Ken said. "I don't think you met before."

"Man, how does it feel to be out of jail after all these years?" Mickey asked.

JoJo simply smiled. "I want to thank you for everything you've done."

Mickey drove two blocks down Tillary, made a left turn onto Court Street, drove five blocks, and left them all off at the restaurant in the middle of the block.

Franco greeted them at the door. "Welcome to the Queen, Mr. Jones. I hope you like my pasta." He led them to a private room. Betsy was there waiting.

"Nice to finally meet you, Mr. Jones," she said. "I've heard so many wonderful things about you."

"Thank you, ma'am. If not for my taking up all your fiancé's time, you'd probably be married by now."

She laughed. "I've made arrangements for you to stay a few nights at the Marriott on Adams Street, just a few blocks from here. Gary's going to spend some time with you to help you get oriented to the world again. He'll take you shopping for some clothes. Maybe you'd like to take in a basketball game at the Barclays Center or a movie. Or maybe you'd just like to walk around, check out the Barnes & Noble bookstore down the block, and just chill out."

"All that sounds cool, Betsy, but I think first I'll stop at that church we passed and have a little conversation with the Lord. And then I would like to go to the Fortune Society to see if they can help me get a job and a place to live. And as for the shopping and all those other things, I don't have the bread for that."

Ken interjected, "We know the Fortune Society. It's a terrific place. It's been around for years, and they do a great job helping ex-cons transition into society when they get out of jail. But you don't need their help. First thing, don't be concerned about the money. Here's an envelope with $2,000 the boys at the Chisholm Club raised for you. And as for a job and a place to live, Gary and I have a proposition for you."

JoJo looked puzzled. "Why are you doing all this for me?"

Ken continued, "JoJo, now the whole world knows how you were railroaded by Racanelli and the DA. But there's more work to do—as you know. Your case is the tip of the iceberg. There are plenty of others rotting in jail who I suspect also were convicted on tainted evidence by the DA and his cohorts. In addition to the ones you've clued us in on, I've recently gotten more than fifty letters from others claiming they have been set up and are innocent. We need someone to work on each of these cases, get all the trial transcripts, check out the evidence, file Freedom of Information Act requests, just like you did, et cetera, et cetera. In short, there's tons of work to do, and you can do it while Gary and I prepare for the Jackson trial. We'll put you on the payroll for five hundred bucks a week. It'll be money worth spending because we're going to sue the bastards for violating your civil rights, and there will be plenty of money around when we win."

"It's a lot to absorb, Mr. Williams. Let me get some rest for a few days and think about it. In the meantime, I'll take you up on your generous offer and stay at the Marriott for a day or so and hang out with Gary. But after that I don't know where to live. I guess I'll try calling my ex-wife and see if she can put me up."

"I think we can help you with that, too," said Ken. "You can stay in the crash pad at the back of our office. We got a couple of cots there where Gary and Mickey, and sometimes even I, sleep after working late. We'll make it into a nice studio for you. There's room to set up a kitchen. Our bathroom has a shower. Gary and Mickey may bunk in with you once in a while, but it will be your place and it won't cost you anything."

Gary jumped in, "We'll bring another desk into my office. Ashanti will set you up with a laptop and telephone, and whatever else you need to work on your cases. We want to blow this whole thing wide open. Think about it."

"I will, but first off to church."

"There's one just a few blocks from here, JoJo. But Betsy and I will take you to our church as soon as you get settled," said Ken.

JoJo then had the best meal he'd had in sixteen years. Two days later he moved in to Ken's office.

∽

It didn't take Ken long to write the song. He had been totally absorbed with JoJo's habeas corpus hearing, but now with the big win his creative juices started to flow again. The night after JoJo moved into the office he tried it out at Arturo's. He showed Frankie the lyrics as he played the melody. Frankie couldn't stop laughing.

"You're a pisser, Kenny. It reminds me of my ex and how she took me to the cleaners. Let me sing it."

Frankie had a deep baritone voice and a natural knack for country. Flaming Jimmy quickly picked up the chords on the bass, and Kenny had a hard time keeping a straight face at the piano as Frankie wailed away. Arturo and the guys at the bar were cracking up.

When we dated many years ago
I'd take her to a bar or to a picture show
No matter where I took her she would never say "no"
She was a cheap date and I loved her so

Cause I had to hustle for a buck
I'd take her to the diner in my pickup truck
She always stood by me when I was down on my luck
She was a cheap date but

Look what she's costing me now
Now this country girl's become a city slicker
Now she's wearing diamond rings and drinking fancy liquor
Look what she's costing me now

Back then when she knew that I was broke
We'd sit and split a burger and a cherry coke
She'd laugh like it was funny every time I told a joke
She was a cheap date how was I to know

Every time she touched me I got hot
One night her pa caught us in the parking lot
That's when daddy's shotgun made me tie the knot
She was a cheap date but

Look what she's costing me now
Only Jesus knows why I had to pick her
My bank account is mighty low and getting even sicker
Look what she's costing me now

Look what she's costing me now
Now this country girl's become a city slicker
Now she's wearing diamond rings and drinking fancy liquor
Look what she's costing me now

When we gave each other wedding rings
We vowed to live a life with just the simple things
We built a house just big enough for our offspring
She was a cheap date but

Look what she's costing me now
Ever since her ma moved in I don't know where to stick her
When I say it's Ma or me she tells me blood is thicker
She's double crossing me

And she's exhausting me
Turning and tossing me
Now she's divorcing me
Look what she's costing me now

13

The next day Ken arrived at the office early and woke up JoJo. "Time to go marching, JoJo."

As JoJo got out of bed and started to get dressed, his voice was strong. "I'm ready, Mr. Williams."

"JoJo, how many times have I told you now to call me Ken?"

"I'll try, Mr. Williams, but after all you've done for me, it's kind of hard."

"Let's do it. By the way, how did you ever get the name JoJo?

JoJo laughed. "When I was in kindergarten my teacher couldn't pronounce my real name. Every time she tried to say Joaquin Jones, it just came out JoJo. Soon, all the kids started calling me JoJo, and I never used Joaquin again. I think my mother named me after a hurricane that ripped through Brooklyn while I was being born."

"Well if you don't call me Ken, I'll start calling you Joaquin. Anyway, we've got to be at Washington Square across the river by noon. The organizers have done a terrific job. All the signs and banners will be there. They expect thousands to show up. We'll be heading north to Herald Square, then cutting south along Broadway and ending in front of One Police Plaza, the headquarters of the NYPD."

"Here's a copy of the press statement we released yesterday," Ken said.

JoJo put his new glasses on and read it:

> We want people to shut down their cities for justice.
> We are continuing where the freedom fighters of the
> civil rights movement left off. We are a new generation
> of young, multiracial activists willing to take up the
> torch and we're not going to stand for this anymore.

When they reached Washington Square they were amazed. The organizers estimated that the crowd was close to 30,000. Somehow Ken and JoJo were able to push through the masses and find Ezekial Thomas by the fountain in the middle of the park. JoJo, enjoying freedom for the first time in so many years, stopped for a moment to look north through the white marble arch that frames the view up Fifth Avenue. Together, they all went to the helm of the procession where they joined the families of Ramarley Graham, an unarmed Bronx teenager shot dead by police in his home in 2012, and sixteen-year-old Kimani Gray, who was recently killed in the streets of Brooklyn by officers because they believed he was carrying a pistol. Along with them were the parents of Jacksonville, Florida teen Jordan Davis, who died while unarmed from gunshots fired by a private citizen two years before. No one involved in any of those killings was ever prosecuted and convicted.

Joining them at the front were Manhattan Councilman Ydanis Rodriguez and his mentor, State Senator Adriano Espaillat. As they all started to march, Councilman Rodriguez bellowed through a bullhorn: "We need to retrain the police! Violence against the people is a systemic problem with the NYPD!" Espaillat called for the governor to push ahead with a proposed bill to create a special prosecutor to handle police abuse cases.

As they all left the park and headed up Fifth Avenue, two of the organizers unfurled a large "Black Lives Matter" banner. Since Ken and JoJo were in the first row of marchers, they gave it to them to carry.

Ken was pleased that the march was for the most part orderly, but there were minor incidents along the way: Someone in the crowd set off fireworks on Madison Avenue, the rear window of an automobile was smashed on Broadway, and protesters kicked two police officers arresting a marcher for throwing a garbage can onto a street in SoHo.

Once they got to 1PP, as evening fell, microphones were set up for speeches. A well-dressed young black man whom Ken didn't recognize was the first to speak. He was articulate and didn't mince his words: "There is a systematic murder of people of color in this country and it is institutionalized racism. The people are here today to convince our leaders, in this city and in this country, to take strong action against this."

Under the watch of riot-geared cops, organizers coaxed the thousands-strong crowd that had assembled in front of the steps into silence so the families could speak. Repeating every word so it could be relayed through the entire gathering by "mic check" responses, Graham's father demanded that borough district attorneys who had failed to obtain the indictment and conviction of police officers involved in the cases be removed from office.

Carol Gray, mother of the dead Brooklyn teen, stirred up the crowd by claiming that police killings are a form of genocide, ending her impassioned comments by shouting, "Today, we stand here. We say 'Black lives matter!' We say, 'All lives matter!' We say 'No more!'"

Soon there were chants of "Killer cops must go!" and as the crowds started to disperse, JoJo turned to Ken and added, "Mr. Williams, James Neary must also go."

Though the march was over, fractious bands remained around lower Manhattan's cluster of government buildings. One group began chanting "March to Harlem," while a few dozen shouted "March on the pigs" and "Stand up, shoot back." They rushed to confront the officers guarding the police headquarters and cursed at them for the next several minutes.

Several hundred others made for the Brooklyn Bridge. The police had taken the precaution of clearing traffic from the Brooklyn-bound lanes. Ken and JoJo were at the head. One of the organizers asked Ken to carry one of the many "Black Lives Matter" signs raised into the sky by the group. He took it and continued to march toward Brooklyn. As Ken was halfway across the bridge, holding the sign above his head, he felt someone shove him. If JoJo hadn't held him up, Ken would have fallen.

Next to him was a tough-looking, African-American police officer who ordered, "Put that sign down and don't make trouble."

Ken was startled. "Officer, I am certainly not making any trouble. I am peacefully marching across the Brooklyn Bridge on my way back home, and there's certainly no law that says I can't carry this sign."

"Don't be a wiseass," responded the cop. "When I order you to do something, you do it, or else."

"Well, I can't believe you are really serious, officer. There's absolutely no reason for me to put the sign down."

"Yes, there is. I gave you an order, sir, and you are to obey it."

"Well, I'm not going to put the sign down, and, furthermore, I want your shield number so I can report you for pushing and harassing me."

"You'll see my number soon enough. Right now you're under arrest for not obeying my instructions, and for a bunch of other things, too."

"What things?"

"You'll find out. Now turn around."

Suddenly a white police officer appeared, and together the two cops handcuffed Ken. He was speechless, but JoJo was not. "You can't arrest Mr. Williams. He's done nothing wrong."

"Keep your mouth shut," snapped back the black cop, "before we arrest you, too."

"JoJo, I'll be okay. Just go back to the office."

The two officers took Ken to a police car that was parked close by on the side of the pedestrian walkway.

"Where are you taking him?" asked JoJo.

"He'll be booked at the 70th precinct," answered the white cop.

As he was being shoved into the police car, Ken quietly told JoJo, "Get ahold of Gary and have him call Kuby. He'll know what to do. This smells to high hell."

Ken had dropped the sign. JoJo picked it up and carried it back to Ken's office. It took him twenty minutes. None of the many police he passed stopped him.

It was early evening when the tall, angular, hippie-looking man from another time strutted into the precinct. Ron Kuby, who boasted that he hadn't had a haircut since 1989, stroked his scraggly beard, ran his fingers through his shoulder-length graying ponytail, and asked Sergeant Markham when he would be able to talk to his new client.

"Kuby, you're looking weird as usual," snarled Markham from behind the receptionist window. "You and Williams make a real pair. Two troublemakers. The last time I saw him before tonight was when he came to see the guy who murdered the rabbi's son. I guess I got to let you see him, but you'll have to cool your heels. They haven't finished booking him yet. Can't wait to see his mug shot."

Kuby was quick to respond. "Same old Markham. Good to see they still got you on desk duty after you beat up that kid last year. Don't play any games with me if you don't want another disciplinary charge to deal with. And by the way, Jackson hasn't been convicted of murdering anybody, and Williams will make mincemeat out of the DA's case at the trial."

"Okay, big shit," growled Markham. "I'll let you know when you can see him, but don't hold your breath that it'll be anytime soon."

Kuby sat down on one of the metal chairs in the waiting area. Soon Gary and JoJo came into the precinct and joined him. They were happy to see Kuby and told him what had happened.

Ron Kuby had a legendary reputation as a no-holds-barred civil rights litigator who had represented the downtrodden and oppressed for many years. He was now in his late fifties but was still at the top of his game. His most recent claim to fame was his representation of the Occupy Wall Street kids who were arrested when they refused to leave Zuccotti Park. But his most famous case was his successful defense of the young black man who was charged with assaulting Bernard Goetz, and the $43 million verdict he got against Goetz for shooting him. Kuby was aptly described by one of his clients as "every prosecutor's worst nightmare; a defense attorney who could charm and incite a jury, and bully most any witness." And he was known for making cops look like liars and fools.

Kuby's upbringing was hardly conventional. He became a radical when, at thirteen, he joined the Jewish Defense League. He was nearly expelled from junior high school for publishing an underground newspaper critical of the school administration and quit in the ninth grade to emigrate to Israel. There he became disenchanted with what he perceived as anti-Arab racism and was deported five months later for participating in antigovernment activities. He returned to Cleveland, where he was born, and lived in a commune for several years. He ultimately went to college and graduated from the University of Kansas with a straight A average and from Cornell Law School, where he was one of the top students in his class.

Kuby then teamed up with famed civil rights lawyer William Kunstler, who had handled many sensational cases, including the defense of the Chicago Seven. Together, they represented some of the most detested criminal defendants to ensure that their constitutional rights to a fair trial were safeguarded. Among them were Sheikh Omar Abdel-Rahman, the infamous "Blind Sheik, who headed the Egyptian-based militant group Al-Gama'a al-Islamiya, accused of planning and encouraging terrorist attacks against Americans, including the 1993 World Trade Center bombing; Colin Ferguson, the man responsible for the 1993 Long Island Railroad shootings; Qubilah Shabazz, the daughter of Malcolm X, accused of plotting to murder Louis Farrakhan of the Nation of Islam. They also defended many American soldiers claiming conscientious objector status during the Gulf War.

Ken knew Kuby well and had a high regard for him. He admired his willingness to take on unpopular cases that no one else would touch. Kuby was currently representing a black man in jail for the last ten years who, like JoJo, claimed that he was wrongly convicted by Racanelli. He was the logical person for Ken to now turn to. Ron Kuby was fearless and would not hesitate to root out official misconduct. Ken hoped that he would help him get to the bottom of his phony arrest.

After about an hour, Markham finally allowed Kuby to talk to Ken. He couldn't resist taunting him. "How does it feel to be on the other side, Kenneth, old boy?"

"Very funny, Ron, but I'm in no mood for your macabre sense of humor right now. I'm in a cell with a real nut job. He's bigger than the guy who tried to rape Troy at Rikers. I'm scared. I need to get out of here fast."

"Simmer down, Ken. You know that they'll keep you in the can overnight because it's too late for you to be arraigned. I'll see you at AP1 tomorrow morning. Then I'll have a chance to see the criminal complaint they trumped up and you'll probably be released on your own recognizance pending trial."

Ken's knees buckled as he was taken back to his cell, and Kuby shook his head in disbelief. He had seen a lot of police misconduct, but this one was right up there with the worst. He picked up Gary and JoJo from the waiting room and, even though it was now almost midnight, told them to meet him at his office in lower Manhattan.

"And try to get Mickey there as well," he told them. "We need his special talents."

~

Ken was home the next day. After Judge Azrack, the judge at the arraignment, read the charges filed against Ken, Kuby convinced the judge that there was no reason to keep him in jail, and he was released on his own recognizance. Ken was charged with harassment, assaulting a police officer, and resisting arrest. The assault charge was, of course, pretty serious stuff. Ken would be disbarred if a jury somehow believed the lying cops and convicted him.

The ADA handling arraignments that day told the judge that the case would go to the grand jury that week, and that he expected an indictment to be handed up within a matter of days. In anticipation that Ken would be indicted, the judge fixed a return date for the following week. Ken would have to then appear before the judge who, in the interim, would be assigned to dispose of the case—either by plea or trial.

The judge did, however, make the ADA give Kuby a copy of the complaint that the arresting officers had prepared. As soon as he and Ken walked out of the courtroom, they sat down on the bench in the hallway—which still had "fuck you" carved into it—and read it together:

> The perpetrator was leading a group of unruly protesters holding up traffic and creating chaos over the Brooklyn Bridge. When the undersigned confronted him and told him to stop inciting a riot, he disobeyed the command and continued to march while waiving a sign that read "Black Lives Matter." When he was told to stop, he pushed the undersigned against the railing of the bridge, causing him to fall. He was immediately placed under arrest by an officer who was nearby, but he would not stand still while attempts were made to handcuff him, and he started to run away before he was subdued.

Naturally, when they left the building, the press was there to pounce. After JoJo's exoneration, Ken was big news. Kuby told Ken to keep silent for now and let him handle the reporters who had swarmed around them. Microphones and cameras were being shoved at them from everywhere.

"Ladies and gentlemen," Kuby politely began. "I've told Mr. Williams not to speak because I'm afraid he'll have a stroke if he does. That's how enraged he is over these trumped-up charges. You can be sure we'll get to the bottom of all this in due time. I've seen a lot of police misconduct in my days, but this one is simply outrageous. Heads will eventually roll. That's it for now. See you all again when we're back in court next week."

14

When Ken returned to his office, Lillian Bloom was waiting. Two other women were with the Jewish community leader and erstwhile Neary confidante. Ken guessed that one was in her late thirties and the other about half her age. They both were thin and had black hair, but the older one's was short and looked like it could be a wig. The younger woman's was shoulder-length and looked real. They were the same medium height and attractive, but the younger woman was particularly good-looking. Ken thought she could easily be a model.

"Mr. Williams," began Lillian, "I want you to meet Rebecca Hyman and her seventeen-year-old daughter, Deborah. Mrs. Hyman came to me last month in tears. She told me that her husband, Shmuel, the grandson of a revered Hasidic rabbi, has been physically and emotionally abusing her from the day they were married eighteen years ago."

Ken was riveted by Rebecca's downcast eyes.

Bloom continued. "She is a deeply religious Hasidic woman who has followed the rituals and lifestyle of the Hasidic world in which she was raised. She will tell you about that world and how women are belittled and abused by their controlling husbands. It has taken extraordinary courage for her to come to me, but the defining moment was when she told me that Deborah's father had recently forced her to have sex with him."

Ken saw Deborah's eyes fill with tears. Rebecca's now were shut tight. He had heard about the way Hasidic men treated their women, but he was shocked to hear that Shmuel Hyman had actually raped his daughter. He told the three of them to sit and buzzed Ashanti over the intercom to bring them some water.

"Lillian, I've admired the work you have done to mend fences between the Hasidic and black communities ever since the Crown Heights riots, but why are you bringing Mrs. Hyman and her daughter to me instead of to the authorities?"

"I don't know who else to turn to. I was going to tell the DA and met with him last month, but before I did, he turned me off when I told him he should do more to address the issue of sexual abuse by Hasidic men. I decided that I couldn't trust him to prosecute the grandson of a prominent Hasidic rabbi and go public with it. I think he's too politically beholden to the Hasidim and believes that they should deal with these types of problems through their own internal religious courts."

"What do you want me to do?" Ken asked.

"I think you can force the DA's hand. Mrs. Hyman and Deborah are willing to file a criminal complaint, but they need a lawyer to make sure they'll be protected once all this gets out and that Shmuel Hyman is properly prosecuted for his outrageous assault on his own daughter."

Turning to Rebecca Hyman, now sitting nervously and holding her daughter's hand, Ken asked, "Is this what you really want, Ms. Hyman? There's bound to be big repercussions back home. I'm sure you remember Sam Kellner, and how the Hasidic community turned against him for insisting that a prominent Hasidic man be prosecuted for molesting Kellner's son. And how Kellner wound up being prosecuted instead."

Rebecca's voice came back with surprising strength. "Mr. Williams, Deborah and I are never going back to that household and that world again. I've put up with a great deal of *tsouris* throughout the years, and raping my daughter is the final straw."

Yiddish was not exactly Ken's mother tongue, but being from Brooklyn he knew what *tsouris* meant. And as a good lawyer, he wanted to find out more. "Tell me about the troubles you have had with your husband."

Rebecca drank a glass of water, took a deep breath, and began to speak in a slow but firm voice.

"My parents arranged my marriage to Shmuel. They did it through a matchmaker. That's the way it works in Hasidic society. I was eighteen. He was twenty-three. They told me that he was a learned and respected Talmudic scholar from an esteemed family, and his grandfather was a legendary rabbi. One day there was a knock on the door, and when my father opened it, to my surprise, a tall, good-looking, dark-haired man with bright blue eyes walked in. He spoke to us softly and politely. I was happy to go out with him on our first date. We went to a big hotel and sat in the lobby drinking Diet Cokes. In our culture, this was the way you got to know your potential husband. But I had immediate misgivings. He seemed more interested in his cell phone than engaging me in any meaningful conversation.

"The next day I told the matchmaker how disappointed I was and that I didn't think we were a good fit. A few days later, my parents got an urgent call from Shmuel's parents. They asked them to talk to me and beg me to give their son another chance. They said that he was nervous around girls and he really had a great personality. In Orthodox dating, you rely a lot on what you are told by the parents, so I agreed to see him again.

"He started to act better, but I still had some reservations. However, we both knew that we were expected to take the next step and get engaged. Then one night he took me to a glitzy hotel in Manhattan, and while we were walking around on the mezzanine, he suddenly dropped to one knee and pulled out a black velvet box with a sparkling diamond ring inside—I could see it was a superb stone—and asked me to marry him. He told me we would have a wonderful life together, that we would be equal partners and make decisions together. I knew that marrying Shmuel would make my parents happy, and since he seemed sincere, I gave in.

"The engagement, like our dating, was very short—that's how it is in our community. I got caught up in all the wedding plans and didn't worry too much about our compatibility. Three days after we were married, I knew that I had made a terrible mistake. It was our first Shabbat together as man and wife. As I started to light the Sabbath candles, he screamed at me and told me I was doing it the wrong way. I was startled and told him that my mother and grandmother had always done it that way. He shouted at me that I must do it his way. I gave in, but he did not speak to me again for the next two days.

"Unfortunately, I got pregnant right away. It was all he was interested in. Sex for married Hasidic men is only for having children. I was afraid to say no. His controlling and belittling only got worse. But I was blessed with Deborah, and for the next seventeen years I tried to make the best of a loveless marriage with an increasingly belligerent man who did nothing but study the Torah every day. I was the sole breadwinner working at the Hellerstein & Stein jewelry store in midtown Manhattan."

Ken was listening intently and did not want to interrupt, but he couldn't help asking Rebecca, "How could he read the Scriptures every day and act like that?"

"It's a good question, Mr. Williams. I would ask myself the same question. But I'm afraid that there's a big divide between reading the Torah and practicing what it tells you. I don't have a good answer."

"How did you manage to stay in the marriage all these years?" Ken asked tenderly.

Rebecca shuddered before answering, "Surely you know about domestic violence, Mr. Williams, and the fear that goes with it. And it's worse in the Hasidic world where the man is the king, and his word always trumps the word of his wife. Whenever I got up the chutzpah to tell him that we should get a divorce, he would hit me and threaten to take Deborah from me if I ever told anyone about our problems.

"But that's all over now. When Deborah came crying to me last month and told me that her father forced her to have sex with him, I called Lillian and asked her to please help us. She has been my savior. Shmuel was at the yeshiva that day, and she came to get me and Deborah right away. Deborah was extremely distraught, and Lillian helped me to determine if she had been injured physically. Lillian at first wanted us to have her examined at the hospital, but of course they would have asked a lot of questions, and Deborah was adamant that she wasn't hurt that much and couldn't go through telling other people about it. Of course we feared the police would get involved. It was all so terrible.

"We just packed a few things and fled. Lillian has been kind enough to let us stay at her apartment until Deborah and I feel better and decide where to go. Shmuel doesn't know where we are but has been sending me threatening emails telling me that he will kill us when he finds us. He has gone mad."

Ken had heard enough. "Lillian, for God's sake, why did you wait so long before doing anything?"

"I told you I spoke to the DA, but as I also told you, I just didn't trust him to handle this the right way. And I thought that Rebecca and Deborah needed some time to decompress and carefully think things through. But I have kept them indoors all that time since my apartment is right in the middle of Williamsburg. There's thousands of Hasidic people there. I didn't want to run the risk of having them spotted if they went out. In retrospect, I should have come to you sooner, but you were tied up with JoJo Jones' case and getting arrested."

Ken realized that Deborah had not said a word. But there were tears in her eyes again, and she had let go of her mother's hand to dab them away.

Ken spoke gently to her. "Deborah, this has to be very painful for you. After all, this is your father we're talking about. If he is prosecuted and convicted of rape, he's looking at a lot of jail time, and you will probably be scorned and ostracized by the Hasidic community for bringing shame upon it."

She began to speak for the first time, quietly, but with resolve.

"Mr. Williams, my father has turned into a beast. For years I watched him hit my mother, and I was afraid to say anything because he threatened to beat me also. In our world, girls are taught to obey their fathers at all costs and to be obedient. But he raped me and threatened to kill me if I told anyone. I had to tell my mother. Who else could I turn to? She would understand. She's been the victim of his abuse since before I was born. Mama called Mrs. Bloom right away, and she came to get us. We have been hiding in her apartment, afraid to go out. We can't keep living like that. We will do whatever you recommend. We have to break free."

"Deborah," interjected Ken, "you're talking about turning your back on your Hasidic world."

"I know, but we must do it. Lillian has prepared us. She gave us a book called *Unorthodox: The Scandalous Rejection of My Hasidic Roots*. It was written by a twenty-five-year-old women named Deborah Feldman. She was never raped by her father, who was mentally ill, but her story is like ours in many ways. I thought it was prophetic that we both had the same first name."

Her mother interrupted, "The book was an eye-opener and gave us the courage we needed to change our lives. Just like me, Deborah Feldman grew up believing her life would be determined by her marriage. When she was seventeen, her grandparents selected her husband, a young man she had never met, who was considered old at twenty-three. They met for thirty minutes, and eight months later they were married. Just like me, she had a child right away. And just like me, her husband was oppressive and abusive, and she knew that she had made a terrible mistake."

Rebecca took a deep breath.

"But unlike me, she rebelled. She read books about feminism, enrolled in a secular college, and had the chutzpah to leave the marriage and move out into the real world."

Lillian looked at Rebecca, "Maybe you or Deborah will write a best-selling book like she did. She really is a role model for all the oppressed women in the Hasidic world."

Turning to Ken, she said, "There is much to respect and admire about the Hasidim, but their view of women as subservient, and the way they keep them uneducated and ignorant about the world simply has to change. Deborah Feldman grew up in Williamsburg in a home with no secular newspapers, no radios, no television, like two hundred years ago."

Ken was taking it all in, but he sat deep in thought for a few moments before speaking. "Here's what we should do. First, we should get Rebecca and Deborah out of Lillian's apartment. You have to be able to move about without fear that you'll be found out. You can't stay holed up. We have to find a place far away from the Hasidic communities so that no one is likely to recognize you on the streets."

"But where will we live?" Rebecca asked.

"I have an idea," Ken said, "but I have to first check it out with the person I'm thinking about. In the meantime, stay put at Lillian's place for a little while longer while I work it all out."

Lillian spoke next. "I assume you will have Deborah file a criminal complaint against her father."

"Eventually, Lillian, but I have to think it through very carefully. Right now, it will be her word against her father's, and who will believe her? I don't want this to be another Kellner situation. I need to figure out how we can get some corroborating evidence."

He looked at the mother and daughter. "Go back to Lillian's apartment now. I'll get back to you as soon as I make arrangements for you to move out."

When they left, Ken picked up the phone and called his favorite number. "Queen's night out tonight, baby."

❧

After Franco asked them how "Mr. and Mrs. Williams" were and made sure the bartender had brought them their usual drinks, Ken filled Betsy in on the fast-moving developments of the last few days. It was the first time they'd had a chance to be together since his arrest. She had been in LA the past week interviewing witnesses for an upcoming trial. Ken told her that he was sure that Racanelli and her boss Neary were behind what happened, but as yet had no concrete proof.

Betsy held Ken tightly and told him, "Thank god you spent only one night in jail. If only I had been here. Everything has changed for us if you are right. The DA's office has been a wonderful place for me to cut my teeth and get great experience. But I'm extremely disgusted by Racanelli's conduct in JoJo's case. It's just really hard to believe that he and Neary would stoop so low as to orchestrate an illegal arrest."

"Well, stay tuned, baby. Time will tell. Mickey will find out one way or another. He and his sidekick Abe have been tailing them night and day. But let's talk about the Hymans. I'd like them to stay with you for a while until I think the time is right to file the criminal complaint. I've got to figure out how to find the smoking gun, otherwise it will be another Kellner fiasco. Your crib in Boerum Hill is far away from the Hasidic communities. They'll be safe there and won't have to be shut in all day. And you relate well to young people. You know, Deborah's a lot like you, trying to break free of her past. While your father never raped you, he sure treated you terribly."

"Let's not go there. I'll talk to her, but I'm in the midst of preparing for this big trial. I don't know how much time I'll have to spend with them."

"I know you'll make them feel at home even if you're not there during the day. And at night you can sit down with Deborah, share your own life story with her, and be of great emotional support. As the Hasidim would say, you'll be doing them a mitzvah."

She laughed whenever Ken would use the few Yiddish words he knew. *Mitzvah* was his favorite. He used it whenever he wanted someone to do a good deed.

"Alright, Ken, I'll do it. I do feel so sorry for that girl. I'll be at the office all day, but should be home by about 8:00. Have them there by then. The double Murphy bed in my study is pretty comfortable. I've got some good books, including a few about domestic violence they might find helpful. I even have a copy of Feldman's book and a terrific interview she recently had in *Slate*. I'll stock the fridge."

"Thanks, sweetheart. My place tonight?"

❧

The sex that night was much better for him. But this time it was Betsy's mind that was elsewhere. After they were done, she started to talk.

"Deborah's plight got me thinking about my marriage to Brandon."

"In what way?" asked Ken, as he cuddled up next to her.

"How you can manage after a bad beginning. I remember how difficult it was for me to leave him. But I had to do it. I was just so lonesome together with him. I had to move on, and I'm in a better place because of it. Debbie Hyman will be, too."

"I think you're right. She's strong, like you."

15

Ken was indicted. All the two cops had to do was to tell their made-up story to the grand jury with a straight face.

The chief administrative judge assigned the case to Judge Louis Velie. He was the prosecutors' favorite. Ken and his team couldn't remember the last time there was an acquittal in his courtroom. They called him "Never Lose Louie."

Kuby just shrugged his shoulders as he and Ken walked into Judge Velie's courtroom for the arraignment.

"Just gut it out, Ken. Let me do all the talking. Our day will come, but not today."

He could not have been more right. The judge marched into the courtroom, quickly stepped up to the bench, and glanced at the copy of the indictment on the top of the desk. With his slick, plastered-down black hair and little mustache, he resembled someone before whom no defense lawyer would ever want to appear.

"Assaulting a police officer," snarled the judge. "Pretty serious stuff, Mr. Kuby."

"So is a phony criminal prosecution by the DA," snapped Kuby.

"Just watch your step. I've held you in contempt before and I'll do it again if you don't behave."

Kuby was undeterred. "Do as you please, but let's get this over with as quickly as possible. My client will waive the public reading of the trumped-up indictment and plead not guilty. We ask for a speedy trial. The sooner the better."

A wry grin crossed the judge's face. "I would like to accommo-date you, but I'm afraid I can't. I'm starting a big murder trial next week, and I have a few other cases that I have on my trial calendar after that. I'm afraid I can't try your case until after the summer."

Ken could no longer follow his lawyer's advice and remain silent.

"Your Honor, with all due respect, I have a major trial set to go before then. I have to get my case out of the way first. There's no way I'm going to be found guilty by a jury once the truth comes out."

The judge's grin got wider: "Sorry, Mr. Williams, it's the best I can do. Next case."

～

Mickey and Abe were sitting in the waiting room talking to Ashanti when they got back to Ken's office. Before Ken or Kuby could say a word, Mickey jumped up and reported what had happened the night before.

"Me and my Jew buddy here followed them to Armando's. I don't think they know me, but I didn't want to take any chances. I sent Abe in. He sat down a few tables away, ordered some pasta, and made believe that he was reading the newspaper that he put on the table. The recorder was hidden inside and was ready to go."

Ken was clearly excited. "Mickey, I knew I could count on you. Play it. Play it."

"Don't get a stroke, my man. There's nothing too helpful on it. They're not that stupid. They ain't going to talk in public about anything they don't want anyone to hear. They're talking about the Mets, the Jets, the Nets, but not about you other than Racanelli mentioning in passing that the judge set your trial down for after the Jackson case."

"So what's the big deal?" asked a disappointed Ken.

"Alright, we don't have anything yet, but I thought you'd like to at least know that Abe told me that I should have seen their shit-eating smiles and winks when Racanelli told that to Neary."

"Well, I knew they had to be behind this. This pisses me off even more."

"We'll keep after them, boss."

"I'm counting on you, Mickey."

❦

Ken felt a little guilty that he had not worked on the Troy Jackson case lately. He'd been preoccupied with all the things that had been happening to him. With the trial just weeks away, it was time to get going. He spent an entire morning checking out Chess Street with Gary, who took pictures of the street and every building on the block, including the two-story, broken-down, wood-shingled building where Troy's grandmother still lived. He was tempted to knock on her door and speak to her, but he thought it would be better to be with Trish when he met her.

The street was a mix of run-down buildings. There were a number of places like Troy's grandmother's, but there were also some commercial buildings. In the middle of the block stood a small bodega. Ken went inside to check it out. The front of the store had bins of rotting fruit, but the apples looked safe and he bought one. There were trays of slimy ham and bologna on the counter, emitting a rancid stink. On the walls behind the counter rested an assortment of cigarettes and rolling papers. A curtain at the back partially concealed a small kitchen table behind it with two folding chairs.

On the southeast corner a video store housed a bunch of video games. Ken played three of them. The first was a car chase; the second, cops chasing and shooting at three hooded men who had just robbed a bank; the last were earthlings shooting alien creatures invading the planet. A counter in the far corner held an assortment of cell phones for sale.

Next, Ken and Gary met Trish for lunch at Junior's. Ken had spoken to her on the phone a few times since her husband was arrested, but this was the first time they had a chance to get together since the arrest.

"Trish, I'm sorry it's taken this long to meet. I've been meaning to do it sooner, but I got distracted with JoJo Jones' hearing and then I got arrested myself."

"I know, Mr. Williams. I read all about it in the papers. Welcome to the club. Those guys are lawless. It would not surprise me if Racanelli was behind it. He must really hate you for making him look so bad in JoJo's case, and now you've got to do it once again in Troy's case."

"We'll be ready, Trish. I've got the world's best private eye on the case, and my brilliant legal assistant, Gary"—Ken put his arm around Gary's shoulder as he said his name—"has been doing a lot of the leg work. He's helping me prepare for the trial. One of the things we're thinking about is allowing Troy to testify. He should make a good witness, but I've got to know everything about his background before I make that decision since it's going to open the door to extensive cross-examination about his past. I'll be going to Rikers this afternoon to see Troy, but you are the logical person to start with. I need to know everything, especially Troy's involvement with drugs. We know that he was arrested when he was a kid on a marijuana charge, but I need to dig deeper. While I know Troy wouldn't lie to me, he may be a little embarrassed to fully open up."

"Troy's a special person, Mr. Williams. Otherwise, I wouldn't be married to him. I was concerned about that neighborhood he was raised in, and Troy told me all about the abuse he suffered from the Chess Street gang. He never wanted to be a part of them, but they kept making fun of him for being serious about school and not hanging with them. The pressure did get to him a bit. He told me that he thought that if he smoked some weed with them they would leave him alone. But Troy was not into drugs. So help me God, I've never seen him smoke one joint since I've known him."

Ken wanted to probe deeper. "You portray him as a perfect person, Trish. But I need you to tell me about his faults."

"I don't know if it's a fault, Mr. Williams, but he hates it whenever someone uses the n-word, even our own people, and even if it's in jest. He's real sensitive about it."

"Well, I don't like it either, Trish. Did he tell you anything about who his friends were?"

"His best friend was Willie Wexler. He was real short. They called him Wee Willie."

"Well, I'm sure Troy has told you that Wee Willie turned against him and will be testifying as a witness for the state at the trial."

"He's shocked. After Troy moved out, we invited Willie to visit us. Troy was concerned because of things he heard about Willie getting into trouble and tried to talk to him about going to school and getting a life, like Troy was doing. We felt sorry for him. He was a good kid, but unlike Troy, he wanted to fit in and not be made fun of. And he didn't have the good fortune of moving from the 'hood."

"And meeting someone like you," Ken added.

"You're very kind, Mr. Williams, but it's true. I think I made all the difference in the world for Troy. We would study together. We would talk about going to college and the good life we wanted to have. And Troy would talk about becoming a guidance counselor and devoting his life to helping kids like Wee Willie."

"But do you know what happened to him?" asked Ken.

"While Troy never wanted to go back to Chess Street, he would always visit his grandmother. I'm sure Troy must have told you that he and his mom lived with her. Grandma Bessie raised Troy while his mother was working her tail off as a home caregiver and trying to save enough money to move out. My mother ran the office and hired her. Troy would get the latest gossip from his grandmother when he visited her. She told him that Willie Wexler had gone bad ever since Troy left and was in prison. She didn't know what for."

"Did Troy ever tell you about anyone else who was a member of the Chess Street gang?"

"He mentioned a few names from time to time, but I don't remember them. Troy was trying to forget his past."

Ken could tell that she was getting upset. "Alright, Trish, enough for now. I'll send Troy your love when I see him in a few hours, and we'll talk again soon."

It was the first time Ken had seen Troy since he was moved out of solitary confinement, and it was the first time that Gary had met him.

Ken broke the ice. "How are they treating you now, Troy? Looks like you lost a little weight."

"It's better here, but I'll never get used to this place. It's pathetic. Almost everyone here is black or Hispanic. But it certainly is a good place to practice my counseling skills."

"Keep your spirits up, Troy. Just a couple of months to go before the trial and you'll be out of here."

"It's good to see you again, Mr. Williams. I was getting a little worried thinking maybe you weren't working on my case because you were preoccupied with JoJo's case—and then the arrest."

Ken could understand how Troy felt, but was quick to reassure him. "It may have seemed that way, but Gary and Mickey have been spending a lot of time working on it, and now that JoJo's out of jail, you've got all my attention."

"Are you sure? How about your own case? I know you told me when we spoke on the phone right after you got out of jail that it's all a set-up, but it must still be a distraction."

"Troy, listen carefully. The arrest has just quadrupled my motivation to get those bastards. Your case will be the first batter up. Mine will be easy after that. Nothing's going to get in my way from exposing them in your trial for what they're worth. Trust me."

"I do, Mr. Williams. My whole life is in your hands."

"Alright, Troy. Right now I want to go over a few things with you. We know Willie Wexler is going to testify against you. And we know that even though you tried to help him get his life together after you moved out, he didn't do it."

"All I know, Mr. Williams, is that one day after the rabbi's son was shot, he disappeared, and I haven't heard from him since."

"Well, they obviously found him, and for some reason he fingered you and cut a cooperation deal."

Troy's eyes seemed to darken, and he sat up straight. He shook his head, and muttered, "I guess some brothers will do anything to save their own necks. I can't explain it."

"Okay, but they say they have two more cooperators. They've got to let us know who they are eventually, but only just before the trial. We don't want to wait that long. We've got to find out who they might be as soon as possible. Can you give us some names of other guys who were pushing dope when you lived there?"

"I remember some of them. There was one called Apollo. We called him that because he thought he was a black Greek god. There was Derrick, Marshawn, and Moses. We called him Big Mo. I remember a guy we called Magic who was always doing card tricks. And there was Rasheen. I remember him because he was a cleanliness nut. They called him Clean Rasheen."

Gary had not said much other than to tell Troy that he was Ken's trusted associate and had been working on his case. He was writing down the names, and wanted to ask a few follow-up questions.

"Do you know, Troy, if they were all members of the Chess Street Crew?"

"I'm not sure. I tried to keep my distance from all of them. They were pretty young. I guess some of them might have been Pawns."

"Do you know who the King was?" Gary shot back.

"Everyone knew him. He was the man. Big and fearsome. He was older than the others. Nobody would cross him. They would do whatever he said. They showed him a lot of respect."

Ken impatiently jumped in. "So, what was his name?"

"I dunno. He called himself Kong and he just wanted everyone to call him King Kong. But sometimes we would call him Video

King Kong because he would always be playing video games in the corner store.

"Did he ever jazz you?" continued Gary.

"He wanted me to become a Pawn. When I told him I didn't want to, he was mad. He called me a wimp because I was a good student. But he left me alone."

"Do you know what happened to him after the shooting?" asked Ken.

"No, I just heard that he disappeared like a bunch of the others."

"Thanks Troy, that's all very helpful. Gary and I have to go now."

❧

Rikers Island didn't allow visitors on Mondays and Tuesdays, but Trish was there to see Troy whenever she could on the other days. They always had to speak through an open window on opposite sides of a wall that physically separated them. She and Troy didn't have a car, so she would often get a Zipcar and drive to the jail. Dr. Gold had told her that taking public transportation might be too taxing.

She tried her best to cheer up Troy during each visit, and she always told him that she and the baby were doing just fine. She never told him about the preeclampsia.

On this occasion she saw a worried look in her husband's eyes.

"What's wrong, Troy. Is something bothering you?"

"Well, Mr. Williams has been asking me a lot of questions lately about the Chess Street gang."

"But, baby, he's tooling up for the trial and wants to be a hundred percent prepared. He's a wonderful lawyer and only has your best interests at heart. And he's a thousand percent confident that you'll soon be out of here. The only thing that's not sure is who is coming out first, you or Troy Junior. You're both due at about the same time."

"I guess you're right, Trish, but nothing is certain. I've been having nightmares lately. What if I turn out to be another JoJo Jones, or any one of the other blacks rotting away in jail because of Racanelli?"

"Get those thoughts out of your mind, Troy! It's never going to happen. JoJo and the others didn't have Ken Williams as their lawyer."

"But Trish, all jury trials are crapshoots. I read someplace that 30,000 innocent people are sitting in jail. It could happen."

Trish tried to put up a brave front but felt a pit in her stomach. She didn't tell her husband that the same thoughts had also crossed her mind.

"Things will turn out okay, Troy. Let's please just try to stay positive."

"And I'll probably still be holed up here when the baby is born, Trish. Our first child and I won't be there to hug and kiss you and hold our son together."

"I know. I miss you so much." Trish tried not to cry as she kissed Troy through the window. She slowly stood, turned around, and quickly walked out of the visiting room.

❦

As soon as the last metal jail door clanged shut behind her and she started to make her way to the parking lot, the cramps returned. Trish doubled over as she crawled into the car. Somehow she was able to drive, but she nearly swerved into three cars on the FDR Drive and had to slam on her brakes to avoid rear-ending another as she barely made it across the Brooklyn Bridge to her home. When she got there she parked in front of the No Parking sign and staggered out of the car. The cramps were excruciating. The doorman grabbed her and took her to her apartment. Trish's mother was off that day and was there. As she opened the door, her daughter collapsed in her arms.

The ambulance passed three red lights before it pulled up to the emergency entrance to the Brooklyn Hospital Center on DeKalb Avenue. Dr. Gold was waiting. Trish was barely conscious. He started the magnesium drip while she was still in the Emergency Room.

"We've got to get more magnesium into her quickly," he told Trish's mom as she stood next to her daughter's bed. "It prevents seizures. We are going to keep her here and monitor her for several days. Her blood pressure is off the charts. Do you have any idea what caused this?"

"Dr. Gold, she was doing fine," her mother answered, "but something must have happened when she visited Troy this morning. How serious is it? Is she going to lose the baby?"

"I'm not only worried about the baby, Mrs. Sampson. But hopefully we caught this just in time, and both baby and mother will pull through. We're going to put her in a private room now. You can stay with her for a while, but she needs rest. We'll be running some tests, and of course we'll keep you notified. Let's be optimistic."

16

Ken would always try to attend the Chisholm Club's monthly meetings. Ezekial Thomas was there that night and wanted to speak to him.

"Ken, the boys are going to vote tonight on whether to support Neary again. If they decide not to, they're going to be looking for a candidate to run against him. As the Democratic county leader, it's going to put me in a tough spot. There are other clubs in Brooklyn which will not turn their back on him out of loyalty. I'm sure he'll have the support of the Irish and Italian clubs, and of course he's got 165,000 Hasidic people in his pocket. He's been our unchallenged DA for twenty-four years and has handed out a lot of patronage. His footprints are everywhere."

Ken couldn't resist. "That's for sure, including the chief administrative judge and Never Lose Louie. And probably the police commissioner as well."

"Be that as it may, we have never had a primary for DA. It will split the party and embolden the Republicans to put up a strong candidate to take over the office for the first time in memory."

"I can't stand the guy, Ezekial. I'd bet my bottom dollar that he's behind my arrest. But rest assured, I won't do anything to hurt you or the party. Anyway, my focus right now is to prepare for the Jackson trial. I won't stay for the vote. I've been spending a lot of time with Troy and Trish Jackson lately. I'm bushed. Call me later and let me know what happened."

When Ken got home, he called Betsy. It was the first night that the Hymans would be sleeping there.

"How are things working out?" he asked her.

"Everything's okay, but Deborah's not feeling well. She threw up a couple of times and is still nauseous. It's probably all the tension and excitement about moving in, but I'll take her to my doctor tomorrow to check her out."

"Call me after. I'll be in the office."

A half hour later, Ezekial called to tell him that the club decided "to sit this one out." They couldn't support Neary because of JoJo's case and the other fabricated prosecutions against black defendants that they heard about, but they didn't want to be accused of splintering the party and make things difficult for their black Democratic county chairman. However, they wanted him to tell Neary that they expected Racanelli to be fired if he wanted their support in the future.

～

Betsy's sensitivity toward Deborah Hyman made Ken more in love with Betsy than ever. He thought it might be time to finally tie the knot. And he hoped that, unlike her first marriage, she would never be lonesome together with him. He sat down at his piano after Ezekial's call. He had to write the song about her past marriage. He couldn't get the hook out of his head. It was his first country waltz.

When he finished singing it he realized that the song could only be sung by a woman like Betsy who had to have the courage to leave a bad marriage and become economically self-sufficient. He knew immediately who to call.

"Wendy, I'm emailing you my latest. Let me know what you think."

Two days later, Wendy Baker had the women in Arturo's weeping as she sang the song:

> I was lonesome together with you
> And I wasn't too sure I knew what I should do

Suddenly, it was plain
There was someone else to blame
For being lonesome together with you

So I needed to learn how to be on my own
Or be lonesome together with you

I couldn't love you the way I did before
But I started to question as I walked out the door
Could I live all alone
Would I wait for you to phone
And be lonesome together once more

Yes, I needed to learn how to be on my own
Or be lonesome together with you

Never thought I could live without you
But now I have a different point of view
By myself I got strong
And learned to get along
No longer lonesome together with you
No longer lonesome together with you

Ken had brought Betsy with him. It was the first time the two women had met. He asked Wendy to join them at a private table in the back of the second dining room. Wendy was quick to check Betsy out as she broke the ice:

"Well Kenny boy, now I know why I could never get to first base with you."

The three of them drank and talked for hours. Betsy and Wendy would become best friends.

‿

There were two surprises the next day. The phone call from Betsy was the first. Deborah Hyman was pregnant. It was a mixed blessing for the lawyer, but tragic for the seventeen-year-old. On the one hand, Ken now had his smoking gun since a simple DNA test would show that Shmuel was the father. On the other hand, Deborah would have to make the excruciating decision to either abort the fetus—an unimaginable sin for a Hasidic woman—or give birth to her father's child.

The letter from the Judicial Grievance Committee was the second. Under New York's Rules of Professional Conduct, each lawyer admitted to practice in the state is subject to the state's disciplinary authority and must comply with its rules. If an attorney violates them, he or she is subject to a host of disciplines, ranging from a simple admonition for minor infractions to disbarment for major offenses, such as a felony conviction.

Ken knew how the system worked. The state was divided into four judicial departments. Each was responsible for processing complaints against lawyers within its department and meting out appropriate punishment if they were found guilty of violating the rules. The Second Judicial Department covered several downstate counties, including Brooklyn. The appellate court of each department was responsible for creating its own grievance committees "to receive, investigate, and, if necessary, prosecute complaints of professional misconduct against lawyers." Brooklyn, being the largest county in the Second Department, had its own grievance committee, consisting of twenty lawyers. The members of the committee were appointed by the chief administrative judge.

Ken was fuming as he read the letter.

Dear Mr. Williams:

The Grievance Committee has been notified by the Brooklyn District Attorney that you have been indicted for feloniously assaulting a police officer.

While you are presumed innocent, the serious
nature of the charge compels us to temporarily
suspend you from practicing law until after your
trial. If you are acquitted, the suspension will, of
course, automatically be lifted. We appreciate your
difficult circumstances as a busy practicing trial
lawyer, but you will have to advise your clients
forthwith that they must seek other counsel. Rest
assured that our decision was not an easy one, and
the Committee's vote was not unanimous. We look
forward to the speedy resolution of this matter.

Ken threw the letter down on his desk and called Betsy's cell. He
didn't mince words.

"I don't know where you are or what you're doing, but drop
everything and come to my office right now. And bring the Hymans
with you."

17

Betsy was appalled when she read the letter. And it didn't take her and Ken long to put two and two together. After being humiliated by Ken at JoJo's habeas hearing, Neary and Racanelli wanted revenge, and they obviously didn't want Ken to try the Jackson case. While there was no direct proof of their shenanigans, the circumstantial evidence was overwhelming: the phony arrest, the selection of Judge Velie as the trial judge, and now the coup de grâce—the suspension of Ken's license to practice law.

Betsy got right to the point. "Well, Ken, who are you going to get to try the Jackson case and take over your law practice while that felony assault rap is hanging over your head?"

"I've got to think about it. But I know now is the time for Deborah to bring her criminal complaint. I'll take her personally down to the DA's office to make sure that it's properly processed. But the Hymans have to understand that the press is sure to pick it up even if we don't go public with it. There is always someone there checking out all the complaints that are filed. This one is a biggie. It will be all over the papers. It's not every day that a revered Hasidic father is charged with raping his daughter."

Looking Deborah directly in the eyes, Ken asked: "Are you sure you're up to it? At first you will be viewed as an outcast, and you and your mom will be scorned by the Hasidic community. But the tide will hopefully turn when the truth comes out."

Rebecca Hyman squeezed her daughter's hand and spoke before she did.

"I will leave all the decisions up to Deborah, but she knows that she has my full support. I think she has the strength of character and the courage to see this through. She is passionate about being a role model for every other child who has been the victim of sexual abuse by their father, regardless of their religion."

"Mama's right," interrupted Deborah. "I'm ready. I'm committed to the life I must live now and the help I want to be for others. Betsy gave me an article by *New York Times* columnist David Brooks about passionate people. He writes that to be passionate 'is to put yourself in danger, to have the courage to be yourself with abandon.'" Deborah was reading from a clip she pulled from her purse. Ken could see it was highlighted with yellow marker. She continued, "People with passion, he said, are 'less willing to be ruled by the tyranny of public opinion.' I think I can handle what people might say about me. It's the right thing to do. And wait until my father finds out that I'm pregnant."

"Let's not say anything about that right away, Deborah. I want to see how the authorities are going to respond to this. My guess is that the DA will try to make you look bad, just like the Kellner case. Let him stick his neck out first before we chop it off."

"I'll do whatever you say, Mr. Williams. I trust your judgment. Thank God for DNA. Otherwise, no one would ever believe me."

〜

Ken was right about the press. Deborah's complaint was lodged late afternoon, but it was all over the evening news, and the tabloids went wild with it the next day. The *Post*, which prided itself on its attention-grabbing headlines, came up with a whopper for its front page: IT AIN'T KOSHER. And Jimmy Margiotta featured Neary's comments in the lengthy story he wrote for the *News*.

The DA was quick to say that people should withhold judgment. He assured everyone that Deborah's story would be carefully investigated, but cautioned that it seemed odd that she would wait for over a month before she brought this to the DA's attention. Neary said that cases that are not promptly reported usually suffer from lack of corroborating evidence and inevitably come down to a "he said, she said" scenario. He also commented that in this case, "It might be difficult to take the word of a troubled seventeen-year-old girl who ran away from home against the word of a highly respected member of the Hasidic community."

~

Ken was in for yet another surprise. When he arrived at the office the next morning, he did a double-take. The sign on the entrance read "BROWN and WILLIAMS, Attorneys at Law."

Betsy was waiting inside with a big smile on her face.

"Good morning, partner."

"What the hell!" Ken exclaimed.

"Thought you might need some help since you can't practice law for a while."

"Don't tell me you quit."

"There's no way I could stay in that office anymore. I tried to turn a cheek to everything that was happening with JoJo Jones and lots of other rotten things I heard about Racanelli's tactics. But the way they treated you was the last straw. That, and how Neary belittled Deborah in his comments to the press. I should have left a long time ago. But now, there's a lot to do. Gary can't handle all the clients by himself. And we have to do something about getting a new lawyer for Jackson."

"Well, maybe you can try it."

"I can't, Ken. There is a policy in place that you can't handle any business with the office for two years after you leave. And Neary would love nothing better than to report me to the Grievance Committee if he could."

"I suppose you're right. Maybe Kuby can step in. I'll get him down here as soon as I can."

❧

That afternoon the DA had two special visitors. Naomi ushered them into his office. It was the first time she had seen them. She was not used to seeing the "Black Hats," as she called the Hasidic men, visit her boss in his office.

Neary recognized the tall, well-groomed older gentleman with his distinctive, well-cropped gray goatee. "Rebbe Horowitz, what an honor."

He was not amused. "It's Rabbi Horowitz. You must stop calling me Rebbe whenever we meet. There's only one Rebbe, our revered Rebbe Menachem Mendel Schneerson, of blessed memory, who departed our world just a few years after the Crown Heights riots. Some Hasidim believe that he was the messiah and is still with us."

"My humblest apologies, Rabbi Horowitz. I know you are the chief rabbi and not the Rebbe. I keep making the same slip of the tongue. I remember the Rebbe well. It was his motorcade that triggered the Crown Heights riots right after I just became DA. I had the greatest respect and admiration for him. He worked so hard with Lillian Bloom, after Lemrick Nelson was finally convicted, to bring peace between the black and Hasidic communities."

Rabbi Horowitz continued, "It's a good thing that Nelson was convicted in the federal court for killing Yankel Rosenblum after your office bungled the state prosecution. But you've been good to the Hasidic communities throughout the years, and we've been good to you, so let bygones be bygones."

Neary breathed a sigh of relief before asking, "What brings you here, Rabbi, and who is this gentleman you brought with you?"

"This is Shmuel Hyman, who has been shamed and defamed by that *mesirah* girl who filed the complaint against him yesterday. We appreciate the statement you made to the press, but Shmuel will be on CNN tonight and wants you to be with him as he tells the world that he is absolutely innocent and has pity for his daughter who suffers from severe mental problems."

Neary looked at Shmuel, who was standing awkwardly near the door, before answering. "I don't think I should be there with him. Let me work behind the scenes. However, I suggest you try to make him look more presentable before the whole country sees him. The way he looks right now, no one will believe him."

He had a point. It was not his Hasidic garb that was the issue. But Shmuel looked unkempt. His gut hung over an oversized, open-collared white shirt that was barely tucked into his black, baggy pants. His long, grayish beard was scraggly, as if it hadn't been washed or combed in days, and when he took his hat off, the yarmulke wasn't big enough to cover the few unruly hairs on his scalp.

Rabbi Horowitz assured Neary, "We'll clean him up. But we really want you to be there. It will add a lot of credibility to his story. And perhaps you can talk about the Sam Kellner fiasco. It will also give you a chance to say some good things about the Hasidim. People do not know enough about our ways, the moral life we try to lead, and all the good deeds we do."

Neary interrupted. "Rabbi, once a criminal complaint is filed, especially one of this nature, I can't just bury it. It's out in the world already. I've been getting calls all day from all sorts of organizations devoted to seeing to it that rape cases are prosecuted and that the victims are not marginalized. What exactly would you want me to say, other than what I've already said in the press release?"

"I know that we have some problems with some of our men. But you can say how well we deal with these types of problems in our own courts. Tell them about our *beth din* and our *vad hatzinus* modesty committee and suggest that it might be best for everyone if Deborah Hyman withdrew her complaint and let her own people handle this. I promise you Hasidic justice will be done. We don't sweep these things under the rug."

"You're putting me in a difficult spot, Rabbi. People convicted of rape, regardless of their religious beliefs and culture, belong in jail. What if I can't do it?"

"This is the biggest disgrace that has hit our community since Kellner. If you can't help us out again after all we've done for you, do not expect any more money from us for your political campaigns and don't count on us to vote as a bloc for you again. Think about it. I'll also be on the show with Shmuel. I look forward to seeing you there. Shalom."

After they left, Neary slumped back in his chair, opened his desk drawer, and pulled out a fresh pack of cigarettes as he pondered what to do.

⤙

While Neary was meeting with Rabbi Horowitz and Shmuel, Ken was meeting with Ron Kuby back at Ken's office. Gary joined them.

Ken put it squarely to Kuby. "Ron, you've got to try the Jackson case. I'm sick about this. Betsy can't do it, and there's no way that Velie will move up my trial. He was an ADA years back under Neary and has obviously been leaned on by him. He's part of the old-boy DA network."

Kuby was more than willing.

"I won't let those sons-of-bitches get away with this. You can count on me. I'll make the time to bone up on the case. Troy will be upset that you got deep-sixed, but I'm sure that I can gain his trust. Maybe he knows my reputation for taking on the system and beating the crap out of rotten cops and prosecutors. But tell me more about their case. Do you have any clue who their witnesses are?"

"There are three cooperators, Ron. We know one of them already and Mickey's at work trying the find out the others. We think the one we know is their main witness. He was Troy's buddy, but he's obviously become a turncoat to save his own ass. Mickey found out that just weeks before Troy was arrested, Wee Willie was picked up in Florida for trafficking big time in coke for one of the Colombian cartels, and if he didn't cut a cooperation deal he'd be facing at least twenty years."

"Did you say Wee Willie, Ken? I handled a case several years ago for a guy named Wee Willie Wexler for selling dope to an undercover agent on Chess Street. Got him a pretty good plea deal. He only got a year."

Gary spoke up. "That's him. Mickey got his rap sheet and that's on it. It didn't show, though, that you were his lawyer."

Kuby was clearly upset.

"Well I was, and we're fucked. If I handled the trial, I would have to cross-examine the shit out of Wee Willie. And as you know, I can't do that. The Supreme Court has made it crystal clear that doing that to a former client is an absolute conflict. I'd be disbarred on the spot. I can't represent Troy Jackson."

Gary Ricco was not given to cursing, but couldn't help himself.

"Holy shit, Ken, what the fuck are we going to do?"

"Looks like you're going to try your first case, Gary."

18

Shmuel looked a lot better when he came into CNN's green room. It was where guests being interviewed waited until it was their turn to go on the air. Rabbi Horowitz, who was sitting next to him, did a terrific job cleaning him up. His black suit was neatly pressed. He wore a new white shirt that was neatly tucked into his trousers. A crisp, black tie made his gut look somewhat smaller. His black shoes shone. His beard had been neatly trimmed, and the few strands of hair on his head were creatively arranged around his yarmulke.

To their surprise, in walked Big Jim Neary.

"I'm not going to say we won't prosecute Shmuel on national TV, Rabbi, but I'll explain how difficult it might be to get a conviction in this particular case, and I'll say some good things about the Hasidim."

"Fair enough," said an elated Rabbi.

Just then the CNN host, Anderson Capers, came into the Green Room to greet his guests and explain how he planned to conduct the interview. After a few minutes, they all walked into the studio and sat around a round table. Shmuel was not used to the bright lights and blinked his eyes several times before a red light flashed and Capers began to speak.

"We have with us tonight Shmuel Hyman. He is accompanied by Rabbi Mordecai Horowitz and the Brooklyn District Attorney James Neary. Mr. Hyman's daughter has filed a criminal complaint against her father accusing him of forcing her to have sex with him. It has brought shame upon the Hasidic communities. Rabbi, let me start with you. Many people in most parts of the United States, especially those outside of Brooklyn, don't know much about the Hasidim. If they know of them at all, they think they are a little strange and don't understand why they live in their own world. Maybe you can shed some light on that."

Rabbi Horowitz was delighted with the opening Capers gave him and talked about the history of Hasidism and its belief system. He explained that the word "Hasidim" means "pious ones" in Hebrew and that Hasidism was a special movement within Orthodox Judaism that at its height, in the first half of the nineteenth century, claimed the allegiance of millions of Eastern European Jews. He talked about how Hasidism gained popularity in all strata of society, especially among the less-educated common people who were drawn to its charismatic leaders and the emotional and spiritual appeal of their message stressing joy, faith, and ecstatic prayer accompanied by song and dance. He explained that like other religious revitalization movements, Hasidism was at once a call to spiritual renewal and a protest against the prevailing Jewish religious establishment and culture.

The rabbi said the Hasidic ideal was to live a hallowed life, in which even the most mundane action was sanctified, and their insular traditions were designed to keep them from being exposed and corrupted by the outside world. He acknowledged that the Hasidic way of life was virtually unknown to most Americans, who were apt to confuse Hasidic men, with their beards, side locks, black hats, and long coats, with the similarly dressed Amish. He explained, however, that while this shared style of dress did indeed reflect similar values of piety, extreme traditionalism, and separation, the Amish were farmers in rural communities, whereas the great majority of the approximately 200,000 American Hasidim lived and worked in enclaves in the heart of New York City amid a number of contemporary cultures very different from their own.

Rabbi Horowitz concluded his remarks by giving several examples of the good deeds the Hasidim have done for the world at large, while at the same time striving to preserve their internal traditional customs and way of life. He proudly pointed out that their organizations provide comfort to the more than 5,000 Jewish military personnel serving in the United States armed forces, and explained that with a global structure of emissaries throughout the world, the Hasidim had the ability to be one of the first organizations able to lend crisis support to devastated communities, regardless of race, religion, or nationality. He cited, as examples, the 20,000 meals they provided for the victims of Hurricane Wilma; their being one of the first responders following the tsunami in Southeast Asia; and their lifesaving airlifts for 2,500 children from Chernobyl.

Capers listened politely to all this, but the time had come for him to get to the point.

"Thank you, Rabbi Horowitz, for giving the public a better sense of your Hasidic world. I can add that I have profound respect for your way of life and how you strive to protect yourselves from what you perceive to be the evils of our secular society. But we're here tonight to talk about Shmuel Hyman and his daughter. We have laws in our country and everyone, regardless of their religious beliefs, must comply with them. Do you think Mr. Hyman should be prosecuted for allegedly raping his daughter?"

Rabbi Horowitz was quick to respond. "You use the word 'allegedly.' How do we know it really happened? Shmuel is the grandson of one of the most revered Hasidic rabbis. He enjoys the respect of the entire Hasidic community. He is a leader at our services on the High Holy days. This has brought shame and disgrace on everyone, including his wife and daughter. They should have first come to us before going to the authorities."

Capers turned to Shmuel. "Mr. Hyman, do you have any reason why your daughter would take the extreme action of going to the police?"

Shmuel looked nervous. "I wish I knew. These charges are outrageous and embarrassing. I thought I raised her to respect her father,

like every good Hasidic daughter. My sense is that she has decided
to rebel against my authority—my not letting her go out with boys
before she is married, not letting her read the smutty trash on the
Internet, and not letting her bring those magazines into the house
showing young girls and boys in scanty clothing. But I never thought
that she would act out this way and accuse me of the most mortal
sin. She needs counseling, and I would like her to come home and be
treated by our own people who will forgive her and guide her back
into our pious ways."

Capers turned next to James Neary. "Mr. DA, notwithstanding
all this, you have a rape charge that has been filed. How do you plan
to prosecute it?"

Neary was ready for the question. "We'll pursue it, of course.
We take these things very seriously. But we have to tread carefully.
We don't have any hard evidence so far. Just the word of the daughter. We've got to question her carefully. There are things we have to
explore, like why she waited so long to file her complaint, where she
has been living, who has been advising her. With all due respect, we
have a bit of a history of Hasidim being less than credible when, for
whatever reason, they publicly turn against their own kind. You may
remember the Kellner case last year when I had to indict him for fab-
ricating his story about his son being molested."

Capers interrupted. "But there are some people who believe
Kellner. I just read a full exposé of his case in *The New Yorker*."

"You can believe whatever you want, Anderson," Neary said, lec-
turing him. "But we just can't take the word of someone like Deborah against her revered father."

Capers was not to be deterred. "Well, what would it take to corroborate her story? Have you considered searching for any DNA
evidence?"

"After a month, there probably isn't any. This is not like Monica
Lewinski's dress. But even if there were, we'd have to get a match
from Mr. Hyman, and I doubt that he would consent, given his

religious beliefs. Rest assured, however, that we will fully and carefully check out this young woman's incredible story and prosecute Shmuel Hyman if we find it believable and get some corroborating evidence."

"Thank you, Mr. Hyman, Rabbi Horowitz, and especially the district attorney, for coming here tonight. I'm sure our viewers will want us to follow this fascinating story as it unfolds."

Ken and Gary were watching. "That's it, Gary. Let's do it. The hell with it. Noon tomorrow in front of Neary's office."

19

Gary had done all the advance work. The press was out in full force. He had given them Ken's press release first thing in the morning. Betsy was standing by his side.

Ken explained the steps leading to his decision to run for district attorney: JoJo's case and the other JoJos who were in the slammer because of the DA's total disregard for the Constitution in striving to convict innocent black men; Ken's fabricated arrest and suspension of his law license, all obviously engineered by Neary and his cronies so he couldn't try the Jackson case, and the DA being in bed with the Hasidic leaders to curry favor with them for their financial and political support. When he finished, he opened up the press conference to questions.

The first was from Sue Wilder from the *Post*.

"You're a suspended lawyer being prosecuted by the Brooklyn DA's office for assaulting a cop. Are you trying to get back at Mr. Neary?"

"No! I'm sick of the injustices being perpetrated in this borough, and I've been thinking about this for a long time."

"Why are you declaring now, Mr. Williams?"

"I guess you can say it was Neary's performance last night on CNN. The nerve of him to make light of poor Deborah Hyman's plight. What a brave girl. She deserves better treatment. Unlike Neary, I will not condone sexual abuse, let alone rape, by anyone, regardless of their race, religion, or national origin. There will be a zero-tolerance policy in my office once elected, and that must include the Hasidim as well. I have a great deal of respect for them, but they must be made to understand that criminal misconduct of that nature must be prosecuted and dealt with under our secular laws."

Jimmy Margiotta asked the next question. "But how about what the DA said about the difficulty of proving these types of allegations, especially when it wasn't reported for over a month and there is no corroborating evidence?"

Ken knew the question was coming. "Good question, Jimmy. Deborah is pregnant. A simple DNA test will prove that the baby is Shmuel's."

There was a muffled gasp as the press was writing it all down, but Margiotta was quick with the logical follow-up question. "But how will you get Shmuel to consent to the test? Neary says their religion won't allow it."

Ken explained, "The Supreme Court says that once the DA asks for it, Shmuel would have no choice. He could be forced to have his saliva tested. Neary must know that. He's got to make him do it here, and when the public hears about all this from me, starting now, he's going to be between the proverbial rock and a hard place. If I don't do this for Deborah, Neary would obviously throw her to the dogs to appease his political base."

Cameras were rolling as Ken spoke. It would all be on the national TV channels within minutes. He allowed Margiotta to ask the last question before wrapping it all up.

"What's the first thing you will do if elected?"

"I'm going to marry this pretty young lady standing next to me."

～

When they returned to the office, the phones were jumping off the hook. Ken got most of the calls, but some were for Betsy congratulating her on leaving the DA's office and becoming Ken's partner. The last one she took was from a deep-voiced male, and made her tremble.

"If your boyfriend gets elected, you'll find him at the cemetery, not the altar."

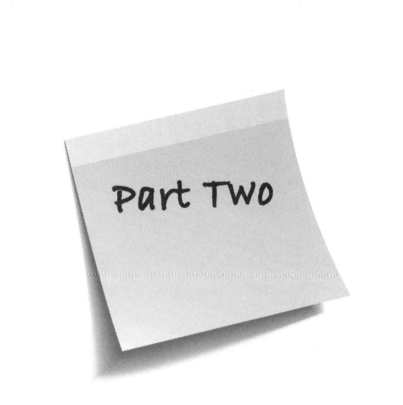

20

"Menachem Mendel Bernstein!" exclaimed Judge Cogan. His law secretary, Tina Cristakis, who was standing at the doorway of the judge's chambers, could not help laughing. Hearing the judge say the name in his Scottish brogue made her crack up.

"Crivvens, Tina, that name sounds a wee bit familiar. There can't possibly be another. It was several years ago, way before you came to work for me, when someone with that name was tried before me. The Jackson trial is our next big one. Menachem Mendel Bernstein must be the same one who the defendant is charged with murdering. And from reading about the JoJo Jones case in the newspapers, his father, Rabbi Bernstein, was murdered in the same neighborhood sixteen years ago. Strange, isn't it? See if you can find the old Mendel Bernstein file."

Tina was used to the handful of the judge's favorite Scottish curse words like "crivvens." The exclamations all seemed to mean the same thing—a range of surprises and astonishments.

Judge Cogan was fond of Tina and hired her as his clerk as soon as she had graduated seventh in her class from Brooklyn Law School two years earlier. He admired how she had worked full time in the court clerk's office while she went to law school at night. Not only was she smart and industrious, but the judge was also taken by her winning personality, and particularly her radiant smile.

Being an attractive, tall Greek American, she was into the latest styles, and Judge Cogan would marvel at the array of high-fashion shoes she would wear to the office.

"How many *paputsia* do you actually have?" he would ask her. Although she had taught him a few Greek words, including the word for "shoes," Tina would always tease him by answering *den ksero*, two Greek words she used whenever she wanted to tell the judge that she didn't know the answer to a question.

Cogan loved Tina's sense of humor and feistiness. She had a particular faculty for impersonating just about every ethnic tongue, and he would get a belly laugh whenever she impersonated his brogue. With all her charm, smarts, and good looks, the judge could never understand why in her late twenties she was still single. But she was a perfectionist, and she told him that she just had never found the perfect guy; he had to be at least three inches taller than her in her high-heeled *paputsia*, have dark hair, a body like Apollo, and preferably be a successful trial lawyer. In addition, her mother's approval would be important—and it was doubtful she would ever approve of someone who was not Greek. In an unintended way, Judge Cogan was the beneficiary of Tina's obsessive-compulsive personality; she was the perfect law clerk.

The judge was also fascinated by two of Tina's tics. Whenever she was deep in thought, she would twirl her long, blond, highlighted hair; and whenever she doubted what someone said, her dark brown, right eyebrow would rise a good half-inch.

❧

It didn't take Tina long to find the file. She knew where the judge kept his closed-out criminal cases. She sat down across from his desk and started to twirl her hair while her boss rummaged through two redwells. The first contained a copy of the indictment and the transcript of the trial testimony; the second a copy of the judge's jury charge, the guilty verdict sheet, and the transcript of the sentence he rendered. Tina kept twirling her hair as Judge Cogan pulled the sentencing transcript out of the second redwell and silently read it.

"Michty me, lassie, it all comes back to me. It was ten years ago when Menachem Mendel Bernstein and two codefendants were all found guilty of conspiring to fraudulently obtain and sell rental cars. Help ma boab, both his coconspirators were also named Menachem Mendel. Bernstein was the mastermind. He had Menachem Mendel Rabinowitz prepare fake drivers' licenses. Then he sent Menachem Mendel Shapiro to rent the cars at Avis outlets in Canada and drive them back to Brooklyn. Bernstein arranged to sell them to South America with phony bills of sale prepared by Rabinowitz."

Tina's curiosity got the best of her: "How did you keep all those Menachem Mendels straight during the trial?"

"Losh, Tina, it wasn't easy." With an elfish grin, he told her, "Instead of counting sheep at night, I started to count 'one Menachem Mendel, two Menachem Mendel, three Menachem Mendel.'" With a straight face, he continued, "I gave them each two years in jail followed by five years' probation. Reading the transcript of the sentencing proceeding brings it all back. The courtroom was packed with Hasidim. One of the rabbis made a pitch that I send them to the Aleph Institute instead of jail. He told me that it was an organization created and run by the rabbis to straighten out young Hasidic men who had violated the secular laws and needed counseling. He said that the Menachem Mendels were good yeshiva boys who studied the Talmud every day. I asked the rabbi, 'Where in the Talmud does it say you can steal cars?' He didn't have a good answer. I told him, 'You can send them to the Aleph Institute while they are on probation after they get out of jail.'"

Tina's right eyebrow went up as she asked, "What about the fact that Bernstein's father was a rabbi who had also been murdered?"

"It did come up. There were lots of rabbis there. Another one said that the Bernstein family had enough *tsouris,* and I shouldn't send Rabbi Bernstein's son to jail."

Tina started twirling her hair again. "Did you know what *tsouris* meant?"

"Of course, Tina, every Brooklyn judge knows that Yiddish word for aggravation. We hear it all the time."

"What did you tell him?"

"I was thinking of taking that into consideration but as I now remember after having read the sentencing minutes I decided that Rabbi Bernstein was more than simply a rabbi."

"What do you mean?" asked Tina inquisitively.

"As you know, Tina, before we sentence someone we get a report from the Probation Department about a defendant's background, including his family. Rabbi Bernstein had a side business as a slum landlord who owned a few run-down buildings on Chess Street and had a reputation in the streets of squeezing rents out of the poor folks who lived there."

"*Den to pistevo,*" she exclaimed.

"You like to use that Greek expression you taught me a lot, don't you? Well, you may not believe it, Tina, but it is true. The good rabbi apparently was not exactly a moral role model for his son. As you say in Greek, the *milo* doesn't fall far from the tree."

Tina was twirling her hair faster. "I wonder how the apple did in jail and how he behaved while on probation?"

"I'm also curious, Tina. The Probation Department will have the records. They keep track of it all. Call them and tell them that Judge Cogan wants to see the Menachem Mendel Bernstein file as soon as possible."

~

It took a few days before the records arrived. Bernstein's probation officer reported that the defendant had been sent to the federal penitentiary in Lewisburg, Pennsylvania. It was a minimum security facility, and he was a model prisoner. With time off for good behavior, he was released from custody after twenty months.

One of the standard conditions of probation is that the probationer must find suitable employment. It's not an easy task for ex-cons to do, but they must convince their probation officer that they are at least trying. In Bernstein's case, his probation officer noted that as soon as he got out of jail, the Aleph Institute found a job for him. It had contacts with many synagogues throughout the world. One of them was in Curaçao, the oldest synagogue in the Caribbean islands. It was founded by Jewish merchants in the 17th century, and because of its historic value the Aleph Institute took responsibility for preserving it. Although there was no current significant Jewish population on the island, the synagogue had become a "must visit" tourist place for the Jews from around the world who would vacation at one of the island's beautiful resorts.

The probation officer gave permission to the Aleph Institute to periodically send Menachem Mendel Bernstein to work at the Curaçao synagogue. It was in constant need of repair, and Bernstein proved to be a good laborer. He also was a good tour guide; he mastered the history of the island and the lives of the Jewish settlers, and would charm the English-speaking tourists with occasional pithy Yiddish expressions when he recounted all the *tsouris* the Jews faced in those days.

Menachem Mendel Bernstein had just completed his first year of probation when he was murdered.

21

It was the first time he had been to One Police Plaza since the march. This time Ken went inside. He was ushered into a spacious office on the second floor by an attractive female police officer. The police commissioner rose from his desk, came to greet him, and shook his hand with an iron-like grip.

Aidan Donnelly looked like he could have been Jimmy Margiotta's sparring partner. He had been appointed by the new mayor as the city's police commissioner soon after the mayor took office. On the wall behind his desk were all sorts of praiseworthy plaques. One in particular stood out. It was a citation from the White House: "For your extraordinary service as Police Commissioner of Los Angeles for quelling racial tensions and reducing crime while respecting the rights of minorities and the Constitution of the United States."

The mayor had promised during his highly charged political campaign that the "stop-and-frisk" practices of the prior administration would end, and that his police commissioner "would reform the force and root out the bad apples who didn't deserve to wear the badge."

"Stop-and-frisk" had become a major issue in the black communities. The past police commissioner—with the ex-mayor's blessing—had vowed to get the guns off the street, and gave merit promotions to police officers who had the best gun-arrest records. Although he never said the gun possessor's constitutional rights should be violated, there had been a marked uptick in stop-and-frisk arrests during the past several years.

Commissioner Donnelly and Ken sat in two gold and blue check-ered winged chairs across a square glass table. On it was a copy of the day's *New York Times*. The commissioner spoke first.

"I'm glad you came. I've been meaning to call you but you beat me to it. We have a few things to talk about. First, let me wish you the best on your efforts to unseat the Brooklyn DA. While I can't come out and endorse anyone because I have to remain publicly neutral, I want to dispel any notion you might have harbored about whether I'm beholden to James Neary."

"Well, Mr. Commissioner, two of your officers falsely arrested me, which then led to my suspension from the practice of law."

"You must understand, Mr. Williams, that I'm not the police commissioner of Brooklyn. I'm the police commissioner of New York City. That means all the five boroughs. I run the country's larg-est city police force. There are currently over 50,000 officers on my watch. It's the finest force in the land. But like every other police force in the nation, there are bound to be some problem cops. I will not condone it. That's why I've brought my own crack people with me from LA to head up the Internal Affairs Bureau."

"Well, I'm glad to hear that you're not in Neary's camp. He's been DA for so long that his cronies are everywhere, and I don't know who in law enforcement I can trust."

"You can trust me," Donnelly shot back. "The mayor appointed me to restore public confidence in the NYPD. He believes that the illegal employment of stop-and-frisks was fueling racial tensions. It was the centerpiece of his election after the federal judge's decision here in Manhattan got the former mayor and his police commis-sioner riled up."

Of course Ken knew what he was referring to. As the campaign for the mayor was in full swing, U.S. District Judge Shira Scheind-lin ruled in a lengthy opinion that the New York City Police Depart-ment was violating the Constitution by illegally stopping and searching blacks and Hispanics who lived in high crime areas. As the judge explained, the concept behind stop-and-frisk was a simple and venerable one. Police officers could arrest a suspect only if they had probable cause to believe that he committed a crime. But they could not base an arrest on mere suspicion. The Supreme Court had ruled many years ago in a landmark decision that the police may stop and search someone only when "a police officer observes unusual conduct which leads him reasonably to conclude in light of his experience that criminal activity may be afoot."

Judge Scheindlin's decision came three months after she heard nine weeks of trial testimony, which established that New York City police officers had stopped and searched about five million people since the previous mayor took office twelve years before. During the testimony, it was revealed that more than 80 percent were black or Hispanic, approximately 90 percent of whom were released after being found not to have committed any crimes.

The judge stated in her decision that the city had adopted a "policy of indirect racial profiling by targeting racially defined groups for stops based on local crime suspect data." The result, she said, was "the disproportionate and discriminatory stopping of blacks and Hispanics in violation of the Equal Protection Clause" of the Constitution.

The battle lines were drawn. The former police commissioner, and his supporters, argued that stop-and-frisk was a key component in the city's largely successful efforts to fight crime, while opponents criticized it as a blatant violation of civil rights.

The former mayor predicted that should Judge Scheindlin's decision stand, crime would rise and would "make our city, and in fact the whole country, a more dangerous place."

Commissioner Donnelly picked up *The New York Times* from the table, opened it to the Metro Section, and placed it in front of Ken before he spoke again.

"I know you've been one of the leaders in the black communities crying out for the end of stop-and-frisks of minorities just because they live in high crime areas."

"It's got to stop, Mr. Commissioner. And I'm pleased that when the new mayor announced your appointment, he said that you shared his views. It's just plain wrong to stop someone because he's black or Hispanic and can't afford to live on the Upper East Side. And I remember when I was an Assistant U.S. Attorney having too often to listen to cops who would shade the truth, if not outright tell a lie when testifying that they arrested a black kid because they supposedly saw him smoking a joint or thought he might have a gun because they saw a bulge in his pocket. It's one of the reasons I quit."

"Unfortunately, Mr. Williams, many police believe that the ends justify the means. When they testify they feel they can count on the judge going along because they know that most judges don't want to run the risk of the press taking them to task for not believing the cops and letting a criminal go free. As you probably know, it's commonly known as 'testilying.' I'm going to put a stop to that. My police officers will testify truthfully."

"I'm sure Judge Black will appreciate that, Commissioner. The *Daily News* recently called him a lunatic for not believing the police and tossing out what he believed was a false arrest. I feel for him. He's an outstanding and courageous jurist, but these are difficult times and the cops know that most judges won't do that."

"Good for Judge Black, Mr. Williams. I hope all the judges have the courage to do the right thing whenever they come across a 'testilying' police officer. I firmly believe that we can keep a lid on crime without sacrificing our fundamental Constitutional principles."

Commissioner Donnelly continued without a pause. "Take a look at this article in today's *Times*. I'm sure Judge Black would be pleased to read that last year under my administration the overall number of arrests, stops, moving violations, and criminal summonses dropped significantly from a peak of 2.63 million in 2011, driven primarily by a steep decline in stop-and-frisks, and that contrary to the dire prediction of the former mayor, crime is actually at an all-time low."

"I'm glad to hear it, but why do you think that happened?" asked Ken.

Commissioner Donnelly was obviously pleased with the question and was quick to answer. "Officers are now encouraged to use greater discretion in exercising their authority and to improve relations between the police and the communities they serve."

"Well, I doubt that our Brooklyn DA shares your sensibilities. He's been putting blacks behind bars for years on trumped-up cases, just like JoJo Jones, and it's going to be a centerpiece of my campaign."

"I share your concerns about him, Mr. Williams, and I've already taken some steps to check up on him. In the meantime, I want you to know that I've instructed my new Internal Affairs guys to check into the circumstances of your arrest. I suspect we have some bad cops, but I also want to find out if anyone in the Brooklyn DA's office had anything to do with it."

"I'm grateful to hear that, Commissioner, but perhaps you could help me with the reason I wanted to come see you."

"What is that, Mr. Williams?"

"Someone called my fiancée the other day threatening to kill me if I beat Neary."

"I'll get on it right away. Rest assured that we'll try our best to get to the bottom of it. Here's my private phone number. Call me whenever you want. By the way, do you have a gun?"

"No."

"I'll get you one."

⟞⟝

It didn't take long before Commissioner Donnelly got back to Ken. He and Mickey were talking about the Jackson case in Ken's office when Ashanti put through the call.

"Maybe we can cut through the formalities," began Commissioner Donnelly. "We may be having a lot of conversations with each other. Why don't you call me Aidan from now on and I'll call you Ken?"

"Fine with me, Aidan, what's up?"

"As I guess we both probably surmised, it was a throw-away cell phone. There's no way of finding out who bought it or what would be on it. The only thing we were able to do was to locate the cell tower for that telephone number. I'm sure you and your investigators know that the towers are spread out all over the place and each one covers a limited geographic area."

Ken could hardly wait. "So, where was this one?"

"Staten Island, Ken. It covered a ten-block area, running from Post Avenue to Dixon Avenue in Port Richmond."

"That's where Racanelli lives," said Mickey.

22

Back at the law offices of Brown and Williams, the boys were working away. Gary was putting the finishing touches to the legal complaint he was preparing for JoJo's civil rights lawsuit for monetary damages to compensate him for his sixteen years in jail. JoJo, sitting at his desk across from Gary's in their joint office, was poring over a bunch of trial transcripts. And Ken was in his own office preparing for his first television debate with Neary.

"Time for a coffee break guys," Ken shouted from across the hall. The coffee maker was in Ken's office. They drank from their favorite mugs. Ken's had a picture of a MINI Cooper. He had to settle for a black one since he couldn't find the yellow model that he drove. Gary had a red mug. It was the one with the big red boot on it that he bought from the concession stand at the Broadway show, *Kinky Boots*, that he recently saw with Ashanti. And JoJo was somehow able to find a mug with a picture of Jesus on the cross.

Gary's curiosity got the best of him. "How the hell can you even think about the debate knowing that if you beat the son-of-a-bitch, Racanelli is going to kill you?"

"Well, what makes you think it's Racanelli?" asked Ken. "There's more cops living in Staten Island than any other place in the city. Anyway, Racanelli is too smart to make that call from his home. And maybe it was someone who was visiting him."

JoJo joined in. "Sometimes smart people do dumb things. Just be careful. I hope you're carrying the gun the commissioner gave you."

"It's in my safe back home. Since I'm only going to get killed if I beat Neary, I don't have to worry about it yet."

JoJo just shook his head. "Sometimes smart people also say dumb things."

Ken laughed, slurped down the rest of his coffee, and swiveling his chair toward Gary, changed the conversation.

"So Gary, how much money are you going to ask for JoJo in the complaint?"

"I thought sixteen mil would be a nice number, one million for each year in the can."

"Sounds good to me," chimed in JoJo.

"Don't hold your breath, big shot," warned Ken. "We've got a long way to go. We'll file the complaint in the Brooklyn federal court as soon as Gary gets it done. That'll kick off the lawsuit. It will be randomly assigned to one of the district court judges. Keep your fingers crossed we get a good one."

"What will happen next?" inquired JoJo.

Gary had the answer on the tip of his tongue. "We're naming Neary and Racanelli as defendants, as well as the City of New York. There'll undoubtedly be a motion to dismiss the case for legal insufficiency. Their lawyers will argue that the DA and Racanelli have prosecutorial immunity, and that the city can't be held liable for their misdeeds."

JoJo was dismayed. "You mean there's a chance we'll get tossed out of court?"

"There is, JoJo," answered Gary. "The law basically sucks. It protects prosecutors and municipalities to a fault. But have faith. I think there's a chance we can survive the motion, and if we do, we'll be off and running."

"Gary's right," interrupted Ken. "We'll then be able to depose Big Jim and Tough Tony under oath, and the case will be ripe for settlement. I'll be licking my chops. I remember how much I relished ripping into the four cops who shot the Dunne kid at their depositions. They were devastated and really pissed off at me. I still got a framed copy of the twelve-million-dollar settlement check on the wall over my desk in my study."

"Do you really think you could get that much money for me, Ken?"

"If we get that far, your case is worth millions, JoJo. I wouldn't settle it for less than ten. What the hell will you do with all that bread anyway?"

"I'll probably give most of it to the church. Probably give a chunk to the Fortune Society. I'll take a little for myself so I can get a nice, little apartment and get out of that fire trap I'm sleeping in now."

"Boy, the gratitude I get for letting you stay in the back of the office," said Ken. "By the way, how's your project coming along? Have you come up with any good stuff yet?"

JoJo put down his Jesus mug and went back to his office. When he returned, he put a stack of papers down on Ken's desk.

"What's all this, JoJo?"

"They're the transcripts of three of Racanelli's criminal trials where three brothers doing twenty-five to life wound up with murder convictions. On top there's a summary of the testimony of the witnesses. There was only one eyewitness to the murders, a crackhead named Patricia Mondre, who testified in each case. Three different murders, three different times, three different locations, and the same eyewitness. She was like Racanelli's full-time professional witness."

"Jesus Christ!" exclaimed Ken.

"Watch how you use the Lord's name," admonished JoJo.

"Anything else?" asked Ken.

"I've got at least fifty more Racanelli cases on my hit list. I'm just scratching the surface. I've got the trial records piled up in boxes in Gary's office and all over that crummy back room where I sleep."

⁓

The debate that night was hosted by Channel 1, New York City's much-watched local TV station. The moderator, Shirley Pollak, was an attractive, dark-haired, young white woman. Neary had a hard

time keeping his eyes off her. It was pretty clear that if he had his dru-
thers he would rather be shacking up with her than having to defend
his office's record. But she had more than her beauty going for her.
A graduate of the Columbia School of Journalism, "Peaches" Pollak
had a quick wit and a disarming way about her that made her a rising
star in the TV news world. Her nickname came from her father, who
always told her she had "peaches-and-cream" skin. "Peaches" was
obviously a better name than "cream."

The two gladiators were dressed alike. They wore the same political uniform: dark blue suit—with an American flag lapel pin—white
shirt, and striped red and blue tie. But that was where the similari-
ties ended. The differences in their ages—and skin color—were pal-
pable. They sat at opposite ends of a rectangular table draped with a
blue bunting, glaring at each other.

Peaches Pollak, who sat between them, started it off by asking
Neary why he was seeking his seventh term.

Predictably, he gave his "tough on crime" stump speech. At the
end, he boasted that ever since the Lemrick Nelson case during the
Crown Heights riots over two decades ago, there had never been
another acquittal in a murder trial handled by his office.

It was the opening that Ken had prayed for. "That's because your
chief prosecutor, Anthony Racanelli, has been getting phony convictions for years against innocent blacks who are doing life for murders
they never committed."

"That's simply not true," shot back Neary. "You're distorting my
outstanding record. You've got one case where someone, who I still
think was guilty as sin, sent a phony letter recanting his trial testimony that got lost in the file and inadvertently wasn't turned over to
his lawyer. Big deal."

"Well, it was a big deal for JoJo Jones, who had to cool his heels
for sixteen years behind bars before Judge Gonzales set him free.
But I've got news for you. Back in my office JoJo's got a stack of trial
records of over fifty other cases that he's poring through that smell

like hell, and he's already spotted three where your chief prosecutor got murder convictions based on the testimony of the same drugged-up supposed witness. I demand that you let those three poor souls out of jail immediately, and fire Racanelli."

Neary's face was beet red, his eyes were bulging, and the fingers of his right hand were tapping around the table, as if he were searching for a cigarette. But before he could respond, Peaches cut in.

"Gentlemen, let's keep the accusations and emotions down. We'll talk about specific things in due course."

"Well, I want to talk about specific things right now, madam moderator," said Ken.

There was no stopping him. In addition to the wrongful convictions, Ken spoke about the need to put an end to illegal stop-and-frisks, the failure of the DA to prosecute trigger-happy cops gunning down innocent black kids, and Neary sucking up to the Hasidic community. As Ken wound up to his finish, he raised his voice to almost fever pitch, jabbed the middle finger of his right hand at Neary, and demanded that he tell everyone watching, "especially the women," when he planned on getting Shmuel Hyman's DNA.

Neary's responses were pathetic. In his entire political career he had never had to deal with such an attack. He had no crutches to help him. He wished he could pull the pack of Marlboros out of his pocket and light up. The best he could do was to "assure everyone" that his office "had properly investigated every criminal allegation against New York's finest," but had found "no wrongdoing." And as for the pending Hyman case, he was "personally on top of it," and "would do the responsible thing once that case is also fully investigated."

When Ken got back to his office, the gang waiting for him was jubilant. Betsy gave him a big kiss; Gary slapped Ken on the back so hard he almost fell over; Mickey wrapped him in a huge bear hug. And the phones were ringing. Betsy answered them while Ken was sipping the champagne Ashanti passed around. Ezekial Thomas called to tell Ken that he had galvanized the black community, and

Lillian Bloom called to tell him that the Brooklyn chapter of NOW was planning to announce its endorsement. But the last call that Betsy took was not so supportive.

"If you marry him you're dead too. But I may not wait so long to get him. And there may be others."

﹏

This time the throw-away cell phone was traced to a five block area in Greenpoint, not too far from the Crown Heights and South Williamsburg Hasidic communities. It was a working-class neighborhood with a large Polish population, but some Hasidim also lived there, as well as a number of Irish and Italian cops.

When he arrived home that night, Ken took the gun out of his safe.

23

This time the DA came to the rabbi. They met in Rabbi Horowitz's small, cramped study on the second floor of the building housing the synagogue and yeshiva along Eastern Parkway. The rabbi was his usual courtly and gracious self as he greeted Neary at the door and offered him some tea and cookies. Neary politely declined; he wished the offer was scotch and cigarettes.

"Rabbi, I don't know if you were watching the debate last night, but I have to do something that neither of us will be happy about."

"I'm afraid I missed it. I had to pay a shiva call on Mrs. Seybert. Her late husband was such a mensch. What happened that seems to make you so upset?"

"I've got to take Shmuel Hyman's DNA. Williams won't let up and I'm boxed in. In addition to the black politicians throwing their support behind him, which I guess does not surprise me, now I'm also losing the support of the women and my re-election is in serious jeopardy."

"But if you do that, you'll risk also losing the support of the Hasidim. Schmuel would never consent, and we would have a difficult time understanding how you can force one of our own to do that."

"I understand," said Neary, "but I'm afraid this is another case where there is a clash between your world and the secular laws we all must live by."

Neary explained to Horowitz, who glowered at him all the while, that the Supreme Court had ruled that you don't need someone's consent, and that it's not an illegal search of a person's body when that person is accused of committing a crime where DNA evidence can make all the difference.

"All we need is a dab of Shmuel's saliva. I'll do whatever I can to keep the lid on things, but I have no choice."

"May God be with you," Rabbi Horowitz solemnly said, as he escorted his distraught visitor out of the room.

～

The chief rabbi had another political visitor later in the day. The rabbi's secretary had told him shortly after Neary left "that a Mr. Williams had called to make an appointment."

Ken was nervous as Tamara ushered him into the rabbi's study. Rabbi Horowitz immediately tried to put him at ease by getting up from his desk and shaking Ken's hand, but could not help smiling when he saw what he had on his head.

"I appreciate your show of respect, Mr. Williams, but you don't have to wear a yarmulke here. Maybe someday you'd like to come to a Shabbat service at the synagogue. Then you can wear it. What brings you here?"

It was Ken's chance to reach out to the Hasidic community. As they sat across from each other at Rabbi Horowitz's desk, Ken leaned forward, clasped his hands and slowly spoke.

"I want you to know that I have no cross to bear with the Hasidim," he began, although he immediately realized that "cross" may not have been the best word he could have used. "But I want to be a good DA for all my constituents and I would like the support of your people."

Ken anticipated Rabbi Horowitz's question. "But how can we support you if you would prosecute someone like Shmuel Hyman instead of letting us deal with these domestic problems in our own ways in our own courts?"

He was ready for it.

"I have the greatest respect for the Hasidim and your desire to preserve your rich culture and traditions in the face of what is often a cruel outside world. I support that and will work with you to protect you against anyone who tries to undermine your way of life. I too am a product of an historically abused people; my ancestors were also effectively enslaved in ghettos and dreaded the secular world's criminal justice system. But I like to think that we have made some significant progress, and we can now embrace fair and just rules of law that should apply equally to all races and religions. We have a criminal justice system in our country that is the best in the world. We believe in the principles—'due process' and 'equal protection' for all—and . . ."

Ken took a deep breath before he finished the sentence.

"And . . . if a father has raped his daughter, which can be confirmed by a simple DNA test, he has committed a crime that cannot be ignored. He has violated one of the sacred laws of society and must be held accountable in the secular courts."

It seemed like an eternity before Rabbi Horowitz spoke again.

"It took courage for you to come here and speak like that. In Yiddish we call that *chutzpah*. I'd like you to come speak to my congregation. We do recognize that we must embrace the secular world while striving to maintain our cherished ways. We do not hide our heads completely. Certainly we do not condone rape, and we are proud to be United States citizens. We pay our taxes and we vote. As for the DA, we have supported Mr. Neary in the past, but I will tell my people to keep an open mind this year."

Ken felt the adrenaline rushing through his body. "Thank you, Rabbi. Please let me know when I can come."

Without missing a beat, Rabbi Horowitz assured him, "I'll get a date for you soon. Just make sure you bring that yarmulke."

Ken let out a huge sigh. The rabbi's warmth and gracious manner emboldened him to ask a few questions.

"While we're talking about what to put on your head, maybe, with no disrespect Rabbi Horowitz, you can educate me a little bit so I don't sound like a dumb goy when I come?"

"Where did you ever learn that word, Mr. Williams? Most non-Jews think 'goy' is a bad word."

"I used to also until one of my investigators, Abe Rosen, told me it only meant that you were not a Jew."

The grin on the rabbi's face was infectious. "A Jewish investigator," he exclaimed. "You're one smart goy."

They both laughed.

"So tell me, Rabbi," Ken continued after the laughter subsided, "why do you always wear a black fedora, even when you are inside talking to me right now?"

Rabbi Horowitz touched the brim of his hat and explained, "God is everywhere, and we will never be in his presence without covering our heads. Either with a fedora or a yarmulke."

"I guess that makes sense," said Ken, "but why do you wear what we call that 'black uniform' all the time, and those strings hanging out of your white shirts?"

"It's the way Jews dressed in olden times," answered Rabbi Horowitz. "Jews always had a way of dress to distinguish them from the people of the lands in which they lived—even when that meant exposing themselves to danger and bigotry. The 'black uniform,' as you refer to it, is our badge of honor and our everyday reminder of who we are, where we came from, and what we're here for. As for the tassels, they would hang from the four-cornered black cloaks as part of our everyday wardrobe in ancient times. And we carry on that tradition to this day."

Ken was fascinated. "Do those tassels mean anything?"

Rabbi Horowitz opened the big, beautifully bound dark-brown leather Bible on the right corner of his desk and turned to a dog-leafed page.

"Here's what the Old Testament commands," he said, as he patiently read, "Speak to the children of Israel and say to them: They shall make for themselves fringes on the corners of their garments.

And this shall be tzitzit for you, and when you see it, you will remember all the commandments of God and perform them."

Ken felt that he was cross-examining the rabbi like a lawyer but couldn't help asking the logical follow-up question. "All the commandments? I thought there were ten. How many are there?"

Rabbi Horowitz closed the Bible, with his left hand lifted up the tzitzit dangling from the left side of his shirt, and explained to Ken, "You will notice that these tzitzit are tassels, but they are not straight, and there are eight strings and five knots on each tassel. It works like this: Each letter in the Hebrew alphabet has a corresponding numerical value. The numerical values of the five letters that comprise the Hebrew word "tzitzit" add up to 600. Add the eight strings and five knots of each tassel, and the total is 613."

"So why 613?" Ken jumped in.

"Patience, patience, my son," said Rabbi Horowitz in a calming voice. "The strings and knots are a physical representation of the Torah's 613 do's and don'ts."

Ken was puzzled. "How do you remember all of them, let alone get them straight?"

"That's what we learn in the yeshiva and why you will see us always reading and studying the Torah and discussing their meanings with the rabbis."

Ken did not want to overstay his welcome. "Thank you, Rabbi. Will you be at the synagogue when I come?"

"It will be my pleasure," replied Rabbi Horowitz as he rose, shook Ken's hand once again and said "Shalom."

"Thank you, Rabbi, or perhaps I should say shalom also."

"Either would do," a grinning rabbi answered.

24

Ken looked across his office desk at the willowy man melded into one of the two soft, green chairs on the other side. He was always struck by how thin and tall, and literally bent out of shape, Mickey's part-time assistant PI appeared.

"Abe, you're coming with me to the synagogue tonight."

Abe Rosen struggled to pull his gangly body out of the chair and had a hard time straightening up.

"You're the same age as I am, Abie. By the time you get to be Neary's age, you're going to look like a pretzel. How'd you ever get that way?"

"Don't piss me off, Williams," snapped Abe amiably. "It's probably because of always having to bend over to talk to that shrimp Mickey. Anyway, why do you want me to go with you?"

"I thought it would be good to have one Jew with me," answered Ken. "We'll swing by the projects on the way over and pick up Mickey."

Ken always worried about Mickey living in one of the several, multi-storied, decrepit red-brick Armstrong Houses apartment buildings. It was in the midst of the most dangerous part of Brooklyn and was controlled by the Bloods. One block away was the Lafayette Gardens project, where the Crips reigned, and just a few streets from there was Chess Street, where Troy Jackson was raised and the Chessmen held court.

"We'll wait for you in the car," Ken told Mickey on his iPhone as he stopped his MINI Cooper in the middle of Clifton Place across from the building where Mickey lived. "I'm not going to risk my life to come get you."

In a few minutes Mickey came bouncing out of the building. He wove his way past three teenaged, baggy-pants kids walking down the street in their hoodies and jumped into the back seat.

"You're going to get shot here one of these days," Ken said, as he peeled away from the curb. "I just read that there were three more gang murders on this street yesterday. Between Lafayette Gardens and the Armstrong Houses that makes more than thirty in this whole rotten, two-block, shooting gallery just this year."

"Well, it's good for our business," retorted the half African-American Mickey sarcastically. "Anyway, it's just blacks shooting blacks. Nobody gives a shit about that. Just as long as they keep it here."

"It sucks," chimed in Abe.

Ken turned right at the next intersection and stopped several blocks down Nostrand Avenue in front of a small, seedy-looking storefront.

"We've got some time for a bite to eat before we put the yarmulkes on, guys," said Ken, getting out of the car. "And believe it or not, they make the best brisket sandwiches in the whole city in this dump. Makes Junior's taste like cardboard by comparison."

"What in the name of Moses is a joint named 'David's Brisket House' doing in the middle of the black section of Bed-Stuy?" asked Abe.

"The place has been here for decades," explained Ken. "The original owner was a Jew named, of course, David. Don't know his last name. There used to be a lot of Hasidim here in those days, but they slowly got out when the neighborhood changed, and moved down the road across Eastern Parkway. For some reason David stayed, and while the ownership changed over the years, it's become an institution where Yemeni Muslim guys serve incredible kosher Jewish deli sandwiches to a predominantly African-American crowd. Who'd a thunk?"

"Only in Brooklyn can this happen," chimed in Mickey. "I heard about this joint but never ate here before. I wonder whether they have brisket melts."

The sign on the blackboard outside the narrow entrance below the red neon light flashing "Open" had the daily special scribbled on it: "1/2 Sandwich and Soup. Your Choice of Pastrami, Brisket, Corn-beef $7.99."

"Salaam alaikum" bellowed the smiling young counter man after Ken, Mickey, and Abe reached the front of the packed line of African-American working men picking up their take-out orders. "Brisket, corned beef, or pastrami?"

Mickey ordered first. "I'll take a brisket melt."

"We don't have brisket melts. If you want one, you will have to go to Junior's. Inshallah."

"I think that means the same thing as 'shalom,'" said Abe.

"I don't think so," said Ken. "I think 'salaam alaikum' is like hello, the same as 'shalom,' which actually is used by you Jews for both 'hello' and 'goodbye,' but I think 'inshallah' is just a common saying in Arabic for 'God willing.' Anyway, I'm not leaving here before I have one of those kosher brisket sandwiches. I can't wait to see how a Muslim cook can make one. Just try the plain brisket for a change, Mickey."

Mickey shrugged his shoulders and gave in. "I'm sure it's not going to be as good as the melt," he growled.

"Three briskets coming up," said the counter man.

There were only three booths, but one was empty. Mickey sat on one side. Abe somehow managed to squeeze his ostrich legs into the other side. Ken took three Stewart's diet root beers from the cooler across the narrow aisle, placed them on the table, picked up three straws and a bunch of napkins from the countertop, and sat down next to Mickey. In a few minutes, a young black kid brought three humongous sandwiches to the table.

"Holy Moses!" exclaimed Abe. "I've eaten a lot of brisket sandwiches in my days but never one this big and juicy."

"It's much better than Junior's," said Ken.

"No more melts for me," said Mickey. "This is pretty fuckin' awesome. Too bad I don't have all my molars anymore."

It was about a half-mile run down Nostrand Avenue before it crossed Eastern Parkway, one of the largest and widest boulevards in Brooklyn.

"I can't believe how the neighborhood can change so fast," Mickey said.

"Well, it's still black," said Abe, "except now it's the color of their clothes and not their skin."

Ken made a left turn and found a parking spot on the next block right by an ambulance with Hebrew lettering on it, just like the one that picked up the injured Hasidic people during the Crown Heights riots.

"We'll walk from here," said Ken. "The synagogue is just a few blocks away."

"Man, do I feel out of place here," snarled Mickey. "The street is swarming with them. Look how they're staring at us."

"Well, it's probably not too often that they see a Jew walking in their neighborhood with a couple of black guys," said Abe.

Within seconds they were surrounded by a bunch of young Hasidic boys. None of them looked old enough to be in the army. The tallest and oldest-looking one approached Abe and asked, "Are you Jewish?

"Yeh," answered Abe, "but I'm not one of the meshuganahs like you."

The young man was not deterred. "It doesn't matter," he said, "As long as you're Jewish you can come to the synagogue with me and lay *tefillin*."

"Who is she?" asked Mickey.

"She's not a broad, Mickey," exclaimed Abe. "It's just their way of asking you to wrap a bunch of black straps around you and pray. I'm not an Orthodox Jew. Only they do that—and these meshuganahs."

"You should be more tolerant, Abe," Ken butted in. "I'm surprised at you. After meeting with Rabbi Horowitz I have a lot of respect for these true believers. Even though they have their issues, especially with the way they treat their women, they're committed to doing a lot of mitzvahs, as you Jews say, in this troubled world of ours."

"Maybe so," Abe said, "but they should stop always trying to convert us to their bizarre ways."

Mickey was taking it all in, and asked the young Hasid, "Why didn't you ask me if I was Jewish also?"

"God forgive me," came the answer. "We don't have Jewish Negroes."

"Well, maybe there are no black Hasidim," said Abe, "but there really are black Jews. In fact, I have a good friend who is one."

"No shit," said Mickey. "Are you playing me?"

"And do you know," Abe continued, "there is a black Orthodox rapper named Yitzhak Jordan who became interested in Judaism as a child in Baltimore, learning from his Puerto Rican grandmother, who had worked for a Jewish family when they came here? At fourteen, Yitzhak started wearing a yarmulke and observing Shabbat. He converted about ten years ago, and he later studied at a yeshiva in Jerusalem."

"I've heard of him, Abe," Mickey said, "but I never knew he was Jewish. I thought it was just his way of having a different name for a rapper."

Abe turned to the young Hasid. "May I ask your name?"

"It's Yankel," he answered quickly.

"That's the same name as the rabbinical student who was stabbed to death during the Crown Heights riots," said Ken. "Anyway, there's nothing in the Torah that says you can't be black and Jewish at the same time. Nobody keeps track of how many black Jews are in New York or across the country. I read someplace, however, that 7 percent of American Jews were either black, Hispanic, Asian, or American

Indian. There is even a tiny branch in New York of a national group called Jews in All Hues."

Another one of the Hasidim boys suddenly spoke up. "Now that you mention it, I do remember seeing a black man praying in our synagogue last month. We don't discriminate. Everyone is welcome. Why don't you two come and watch your Jewish friend put on *tefillin*?"

"Do it, Abe," said Mickey. "It'll be cool to see how it's done."

Abe relented. "Alright, I'll do it for you guys, but just don't make fun of me."

The synagogue was not what they expected. Ken and Mickey had been in a number of them for clients' bar mitzvahs and weddings, but this one was different. They walked down four steps into a huge fluorescent-lit room lined with wooden benches and rectangular tables stacked with black-bound books. Ken estimated that there must have been over a hundred Hasidim, either sitting or milling about, each bent over a book.

"I've seen eating frenzies, boss," said Mickey. "But this is the first time I've seen a reading frenzy. They must be searching for all those commandments you told me about."

Yankel took them to the right side and opened up a black plastic bag he was carrying. Out came a pair of small black leather boxes and long black leather straps. Yankel asked Abe if he was righty or lefty. When Abe said he was right-handed, Yankel then told him to roll up his left sleeve, and placed one of the boxes on top of Abe's bicep, just below the halfway point between his shoulder and elbow—right across from his heart. Yankel then made a loop with the strap, placed Abe's arm through it, and asked him to repeat after him:

Baruch atah Ado-nai, Elo-heinu melech ha'olam, asher kideshanu b'mitzvotav, v'tzvanu l'haniach tefillin.

"I guess that's Hebrew, but what does that mean?" Mickey asked.

"It's simple," Yankel said. "Blessed are You, Lord our God, King of the universe, who has sanctified us with His commandments, and commanded us to put on *tefillin*."

He then told Abe, "Focus on what you're doing. From the time of the blessing until both *tefillin* are in place, do not talk. Don't even wink. Just concentrate on hooking up your mind, heart, and deeds, and binding them to God."

Yankel wrapped the strap around Abe's bicep two more times, and then seven times around his arm and once around his palm, leaving the remainder loose. Next, he placed the other box on top of Abe's head just above his forehead. Two straps dangled from it down the front of Abe's shirt. Yankel wrapped the remainder of the strap on Abe's arm three times around his middle finger, once around the base of his arm, then once just above the first joint, then one more time around the base. There was some strap left over, so Yankel wrapped it around Abe's palm and tucked in the tail.

Yankel then had Abe repeat a long prayer in Hebrew praising God.

After they finished, Mickey asked Yankel to explain "What that *tefillin* stuff was all about?"

Ken breathed a sigh of relief that Mickey didn't say "fuckin' *tefillin* stuff."

Yankel knew the question was coming, and was happy to explain.

"You have a brain. It is in one world. Your heart is in another. And your hands often end up involved in something completely foreign to both of them. Three different machines. So you put on *tefillin*. First thing in the day, you connect your head, your heart, and your weaker hand with these leather straps—all to work together. And then, when you go out to meet the world, all your actions find peace and harmony as one—your soul, your mind, and your body."

Soon Ken was standing on a raised platform in front of a couple hundred Hasidic men, who were now all seated on the wooden benches. His black yarmulke looked out of place dancing on top of his swept-up black hair, but he said to himself that at least it didn't clash with the color of his skin.

Rabbi Horowitz gave him a wonderful introduction, praising him for coming to ask for his support, and for his "chutzpah" in speaking to him honestly and forthrightly about Shmuel Hyman, and the reason why he believed he must be prosecuted in the secular courts.

As Ken looked out at the sea of beards and black coats, he wondered whether these pious-looking men had a sense of humor. He always prided himself on warming up his audiences with a good joke before getting down to serious business. On this occasion, however, he thought it might be best to play it safe. But as he saw how skeptical the audience looked at him—a black man standing before them where the Rebbe used to speak—he thought he needed to say something to try melting the icy stares before he began his talk.

"Well, I imagine this may be the first time you've had some black dude come speak to you," he said.

Before he could say another word, the audience broke out laughing. It would be a smooth ride after that.

After the laughter had subsided, Ken scrapped his usual stump speech and went right to the heart of what he suspected was on everyone's minds—the fate of Shmuel Hyman. He didn't mince words and told his audience what he had said to the rabbi last week about why Shmuel must be prosecuted for rape in the criminal courts under the laws of the United States. He told them, however, that he believed that many nonviolent domestic disputes could probably be better handled outside of the strictures of the criminal law, and more than a few eyebrows were raised when he said that he would rely on the *beth din* and *vad hatznus* to resolve such disputes within the Hasidic community.

He drew more laughter when he concluded his remarks by recognizing that "there were a lot of meshuganahs out there whose *tsouris* should not be criminalized."

When he sat down, the Hasidim stood up. It was clear from their applause that Ken was a hit. As he was walking out, one of the Hasidic men—who looked like he could have been be a hundred years older than Ken—hobbled over to him with a walker, and with a twinkle in his eyes asked, "Kinder, with all that Yiddish that you speak, are you sure you never were bar mitzvahed?"

Little did the old man know that Ken had used up his entire Yiddish vocabulary. The first thing Ken did when he got home was to flip to the word "kinder" in his Yiddish dictionary. He now knew the affectionate Yiddish saying for "my sweet little child."

After that evening, although he certainly still did not approve of all their ways—especially their byzantine view and treatment of women, and their over-the-top resistance to secular laws—Ken Williams felt a fondness for the Hasidim.

25

Ken had religion in his heart. After being with the Hasidim at their synagogue, he wanted to take JoJo to his church to meet its charismatic pastor. The next Sunday morning they drove from Ken's office in his MINI Cooper to the far eastern end of Brooklyn. After they had been driving for about a half hour JoJo broke the silence.

"Where is this place, Ken, in heaven?"

"It's certainly not around the corner, JoJo, but wait till you see how many folks manage to get there."

Suddenly, as they turned down Louisiana Avenue a huge, light gray concrete building, the size of a large warehouse, loomed ahead surrounded by a sea of parking lots.

"Wow, Ken, this place is in the middle of nowhere, and those parking lots are bigger than the ones at Rikers."

The security detail at a small, private parking area next to the building ushered their special guests into a private parking space. Soon JoJo and Ken were sitting in the second row of reserved seats of a huge auditorium of soft green theater-type seats.

"This place is like three times the size of the Apollo," exclaimed JoJo, as he gazed at the throngs of African Americans rapidly filling up every chair in the orchestra and balcony. "How many people are here, Ken?"

"They say it holds 3,500. There are three services every Sunday. There's never an empty seat."

"That means that over 10,000 brothers and sisters will be praying here today," said a bewildered JoJo.

"It's the largest mega church in the city, JoJo."

The 96,000 square foot Christian Cultural Center, as the church was known, was built in the mid-nineties by Pastor A.R. Burnham. Cameras on telescoping booms were cantilevered over its blue carpeted stage. There was a giant TV screen on the soaring wall behind the stage flashing coming attractions of church events. Soon the stage was filled with a chorus clapping their hands and singing over and over, "Jesus is our Lord."

"There must be a hundred of them, Ken," said a startled JoJo.

"Not quite, but they sure can sing."

Soon everyone stood, and for the next hour there were Hallelujahs and "Thank you Jesuses" coming from every corner of the church. Then, a tall, slender man ascended the stage from its far right side. He looked to be about sixty and was impeccably tailored in a light brown wool suit and with his tortoiseshell glasses, looked more like the banker he once was than the pastor of a congregation of nearly 40,000. He carried a smartphone and a bottle of water. Behind him was a large glass marker-board that the magnetic Pastor Burnham would soon cover with bullet points as he delivered his forty-five-minute sermon. After endlessly exhorting everyone to "let Jesus in your lives," he ended the sermon with biblical references to Adam and Eve while extolling the importance of women for the less-enlightened male:

"Adam, alone at first, is a clueless workaholic. Eve, created by God to help Adam get his act together, has better people skills and can multitask, even though Adam thinks she's a nag. So, man up, men, or you'll lose her."

Pastor Burnham's sermons about male responsibility attracted a lot of young men, which in turn, brought in more women. Because of his huge following he had developed a reputation as a kingmaker, or "spiritual power broker." Every powerful political figure courted his support, and even the last two popes as well as the president of Israel would not leave the country without paying their respects. He was the spiritual adviser to Denzel Washington and a host of famous black athletes.

Ken and Betsy were two of his favorite parishioners.

~

After the services Ken followed A.R. Burnnham into his stylishly furnished study. "Pastor, I want you to meet JoJo Jones. It's the first time he's been to your church, but I'm sure he would have come before if he wasn't holed up in prison for the last sixteen years."

Pastor Burnham stood from behind his desk and shook JoJo's hand. "Welcome, Mr. Jones. Please make the church your second home. Of course, I know all about your suffering. It's been all over the media, and also the story of how brilliantly Mr. Williams has represented you."

JoJo was nervous and stuttered as he spoke. "Pastor, I've studied the scriptures while in jail. Jesus was what kept me sane. I would like to become a member of your church if you would have me."

The pastor smiled. "JoJo, you can come here anytime you want. Here you will always find Jesus."

JoJo took Pastor Burnham at his word. He became one of the church's most active members, involving himself in virtually all of the church's activities. He even found out that he could sing and became a member of the choir. And, of course, he decided he would never miss the Sunday services.

26

Betsy had taken Debbie under her wing. She felt so bad for the pregnant young Hasidic girl that she wanted to expose her to the cultural and intellectual life of Brooklyn that she had been missing while she was virtually imprisoned by her brutish father. Debbie's mother's job gave them enough money to move out of Betsy's place and rent a modest one-bedroom apartment on Union Street in Park Slope. Rebecca had loved working at the Hellerstein & Stein jewelry store in Midtown Manhattan but switched jobs after she moved out of her home to make it difficult for her husband to find her. She now worked at Fitzgerald & Sons jewelry store on Madison Avenue. Debbie also occasionally worked there.

Betsy arrived there early in the morning. It was a beautiful day, and Debbie's mother had already left for work. The apartment was small, but it was neat and clean. Debbie insisted that her mother have the bedroom. She slept on the fold-out couch in the living room, which accommodated a small dining table next to a tiny service kitchen. Park Slope was next to Prospect Park and was home to lots of upwardly mobile young people and thirtysomething couples with families. The park was designed in the middle of the 19th century by the famous landscape architects Frederic Law Olmstead and Calvert Vaux after they completed Central Park in Manhattan. It was opened to the public in 1867. In every respect, it rivaled its counterpart across the river.

Debbie's father never allowed his daughter to spend much time in the park. He thought it was too dangerous and not a proper place for a good Hasidic girl to hang out. Now she enjoyed walking through the park's ninety-acre Long Meadow, visiting its zoo, and marveling at its neoclassical buildings. Her favorite was the Boathouse by the beautiful lake, and she would enjoy renting a row boat and exploring every part of the lake's sixty acres. On the weekends, daughter and mother would never miss the free concerts at the Bandshell.

"So what are we going to do today?" asked Debbie as the two women sipped cups of tea at the dining table.

"Brooklyn has so many diverse neighborhoods and is so rich in history, culture, and historic buildings that one day can't possibly do justice to it," Betsy explained. "But I've borrowed Ken's MINI so we can drive around a little, and I can show you some of my favorite places."

Debbie was more than willing. "I'm familiar with the part of Eastern Parkway where we lived around the corner from Kingston Avenue, not far from the synagogue, and your neighborhood around Boerum Hill. And I know how to take the subway to the jewelry store in Manhattan, but most of Brooklyn is still a mystery to me. My father had an iron grip on my life."

They walked down the two flights of stairs from Debbie's apartment and jumped into the MINI Cooper parked around the corner. Soon they were driving down Ocean Parkway.

"I remember my father taking me once to visit a cousin who lived somewhere on Ocean Parkway," Debbie said. "I remember how wide and beautiful it was, especially the bike path down the middle. But I have no idea where it takes you."

"Well, it runs from Prospect Park all the way down the spine of Brooklyn to Brighton Beach and Coney Island—about five miles," explained Betsy. "The landscape architects who designed Prospect Park and Central Park also designed the Parkway, and fashioned it after the great boulevards in Berlin and Paris, with its central roadway and grassy median-pedestrian path. The bike path has been there since the 1890s. Ken told me it was the first in the United States."

Debbie was excited. "Let's bike the whole path someday, Betsy."

"We will," she said. "But today we're driving."

After cruising for twenty minutes past stately mansions and homes dating back to the early 1900s and modern high-rise apartments, the giant Wonder Wheel Ferris wheel and classic Cyclone rollercoaster at Coney Island loomed ahead.

Debbie couldn't keep her eyes off of them. "Wow," she exclaimed, "I've heard about them but my father would never let me go."

"Well, here's your chance, baby girl," said Betsy with a mischievous look.

Betsy found a parking space on Surf Avenue and in a matter of minutes they were staring at the Cyclone—the world's most iconic roller coaster since it was built in 1927. "Ken talked me into doing it last year, Debbie. I was scared out of my mind, but I loved it. It's both death-defying and addictive. Are you game?"

Debbie stood in front of the ticket booth and watched in awe as the passengers screamed during the 85-foot first drop and the harrowing barrage of 60-mile-per-hour twists and turns. She looked at Betsy incredulously. "Is this some sort of test of my newfound freedom?"

"Well I guess you can look at it that way," answered Betsy.

"Okay. If you can do it so can I."

They clutched each other and screamed as the giant machine soared up and down through the cool air. After the attendant opened the metal gate that encased them and helped them out of their seats, Betsy held her breath waiting for Debbie's reaction. It didn't take long.

"Let's do it again, Betsy."

"Not so fast, sweetheart. We probably shouldn't have done it at all. Remember, you are pregnant. Anyway, we've got lots more to do today."

"You're right. But the baby and I are in good hands with you, Betsy."

"Does that mean you've made the big decision, Debbie?"

"No, Betsy. I'm still torn."

Betsy hugged her. "Well, the clock is ticking, and you have to do it soon."

"I know, I know. Please, Betsy, let's not spoil the day and talk about it anymore right now."

Soon they were on the wide boardwalk just a short way from the amusement park, watching the waves of the Atlantic Ocean lapping the shoreline. They stopped at a Nathan's Hot Dog stand.

"They're the best," said Betsy. "I've got to have one."

"Are they kosher?" asked Debbie.

"I guess I should know that, Debbie, but I always wondered, what exactly is the difference between kosher and nonkosher food?"

Of course, Debbie knew the answer. "According to the laws of the Torah, kosher food must be slaughtered by a *schochet*. Jewish law prohibits causing any pain to animals, so the slaughtering has to be done in such a way that unconsciousness is instantaneous and death occurs right away. A 'schochet' is a specially trained Jew who is taught to do that."

Betsy was quick to put her newfound knowledge to use. "Are Nathan hot dogs kosher?" she asked the male Latino behind the counter.

"I have no idea, señora," came the answer. "But there's a place a few stores away that says they only serve kosher dogs."

Soon Betsy and Debbie were eating certified kosher hot dogs.

After she wiped some mustard off her face, Betsy asked Debbie, "Have you ever eaten nonkosher food?

"Not to my knowledge," Debbie answered. "There are certain things that are so ingrained in me I don't think I can ever do it."

They returned to the car, and Betsy started to drive back up Ocean Parkway.

"Where to now?" Debbie asked.

"I think you need something calm and peaceful after your traumatic rollercoaster ride."

They drove into the middle of Prospect Park, and Betsy parked in the Brooklyn Botanic Garden parking lot.

She was the consummate tour guide. "This place is heaven on earth," Betsy told Debbie as they were walking to the Garden's entrance. "It's been here since 1910 and there are about a million visitors a year. The fifty-two acres hold over 10,000 types of plants. Inside there are three climate-themed plant pavilions, a white cast-iron and glass aquatic plant house, and an art gallery. It's also home to the world-famous Bonsai Museum and has a bunch of specialty gardens. My favorite is the Japanese Hill-and-Pond Garden."

Soon they were walking over a wooden bridge with stone lanterns leading to a Shinto shrine. They stopped and sat on a stone bench in front of one of the many ponds filled with hundreds of Japanese koi fish.

"It's beautiful, Betsy," marveled Debbie as she was taking in the hypnotic tranquil landscape. "I never knew this place existed. And only a short distance from where I used to live."

Betsy was not done with showing off her textbook knowledge of one of the wonders of Brooklyn. Familiar with the borough's landmarks and history, courtesy of dyed-in-the-wool Brooklynite Mickey, she had also brushed up the prior evening with a coffee-table book on Brooklyn that he had given her.

"The Japanese Hill-and-Pond Garden was the first Japanese garden to be created in an American public garden. It opened to the public just before the First World War. It's considered a masterpiece of the Japanese landscape designer Takeo Shiota, who was born in a small Japanese village not far from Tokyo but emigrated to our country at the beginning of the last century. Lucky for us. They say it compares to anything you might find in Japan."

"Who says that?" Debbie asked.

"Uh, this book I was reading, written by a Suzie Matsumoto, who I think is a living descendant.

"I wonder whether he was put in one of our Japanese camps during World War II?" Debbie mused.

"You know, Debbie, I don't know. Maybe he was. There's a plaque somewhere here that says he died in 1943. I hope he was spared that humiliation. What a gift he and so many other immigrants have given to our country! It's a shame they've become such a political football."

"It's a good thing he wasn't deported," Debbie wryly commented.

They spent the afternoon at the Brooklyn Museum. It was right next to its sister Beaux Arts building on Eastern Parkway, the Brooklyn Public Library, and the museum's massive portico columns rose over Eastern Parkway like the Vatican looms over St. Peter's Square.

"Like the Library," Betsy explained, "it's one of a handful of classical buildings built in Brooklyn throughout the 19th century that are the remnants of a bygone era, when Brooklyn architecture was influenced by the great ancient Greco-Roman edifices, and Brooklyn was home to a landed gentry that really cared about aesthetics."

"I think I've seen some of them," said Debbie, who had read a bit of classical history when her father wasn't looking. "There's the Brooklyn Borough Hall . . ."

"That's Greek Revival style," Betsy interjected, then quickly realized she should let the girl talk.

". . . and the old Post Office building on Cadman Plaza East across from the new Federal Courthouse," Debbie continued. "That's Romanesque Revival style, right?"

Betsy was impressed. "And the magical Peter Jay Sharp Building," she added. "It's the home of the Brooklyn Academy of Music, where we're going to wind up tonight."

Debbie was taking it all in, but Betsy wasn't finished.

"And there are also some beautiful churches, Debbie. My favorite is the old Plymouth Church in Brooklyn Heights. That's an affluent neighborhood with low-rise architecture and many brownstone row houses, most of them built prior to the Civil War. The church is on a beautiful tree-lined street, close to the Federal Courthouse. It was built in the mid-1800s and is an example of 19th century urban tabernacle architecture with Italianate and colonial motifs. But it is most famous for its first pastor, Henry Ward Beecher, a leading abolitionist and the brother of Harriet Beecher Stowe who wrote *Uncle Tom's Cabin*. Have you ever read it?"

"No, but I will. I have a lot of catching up to do."

Betsy continued with her history lesson. "The Plymouth Church became an important station on the Underground Railroad, through which slaves from the South were secretly transported to Canada."

"Where did you learn all about these things?" asked Debbie, "From that book of yours?"

"Well, Debbie, I knew all about the church and the Underground Railroad from my Black History studies during my undergraduate days at Howard, but the history and architecture of Brooklyn during the 19th century came from Mickey. Believe it or not, he's quite an intellectual and a Brooklyn history nut. He keeps getting books about Brooklyn out of the big Library and gives them to me."

"He doesn't look the type, Betsy."

"Well, looks can deceive you, Debbie. For all his nutty ways and despite his funny looks, Mickey is a real diamond in the rough. He's intellectually curious and smart as a whip. He did a great job on JoJo's case, and I'm sure he'll be invaluable on the Jackson case also."

"I suppose one never knows," commented Debbie. "You would never think my father was so mentally disturbed from his outward looks."

"Debbie, I hate to bring up your pregnancy again, but the mention of your father just now makes me think that you might benefit from some professional counseling. I'm sure I can find a good therapist for you to see."

"But I have you to talk with, Betsy."

"I'll be by your side, all the time, Debbie. You can count on me. But I'm simply not trained to professionally counsel a young girl who must still be traumatized from what you've been through."

"Do you really think I need someone to talk to about my father and . . . ."

"Yes, I do. You just can't make the choice by agonizing over it all by yourself. There's just too much emotional baggage here that you have to sort out. If you have the baby, your child will be a daily reminder of that horrific moment."

"But it's a sin to take a life. I just don't believe in abortions. I think my religion is right when it comes to that. Anyway, I guess I could always give the baby up for adoption."

They had been walking through the museum side by side while they were talking, but Betsy gently sat Debbie down on a bench across from a Chagall painting, grasped her hands and looked her straight in the eye.

"Debbie, as difficult as this is for both of us, I just can't pull any punches anymore. You've been raped by your sick father. I just don't see how you can have this baby."

They both started to cry.

"Maybe you're right, Betsy. I just don't know what to do."

"I'll have some names of psychologists for you by tomorrow. And don't worry about the cost. Ken and I will take care of it."

As they hugged, Debbie wished she had Dr. Gold's tissue box.

❧

They then visited the huge collection of Egyptian antiquities spanning more than three thousand years, as well as a stunning array of African, Oceanic, and Japanese antiquities, and spent most of the rest of the afternoon viewing the extraordinary collection of post-colonial American art, including notable works by Mark Rothko, Edward Hopper, Norman Rockwell, Winslow Homer, Georgia O'Keefe, and Max Weber. Debbie's favorite was Gilbert Stuart's famous portrait of George Washington.

They ended their museum visit at the Elizabeth A. Sackler Center for Feminist Art, dedicated to preserving the history of the

feminist movement since the late 20th century and raising aware-
ness of feminist contributions to art. Debbie stood for a long time in
front of Judy Chicago's large installation, *The Dinner Party.*

She looked distraught. "I'm sure she was not a Hasidic woman,
Betsy. How could the world I was raised in so totally inhibit female
creativity and keep us so ignorant? How many Judy Chicagos could
there have been among us if it were otherwise?" she asked rhetorically.

"Fortunately, it's not too late for you, Debbie. Let's get a bite to
eat before the show."

"What show?" Debbie asked.

"I'll tell you later, but I thought the BAM would be a perfect
way to end this very special day. But as for dinner, Ken told me we
must check out David's Brisket House. He ate there with Mickey and
hasn't stopped raving about the kosher corned beef, pastrami, and
brisket sandwiches."

"After the roller coaster I guess I'm game for anything," said a
willing Debbie. "Is it really kosher?"

They drove a mile or so along Eastern Parkway to Nostrand Avenue, not too far from where Debbie used to live. After turning left on
Nostrand, Betsy parked the car a few miles down the road in front of
the restaurant.

"I can't believe this," said a bewildered Debbie, as they entered
the place and walked toward the counter. "This hole in the wall is a
dump, and what are all those Muslims doing in the kitchen? Nothing
about this place looks kosher to me, let alone the food."

The counterman, Mohammad, overheard Debbie's comments,
and smiled.

"We Arabs cook just like the Jews," he told the two women. "You
call it kosher, we call it halal. We slaughter the animals just the same way
you do. Just try one of our sandwiches. You'll be surprised. What will it
be, corned beef, pastrami, or brisket? We can also do combinations."

In a few minutes, a young Muslim boy brought a pastrami sandwich and a brisket sandwich to the booth where Betsy and Debbie

sat, and with a big friendly smile said, "I hope you enjoy them. Can I get you some mustard or something to drink?"

"I guess mustard and some diet cream sodas would be fine," said Debbie, smiling back at the boy. "What's your name and how old are you?"

"My name is Omar and I am fourteen, ma'am. I get straight A's at school. My father is the number one chef here and I'm saving money for college. When I grow up I want to be president of the United States."

"Lots of luck," whispered Betsy despondently under her breath, but she gave Omar a big smile.

The sandwiches were as advertised. "I've never had such a great pastrami sandwich before," said Debbie.

"And likewise for the brisket," chimed in Betsy.

When they left, Betsy gave Omar a five-dollar tip as he was cleaning off the table.

"Thank you from the bottom of my heart, miss," the overwhelmed young boy said. "You made my day."

"They're so like us," said Debbie as they were walking out. "Why can't we make peace?"

"I guess only God knows," was the best answer Betsy could muster.

～

Debbie was struck by the Brooklyn Academy of Music's complex of buildings at the intersection of Fulton Street and Ashland Place—not far from Ken's office. She had never been there before.

Betsy explained, again informed by Mickey and his Brooklyn books, "BAM is Brooklyn's major performing arts venue, and it began operations in its present location in 1908, with the construction of the Peter Jay Sharp Building you are looking at."

"This building is awesome!" Debbie exclaimed. Betsy called her attention to the massive gray granite base and cream-colored terra cotta trim. "I love it," said Debbie.

Inside the building, Debbie picked up a brochure, which boasted at the top of the front cover that "annually, more than a half a million people experience a broad range of aesthetic and cultural programs at the BAM." She read the rest of the cover page:

> The BAM complex is now home to a number of theaters, including the old historic Harvey theater, which seats over 800 people. CNN has named the Harvey "one of the World's 15 Most Spectacular Theaters." It has become the first choice of venues at BAM among directors and actors for presenting traditional theater. But the centerpiece of the BAM remains the massive Peter Jay Sharp Building—the building which heralded the advent of the BAM in 1908—housing the 2,200-seat Opera House. Geraldine Farrar and Enrico Caruso performed in a Metropolitan Opera production of Charles Gounod's *Faust* at its gala opening.

Betsy pulled out two tickets from her pocketbook. "Debbie, we're going across the street to the Harvey Theater to see a production of Shakespeare's *The Merchant of Venice*."

Debbie was surprised. "My teacher said we should never read that 'anti-Semitic trash.'"

"Whether it's truly anti-Semitic has been a subject of debate for centuries," said Betsy, "but it's a powerful masterpiece that has some relevancy to the life you've left and the new life you are now embarking upon."

"How so?" asked Debbie.

"We'll talk about it afterward," answered Betsy.

About two and a half hours later they sat in the BAM café back in the Peter Jay Sharp Building.

Debbie spoke first, "Shylock gives Jews a bad name. A moneylender from the ghettos wanting a pound of flesh if Antonio didn't pay back the money if Bassanio defaulted, which turned out to be the case."

"But Antonio wasn't Jewish," explained Betsy. "As an aristocrat in those days back in the 16th century it was not appropriate to pay interest on borrowed money, so he made the deal that almost cost him his life. In the end, many modern readers and theatergoers have read the play as a plea for tolerance, noting that Shylock is a sympathetic character because Shakespeare made a mockery of the Christian world's perverted sense of justice and its resorting to trickery and dishonesty."

"And he did have Shylock make that powerful speech," added Debbie.

Betsy took a paperback of the play out of her pocketbook. "Hearing it tonight and reading it again always brings chills to my bones, Debbie. 'I am a Jew. Hath not a Jew eyes? Hath not a Jew hands, organs, dimensions, senses, affections, passions? Fed with the same food, hurt with the same weapons, subject to the same diseases, healed by the same means, warmed and cooled by the same winter and summer as a Christian is? If you prick us, do we not bleed? If you tickle us, do we not laugh? If you poison us, do we not die?'"

"So why did you think this was a play I should see?" Debbie asked.

Betsy was waiting for the question. "For a couple of reasons. First, it vibrates to this day. The play is an object lesson of the evils of discrimination, be it against Jews or blacks—like we have had to endure—or Muslims, or any minority. Second, the ghetto world in which the Jews lived in those days and their insular lives still resonate today in the world you have chosen to leave behind. And last, Shylock's daughter, Jessica, left that world to become part of the secular world, just like you are doing."

"True," Debbie interjected. "But I didn't particularly like her character or the way she victimized her father."

"I didn't particularly care for her either. She was no Deborah Hyman. But it shows that you don't have to be locked into an unsavory environment."

"I suppose," Debbie sighed. "I'm exhausted Betsy. It's been a super day and I want to thank you."

She fell asleep on the way home.

27

It had been a while since Ken had spoken to Rebecca and Deborah Hyman. But he wanted to tell them in person that, as expected, Shmuel's DNA proved that the baby growing inside Deborah was her father's child. The next week he and Betsy came to Rebecca and Debbie's apartment and the four of them sat around the dining table.

"So what happens now?" asked Rebecca.

Ken laid it all out. "He's being charged with first degree rape as we speak. The DA has no choice. He can't wiggle his way out of this one. Shmuel will be arraigned tomorrow morning. I plan to be there, although I'll only be a spectator. I'm curious to see what Neary's position will be on bail and the fixing of a trial date. My guess is that he won't oppose a token bail package and Shmuel will be free until the case is disposed of either by a negotiated plea or a trial. If he goes to trial and is convicted he's looking at twenty years."

Deborah was startled. "My father will be going to jail for twenty years?"

"Probably not that long," interjected Betsy. "The sentencing judge has some discretion. He'll probably fix an indeterminate sentence below that, but he's looking at serious jail time."

"Oh, my God!" exclaimed Deborah as she broke into tears. "What have I done?"

Her mother jumped up from her chair and reassuringly embraced her daughter. "You've done nothing wrong, my child. We've been through this over and over. This day had to come. We are both making new lives for ourselves. We will get through this ugly passage together and will pray to God that we stay strong."

"I know you're right, Mama, but it's still hard for me—and you. I don't have a father anymore."

Betsy and Ken looked like they might cry at any moment, and Ken tried to reassure Deborah. "I'll help as best as I can, Debbie. I still can't practice law but I can be your spokesperson and handle the press and PR."

Rebecca cried out, "What do you mean about the press and our needing PR? I know there will be stories in the papers about my husband. But why won't they let me and my daughter alone and respect our privacy? Do they want to make things worse?"

Ken gently held Debbie's hands before answering her mother. "We can't be naive about this Rebecca. Shmuel Hyman's arrest has already been big news. Now that he's being indicted for raping Debbie and the DNA test confirms her story, it's guaranteed to be in every major newspaper and TV channel in the country, and every rag will be having a field day with it."

"I guess I just don't understand why they are so interested in Mom and me," said Debbie, while Ken was still holding her hands. "Why can't they just leave us alone?"

Ken had to level with her. "You've got to understand, Debbie, everyone is going to want the answer to one question."

"What question?" she sheepishly asked Ken.

"Will you, a Hasidic Jew, have an abortion?"

❧

Ken was right. When he arrived at the old Criminal Court building the next morning, he was accosted by a phalanx of press. They were lined up at the entrance like birds of prey, and the cameras were clicking away. Marigotta was leading the charge as he wiped a pigeon dropping off his head. "How appropriate," Ken mused.

Ken knew that the predator reporter would be drooling over the story.

"Have you asked the Hyman girl if she plans to have the baby?" Margiotta shouted.

Ken was not going to get sucked in. "We'll have to wait and see. No decision has been made yet. This is obviously all very painful and traumatic for her. Please respect her privacy during this difficult time of her life."

It was wishful thinking. As he told Rebecca and Deborah, it was bound to be a big national story. He didn't realize, however, just how big it would be.

Once inside, Ken sat in the back row and listened to a young male ADA he had never seen before tell the judge that Shmuel was not a flight risk and "the office would have no objection to his being released on his own recognizance." Ken was not surprised. It was the least Neary could do to try to appease the Hasidim.

He was also not surprised when the ADA asked that the trial date be postponed until after the general election. Shmuel's defense counsel quickly joined this request. Except in unusual circumstances, like JoJo's case, most criminal defense lawyers wanted to delay judgment day for as long as possible. Memories fade. Evidence becomes stale, or even lost. Things happen. Ken still talked about how he jerked one case around for more than a year with all types of motions—none of which had a scintilla of merit—until it had to be dismissed because the prosecutor's star witness was killed in an automobile accident.

Shmuel walked out of the courtroom a free man—at least temporarily—and the judge fixed the trial date for three months after the general election. It gave Ken the opportunity to tell the press waiting outside that "the DA is still in bed with the Hasidim and doesn't want Shmuel to get convicted on his watch." He also assured them that "Once elected, I will see to it that there are no trial adjournments and Shmuel Hyman will be swiftly prosecuted and, hopefully, convicted for raping his daughter."

⌇

Deborah Hyman's plight did indeed go viral. It stoked a national firestorm, engaging the country's political leaders on each side of the pro-abortion, anti-abortion divide. And the pro-life contingent had to stake out its position on whether it would approve of any exceptions at all. The Democratic leadership supported a woman's right to choose. But, as Irin Carmon reported for MSNBC, "The question was not whether or not to ban abortion or to defund Planned Parenthood. It was about whether exceptions in the case of rape, incest, or a woman's life endangerment are legitimate."

A number of GOP leaders, namely Scott Walker, Marco Rubio, Mike Huckabee, Rick Santorum, and Ted Cruz, had expressed their opposition to any exceptions. If it were up to them, Deborah Hyman should give birth to her father's child.

Deborah knew all the pros and cons. Even at seventeen and despite what had been taught to her as moral law, she understood the logic of the thinking across the political spectrum. Many on the right supported an abortion exception for rape victims, and the thought of her father's baby lying in her belly repulsed her. But an abortion was so contrary to her religious beliefs and upbringing that Rick Santorum's words—perhaps the most outspoken of the GOP "no-exception" pro-lifers—resonated with her when she read his response to a question about his position on criminally charging doctors for performing abortions on women who were victims of rape or incest:

> The U.S. Supreme Court on a recent case said that a man who committed rape could not be killed, could not be subject to the death penalty, yet the child conceived as a result of that rape could be. That to me sounds like a country that doesn't have its morals correct. That child did nothing wrong. That child is an innocent victim. To be victimized twice would be a

horrible thing. It is an innocent human life. It is geneti-
cally human from the moment of conception. And it is
a human life. And we in America should be big enough
to try and surround ourselves and help women in those
terrible situations who've been traumatized already.
To put them through another trauma of an abortion
I think is too much to ask. And so I would absolutely
stand and say that one violence is enough.

Deborah was exhausted from lack of sleep. She had recurring
nightmares and had lost a lot of weight. She didn't know what she
should do. How could her father have done this to her? Why had
God done this? She wished she could be an ordinary "unwed pregnant teenager" deciding whether to get an abortion or have a baby
or give it up for adoption. But why, she thought, would any young
woman, or a woman at any age, want to remain pregnant when she
had been raped by a stranger or a family member?

She knew she was also fortunate in many ways. Her mother
would help her in any way she could if she wanted to have the baby
and keep it or plan to have the infant adopted. But the clock was ticking, and she had to make up her mind soon. She called Betsy.

"I think you're right, Betsy about getting some professional help.
Who would you recommend?"

❧

Three days later Debbie nervously sat in Dr. Iris Feuerstein's
waiting room. Her mother sat next to her. Debbie picked up a copy of
Psychology Today from the magazine rack next to her but before she
opened it a short, thin, bespectacled middle-aged woman with frizzy
grayish hair opened the door leading to her inner office. She had a
kind face and spoke in a soft voice.

"Rebecca and Debbie, please come in."

They sat in three cushioned velvet chairs placed in a semi-circle across from an empty plain, mahogany desk. Dr. Feuerstein broke the tension.

"Let's just all chat a bit, and then Mrs. Hyman, after I get a little history, I'd like to speak to Debbie alone."

Debbie sat silently, but started to cry as her mother told the psychologist all about her troubled marriage to her abusive husband and how she and Debbie decided to leave their home after Debbie told her that her father had forced her to have sex with him.

Dr. Feuerstein dropped her pen on her lap, stopped taking notes, handed Debbie some more tissues, and tenderly held Debbie's hands.

"How traumatic this must be, Debbie. I've counseled some Hasidic women who were treated terribly by their husbands, but nothing quite like this before."

Debbie took a deep breath, wiped tricklets of tears from her cheeks and blurted out. "Dr. Feuerstein, I'm pregnant. I'm frightened, I'm confused. I don't know what I should do. Please help me."

"Mrs. Hyman, please wait in the waiting room now while I speak to your daughter."

Debbie blurted it all out as soon as her mother left. "Dr. Feuerstein, I cry myself to sleep every night. I try to put on a brave face for my poor mother who has also suffered so much, but I don't know what to do. I am so much against abortion. I do believe it is a mortal sin to take the life of one of God's creatures. And the thought of killing the life inside of me is too much for me to bear."

"Debbie, time is short. There's lots to talk about. I want you to come here every day this week. I think I can help you get through this. But for now, let me leave you with something to think about until we meet next time. If God were with us in this room I'm pretty sure he would tell you that you are a good person and what has happened to you is a tragedy. I imagine God loves you and would forgive you and want you to forgive yourself at a time when perhaps there's no way to make a really good decision, only a choice that seems the best you can make in a terrible situation. Can we talk more about this at three tomorrow afternoon?"

Debbie met with Dr. Feuerstein every day that week.

28

JoJo's civil lawsuit was randomly assigned to Judge Black. Ken was pleased. Black had received high marks from the bar for his handling of the last Lemrick Nelson trial. He had a solid reputation for legal scholarship, and Ken liked the fact that he had written a number of opinions critical of civil rights violations, and also because of a book he had written, *Disrobed*. In it he called for more openness from judges, believing that they had a moral responsibility to demystify and humanize the judicial process.

Because Judge Black did not shy away from speaking out and saying precisely what was on his mind, he was often good copy and fair game for Jimmy Margiotta. Jealous of the judge's huge mane of unruly black hair, the predator reporter would frequently refer to him as "Judge Blackhead." When the judge spoke out against the death penalty during a murder trial, Margiotta—an obvious fan of the needle—took it one step further, writing that "Judge Blackhead is a Blockhead."

Margiotta's latest blast about "Judge Blockhead" was when Black had recently ruled that the cops did not have justification to stop and frisk Killer Kalafer, a felon in possession of a gun. Ken had read about the case and Margiotta's vicious attack against Judge Black. After a hearing, the judge granted the defendant's motion to suppress the gun. Since without the gun in evidence the government had no case, and Killer Kalafer—who was being held without bail and facing a minimum of ten years—could not be convicted. The next day Margiotta took the judge to the woodshed for "letting Killer

Kalafer—a career criminal packing heat—back on the streets to ter-
rorize once again the helpless public." Even worse, the lead editorial
called the judge "a lunatic."

Because Black would now be handling JoJo's case, Ken wanted
to bone up on the judge's latest cases and obtained a transcript of
the suppression hearing. As he suspected, the judge's decision was
clearly correct, and he hoped that any judge committed to upholding
the rule of law would have rendered the same decision.

Two cops had testified at the hearing. Ken remembered the tall
stories police would tell when Ken was handling these types of cases
as an AUSA, and after reading their testimony he told Gary "If you
believe their story, then you believe in Santa Claus." According to the
cops, they just happened to be driving by in their patrol car early in
the morning on Chess Street when they happened to notice the defendant—who was walking on the street just a short distance away—"lift
his sweatshirt revealing what appeared to be the butt of a gun."

The cops had good practical reason to search Killer Kalafer. They
knew that he had been a Rook of the Chess Street gang, who had just
been released from jail after doing ten years for attempted murder.
The chances of him roaming Chess Street in the middle of the night
unarmed were nil. But they did not have a constitutional reason to stop
and search him, unless the judge credited their clearly incredible story.
If so, the search would have been based on more than a hunch, and the
officers would have had the requisite specific knowledge to justify it
under the "reasonable suspicion" standard of the Fourth Amendment.

Margiotta gleefully reported the next day that the government
lawyers would be "constrained to tell the lunatic judge that without
the gun there was no evidence against the defendant, and the court
would have to dismiss the case and let Killer Kalafer go free."

Not surprising, Margiotta didn't exactly get his facts right—not
that he cared. Actually, although the gun charge would have to be
dismissed, Killer Kalafer could still be sentenced up to two years for
being caught carrying the gun because, having just been released

from jail, he was on probation for five years. Two of the many conditions of his probation that the sentencing judge had imposed were that he would not carry a gun and must remain in his home between 10:00 p.m. and 6:00 a.m. Oddly, the Supreme Court had held a number of years earlier that an illegal search and seizure would result in the exclusion of the found evidence for purposes of a new criminal indictment—but *not* for the violation of probation.

So when the government appeared before Judge Black a week later to consent to the dismissal of the gun charge, the judge nonetheless sentenced Killer Kalafer to two years—the maximum permitted under the law for the probationary violations.

Ken felt sorry for the judge. A responsible press would have sung the praises of the independence of the judiciary and the courage of jurists like Judge Black in upholding the Constitution at the risk of being called a lunatic. He wished that the irresponsible predator reporter had written that Judge Black had put Kalafer back in the slammer, as well as what the judge had said to the AUSA when he did that. But he knew that would never happen. Margiotta did report, however, that "Killer Kalafer had written a 'thank you' letter to the lunatic judge."

He had Gary read from the transcript what Judge Black said to the AUSA.

"THE COURT: It would be nice if your office could possibly find an occasion to say that we don't tolerate and condone assaults against the independence of the judiciary, but I leave that to your office. Because we all are in the same world together, whether we agree or disagree. The one thing that's so important—and we all know this and mouth this, but then we have to apply it sometimes— is to respect the independence of the judiciary whether we agree or disagree. We understand that.

"THE AUSA: Your Honor, there is a First Amendment and we do not control the press. So, to the extent that the press is going to write about a case, it is their prerogative.

"THE COURT: Of course they can do what they want. But I think that there's a separate issue in terms of any time there's an attack against the judicial process, what is the responsibility of the organized bar? What is the responsibility of all of us?

"My concern is that things like that have a chilling impact, maybe upon new judges, maybe upon state court judges. Separate and apart from me, I see that as a serious problem and there's a chilling impact potentially that you know is visited upon the bench. These are bar association matters, but I think all of us should be a little bit sensitive to that.

"THE AUSA: And I, Your Honor, I respectfully disagree with that narrative. Our assessment is that these officers testified credibly.

"THE COURT: I'm not talking about that issue. Let's not talk about that. We are really not on the same wavelength. I'm talking about any assault against the independence of the federal judiciary. That's all I'm talking about. That's a different issue, okay? I don't know whether you get it or not. Second suppression motion I granted in twenty-one years, alright? I think 98 percent have gone the other way. Anyway, let's move on because there's a record here being made and you have my thoughts about this thing."

After Gary finished reading it, Ken said, "I'm confident that Judge Black will not cower to the press and he'll do the right thing by JoJo, even if he's called Judge Blockhead and a lunatic again. But who knows?"

❧

Ken had great respect for Judge Black and most of the federal court judges. The founding fathers were intent on making them independent and provided in the Constitution that they would be appointed by the president—with the consent of the Senate—for life. By contrast, the state court criminal judges handling felony cases in the city were elected for fourteen-year terms and had to retire at seventy. But even though they were elected, in reality they owed their jobs to the political bosses. Moreover, if their fourteen-year term ended before they reached the mandatory retirement age, they would have to run for reelection.

Therefore, unlike federal judges, New York state judges were more concerned about public opinion and alienating the likes of Jimmy Margiotta. While some of them like Judge Cogan had outstanding reputations, Ken's gut told him that if they wanted to be reelected few would have had the courage to do what Judge Black did and run the risk of being called another "lunatic" judge.

Because they never had to retire, there were some drawbacks. Four of the Brooklyn district judges were over ninety years old. Judge Black was considered a youngster at the tender age of eighty-one. The nonagenarians were still functioning well, but Ken never wanted his clients to be sentenced by one of them. He remembered years back when one of his convicted defendants had to appear before the late Judge Bartels—who died with his boots on just days before his hundredth birthday—when the judge was ninety-six. The defendant was facing a maximum twenty-year term. Ken pleaded for a short sentence because of his client's age. The judge asked Ken how old his client was. When Ken said he was seventy, Judge Bartels snarled, "seems like a young man to me," and gave him the full twenty years.

The Brooklyn federal courthouse was right across from Cadman Plaza Park, just a short distance from Ken's apartment. He would often jog through the park late at night and admire the beautiful fourteen-story modern building. With its sparkling while marble facade and striking outdoor statues it stood in marked contrast to the crummy State Criminal Court building. And there were never pigeons on the top of the federal courthouse. "No pigeon would ever crap on a federal judge," he would muse to himself.

A week before Judge Black was called a lunatic by the *Daily News*, Ken sat in the judge's courtroom on the tenth floor, listening to the oral argument on the defendant's motion to dismiss JoJo's case. Since he was still suspended from practicing law, he had Gary handle the argument for JoJo. Ken thought Gary did a terrific job, but he was also impressed with the Corp. Counsel lawyer, who was making a cogent argument for the dismissal of the complaint for "legal insufficiency." After listening intently, Judge Black reserved decision and said he would try to issue a written opinion within the next few weeks.

Several days later, when Ken was taking one of his nightly jogs through the park, he noticed the lights burning in the right corner office on the ninth floor of the courthouse. Ken knew it was Judge Black's chambers and guessed he might be working late at night on JoJo's case.

Ken was right.

～

Jason Johnson was sitting next to Judge Black in the middle of the large conference table in the judge's private office, and he placed the proposed opinion he had drafted in JoJo's case in front of his boss. This year the judge had three outstanding male law clerks. Each had recently graduated high in his class from a top law school. Federal court clerkships were coveted jobs for newly minted lawyers. Most judges, as Judge Black did, hired them for one year before sending them on their way to start their promising legal careers in the public or private sector. He had already hired three female clerks for the following year.

Jason, who had graduated at the head of his class from Penn Law, was one of the judge's favorites, and Black gave him the JoJo Jones case. Jason's job was to carefully read the briefs, do all the necessary research, and draft the proposed opinion for the judge's scrutiny. It was rare that Judge Black, after reading the briefs himself, did not rewrite the opinion, but Jason's were among the best he'd seen in twenty-one years on the federal bench.

Jason was madly in love with his gorgeous, voluptuous girlfriend, Kathryn, but you would never have guessed that he was not gay. If he were a woman, he would have been a knockout: slender build, narrow hips, curly black hair, milky-white skin, and piercing light-blue eyes. When Judge Black found out that he was a devout Catholic, the judge asked Jason if he'd ever been an altar boy and was relieved when Jason told him his father would not let him become one. The judge told his wife that "any gay priest would have licked his chops if he were."

As usual, whenever Judge Black sat, he would habitually press his two large hands on the top of his pot belly, as if the pressure would make it disappear. As he started to read the draft opinion that Jason had placed in front of him, he lifted his left hand off his gut to turn the pages, rummaged the fingers of his other hand through his unruly hair, and tossed his horn-rimmed glasses down on the table after he finished reading what his clerk had written. He was not pleased.

"Are you sure we have to dismiss the claims against Neary and Racanelli?" he asked.

"I'm afraid so, Judge. The law is pretty clear. They have prosecutorial immunity."

"Isn't there any way we can get around it?"

"I don't think so, Judge."

"I just can't fathom letting those 'guardians of the law' get away with all this, Jason. And you question whether the city can be held responsible for their misdeeds, as well. That means we would have to dismiss the case."

"That's a closer call, Judge. It all depends on whether you think *Monell* liability could be in play. I have my doubts."

"I've got a headache," Judge Black said. "Thanks for staying late. I'll have to hit the books myself on this and think about it. See you tomorrow morning."

Jason lived near the courthouse and walked home. The judge took the elevator to the garage and drove his three-year-old, black, four-door Chevy across the Brooklyn Bridge to his Greenwich Village apartment.

The following week he issued his decision in a thirty-two-page written opinion.

~

Ken received some great news from Commissioner Donnelly the next day. The NYPD Internal Affairs Bureau had completed its investigation into Ken's arrest. The Brooklyn Bridge was under constant video surveillance, and it seemed to confirm—though not too clearly—that the black cop had shoved Ken while he was peacefully carrying the "Black Lives Matter" sign. The surveillance camera also picked up the pictures of a few other cops—in addition to the one who helped with Ken's arrest—who were in close proximity. They were questioned extensively under oath, and all said they heard the officer tell Ken to put down the sign.

The two cops who arrested Ken had been suspended by the commissioner and would be subject to an internal disciplinary proceeding. And—not trusting Neary—Donnelly had requested that the governor appoint a special prosecutor to bring criminal charges against them.

Moreover, Commissioner Donnelly had brought all this to the attention of the Second Department's Grievance Committee. Ken's law license would immediately be reinstated.

~

Judge Black began his opinion by recounting all of the complaint's detailed allegations of Racanelli's wrongful acts—the same that underlay Judge Gonzales's grant of JoJo's habeas petition. It was all there: the failure to turn over the exculpatory letter, the solicitation of false testimony, the threats to the lying witnesses. The judge then painstakingly discussed the law of prosecutorial immunity, explaining that "absolute immunity protects prosecutors from liability for virtually all acts, regardless of motivation, associated with his function as an advocate." He explained that the policy behind the rule "was to allow prosecutors to do their job without fear that they would be held accountable in the courts of law for their mistakes, or even their egregious behavior." In his research he uncovered a decision from the Second Circuit Court of Appeals, which he was duty-bound to follow. He quoted a paragraph of the court's language. It was right on point. The court could have been writing about JoJo's case.

> The falsification of evidence and the coercion of witnesses . . . have been held to be prosecutorial activities for which absolute immunity applies. Similarly, because a prosecutor is acting as an advocate in a judicial proceeding, the solicitation and subornation of perjured testimony, the withholding of evidence, or the introduction of illegally-seized evidence at trial does not create liability in damages. The rationale for this approach is sound, for these protected activities, while deplorable, involve decisions of judgment affecting the course of a prosecution.

The judge hated to let Racanelli and Neary off the hook, but he would adhere to the law—just like in the Killer Kalafer case—and had no choice.

He next turned to the issue of the city's liability and the *Monell* case that Jason had mentioned. In *Monell v. Department of Social Services,* the Supreme Court held, back in 1978, that a municipality could not be held vicariously liable in monetary damages for the constitutional violations of their employees "unless a municipal policy or custom caused the constitutional injury."

Judge Black seized on this exception. He explained that Neary was clearly the policy maker for the Brooklyn DA's office and quoted from that section of the complaint which stated that "Judge Gonzales, in her comments from the bench during the habeas hearing, had lambasted the DA's office—and in particular its continued denials of wrongdoing." Black also referred to those portions of the complaint recounting that after Gonzales' decision, "District Attorney James Neary announced to the news media that Racanelli would not face disciplinary action and that there would be no investigation into his office's conduct."

The complaint also alleged that "Racanelli's conduct was part of a pattern of wrongdoing that has resulted in numerous other bogus convictions." Attached to the complaint, and incorporated by reference, was a lengthy document that JoJo had prepared reporting on a number of the cases that he had researched up to that time. The judge read carefully what JoJo had written.

First, JoJo cited the case of Shabazz Blackmon, still in jail twenty-one years after being convicted—just like JoJo—for murdering a Hasidic rabbi. Shabazz was Racanelli's first scalp. After poring over the trial transcript and evidence, JoJo concluded that Shabazz' conviction resulted in large part from a flawed investigation by Racanelli, who failed to pursue a more logical suspect. And word on the street was that Racanelli had removed violent criminals from jail to let them smoke crack cocaine and visit prostitutes in exchange for incriminating Blackmon. Finally, ever-resourceful JoJo was able to contact the supposed eyewitness who picked Shabazz out of a lineup. She told him that Racanelli told her who to choose.

Next, was the case of Keenan Anunaby—still rotting in jail after eighteen years for a murder he never committed. Anunaby was one of the three that Patricia Mondre had fingered. He was accused of shooting a Hasidic man on a Crown Heights street corner and then, curiously, putting the dying man inside a livery cab and ordering the driver to take him to the hospital. The trial transcript revealed that Mondre was so belligerent on the witness stand that the judge threatened to strike all of her testimony. And Mondre contradicted the evidence in several ways, including the direction the shot was fired and the color of the cab. She even admitted that she had lied at other trials where she had testified.

Judge Black was appalled by what JoJo had documented, and carefully read the rest of his report. There was much more. And it got worse.

There was Eric Fielder, convicted thirteen years ago for murdering a young Hasidic boy who was collecting rents for his grandfather from black tenants living in a dilapidated apartment around the corner from Chess Street. And Buster Bailey, convicted of the fatal shooting of another Hasidic rent collector; remarkably, JoJo found out that the main witness was in police custody at the time of the shooting. And Willie Sanders, convicted of kidnaping and killing Steven Kaufman, a wealthy Orthodox Jew in Queens as he was coming home from Sabbath services at the local synagogue. Racanelli wrung a confession from him after fifteen hours of grueling interrogation without sleep or food. JoJo knew Sanders from Green Haven, where he was still serving his twenty-five-to-life sentence. Sanders had told him that—just like Solomon Butler—the day after his coerced confession, he recanted everything Racanelli had written down. And also like Butler, Racanelli never told that to Sanders' lawyer. Willie Sanders was convicted without a single piece of forensic evidence—or evidence of any kind—tying him to the crime.

There were six other equally eye-popping cases that JoJo had written about. He ended his report by writing: "I believe I've only just begun. There are forty-seven other cases I have on my radar screen. This is my life's work. I will never rest until every brother who has been wrongly convicted because of Anthony Racanelli is exonerated."

Judge Black was overwhelmed by what JoJo had written and reasoned that if Neary knew about Racanelli's illegal activities and had condoned them, or if his office systematically failed to train his other prosecutors regarding their *Brady* obligations, the proper way to conduct an interrogation, and the impropriety of coercing witnesses to provide false inculpatory evidence, either would satisfy the "policy or custom" prong under *Monell*, and the city could therefore be liable.

To Ken's delight, Judge Black concluded: "The plaintiff has alleged a plausible case against the city in his complaint, and was entitled to flush out the facts during pretrial discovery." He ordered the city to allow the plaintiff to have access to the files of all of Racanelli's trials and wrote that "plaintiff's lawyer would be permitted to depose Racanelli and Neary under oath."

His law license reinstated, Ken couldn't wait to grill them, just like he did when he tore into the four cops who shot the Dunne kid. As soon as he finished reading the judge's opinion, he had Gary prepare the requisite "Notice to Take Witness's Deposition," and had him run it over to the Corporation Counsel's office in Manhattan. In it he set the date for the depositions for the following Monday "at the Law Offices of Brown and Williams."

⌇

"Fuck him," Neary yelled at Carla Amon over the telephone. Amon was the chief of the Corp. Counsel's litigation bureau and had just told Neary she had received the deposition notice.

Neary continued to rant, "I didn't let the prick put me and Racanelli on the stand in the habeas case, and I'm certainly not going to let him tear into us now. Try to settle the fuckin' case."

Amon was shocked at Neary's language and began to think that there might be a lot of merit to the lawsuit. Although the DA and his chief prosecutor were off the hook, the city could be hit for millions. If there were to be a trial, Ken would parade witness after witness—many still serving life sentences—before the jury to testify how they were railroaded by Racanelli and the DA's office. It would be a three-ring circus and a feeding frenzy for the national press.

Three days later, Ken told JoJo that the city had offered $14 million to settle the case.

"I'm prepared to go to the well for you, JoJo, but it's a lot of money. Two million more than I got for the Dunne case. But it's your decision."

JoJo didn't hesitate. "I want to get on with my life, Ken. It's more money than I ever dreamed of. We'll have enough to get to the bottom of all the other cases I'm working on. The old church I used to belong to will be able to repair its run-down building, and I'll have enough to get myself a decent crib."

"Well, we'll miss you, JoJo. Gary and I kind of got used to you living in the back room. I guess you can start making your plans to move out. We have some paperwork to do to wrap things up. General releases and all that technical legal stuff. And we want to make sure that the settlement papers earmark the money for 'pain and suffering,' so it will be tax free. We should have the money by next month. Though our retainer agreement would allow me to take one-third as my fee, I'll be happy with 10 percent, if it's okay with you. It's still a lot of money. I'll put it to good use. I'll be able to take on a lot of JoJo cases."

"Ken, as far as I'm concerned, you are entitled to the whole fee. You've been my man from day one. Without you I'd still be in jail. Let's put three mil in an escrow account and use it to free all the others."

"It's a deal, JoJo. Let's get the gang and celebrate. I think we can afford some good food at our favorite watering hole."

It would be all over the news the next day. Amon had prepared a joint press release announcing the settlement. Ken insisted that it be issued at his office. The TV coverage showed JoJo coming out of his back room smiling and commenting, as he showed them all the boxes of files he was working on, that he "had just begun to scratch the surface of all the other phony prosecutions by Racanelli of brothers who are still rotting in jail."

29

It's not every day that the FBI pays a visit to a federal judge. But as Special Agent Nick Phillips flashed his photo ID to Judge Black when Jason ushered him into the judge's chambers, he asked the somber-looking judge if he could shut the door "so nobody can hear us." Agent Phillips was accompanied by Charlie Dunton, the Eastern District of New York's chief marshal. They all sat around the judge's conference table.

The agent and the marshal each looked and dressed exactly as one might expect: crew cuts, sculpted bodies, dark blue suits with American flag lapel pins, white shirts, and striped red and blue ties. Agent Phillips spoke first.

"I'm one of several full-time agents of the special FBI office that does nothing but investigate threats against judicial personnel. Most are against judges. The public doesn't have a clue how much at risk you are. There's in the neighborhood of eight hundred federal judges across the country. We average over three hundred threats a year. We take them all seriously. Each one is meticulously investigated."

Black was quick to respond. "I know that, Agent Phillips, and my colleagues and I are grateful you do that."

Phillips continued. "Judge, I'm also sure that you know that ever since the letter-bomb that killed Judge Vance in Atlanta several years ago, all mail addressed to federal judges at their courthouses is opened by the marshals before being sent to their chambers."

"I knew Judge Vance," Judge Black acknowledged. "What a tragedy. It was sent by a delusional, *pro se* civil litigant who mistakenly thought the judge had ordered that his home be foreclosed. Vance had nothing to do with the case. But about 20 percent of our calendars are *pro se* cases, and most of them are from crackpots angry at the system. Anybody can bring a lawsuit without having a lawyer. The judicial system is open to all. We spend an enormous amount of judicial resources processing them. I've had cases suing Jesus, Mohammad, and Moses. It's a great country."

"Well, you may want to take a look at the letter that Marshal Dunton's office opened yesterday."

Judge Black slowly read the one-page typed letter that Agent Phillips handed to him. It was short and to the point:

> You let Killer Kalafer go. Now you let the nigga get millions out of my hard-earned tax dollars. You have it in for the cops and the DA who are trying to keep the niggas off the streets. We can use one less nigga-loving, cop-hating Jew judge. I've put you on my hit list. You and Williams both gotta go.

Black handed the letter back to the agent before commenting. "I've had death threats before, Agent Phillips. It kind of goes with the job. I think this is the fourth. Over twenty-one years I guess that's not too bad. The last one was a number of years ago from Anthony Casso after I had to give him a life sentence. I guess I was due for another."

❧

Anthony Casso, who went by the charming nickname of "Gaspipe," was an underboss in the Lucchese crime family. The government was willing to enter into a cooperation deal with him because prosecutors thought he might be needed as a backup to Salvatore Gravano—Sammy the Bull—in the John Gotti trial. Gaspipe was also considered a valuable potential witness in other pending prosecutions against the Mafia. In his cooperation agreement, Gaspipe had to plead to orchestrating fifteen murders. If the government was not satisfied with his cooperation, for good and sufficient reasons, Judge Black would have had no choice under the law but to sentence him to life for all the murders.

That turned out to be the case. The government pulled the plug on Casso and told Judge Black that Gaspipe had indeed breached his cooperation agreement because he had written a letter that falsely disputed the trial testimony of Sammy the Bull during the Gotti trial. The letter contained a number of lies, including that the Bull had ordered the stabbing of Al Sharpton.

Black had no choice but to give Gaspipe life. Not surprisingly, Gaspipe did not take kindly to the judge's sentence. He could not understand why he was being salted away forever when the Bull—who also confessed to killing lots of people—only got five years, and other cooperators also received significantly lighter sentences. Judge I. Leo Glasser, who presided over the Gotti trial and was the Bull's sentencing judge, gave him just five years to reward him for testifying against Gotti, who was finally convicted after two failed attempts. Gravano was one of the highest-ranking Mafiosi to break the code of omertà.

Because he testified to save his own neck—and got such a big break—many others came forward, and the New York Mafia was decimated in a number of trials that followed.

Gaspipe complained to the press that his crimes "weren't any worse than all those other cooperators" and he was "being singled out." He later wrote a book in which he said that his "biggest problem" was Judge Black, and that the judge was prejudiced against him because the prosecutors had told him that he was going to kill one of Black's colleagues, which "was a bold-faced lie."

A few months after Black put him away for life, the FBI told the judge that it had learned that Gaspipe was trying to arrange a contract killing from his jail cell to kill him. If Gaspipe had gotten his way, Black would have been the fourth federal judge assassinated in recent times.

In addition to Judge Robert Smith Vance of Atlanta, a district court judge for the Western District of Texas, John H. Wood, was killed by James Harrelson—the father of the actor Woody Harrelson. It was a contract killing orchestrated by the Texas drug lord Jamiel Chagra, who was waiting to be tried before Judge Wood. The San Antonio federal courthouse now bears Wood's name.

Richard J. Daranco was a district judge closer to Judge Black's home. He sat on the Southern District bench in Manhattan. Judge Daranco was murdered by the father of a deranged civil plaintiff whose frivolous case Daranco had dismissed. The judge was shot when doing yard work in front of his home.

Judge Joan Lefkow, sitting on the district court in Chicago, would have been another casualty if she were home when her would-be killer came to find her. While she escaped with her life, her family was not as fortunate. When the judge returned home late one evening after a long day on the bench she found her mother and husband in the basement, shot to death. They had been murdered by Bart Ross, a disgruntled plaintiff in a medical malpractice case that the judge had tossed out of court.

State judiciaries have also hardly been immune from violent attacks by crazed litigants. In the same year that Judge Lefkow's mother and husband were killed, shootings outside of the local courthouse in Tyler, Texas, left two people dead and four others wounded. A judge, a court reporter, and a deputy sheriff were also murdered in the Fulton County courthouse in Atlanta. After that, Marshal Dunton took extra precaution to make sure that nothing like that would ever happen in his courthouse. A marshal, visibly armed with an AK-47 automatic rifle, was posted at the entrance to the building.

Even so, bad things could still happen.

Victor Wright had been brought into Judge Black's courtroom to be sentenced to life after being convicted for serious drug crimes. He seemed to accept his impending fate because he had not shown

any signs of hostility at any other time when he had been in court—
but not on this occasion. As he walked into the courtroom, followed
closely by two marshals, he bolted past his lawyer, razor in hand, and
lunged at the prosecutor, Carolyn Pokorny, a thirty-eight-year-old
AUSA, and started to choke her. All mayhem broke loose. Within
seconds, Ron Tolkin, the court reporter who was right there, and
the marshals jumped on Wright. The razor fell to the ground, and
one marshal was on the verge of inflicting a deadly choke hold on the
defendant when he took his hands off Pokorny's throat. Judge Black
pressed the security button on the bench and within thirty seconds
marshals were swarming all over the courtroom, and the frightening
potential disaster had been averted.

Carolyn Pokorny had barely escaped with her life, but the
imprint of Victor Wright's fingers on her neck—which did not disappear for two weeks—made her realize how close she had come
to dying.

Jerry Markon, a respected reporter for the *Washington Post*, noting that threats to federal judges and prosecutors were on the rise,
attributed the trend to "disgruntled defendants whose anger is
fueled by the Internet; terrorism and gang cases that bring more violent offenders into federal court; frustration at the economic crisis;
and the rise of the 'sovereign citizen' movement—a loose collection
of tax protesters, white supremacists and others who don't respect
federal authority."

There were, in short, a lot of loose screws out there. Harold
Turner was one of them. Since 2001, he had been broadcasting an
incendiary Internet radio show from his home studio in North Ber-
gen, New Jersey, gaining notoriety because of his anti-immigrant
and anti-Semitic remarks. He was arrested in 2010 for making death
threats against three federal circuit court judges from Chicago. He
took exception to a decision they had rendered upholding a hand-
gun ban and posted a message on his website expressing his outrage.
He called the judges "cunning, ruthless, untrustworthy, disloyal,

unpatriotic, deceitful scum." The Free Speech Clause of the First Amendment of the Constitution gave him the right to make these obnoxious comments, but he didn't stop there. He went on to write that, "These judges deserve to be killed," and later, "If they are allowed to get away with this by surviving, other judges will act the same way." To make matters worse, he posted their home addresses and photos.

Judge Black knew about all of this, and particularly the Turner case, because he was convicted for his frightening conduct in the judge's courthouse by a jury before one of Black's colleagues. The jurors determined that Turner had crossed the line that the First Amendment draws. The prosecutors had made it clear to them that "You can't yell 'fire' in a crowded theater."

Marshal Dunton, as the EDNY chief marshal, was also familiar with the Turner case. He had been sitting quietly up to that point, but now spoke.

"Even though Turner was sentenced to three years in jail, the three judges that he wanted dead have to wonder if some kook out there might be hiding in wait for them or their families," said Dunton.

Agent Phillips was quick to agree. "It just goes to show how vulnerable judges are."

"There's no doubt about that," Judge Black interjected. "I don't think the public fully appreciates the risks that come with the job of being a judge. But it has not affected my ability to handle my cases. I had no idea what was in store for me and my colleagues when I took the oath of office two decades ago, but I've managed to take it all in stride."

"Be that as it may, Judge," said Phillips, "but we still have to alert judges to any threats against them and assess the risk to their lives. In Gaspipe's case, the FBI classified it as low risk because there was no tangible evidence that any contract had been placed on your life, and since Gaspipe had a life sentence in a maximum security prison, there was no risk that he could kill you as long as he didn't escape. I'm afraid this case is different."

"In what way?" Judge Black asked.

"We've classified it as the highest risk," answered the agent.

Black was startled. "Why?"

"Because whoever this is has you lumped together with Ken Williams. It's apparently the same person. There's a very angry nut out there who is motivated to kill both of you. He obviously hates blacks and Jews, and the pattern of his threats against Williams, and now you, put both of you at extreme risk of being murdered. He obviously has a score to settle with Williams, and now he thinks you're in league with him because your decision in the Jones lawsuit opened the way for Williams to get Jones lots of money."

"What am I supposed to do about it?" Judge Black asked.

"Not much. Go about your business as usual. But Marshal Dunton has arranged for you and your family to have round-the-clock security. There will be a marshal following you and Mrs. Black wherever you go. As for your two children, they live in California and I don't think they need protection."

"What about at night when we're at home sleeping?"

Marshal Dunton answered: "One will be posted outside your co-op."

"I'm not so sure all my neighbors will be so happy with that, Marshal."

"We'll talk to all of them and try to put them at ease."

"When does this start?" asked the judge.

"Right now," came the answer from the chief marshal.

❧

Judge Black drove his car home. Sitting next to him was Deputy Marshal Ryan Corcoran. The judge introduced him to his wife as soon as they entered their sixth-floor apartment. She did not know why he was there. As they all sat around the kitchen table, Corcoran explained everything to her, and her husband showed her a copy of the death threat. The deputy marshal told them how he and his colleagues would work in shifts. He would be staying with the Blacks that night until he was relieved by another deputy marshal at 8:30 in the morning. Corcoran would then drive the judge to court, and his relief would stay with Mrs. Black—wherever she went—until the judge came home after work.

Kyra Black was at a loss for words. The best she could do was to ask the marshal if he would like a cup of tea or coffee. He politely declined. She went to get the whistling tea kettle and a Lipton tea bag and with her gnarled fingers grasped the kettle in her right hand. Kyra dropped the tea bag into a cup on the kitchen counter with her left hand, and with both shaking hands managed to pour the hot water into the cup and put it down by her husband. The deputy marshal didn't know whether the shakes were from Parkinson's or because of the death threat.

Nevertheless, the judge's wife had aged well. Though the same age as her husband, she was—unlike the judge—trim, and looked several years younger. There was a certain elegance about her and a fierce look of defiance.

"Marshal Corcoran," she began. "Is there really a need to make such a fuss about all this? My husband has been on the bench for over twenty years; he's had threats before and lots of letters from a strange assortment of folks who have come before him. I really don't think our lives have to be upended like this and that we need the government to invade our privacy."

"I understand your feelings, Mrs. Black. But the FBI and the Marshals Service would not be imposing on you if we did not have you and the judge's best interests at heart. Let's be patient while we hunt down who is doing this. Hopefully we'll get to the bottom of it quickly."

"He's right, dear," interjected Judge Black. "Let them do their job as they deem necessary. While I'll be safe in the courthouse, remember poor Judge Lefkow. I sure don't want to worry about you winding up like her mother and husband. I'll have peace of mind while going about my work."

"I suppose you're right, Felix. My girlfriends might even be a little jealous to see me being escorted all around by such handsome young fellows."

We'll try to be as unobtrusive as possible, ma'am," reassured the Deputy Marshal. "We'll just be sitting in the hallway in our plain clothes when you or the judge are in the apartment."

"But what should I tell my neighbors and the doormen?" Mrs. Black asked.

"There are only four apartments on the floor," Corcoran answered. "I'll speak to all those folks and try to put them at ease. I'll tell them how proud they should be that such a highly regarded federal judge is their neighbor. I'll also talk to the doormen and try to make them feel very special, like they are part of law enforcement."

The judge's wife said, "I'm not so sure they'll be happy to see you. They're all here from Albania, and I doubt that they are all kosher."

Marshal Corcoran tried to reassure her. "I'm not going to ask them for their papers. Leave it to me."

"Thank you," said Mrs. Black "Is there anything we can do for you while you're standing guard?"

Marshal Corcoran smiled. "Well, I'd really prefer not to stand, Mrs. Black. Perhaps I can borrow a kitchen chair for the night."

"Please take the small leather one from the living room."

"Thanks. And since we'll be seeing a lot of each other, please feel free to call me Ryan."

After he left, Corcoran went to the lobby to talk to the night doorman. When Corcoran showed Osman Leprevic his government credentials, the doorman became pale. The marshal realized that Mrs. Black might have been right about the immigration status of the doormen in the building.

Corcoran tried to put him at ease. "Osman, I'm not from Homeland Security and I'm not here to check you out. We're only concerned about the safety of the judge and his wife. We'll be putting some high-quality surveillance cameras around the building and throughout the interior. Do as we tell you and everything will be fine."

The color returned to the doorman's face.

30

At the same time that the FBI was visiting Judge Black, the police commissioner was walking into Ken Williams' law office. Commissioner Donnelly gave him an update on the recent events before Ken could say a word.

"Ken, you got company. You are no longer the only one with death threats. He's now threatening to also kill Judge Black. The marshals are giving the judge and his wife twenty-four-hour security. I think you need it, too."

"I appreciate your concern Aidan, but I just can't have the cops living with me all the time. It'll just cramp my style and won't work. I'm not eighty-one years old like the judge. I can take care of myself."

"Don't be such a hero," snapped Commissioner Donnelly.

"Don't worry. I've got the gun you gave me, and I know how to use it. Mickey's got one also, and so does Betsy. I'll have Mickey with me all the time starting tonight. He'll be waiting for me in the Green Room while I'm being interviewed on Channel 1. It should be good stuff. JoJo will be on TV with me talking about all the rotten prosecutions he continues to uncover by Racanelli and the DA's office. And I'll be stoking the fires, too. The primary is right around the corner and I've got to keep the heat on Neary."

As he left, the police commissioner gave Ken a sympathetic look and a word of caution.

"Alright, Ken. Do it your way, but just be careful."

"Peaches" Pollack quickly set the agenda.

"Folks, we have with us tonight Ken Williams, who hopes to be Brooklyn's next DA, and his newly minted millionaire client, JoJo Jones. Let me first ask JoJo a question. You sat in jail for sixteen years a pauper. Now you've got fourteen million bucks. What does that feel like, and what are you going to do with all that money?"

JoJo knew the reporter would ask this question.

"I've gone over this with Mr. Williams. He's entitled to one-third for his fee but only wants 10 percent. We agreed that the rest will go into a special pot to finance the work we're doing to free all the other victims of the corrupt DA's office who've been sitting in jail for years, some of them for longer than I did."

Ken interjected, "JoJo's done a terrific job so far. But he's got a long way to go. When he's not in church he's poring over the boxes of files sprawled around our office. Most are stacked up in the back room where he sleeps. He's buttoned down several cases so far. I'll be going over them carefully myself once I take office. If they are what JoJo says they are, I'll free those poor men as soon as I can."

Shirley Pollack asked Ken, "While we're on the subject, what else do you plan to do if you become the next DA?"

"At the risk of sounding smug, Peaches, it's not 'if' but 'when.' I'm way ahead in the polls. I've picked up the endorsement of every major newspaper. Neary's days are numbered, and he must know it. But he has no one to blame but himself. He continues to protect Racanelli and his henchmen who are only interested in getting convictions at any cost. He continues to placate the Hasidim. And, though I can't prove it, I'd bet my bottom buck that he was behind the orchestration of my phony arrest and the suspension of my law license."

"With all due respect, you haven't answered my question," said Pollack. "What will you be doing?"

"Sorry for getting off track. But to specifically answer your question, in addition to freeing all the wrongly convicted blacks as soon as I can, I'll appoint a special prosecutor to expeditiously try Shmuel

Hyman for raping his daughter. I'll also appoint a special committee to work with the leaders of the Hasidic community, like Rabbi
Horowitz, to assess which violations of the secular laws are best
handled by them internally and which must be prosecuted by our
courts. And finally, I'll have the special prosecutor launch an investigation into Racanelli and the soon-to-be ex-DA's conduct while in
office to see if any criminal charges are warranted."

"Wow. Those are all pretty strong words. You may be making a
lot of enemies. Rumor has it that there are already death threats out
against you. But getting back to JoJo, what will you be doing with
your millions?"

"I'll be giving some of it to my old church and a lot to my new
church, Miss Pollack. They just made me a deacon. But I'll indulge
in one luxury. I'll be closing on a new condo in Dumbo next week.
It's top of the line and has a huge balcony with a great view of the
Brooklyn Bridge and the Freedom Tower across the river. Mr. Williams has been kind enough to let me stay in the back room of his
office. But it's time to move out. I can't wait. I'll have you all over for
dinner."

"Well, you certainly deserve it, JoJo," Pollack said.

She thanked them both for coming and ended the program by
telling Ken, "We'll all be watching the race as it unfolds and if you
win we'll look forward to having you back as the new DA."

⌒

Mickey slapped Ken on the back as soon as he and JoJo walked
back into the Green Room.

"Great job, boss. You really gave it to them. And JoJo, I almost
had tears in my eyes, and you know how tough I am. Where do we
go now?"

"Back to the office for me," said JoJo. "I'm bushed. Got to get to
the church early tomorrow morning. And I got to start wrapping up
things before I move out."

"How about you, Ken?" asked Mickey.

"No partying tonight, Mickey. Home for me also. Got a big day tomorrow. I want to touch base with Deborah Hyman. And then I'm going to see Trish. I'll also try to visit Troy afterwards. The trial's in just three weeks. They have him at the MDC now and Gary and I have to start prepping him in case we decide to let him testify."

Mickey was disappointed.

"Well, you're not much fun lately. And I don't remember the last time you even wrote a song."

"Mickey, I've got death threats against me. I got the most important trial of my life right around the corner, and the primary is just months away. I've got too much on my plate to write more country songs right now. And not only that, you haven't given me any inspiration lately."

31

The last time the phone rang in the middle of the night was when Trish called to tell him that Troy had been arrested.

"Sorry to wake you up, Ken, but I'm afraid I have some terrible news."

Ken recognized the police commissioner's voice at once. "What happened, Aidan?"

"Your office has been firebombed. It's pretty much destroyed."

"I'll be right down," said Ken, suddenly wide awake.

"I think you might want to go to the hospital instead. They pulled JoJo Jones out. He's in the critical care burn unit at Downstate. I think it's pretty serious. I'll meet you there."

"Holy shit," shouted Ken as he slammed down the phone.

❧

Commissioner Donnelly was waiting for Ken in the emergency room when he arrived. Ken wasted no words.

"Where's JoJo?"

"I'm told we can't see him now, Ken, but the doctor will be down shortly to talk to us."

They sat silently staring into space for what seemed like an eternity before a tall, handsome, dark-haired man in a pale-green hospital gown walked slowly through an interior double door. Ken thought he probably wasn't older than his mid-thirties, but the solemn look on his face made him look years older.

Dr. Anagnostou told them to stay seated as he pulled up a chair and sat in front of them.

Ken couldn't wait. "How bad is it doctor?"

"I'm afraid it's very bad," he answered somberly.

"Third-degree burns, doctor?" Commissioner Donnelly asked.

"Most people think that third degree is the most severe, but there actually is also fourth degree. It is potentially the most dangerous. Third and fourth will both result in partial or total burning away of the skin, and any remaining skin will often appear blackened and charred. They both have a high risk of infection and if major blood vessels are destroyed, lack of blood circulation may result. All of this can result in permanent damage to limbs."

"What's the difference between third and fourth?" asked Ken.

"In the case of fourth-degree burns, the hypodermis is burned away. This is the deepest layer of skin that is closest to the muscles. The burning away of this layer may cause what we call compartment syndrome, resulting in extensive nerve and muscle damage. Death may result."

"How severe is JoJo?" asked Ken.

"I'm afraid it's very severe," replied Dr. Anagnostou. "His body is charred all over, and there is a lot of nerve and muscle damage. It's fourth degree."

Tears welled up in Ken's eyes. "Does that mean JoJo is going to die?" he asked.

"Not necessarily, we'll do everything medical science offers to keep him alive."

Ken asked the logical follow-up question. "What are his chances, Doc?"

"Fifty-fifty, Mr. Williams."

~

Dr. Anagnostou told them they could not see JoJo that night. He was heavily sedated and fluids were being intravenously pumped into his body. The doctor told Ken to check back later in the day to see if JoJo would be able to talk to him.

Ken knew that he'd never get back to sleep. He called Mickey, Gary, and Betsy and told them what had happened and then drove to his office. He could not believe what he saw. The outside was just a shell, and between the fire and the water damage from extinguishing the flames, everything on the inside was destroyed; the wooden desks and chairs were cinders, and all the file cabinets in Ken's and Gary's offices, as well as all the boxes that JoJo had in his office, were incinerated. Police had cordoned off the building with yellow crime-scene tape, and several officers stood guard while investigators from the bomb squad were working their way through the rubble.

Mickey, Gary, and Betsy met Ken for breakfast at Junior's. But they all felt too miserable to eat, and their thoughts were only on JoJo.

Ken said, "It just doesn't seem possible that this is happening after everything that JoJo went through."

"Will we be able to see him today, Ken?" asked Betsy.

"The doctor said he'd let me know."

"Well I can't sleep, so I guess the best we can do is just pray," said Ken. "But why the hell did I ever let JoJo sleep in that crummy back room with all those corrugated boxes."

"Don't be so hard on yourself, dear," said Betsy, "after all you've done for him."

"Betsy's right," interjected Mickey.

"Mickey, this is all my fault. Whatever son-of-a-bitch did this was after me."

"Let's all go to JoJo's church and pray for him," Gary suggested.

"Good idea," Betsy said. "Then, while we're waiting to hear from the doctor we can go see Deborah Hyman, Trish, and Troy. Maybe it will help keep us sane."

❧

Pastor Burnham was conducting morning services when they arrived. There were the usual 3,500 parishioners there.

After the service, they met the pastor in his office.

Ken delivered the bad news. "Pastor, JoJo's in the hospital fighting for his life."

Before another word was spoken Pastor Burnham, clasped his hands, lowered his head and prayed. "Oh Lord Jesus, please save one of our flock."

He then tried to offer encouragement. "JoJo's just been made a deacon. He's a true disciple of the Lord. And his strength has been tested during the many years he was in jail. He'll make it. He has so much to live for now and so much unfinished work to do to free the brothers who should not be sitting in jail."

"I'll let you know when you can come see him," said Ken.

"I won't wait, my son. I'll be going to the hospital to be by his side right now."

"I imagine the doctors will let his pastor be with him. We'll be there as soon as Dr. Anagnostou tells us it's okay."

Ken told Gary and Mickey to head over to the police commissioner's office to find out how the investigation was coming along, while he and Betsy dropped by the jewelry store where Deborah Hyman was working that day to find out how she was feeling.

Deborah was waiting on a customer when they arrived. She greeted them warmly.

"Please wait in the office until I finish selling Mrs. Kuhlman this lovely necklace," she said.

"As you can tell, Deborah is a terrific saleslady," said the well-coiffed older woman as she took off her mink stole and put the diamond necklace around her wrinkled neck.

"Take your time," said Betsy. Turning to the woman, she said, "the necklace looks beautiful on you!"

While they sat down to wait in two plush, gold-embroidered chairs, a young Chinese man asked if he could bring them some tea or coffee. Ken took coffee black; Betsy asked for tea with lemon.

Soon Deborah joined them. She thanked Betsy for helping her make the diamond necklace sale and said how much she missed them. She told them her mother would be coming to the store later in the day, and she would give her their best wishes. Ken told her about JoJo and brought her up to date on everything that was happening since they last met. As they were walking out of the store, Betsy gave her a tender kiss on each cheek, commented on how beautiful she looked, and asked, "Have you made your decision yet?"

"Yes, I have, Betsy. Thank you for sending me to Dr. Feuerstein. She was a godsend. She helped me get in touch with all my pent-up anger towards my father. In a strange way, I actually feel sorry for him. He's cursed and a sick man. Dr. Feuerstein helped me clarify things."

She paused, took a tissue from her pocketbook to dab her tearing eyes, and spoke in a barely audible voice. "I'm no longer pregnant."

~

It was the second hospital he had visited within the last twenty-four hours. This one was a lot better. Trish Jackson had given birth the day before. She smiled faintly as Ken and Betsy came into her room at Kings County Hospital's maternity ward. The baby was lying on her stomach.

"Say hello to Troy Junior," she said proudly.

"He looks a lot like his father, but I can understand why you're not as happy as I wish you were," Ken commented.

Trish tried to force a better smile. "Please take a picture of Troy's new son with your iPhone, Mr. Williams, and go show it to him."

After Ken took the picture, he said: "I'm one step ahead of you, Trish. I've already made plans to visit Troy at the MDC today. I'll either go before or after I see JoJo, depending on what JoJo's doctor tells me."

Trish thanked them for coming to the hospital and asked whether they might visit her when she took the baby home. They assured her that they would and that nothing that had happened to JoJo or to their office would interfere with them handling her husband's trial.

"It's just a few weeks away, Trish," said Ken. "You'll be there in court. By this time next month Troy will be home bouncing his baby boy on his knees."

⌐

After they left, Ken called Dr. Anagnostou on his cell phone.

"Can I come see JoJo yet, doctor?" he asked.

"Maybe in about two hours," the doctor told him. "We're working around the clock on him. He's semiconscious, but has asked for you. We told him that we'll let you visit him soon. In the meantime, his pastor is by his side asking Christ to save 'one of his flock.' Mr. Jones seems happy to have the spiritual support."

"We'll be there," Ken said. "How's he really doing, Doc?"

"Fortunately, as strange as it may sound, with fourth-degree burns, there's no pain. But he's at heightened risk of infection. We're hopeful, though."

"Thanks, Doc."

After he hung up, Ken and Betsy went to the photo store a block away from the MDC and had an 8 x 10 color glossy picture of Troy Jr. made. Moments later, they were showing it to the proud father in the jail.

"He looks just like you," said Betsy. "Like father, like son."

"How's Trish doing?" Troy asked.

"She's holding up okay," Betsy said. "Obviously, she's feeling so many emotions. Trish is happy the baby is beautiful and healthy. He's got your mischievous eyes. But naturally she's a little down that you could not be there to share the moment. She should be able to visit you again by next week after she gets out of the hospital."

Ken then told Troy about JoJo but assured him that it would not affect his trial.

"All the files are gone, but we'll somehow be ready in spite of this. Gary and I will be spending more time with you the next several days preparing you to testify. But we'll see how the trial goes before we decide whether you should take the stand. I doubt if it will be necessary. Hang in there. You'll be home with Junior before you know it."

Before Troy could say another word, Ken's cell rang. While cell phones normally were not allowed in the jail, the warden had made an exception for Ken after he explained that he was waiting for a call from the hospital about JoJo.

It was Dr. Anagnostou.

"He's not in good shape, but he's asking for you."

"I'll be right there, Doctor."

～

Ken and Betsy waited in the lobby for just a few minutes before the doctor came to meet them.

"The pastor is still with him," he told them. "JoJo wants him to stay, but it may be best if Betsy waited here. He doesn't want anyone to see him in his condition. He only wants to talk to Ken."

"I understand," said Betsy.

Ken had a hard time trying not to react as the doctor ushered him into JoJo's room. But it was not easy to keep his emotions in check. He flinched as he saw JoJo looking like a mummy; the only parts of his body that were visible were his eyes, nose, mouth, and charred left arm, where an intravenous tube was dripping fluids into him.

JoJo could barely talk, and Ken kneeled by the side of the hospital bed to try to hear him.

"Ken, you've been my savior on Earth," JoJo whispered. "Now I'll be meeting my savior in Heaven."

Ken tried to hold back his tears.

"Don't talk like that, JoJo," he said. "You have wonderful doctors, and even though you're going through a tough time now, you'll be much better soon."

"I'm not so sure . . . I'll try. But if I don't make it, promise me you'll beat the living daylights out of Neary and free all the brothers when you're DA."

"You can count on it, JoJo."

"And make sure you win the Jackson case . . . poor kid suffered so much rotting in jail for no reason like I did."

"He'll be home with his wife and new son soon," Ken said.

"One more thing," JoJo said, but his breathing was more labored. "You should marry Betsy. Please move into my condo . . . my wedding gift to you."

"Thanks, JoJo. I'll marry her as soon as the DA race is over. But you're not going any place. The first thing we'll do when we get back from our honeymoon will be to visit you at your beautiful new home."

JoJo gasped for air, but managed to mutter. "I don't think so, Ken."

There was more gasping, and then silence.

JoJo had died.

32

The Christian Cultural Center was packed for the funeral service. In the brief time he was out of jail, JoJo had touched many people. Ken, Mickey, and Betsy sat in the front pews on the left of the center aisle. Commissioner Donnelly sat next to Ken. Behind them were members of the Fortune Society. Ron Kuby sat with them. Near him were Judge Gonzales, Judge Black and his wife, and Judge Black's law clerks. Sitting in the first row on the other side of the aisle was James Neary. Ken thought, "that rat bastard would never have come if he wasn't running for re-election." Racanelli was not with him.

The service began with the reading of the 29th Psalm. It was followed by a number of gospel songs from the choir. After a few readings from the Bible, Pastor Burnham rose to speak. "We have lost Deacon Jones, but everybody wants to go to Heaven, and JoJo's now with the Lord Jesus."

"Amen," came the congregation's response.

He continued, "But we celebrate his life on Earth today. Jesus must be proud of Deacon Jones. He could have been a bitter and revengeful man when he got out of jail, but he turned the other cheek, just like Jesus and devoted his life to helping other brothers who were suffering, just like he had suffered."

"Right on," came several voices from the congregation.

"Tell it like it is," came another voice.

After a brief pause, Pastor Burnham continued. Looking up with his hands outstretched and his voice an octave lower, he looked and sounded like he was speaking to heaven.

"Lord Jesus, look after our son. He has not known much peace on Earth. Make his heavenly days tranquil. Shower him with your love. He has done your work on Earth. He deserves your grace and eternal heavenly rest."

More "amens" from the congregation.

"And one more thing, Lord," shouted the pastor. "Whoever did this dastardly deed should go where the devil resides. We trust that Commissioner Donnelly, who prays with us today, will find this coward, and justice will be served."

Yet more "amens."

Pastor Burnham was not finished. "But JoJo would ask forgiveness. And we trust that Ken Williams will complete JoJo's work on Earth by freeing all those poor brothers still in jail for crimes they never committed once he is the DA."

More "right ons."

Ken looked over to Neary, who looked like he wished he never came.

The service concluded with everyone standing and singing "Amazing Grace." As they filed out it seemed like everyone—other than James Neary—wanted to shake Ken's hand and wish him well.

Ken asked Ron Kuby to join him, Betsy, Mickey, and Gary at the Queen for lunch. They had important matters to discuss.

❧

The five of them sat at the usual round table in the corner. Franco had not arrived yet. They were all tearful and looked at each other in silence for several minutes before Mickey broke the ice.

"Maybe everybody wants to go to heaven like the pastor said, but nobody wants to die."

"That's not exactly true, Mickey," chimed in Gary. "How about all those Muslim suicide bombers?"

"You got a point there," replied Mickey. "But I'm talking about normal people, not those crackpots."

Ken joined in. "Everybody wants to go to Heaven but nobody wants to die! Sounds like a good title for another song. But let's be serious now. We have just a couple of weeks to go before the Jackson trial and the primary is right around the corner. All our files and campaign material are gone, as well as all the trial transcripts and evidence that JoJo had assembled and stored in all those boxes in his room. And we have no office to work out of. We've also lost all the discovery material that we got."

"Looks like whoever did this wasn't too keen on you winning the trial and becoming DA," said Kuby.

Ken wasn't laughing.

Under the rules, the state was required to turn over, well in advance of the trial, any photographs and drawings made by its investigators that it planned to introduce at the trial, as well as scientific tests, such as reports from the coroner and medical experts detailing the exact cause of the victim's death, the entry and exit points of the bullets, and the type of gun the bullets came from. They were also required to disclose any of the defendant's prior convictions that the prosecutor planned to use to cross-examine the defendant if he chose to testify. Ken had received numerous photos of the crime scene, a ballistics report, and the coroner's report. He needed all this material for cross-examining the experts and the cops who investigated the crime scene. He also was given the details of Troy's prior drug conviction. He no longer had any of this original material.

Kuby apologized for his flippant comment and told Ken that he would do whatever he could to help.

"You can use my office. It will be a little tight, but we'll manage. I got a couple of interns working for me now that we'll put at your disposal. We'll all work like hell to see that these bastards don't get away with this."

"As you know, I'm conflicted out from working on the Jackson case," said Betsy, "but I'll contact Ken's other clients and try to keep the practice alive."

"I knew we could count on you," Ken said to Kuby. "But we've really been set back. We also lost all the cross we've scripted for Wee Willie and the other dirtbags that Troy has told us he knew, two of whom may possibly be the other cooperators. Unfortunately, we don't have their names yet. Racanelli is playing it close to the vest and won't tell us who they are and give us any info about them until he calls them to testify."

"I know that case law, Ken, but the trial judge has discretion to give us that information before then. Cogan's a fair-minded judge. Why don't you ask him to make Racanelli tell us who the other cooperators are now, and the names of all the other witnesses he plans to call? And I'm sure he'll make the DA give you another copy of all the destroyed discovery material."

"You've read my mind. I've had that on my list of things I'm planning to do. I'll call the judge's clerk this afternoon and ask for an immediate conference with his Honor."

"And I'm sure he'll also adjourn the trial because of the fire," said Kuby.

Ken quickly rejected Kuby's suggestion.

"Look, Ron, whoever did this would like nothing better than to have the kid holed up in jail for as long as possible. I'm not going to play into his hands. We're going to trial on schedule come hell or high water."

"It's your call, Ken," said Kuby.

The waiter placed some pasta dishes on the table. Nobody seemed interested in eating, but they picked at the food for a few moments before Kuby spoke again.

"By the way, Ken, do you have any new info on who the hell torched your place and is planning to kill you and the judge?"

Mickey answered. "Only that the death threat letter to the judge was mailed from a post office from the Bronx. But that doesn't mean squat. Maybe the fire bomb investigators will find something."

"Well, it's got to be someone who Ken really pissed off in the past," Kuby commented.

Ken just shrugged. "That could be a lot of people, I suppose. Whoever it is also hates blacks."

"And liberal Jewish judges who he thinks has it in for the cops," added Betsy.

"And someone who obviously went bonkers when you got all that money for JoJo," said Kuby.

"Here's my take on it," interjected Mickey. "The first death threat against Ken came from a cell in Racanelli's neighborhood. I don't think he did it, but it may have been someone who was visiting him. And the second death threat came from a cell in Greenpoint. The guy probably lives there."

"It's all conjecture, Mickey," said Ken." And how about the death threat against the judge? It may not even have been from the same guy. Some law and order guy who thinks the cops should be allowed to stop and frisk anyone who they think looks suspicious could have it in for poor Judge Black. As for me, it could be any one of a number of nuts who don't like what we're doing or what I've done in the past. Maybe it really is Racanelli, or someone close to him; maybe it's a crazy Hasid who thinks that JoJo really killed the rabbi; maybe it's even Shmuel Hyman who's gonna be prosecuted for raping his daughter. In any event, I'm not supposed to be killed unless I win the primary."

"I've had lots of threats against me for all my civil rights cases, but nothing quite as serious as this," said Kuby. "Is it really all worth it, Ken?"

Ken just glared at him.

"Let's just concentrate on winning the Jackson case and the election."

⁓

Ken appeared before Judge Cogan the next day. Mickey was with him. Before Ken could say anything, the judge spoke.

"Losh, it's a terrible thing that has happened. Under the circumstances I'll adjourn the trial."

"That won't be necessary, Your Honor," replied Ken. "But I would like you to order the prosecutor to give me another copy of all the discovery as soon as possible. And I would like to know the names and addresses of the cooperators who will be testifying for the People."

Ty Cohen was quick to respond. "We'll of course give Mr. Williams the discovery material, but under the law, we don't have to disclose the names of the witnesses until they testify."

Judge Cogan put down his glasses before he spoke, and leaned forward.

"I know all that very well, Mr. Cohen. But the law also allows me to exercise a sound discretion. It's manifestly unfair to spring the government's critical witnesses on defense counsel at the last minute. Is there any reason why Mr. Williams should not have their names now?"

Cohen was on top of his game. "It's a matter of their safety, Your Honor. The court must consider the witnesses' safety when deciding on the time for disclosing their identities, and it would be improper to disclose their names before the trial where it would create a manifest danger. And when it comes to cooperators, their safety is always at risk. We're dealing with very dangerous people here, and in that world a stool pigeon is a prime candidate for all sorts of bad things."

Ken didn't have to say anything. The judge said it all.

"Be that as it may, but I think in this case, considering that everything happened so long ago and Mr. Jackson doesn't strike me as a violent young man, I'm going to require you to disclose all your witnesses, including the names of the cooperators, by the end of the day. And remember, as I'm sure you realize, you have to turn over all statements you have taken from the witnesses and anything that could be used to impeach them. And don't forget your continuing *Brady* obligations to disclose any exculpatory information. We don't want another Joaquin Jones case. Jury selection will be three weeks from Monday. See all of you then."

As they left the courtroom Ken told Mickey, "I'll let you know as soon as I get everything. You'll have a lot of work to do in a short time."

33

Commissioner Donnelly had told Ken at JoJo's funeral that he should stop by his office as soon as he was up to it. He had some things to tell him that were about to go public about the DA and Judge Velie. After lunch, Ken told Betsy and Gary to get settled into Kuby's office, and he took Mickey with him to One Police Plaza.

The commissioner said he had some good news for Ken. "The New York City Department of Investigation has been looking into the DA's use of forfeiture money seized from drug dealers and other criminal defendants."

As an AUSA, Ken had collaborated on occasion with the DOI, the city's agency responsible for investigating corruption, fraud, waste, and abuse by government entities and officials.

Donnelly continued, "Forfeited monies from criminal activities are public funds. I've just been given a report from the DOI that says Neary illegally tapped into this fund to pay tons of money to a political consultant for over a decade, and that since you announced that you were running against him in the primary, he has taken more than $200,000 from the fund to help finance his campaign against you. I thought you might like to see the report before the press gets its hands on it today."

Ken could hardly believe what he read. The report ran for twenty-seven pages. It first explained that "State law requires that asset-forfeiture funds be used only for law enforcement purposes." But the money was paid to one Mortimer Marsh, who had long advised James Neary on public relations.

As detailed in the report, during the last two years Marsh's firm was paid $219,824 for "public relations and communications services." However, during that time, his firm "provided few if any actual public relations and communications services" to the DA's office; rather, Marsh served "primarily if not exclusively as a political consultant" to the DA "personally."

The DOI investigators found that during the last year the DA's office typically issued two or three checks each month to Marsh's firm from asset-forfeiture funds from convicted criminals, and that over the past decade the office paid his firm about $1.1 million from those funds.

The report noted that the DOI inquiry included the review of about 6,000 e-mails sent to or from the DA's official e-mail address for the prior eighteen months, and painted a picture of a DA who, after two dozen years in office, used staff members, colleagues, and whatever resources he could tap to help shape his primary campaign against Ken. It concluded by commenting that the DA potentially violated the New York City Charter, which could constitute a misdemeanor, and also the State Penal Code for official misconduct, which, given the large amounts of money entailed, would be a felony.

Ken was flabbergasted. "If the report is accurate, Aidan, Neary could be criminally prosecuted. Maybe he'll get to join JoJo's brothers in jail."

Mickey had been sitting quietly, taking it all in, but couldn't contain himself. "That's fuckin' great news, Commish," he blurted out.

"It's pretty serious stuff," Commissioner Donnelly commented. "The report has been referred to the attorney general in Albany. He'll have to appoint a special prosecutor to look into this and, if it pans out, indict Neary. In the meantime, Ken, you can make political hay out of it. It pretty much insures your election. But you should read the rest of the report. You'll get a big kick out of what it says about your favorite judge."

The second part of the DOI report concluded that Never Lose Louie had violated the Judicial Code of Conduct by advising the DA on his campaign, offering legal advice, and discussing matters that the district attorney's office was pursuing. It detailed a number of instances from a host of e-mail exchanges of Judge Velie's improper behavior of engaging in political activity and using his office to support Neary's reelection.

In one example, Neary asked the judge for suggestions on how to attack Williams on his qualifications. "Lack of experience in supervising a large number of attorneys," the judge replied. "Until he puts forth a plan or set of goals, put it out there that he is not qualified to run for office." In another exchange, Judge Velie told Neary that he believed the structure of a planned debate between him and Williams would favor the incumbent DA. The judge wrote that the debate would "focus on the nitty-gritty of what the DA does each day to run the office" and that Williams "has no clue, and that will come out."

The report also said that Judge Velie "used his apparent connections" to the editors of the *New York Times* and *New York Law Journal* "to further Neary's political interest." At one point in the report Velie told Neary about a conversation he had with a *New York Law Journal* reporter disparaging Williams' character and legal skills and suggesting that Neary do the same.

The DOI report also recounted "discussions" between Velie and Neary regarding "pending criminal matters and investigations." It also referenced an editorial criticizing Neary on his poor record of prosecuting sex-abuse cases among the Hasidic Jews, and Judge Velie's advice that Neary should have a news conference "with victim advocates at your side."

And to Ken's dismay, Never Lose Louis also gave Neary advice on how to respond to questions about JoJo's case and to the rising number of claims of wrongful convictions under Neary's watch.

The final paragraph stated that the DOI report would be sent to the State Commission on Judicial Conduct, which is empowered to initiate judicial removal proceedings. It concluded that "the DOI is of the strongest opinion that such proceedings are warranted."

Ken had previously told the commissioner about how he always suspected that "Judge Velie was morally corrupt and nothing more than a political hatchet man for the DA."

Mickey spoke for a second time. "I hope they kick his ass off the bench."

"Before that could happen he's entitled to a hearing," said Commissioner Donnelly. "But he's got a lot of explaining to do."

"I just wish JoJo was here to hear all this good news. I miss him so much and can't believe we aren't doing this together," Ken said.

"Things have certainly turned your way, Ken," said Donnelly. "With what you've been through, you deserve it. Now all you have to do is win the Jackson trial."

"It's more apparent than ever, Aidan, that Troy has been railroaded. That poor kid. What I've been through is nothing compared to what he's had to put up with. And he hasn't even seen his new son yet."

When Ken and Mickey got to Kuby's office after they left Commissioner Donnelly, Gary told them that he had received a copy of the discovery material that had been destroyed in the fire. He also told them that Ty Cohen had complied with Judge Cogan's order and disclosed the names of the cooperators. In addition to Wee Willie Wexler, Rasheen Ross and Marshawn Brodie would also be testifying that they were at the scene and saw Jackson shoot the rabbi's son.

～

Ken and Gary burnt the proverbial midnight oil in Kuby's office for the rest of the week, prepping for the big day. Ken needed a break. That Friday night, Mickey sat next to him at the piano at Arturo's. The night before, at Ken's apartment, Ken had played the song he wrote for him. He told Mickey it came to him "as soon as you said, after JoJo's funeral, that while everybody wants to go to heaven 'nobody wants to die.'"

"It's cool, Ken." Mickey had told him. "It's made to order for Garth Brooks. You may not believe it, but I can sing that sucker better than he could. Let's do it at Arturo's."

Frankie and Jimmy were dumbfounded when Mickey grabbed the mic. "You really gonna sing?" asked Frankie incredulously.

"You bet your sweet ass I am," said Mickey.

The place was packed, but everybody stopped talking when Mickey started to sing in his deep, earthy, Garth Brooks voice. But they all joined in on the choruses.

> Everybody wants to go to Heaven
> But nobody wants to die
> And anyone who tells you differently is lying
> While I want eternal peace of mind
> I'm not ready to leave this world behind
> Cause nobody's seen that big guy in the sky
>
> That's why I'll always be the loving kind
> And I'm not living life wasting my time
> I try to make the most of every day
> I drink good whiskey, I have good friends
> I'm livin' and lovin' 'til my earthly end
> Cause waiting for the next life ain't the natural way
>
> If I ever go to Heaven
> I'm never gonna tell a lie
> You'll never see me looking miserably or lying
> When I'm in my final resting place
> There'll be a big smile upon my face
> Cause here's what I'll tell that big guy in the sky

I always was the loving kind
I never lived life wasting my time
I tried to make the most of every day
I drank good whiskey I had good friends
I lived and loved 'til my earthly end
Cause waiting for the next life wasn't the natural way

I'm not sure I'll go to Heaven
Or the place where the devil resides
Whether I'll end up angelically or frying
But on my judgment day I'll say amen
And say the same things to both of them
The devil himself and the big guy in the sky

I'll say I'm glad I was the loving kind
I never lived my life wasting my time
I tried to make the most of every day
I drank good whiskey I had good friends
And lived and loved 'til my earthly end
Cause waiting for the next life ain't the natural way

Ken then asked everyone to "please be quiet." He told them that
when he was a little boy he lived on his grandparents' farm in South
Carolina with his parents, and his grandfather would sing him a song
that was written by Ken's great-grandfather when Ken was born. It
passed through the generations and was sung by Ken at his father's
funeral several years back. It was so personal that he never sang it
again. He decided he would do it now because he was so moved by
Troy's tears of joy when he had showed him his new son's picture.
But he was so choked up when he started to sing it, he asked Frankie
if he could do it for him.

Like father like son
And so goes the chain
The young never learn

From the older one's pain
Whatever may come
Just love him don't run
And he'll do the same
For his father and son

When my son was born
I held him tenderly
He was his daddy's pride
But I won't forget who was standing by my side
And what my daddy said to me

Like father like son
And so goes the chain
The young never learn
From the older one's pain
Whatever may come
Just love him don't run
And he'll do the same
For his father and son

Many years have passed
I've lived enough to see
My son and his son become men
But each one in turn has learned what my daddy said to me

Like father like son
And so goes the chain
The young never learn
From the older one's pain
Whatever may come
Just love him don't run
And he'll do the same
For his father and son

34

Ken, Gary, Mickey, and Troy were each taking notes as Judge Cogan began vetting the jury. The big day had finally arrived. Racanelli sat next to Ty Cohen at the prosecutor's table. The judge's law clerk sat next to the court reporter just below the judge's bench. Gary had a hard time keeping his eyes off of Tina. She twirled her hair and smiled at him.

The courtroom was packed. The first row of public benches was reserved for the press. Trish sat in the second row. Troy Jr. was on her lap wrapped in a light blue blanket. He was now a month old. The prospective jurors saw Troy blow them kisses—it was the first time he saw his son, and Troy beamed. Sitting behind Trish were a number of kids from Bushwick High whom Troy had counseled, as well as the school's principal.

Ken was psyched. He couldn't wait for the opportunity to cross-examine the cooperators. But his total focus was now on jury selection. It was all important. Strange things had been known to occur. Criminal defense lawyers would always tell stories at bar association meetings of problem jurors who, during the vetting process, had cleverly answered the judge's questions to avoid being tossed, especially in a high-profile case that would be all over the press. Some just wanted the limelight.

In spite of its importance, the jury selection process usually passes by in a flash. It was commonly known among the trial lawyers that judges have some sort of perverted competition among them over who's the quickest to pick the jury.

On that, Judge Cogan prided himself; he had no doubt he was the fastest. But this case slowed him down. In addition to the requisite twelve jurors, Judge Cogan decided, in his discretion, that there should be six alternates. The judge first spoke generally to a random panel of ninety-five prospects who had been called up from the central jury room. He told them about the type of case they might be sitting on, the expected length of the trial, and how the jury selection process worked. Also, he told them they would not be sequestered. Since this was a criminal trial, he lectured them that the prosecution was brought in the name of The People of the State of New York, and that the People had the burden to prove the defendant guilty beyond a reasonable doubt. He also told them that under the Constitution, the defendant was presumed innocent and did not have to testify; if he chose not to, it could not be held against him.

Tina then randomly selected twelve from the group of ninety-five and had them sit in the jury box. Judge Cogan spoke to each of them. He asked which community they came from, their occupation, and some general questions about their families and hobbies. The judge then asked them whether there were any reasons they could not sit and "listen carefully to the evidence, hold the government to its burden of proof, follow the law, and render a fair and impartial verdict—without prejudice because of the defendant's color—based solely on the evidence." They all said they could. The judge then gave the lawyers an opportunity to question them as well.

Jury selection proved far more tedious than Judge Cogan had anticipated. Many of the prospective jurors knew about the case and the DA campaign from the extensive media coverage, and they told the judge that they did not think they could be fair to the prosecution. Some also said they were Jewish and knew Rabbi Bernstein. They were not sure they could put his murder and now the murder of his son by "schwartzes" out of their minds and render a verdict for the defendant.

Cogan had to dismiss both groups "for cause." Others then were called to take their places, and the process repeated. After twelve were qualified, the lawyers then exercised peremptory challenges, meaning that they were permitted to excuse any of the twelve for any reason whatsoever, except for race or color. This being a murder case, they each had twenty perempts. Those excused would then be randomly replaced by new prospective jurors, and the questions and challenges went on until all the prosecution and defense perempts were used up and twelve qualified jurors remained. The alternates were then selected.

By the end of the first day, only seven of the jurors had been selected. Judge Cogan ordered everyone to return by 9:00 a.m. the next day to complete jury selection and, if time permitted, to hear the opening statements by the lawyers.

Ken, Gary, and Mickey decided to review their notes at the Queen and then try to get a good night's sleep. By ten o'clock they were all in bed. Mickey slept on the Murphy bed in Ken's place. He had been doing that ever since the last death threat.

Ken made coffee in the morning, picked up the morning edition of the *Times* in the hallway, and turned to the New York Region section to see if the newspaper was covering the trial. It was. There was a small article that jury selection was underway and it was possible that Wee Willie Wexler would be testifying for the People early in the week.

But the article that really caught Ken's eyes was the one midway down the page with the headline:

FACING REMOVAL, JUDGE WILL LEAVE BENCH.

The lead paragraph reported that Judge Louis Velie "had agreed with the New York State Commission on Judicial Conduct to resign rather than face the prospect of removal for allegedly discussing pending cases and engaging in improper political activity."

The article explained that the judicial commission began its inquiry into Judge Velie's behavior after having received a preliminary report from the New York State Department of Investigation. Rather than wait for the final report, the judicial commission had opened an inquiry that included interviewing witnesses, reviewing documents, and hearing from the judge. At the conclusion of the investigation, the commission's counsel notified the judge that "he would recommend that the eleven-member panel remove the judge from office, an action that would lead to formal removal proceedings."

Never Lose Louie finally lost. Rather than risk removal, he agreed that he would step down from the bench at once, and he also agreed that he would not seek or accept judicial office again. He issued a face-saving statement that "working for the people of the city and state has been a distinct honor and privilege."

Ken was ecstatic and called Betsy to share the good news with her.

"I guess there's a God in Heaven after all," he told her. "I hope JoJo is watching. That son-of-a-bitch finally got what was coming to him."

⁓

At the end of the second day, all the jurors had been chosen, plus the six alternates. It was a fairly diverse group of men and women: Of the twelve, two were Hispanic, one was Asian, four were black and five were white. One of the whites was Irish, two were Italian, and two were Jewish. Two of the alternates were black, two were Jewish, one was Asian, and one was Irish. None of the Jewish jurors or alternates were Hasidic or came from the Hasidic community. And none of the blacks came from the neighborhood where the murder occurred. The eighteen were then given the jurors' oath by Judge Cogan: "To render a fair and impartial verdict based solely on the evidence, without fear of favor or prejudice." They were then told by the judge to return the next morning promptly at 9:00 a.m. for the beginning of the trial, at which time he would give them preliminary instructions and the actual trial would begin.

When the jurors returned the next day, Judge Cogan welcomed them and began to explain the process and how he ran his courtroom.

"Have you all had a good night's sleep?" he asked.

The jurors nodded.

"Good. We'll go until five every day with an hour for lunch and a fifteen-minute morning and afternoon break. Do not talk to anyone about the case, not even among yourselves, until you start your deliberations. Do not read anything about the case in the press or watch TV coverage. And don't check things out on the Internet. If you inadvertently do, you must tell the court clerk about it, and then I will determine if I think you can still render an impartial verdict. If not, you will be replaced by an alternate."

Judge Cogan continued, "Since the People have the burden of proof, the prosecution presents its case first, and after I finish giving you these preliminary instructions, the lawyers will make opening statements. The purpose of the People's opening is to give you a sort of roadmap of what the prosecutor expects to prove. The defendant's lawyer does not have to make any opening comments, but he can if he wishes, and defense counsel has advised me that he will do so. The prosecutor will then call his first witness. After the prosecutor calls all his witnesses and presents all his evidence, it will be the defendant's turn. But the defense does not have to put on any case at all. It can rely on the presumption of innocence and simply take the position 'that the People of the State of New York has not proven its case beyond a reasonable doubt.'

"After all the evidence is in, the lawyers will each sum up, and I will then instruct you on the law governing the case, and you will start your deliberations. Your verdict has to be unanimous. When you arrive at a verdict the foreperson will give the verdict sheet to the bailiff, who will be sitting outside the jury room. He will then bring it to me. After I look at it, all the parties will be summoned back to the courtroom. The verdict sheet will then be returned to the foreperson. I will then ask the foreperson to stand and publicly announce the verdict."

The judge then gave a nod to the People's lead prosecutor: "Mr. Cohen, time for your opening statement."

~

Ty Cohen quickly walked to the wood podium and stood firmly just a few feet in front of the middle of the jury box as he spoke in a sturdy, confident voice. "Members of the jury," he began, "I will save the details of the shooting of Menachem Mendel Bernstein by the defendant for the trial. But I will tell you right now, quite frankly, that the case will turn largely on the testimony of three cooperators. And they each have criminal records and were members of the notorious Chess Street Crew. Nonetheless, they knew what was happening in that neighborhood, and sometimes it takes a small fish to catch a big one.

"But under their cooperation agreements they had every incentive to tell the truth. They were each eye witnesses, and their cumulative testimony will convince you that the defendant is indeed guilty beyond a reasonable doubt. You will also hear testimony from the owner of the bodega where the murder happened that Jackson carried a .38, and the coroner will testify that a bullet to the heart had come from that type of gun. While their testimony standing alone is admittedly not sufficient to convict, it lends credibility to the testimony from the three eye witnesses.

"Although they are all cooperators, ask yourselves how likely it is that each of them would be lying under oath and risk going to jail for many, many years. You may possibly doubt the testimony of one of these witnesses, but what are the odds that all three would be committing perjury? No! There is only one verdict you can honestly render, and that is that Troy Jackson is guilty."

It was time for Ken. He also stood just a few feet from the jurors, and like Cohen, spoke without notes.

"Ladies and Gentlemen of the jury, as Judge Cogan has told you, the People must prove a defendant's guilt by proof beyond a reasonable doubt. Fair enough. But when you are sent into the jury room to deliberate Troy Jackson's fate after hearing all the testimony, you will not have a reasonable doubt, you will have absolutely no doubt that he is an innocent man who has been wrongfully charged with murder."

Ken then asked Troy to stand. He was wearing his prison grays.

"Okay, Troy, thank you. You can sit now," Ken said before continuing.

"When defendants are brought to trial before a jury, they are allowed to dress up in order to make a good impression and look like law-abiding citizens. Their lawyers will make sure that they are neatly dressed, usually in a nice suit, and cleanly shaven. If they are in jail, their clothes will be brought to them by a correction officer, and they are allowed to change from their prison garb before coming into the courtroom. The idea is that the jurors will not see prison jumpsuits and assume that defendants are really bad people who belong in jail; otherwise they would be out on bail.

"But who are we kidding? When you've been charged with murdering someone, you're not going to get bail and you'll be sitting in jail until your trial, which may take many months. We're not playing games here and trying to hide the truth. Troy has been sitting in jail for a long time. He's not going to dress up like a dandy and pretend otherwise."

Judge Cogan looked surprised. In all his years on the bench he had never heard such an opening. Defense lawyers invariably hammer home the constitutional mandate that the government must prove guilt beyond a reasonable doubt, and he never saw a defendant come to court dressed like a prisoner.

Ty Cohen was also clearly taken by surprise and thought he should object.

"I don't think those are proper comments for the defense to make, Your Honor."

"Well, it may be a little unorthodox, but why not?" Judge Cogan said and told Ken to continue.

"Troy is an outstanding citizen and a role model for every kid who has had the misfortune of being born into one of the black ghetto neighborhoods that still fester in certain parts of Brooklyn. He is a star guidance counselor at Bushwick High. I see a number of his students sitting here in the courtroom. He has an adoring wife and family—and a newborn baby."

Ken asked Trish to stand. She was dressed in a light blue pantsuit and holding Troy Jr.

"Trish Jackson will be testifying. She will tell you about how they met in high school after Troy's mother saved enough money to escape drug-infested Chess Street. They have been married for two years; this is their first child. Trish teaches science at Corpus Christi Junior High. They just bought a beautiful condo in Williamsburg with a great view of the Brooklyn Bridge. And now, the DA, who has a history of currying favor with the Hasidic community, and his chief prosecutor, who has brought phony prosecutions against blacks for robbing and even killing Hasidic Jews, have decided to make Troy Jackson their next victim, seven years after a murder. Can you believe it?"

Ty Cohen was livid. He had heard enough and asked for a sidebar.

"Judge, this is totally improper. We're trying Jackson, not the DA or Racanelli. These are inflammatory and baseless remarks that have no place in this trial."

"I think Mr. Cohen is correct, Mr. Williams. This is not the forum to raise prosecutorial misconduct. You can have a separate proceeding for that, but not here. The People's motive is not on trial now. Only whether the prosecution can prove your client guilty."

"Very well," agreed Ken. But the jury had heard what he'd said, and even though Judge Cogan then told the jury to disregard those comments, Ken was glad he'd said them.

Ken was a pro and he knew what to tell the jurors when he continued.

"Folks, sometimes I get so impassioned when defending an innocent man, I may say things in the heat of battle that might be viewed by his Honor as better left unsaid, but let's move on. I can wrap this up very quickly. As Mr. Cohen told you in his opening remarks, the People's case turns largely on the words of three convicted criminals who have cut a deal to save their own necks. I have reason to believe that the number one cooperator, Wee Willie Wexler, will testify that he was with Troy Jackson when he saw him shoot Bernstein, and the other cooperators are prepared to corroborate his story. I caution you, however, not to jump to conclusions until you've heard all the evidence. You will then conclude that you can't believe a word of what Wee Willie said and will be shocked that Troy Jackson's law-abiding life has been turned upside down."

Ken took a measured pause, looked straight into the eyes of each juror, and solemnly concluded: "At the risk of having to eat my words, I don't think it will take you more than fifteen minutes to walk back into this courtroom after you start your deliberations and return the only verdict you can. Not guilty."

"Call your first witness, Mr. Cohen," ordered the judge.

Cohen led with the owner of the bodega. He testified that he was in the backroom when he heard the shot but did not know who was in the store at the time, "and didn't see nothing." But he "thought" he had seen Troy with a .38 two days before the murder. Under Ken's cross-examination, he admitted that he "couldn't be sure."

Wee Willie Wexler was next. The cooperation agreement was put into evidence, and Wee Willie swore that he had every reason to testify truthfully; otherwise he would be facing twenty years for having pled guilty to being a major drug distributor as the number two man of the Chess Street Crew. Ty Cohen then asked Wee Willie the question everyone in the courtroom was waiting to hear." "Did you witness who murdered Menachem Mendel Bernstein? Wee Willie didn't hesitate to blurt out his answer. "It was Troy who shot him."

Cohen was quick with the logical follow-up. "Tell the jury every-thing you know about the murder and why Troy Jackson pulled the trigger." Wee Willie was well prepared. "Me and Troy were best friends when we were growing up in the hood. Though he moved out when he was like fourteen, about ten years ago, he never really left. He always came back to visit his grandmother and hang with us. As junior members of the Chess Street Crew, we were allowed to hustle some weed. We were just kids and were known as Pawns. We had to give the King a cut.

"Eventually, I became the Rook. The rest were either Bishops or remained Pawns. To become more than a Pawn you had to do some bad stuff.

"One day, I got a call from a Jewish kid. I don't know how he got my cell number. He told me his name was Manny and was told that I had some good crack. I didn't learn his real name until after he was done in and I saw on TV that he was a rabbi's son. We agreed to meet at the bodega. Troy happened to be with me. I sold the white dude a few grams. He would come back every so often for more. A lot more. He was obviously pushing the stuff. I guess he wanted me to think he was cool 'cause he told me after he had bought a lot of shit one night that he was on probation for doing cars. He was like doing Jew-ish community service. I told the King about it."

Ty Cohen interrupted: "Tell us the King's name."

"He only told us his last name was Kong. Wouldn't tell us his first name. Said he hated it. Told us to just call him King Kong, like the gorilla in the movie."

Cohen then showed him a picture of a mean-looking black man with a tapered goatee. He looked about thirty years old. "Is this King Kong?" Cohen bellowed.

"That's him."

"I offer it in evidence, Your Honor."

There was no legal basis for an objection. It was marked Exhibit A, and Cohen instructed Wexler to continue.

"The King got this brilliant idea. He told Manny that he could make a lot of bread if he could get the drugs into the country. The King told him: 'We got the contacts in the Dominican. You figure out how to get back and forth. Put on those Jewish threads, carry a bunch of those Jewish books with you, and they'll never stop you. I'll pay you 10k for every ten kilos you smuggle in.'

"Manny bought in. And he figured out how to do it. There was this old Jewish church down in Curaçao. It's got history, especially for those real religious Jews with the funny clothes. There was no Jews on the island now, but the Hasid folks would send kids there to maintain it and conduct services for Jew tourists.

"Manny had talked his probation officer into letting that Aleph place—that's like a reform school for Jews—send him there. He would make a trip every month, stay for a few days working in that church, and meet up with the Dominicans. With that black hat on his head, that black robe, and those funny-looking white threads hanging out of his white shirt, he was never stopped by the customs guys. He carried a suitcase full of those books they call Talmuds, with false bottoms. The dope was hidden in them.

"The king would send Troy and me to do the money stuff. He was the man and never wanted to get involved. We did the exchanges in the bodega. The King, who had this thing with taking videos—we called him the Video King—would watch from outside in case there was trouble. We would carry heat just in case. Troy's was a .38.

"Troy would take the stuff and put it in a storage room in the basement of his grandmother's crib. It was safe there. She could hardly walk and gave Troy the key. He would get her whatever she needed from it. No one ever figured the old lady's digs was being used for the Crew's stash house.

"But there was one shipment that was bogus. The King was pissed that the Jew had been passing off some bad stuff on us. He told me and Troy to tell him to make it up to us and give us ten kilos of good shit. He wouldn't get paid for it, and if he didn't agree, he would be in big trouble. The King told me and Troy to show him our heat to scare him big time.

"We told him. It was late at night and only me, Troy, and the Jew was inside the bodega. The King was watching from outside. The Jew started to yell and scream that he was being jazzed. He took a bag of coke out of the bottom of one of those Jewish books and we took it from him. He said the stuff was good. Troy said it better be or else, and pulled out his .38 to scare him. The Jew called him a dirty nigger. Troy lost it, and plugged him."

There was stunned silence in the jury box. Judge Cogan thought it would be a good time for the morning break. The jury was led out and admonished not to talk about the case. They were instructed to return in fifteen minutes.

When the trial resumed, Wee Willie wrapped up his testimony by telling the jury, "After Troy shot the Jew we all took off. I skipped town and didn't come back for two years, and I never saw King Kong again."

On cross-examination Ken Williams did not touch Wee Willie's story. As a good lawyer he knew that it would only give him the opportunity to repeat it. He did, however, try to discredit the People's number one cooperator by bringing out his bad rap sheet—he had spent a year in jail on the drug charge when Kuby was his lawyer and two more years on another drug conviction—and asking him rhetorically whether "as a cooperator he would do anything to get out of jail?" After Willie meekly answered "no," Ken ended with a flourish:

"If you didn't make this deal with the DA you would be facing twenty years, right?"

"Yeah, but I'm telling the truth."

"We'll let the jury decide that."

Ty Cohen then called his next witness. It was the number two cooperator, Rasheen Ross.

Rasheen limped into the courtroom, the lingering effect from a bullet wound when he was shot by a rival drug dealer several years ago. He had a worried look on his pock-marked face, but his tall angular body was neatly dressed in khaki pants and an open-collared light blue shirt that did not hide the snake tattoo wrapped around his neck. He had been waiting outside with Racanelli. Witnesses were not allowed inside until it was their turn to testify. Racanelli was there to make sure no one would try to speak to him. After Rasheen took the stand and was sworn to tell the truth, he candidly told the jurors about his criminal past and about his cooperation agreement. Under Cohen's direct examination, he then told the story that Racanelli had expected:

"Me and Marshawn Brodie were walking past the bodega. The door was open, the King was standing outside. We asked him why he was there. He told us that a deal was going on and he was there in case there was trouble. We all looked inside. Troy and Wee Willie were arguing with some white dude. Suddenly Troy shot him, point blank, right in the chest. Everybody ran like hell."

Ken rose slowly from his chair but raced to the podium to start his cross examination. He could not wait to begin.

"Did you ever tell the police that what you just testified to under oath was not true?"

Rasheen squirmed a little but said "never."

"You and Marshawn are both doing time now at Dannemora, right?"

More squirming: "Yeah."

"Do you guys know Shaquille Mann?"

"Yeah."

"Isn't he also doing time with you at Dannemora?"

"I dunno."

"Didn't you tell him that you and Brodie had lied to the cops, that Wee Willie Wexler had put you up to it and you never saw Troy Jackson shoot the Jew?"

Ty Cohen jumped to his feet, yelled "Objection," and asked for a sidebar. Sidebar conferences with the judge were rare. They would take place outside of the earshot of the jury at the far end of the bench. Judge Cogan had told the lawyers he would only allow them if they were critical.

Anticipating the basis for the objection, Judge Cogan stared at Ken.

"Mr. Williams, there better be a good faith foundation for your questions."

"There is, Your Honor. I have a recorded conversation between Rasheen Ross, Marshawn Brodie, and Shaquille Mann in the weight room at the jail. And if necessary I've subpoenaed Shaquille to testify."

"I'll let you play it. It strikes me as proper cross. After all, the cooperators' credibility is at the heart of this trial."

Cohen feebly objected "for the record" and slowly walked back to counsel's table. He tried to put on a game face for the jury, but inside he had a pit in his stomach.

The tape was marked as Defendant's Exhibit 1. Ken pulled out a tape recorder from his briefcase, gently put the tape in it, and pushed the play button.

"Rumor has it you guys cut a deal with the DA to rat out a brother. Guess I can't blame you. It's every man for himself here. If you can get out of this stink hole, go for it."

Ken pressed the stop button.

"Is that Shaquille's voice?"

"Yeah, I guess."

Ken played more.

"Did you and Brodie really see who shot the Jew?"

"Nah, but I don't really give a shit. I want out. Nate Jones, that other brother in our cell, told us Willie Wexler told him that he was in the bodega and saw the kid shoot him. Willie just got picked up and unless he cut a deal with the DA he gone be joining us here pretty soon. But Nate said Tough Tony told Willie he had to get two dudes to back him up, and said they better make up a good story. Me, Marshawn, and Nate were all Bishops in the Crew. Willie got word to Nate that he needed someone, but Nate's getting out next month and didn't want to get involved. He said he would talk to us. We agreed to cover Willie's ass. Anything to get the hell outta here. It's tough shit for Jackson. I guess Nate told you about it."

"He also told me that Racanelli and the DA put you up to it."

"Yeah."

Ken took the tape out of the machine and placed it carefully on the table in full view of the jury. They looked disgusted. Judge Cogan told the jurors he would probably call them back in about a half hour and sent them out of the courtroom. After they left, he asked to see the lawyers in chambers.

"How did you get that tape, Mr. Williams?"

"Your Honor, my client's life is at stake. I believe the DA and Anthony Racanelli would stoop to nothing to convict Troy. They didn't turn over exculpatory material in JoJo's case, other phony convictions have recently come to light, and I had every reason to believe that this would be another one unless I did something bold. My investigator did it all. Mickey Zissou got to Shaquille Mann. Shaq was also getting out soon. He had been convicted on a robbery count by Racanelli on one of his shaky ID cases. He swore he was innocent and hated him. It was his opportunity to get sweet revenge. Mickey visited Shaq in jail. He smuggled in a wire. The trap was set."

"Mr. Cohen, do you want to move to dismiss the indictment?

"I'll have to talk to the DA, Your Honor."

"You have fifteen minutes."

❧

Neary was furious. "How the fuck did that Zissou get a wire past security? But we're in for the ride. Let the jury do its job. I'm not going to toss it. Wexler has never recanted. We've grilled him to death. Everything he told us adds up. We believe him; maybe the jury will, too."

"Not in a million years, but you're the boss," Cohen said deferentially.

Ty Cohen told Judge Cogan that he would not be calling Marshawn Brodie. His only other witness would be the coroner, Dr. Jacob Weinstein. The trial continued.

After Dr. Weinstein identified the bullet as a .38, Ken didn't bother to question him. The prosecution rested. It was the defendant's turn.

Ken did not have to do anything. He could simply remind the jury that under the Constitution he didn't have to do a thing and the defendant did not even have to testify. Ken could give a fiery summation blowing the DA's case out of the water, drill home the fact that Neary and Racanelli were hell-bent on getting another bogus conviction, and ask the jury to vindicate Troy Jackson by immediately returning a verdict of "Not Guilty." But Ken wanted blood. He would have Trish, Troy's mother, and his grandmother testify. It would make the jurors even more irate. He decided that there would be no need to have Troy testify and give Cohen the opportunity on cross to question him about his drug conviction; unless he testified, it could not be introduced into evidence.

Ken let Gary handle the direct testimony. The three women made compelling witnesses. They testified about Troy's wonderful scholastic achievements, his passion as a role-model for the kids he counseled, his love for his wife, and his joy in becoming a father. Some of the jurors had tears in their eyes. Tina sat mesmerized by Gary's deft questioning and cool composure.

Cohen meekly asked the three witnesses a few perfunctory questions under cross, just bringing out that they were hardly unbiased. He wondered whether the jury would even be out for five minutes.

Summations didn't take much time. Cohen tried to make the best of it, but it was clear that he didn't have much fire in his belly. He slowly walked to the podium and had a difficult time making eye contact with the jurors as he concluded his brief comments by telling them: "Whatever you thought about Rasheen Ross, Willie Wexler was testifying truthfully because if he lied he would be going away for a very long time."

Ken chose not to gild the lily. He simply rose from his chair – instead of walking to the podium. He asked Troy to stand and Ken put his right arm around his shoulder before he started to speak. His voice was strong.

"Folks, I may be wrong but I don't think I need to give a long summation. I saw the shocked look on your faces as you heard that the DA's chief prosecutor had lined up Ross and Brodie to lie. And since they were willing to perjure themselves, can you believe anything that the convicted drug dealer Wee Willie said? Anthony Racanelli should be on trial, not Troy."

"I ask you to quickly return the only verdict that you can, and exonerate Troy Jackson."

Judge Cogan then explained the law to the jurors from the bench. When he finished he glanced at his Citizen's silver wrist watch and told them: "Ladies and gentlemen, it is now 11:40 a.m. The bailiff will now lead you out of the courtroom. Once inside the jury room you may start your deliberations. Lunch will be brought in at noon. You may take whatever time you need to deliberate, but if by chance you reach a verdict before noon, you could either tell the bailiff right away or you can wait until you finish eating. Remember that your verdict must be unanimous."

❧

After the twelve jurors were escorted by the bailiff into the jury room to begin their deliberations, Judge Cogan excused the six alternates and thanked them for their service. As they were leaving the courtroom several stopped to tell Troy how sorry they were that he had to be the victim of a corrupt DA. One gave him his cell number and asked him to please call to let him know where the victory party would be.

It didn't take long for the jury to respond. Only fifteen minutes had passed when the bailiff handed Judge Cogan the foreperson's paper. Everyone was still in the courtroom; it was all over but the shouting. But the look on the judge's face said otherwise. Instead of returning it to the foreperson, he read what was on it out loud.

"Judge Cogan, eleven of us want to end this charade but the other one refuses to go along. He says his mind is made up and he won't vote to acquit under any circumstances. What should we do?" It was signed by the foreperson, Charlotte Moore.

It was not the first time that the judge had a holdout juror. While it was not common, it happened. Judge Cogan told the lawyers that he wished he were a federal court judge like his good friend Judge Black, because if this were a federal trial, the Federal Rules allow a judge to dismiss a juror who refuses to deliberate and to take a verdict from the other eleven. But under the laws of the State of New York, he could not do this. Nor could he speak to any of the jurors. The judge had been a member of a committee to lobby the legislature for a change, but to no avail. He had no choice. He would have to declare a mistrial. If the DA didn't move to dismiss the case, he would have to set it down for a retrial.

Ken Williams was annoyed, but not too upset. The trial had once again dramatized how rotten the DA was. The primary was just a few months away. Every poll projected Ken as the likely winner. The *New York Times* had given him a glowing send-off, and even the *News* and the *Post* said it was time for a change. If Neary didn't have the common sense to dismiss the indictment, it would be the first piece of business he would attend to once he took office.

But true to his stubborn Irish roots, Neary wouldn't budge. He knew he was going down to defeat and was an angry man. "To hell with it," he told Racanelli back at his office: "Let Williams do it and set a guilty man free."

～

The next day Judge Cogan released Troy Jackson.

"Crivvens," he bellowed. "You've been through hell. Under the circumstances I'm granting your lawyer's application to release you on your own recognizance while the case is still technically alive. I'm confident you will show up in court if and when necessary."

Troy bolted from his chair and ran to Trish and his son. She was in tears. Troy lifted his baby up over his head and whirled him all around. Everyone in the courtroom applauded.

The *Times* found out who the holdout was—one of the white male jurors. The newspaper learned that his father was once a member of the Klan. No one ever knew. He had answered every question the judge and Ken had asked him without giving any indication that he could possibly be a racist.

Ken threw a big victory party at Junior's. Most of the jurors showed up to tell Troy how happy they were for him and how sorry that he was put through all the agony. After the trial, they had read the newspaper accounts of JoJo's case and wondered why Racanelli was not prosecuted instead of Troy.

While Judge Cogan thought it would not be appropriate for him to attend the party, he gave Tina permission to go. She told Gary how impressed she was with the way he handled his role in the trial. She liked the fact that he was a good six inches taller than she was, and thought his light-skinned black body perfectly complemented his good looks. Tina gladly accepted his offer to have dinner with him the next night. Naturally, he took her to the Queen. They became inseparable.

～

The following week Ken was the featured speaker at Bushwick High School's assembly program. The school's principal, Henry Miller, decided to make a big deal over the return of its number one guidance counselor.

The assembly was packed. Sitting with Principal Miller, Ken, and Troy on the stage were Troy's fourteen current counselees.

"Welcome home, Troy," shouted the principal into the microphone as he stood at the podium. For a high school principal, he was not terribly well-dressed. His blue suit looked like it needed to be pressed, and his baggy pants were held up by a pair of red suspenders. With his shaggy white hair he resembled Clarence Darrow at the Scopes Monkey trial.

"You've been missed," Miller began in his garrulous voice. "You've suffered through terrible times but you're back home now with your colleagues and admirers. If there's any solace we can take from the horrific ordeal you've been put through, it probably will make you an even better guidance counselor and role model to our students. Knowing you as I do, you will teach them that physical revenge for injustices visited upon us is not the way. The way to get even is to become leaders in their communities and help solve the problems that still infest pockets of poverty right here in the projects of our borough."

There was polite applause before the principal handed the microphone to Troy.

"Good to be home, guys," he began. "I don't know if I could have gotten through all this if I didn't know that you had my back. Many of you came to the trial. There was never a day when I was in jail that I didn't get tons of letters telling me to keep my cool and how much you miss me. And you've been great to Trish, who's sitting in the front row here with our new baby boy. But I wouldn't be here today if not for Ken Williams. He's the real role model. He has shown us that a black activist can become the district attorney of our borough. How cool is that? That's what I want all of you to take away from this. Sure I've suffered. But in the end it was kind of worth it. I'm not bitter about what I've been through. It has all turned out perfect."

The kids all stood and cheered.

35

Over the next few months the primary campaign was in full swing, and on the second Tuesday in September Troy and Trish were second and third in line on the bright, sunny day when the polls opened. Troy held his son tightly as he walked into the voting booth. The Jacksons couldn't wait to pull the lever for the man who was their family's "savior."

Ken, Betsy, Mickey, Gary, and Ron Kuby waited after the polls closed at the Queen for the results, but as everyone anticipated, the primary election was a landslide. And even the Hasidic community, for the first time, did not vote in a block for Neary; the majority voted for Ken. Neary did not even win the Irish vote.

Since the Republican Party could not find a sacrificial lamb to oppose the Democratic candidate for the general election in a borough that had never in recent times voted for a Republican DA, Ken's election was guaranteed. But, the general election would not take place until November. In the meantime, Ken had to wrap up his law practice. He also had some personal business to attend to. He asked Betsy to meet him the next night at the Queen and told her to wear something special.

After Franco escorted them to their usual table, Ken opened a small velvet black box and took out a beautiful 3-carrot square-shaped ring. "Time to tie the knot, Betsy."

"It's about time, dear. What took you so long?"

"Well, it took the Hyman women a little time to help me find the perfect ring."

"Just like you to look for bargains at their jewelry store, but all kidding aside, I love you, always have, and always will."

The elderly couple sitting at the next table applauded as they kissed.

It was at least thirty seconds before their lips parted when Ken spoke again. Betsy had never before heard such rapid fire speech from him. "And, in case you haven't noticed, we've been a little pre-occupied with a few other things. But I wanted you to be by my side as my wife when I take the oath. And we should take JoJo up on his deathbed wish to move into his new condo. It's really a terrific place. And I thought I'd ask Pastor Burnham if he could marry us in JoJo's church. That way, we'll feel that he's still with us."

"Well, it's our church also," corrected Betsy ecstatically, "but it's the perfect place."

Franco was snooping nearby. "It's about time. Now I don't have to apologize anymore for calling you Mr. and Mrs. Williams."

"And you'll be at the wedding, too," said Betsy.

When they told the Police Commissioner the next day, Donnelly was concerned.

"Remember the death threats. It's supposed to happen if you beat Neary. Whether you like it or not, we're not just relying on Mickey anymore to keep you from getting killed. I'm putting a detail on you and Betsy until we find this guy. And I will alert Pastor Burnham about the security we'll have inside the church during the wedding ceremony.

⌁

He had been waiting for the right moment. The wedding would be it. The press had announced when and where it would happen. He knew that the police would be all over the place, but he could easily fit in. The dingy corner of his basement apartment had newspaper accounts of all of Ken's trials where he preyed on the police and made them look like fools and racists. Included were the details of the criminal charges pending against Shmuel Hyman and excerpts from speeches that Ken had made during his campaign about holding the Hasidic community responsible for their criminal misdeeds. He also had copies of the newspaper stories about Judge Black and how the "lunatic judge" had ruled that Killer Kalafer's arrest was the product of a classic "stop and frisk" by cops just trying to do their job.

He knew the location of the Christian Cultural Center. He had kept his police uniform. It was the first time he would be wearing it since he was thrown off the force. He recently had it dry-cleaned so it would not look like it hadn't been worn for years. He checked his 9mm Glock 19 sixteen round pistol to make sure it was fully loaded. He could hardly wait for the blessed event.

~

Ken had told Gary that he and Betsy wanted him to be part of the wedding ceremony. "I guess I'll have Mickey be the best man, but you'll be right with me. Maybe you and Tina will be next. How are you two lovebirds getting along?"

"I love her, Ken. But, boy, her Greek temperament sometimes makes me nuts. There are times when she blows hot and cold, just like the weather, but I know she loves me too."

It had been a while since he had the inspiration for another country song. Ken wrote it shortly after he had asked Betsy to marry him and thought it would be perfect for the Oak Ridge Boys. He sent it to Mickey, Frankie, and Jimmy, and the night before the wedding he and the gang were singing it at Arturo's:

> When we were young and innocent
> And just began to kiss
> We thought each day would bring
> Only happiness
> But though I'm still in love with you
> I'm sorry dear to say
> It hasn't quite worked out that way

Our love blows hot and cold
Just like the weather
It changes all the time
As the days go by
But while we have stormy days together
I pray to the Lord you'll never leave me
High and dry

Our love blows hot and cold
Just like the weather
It changes all the time
As the days go by
But while we have stormy days together
I pray to the Lord you'll never leave me
High and dry

And while we want our love to be a pretty melody
We haven't always sung in two-part harmony
And while we want to be on key
I have to tell you that
Our love has been both sharp and flat

Our love blows hot and cold
Just like the weather
It changes all the time
As the days go by
But while we have stormy days together
I pray to the Lord you'll never leave me
High and dry

Don't leave me high and dry
Don't leave me high and dry
Never, never leave me high and dry

Ken sent "High And Dry" to Dusty in Nashville later that night.

36

It was a perfect crisp, sunny, fall Sunday for the wedding. Pastor Burnham met Ken and Betsy in his study right after the last of the three morning services and signed the marriage license after Gary and Mickey put their John Hancocks on the witness lines.

There was no marching down the aisle—the bride and groom wanted to keep it simple. There was no flowing wedding gown. Betsy thought it inappropriate at her age. But she couldn't help looking beautiful in her demure champagne-colored dress and right in style in her peep-toe Jimmy Choos. Ken wore a blue suit. Together, they made a striking couple, befitting their soon-to-be new status as Mr. and Mrs. District Attorney.

It had the feel of a celebrity wedding. The usual 3,500 parishioners had remained after the last service, and an overflow of hundreds were standing in the aisles. All the politicos were there; it seemed as if everyone from the Chisholm Democratic Club was surrounding a smiling Ezekial Thomas.

Commissioner Donnelly was taking no chances. Although Pastor Burnham was not happy to have uniformed police officers at every exit, he reluctantly agreed after the police commissioner had convinced him that in addition to a number of plainclothes police sitting in the audience, a visible show of force was also necessary for such a high-risk situation.

It was a big moment for Pastor Burnham and his church when he walked to the pulpit with the wedding party at his side. His booming voice was as loud as ever as he administered the vows and presided over the exchange of the wedding rings.

Pastor Burnham then cleared his throat. He was hardly done speaking.

"Lord Jesus, we were last assembled with a crowd of this magnitude for the funeral of our beloved departed Deacon JoJo Jones. But we are here today for a joyous occasion, and I pray to the Lord that JoJo is looking down on us now with a big smile on his face."

He was just getting started.

"I know that with Betsy at his side, Ken will be completing JoJo's work on Earth and will be making JoJo proud of him as he embarks on what will surely be a brilliant career as Brooklyn's next district attorney. Ken will make sure that there will be no more black brothers who will be sitting in jail like JoJo. And he will make sure that there will be no more special favors for white folks who deserve to be prosecuted for heinous crimes, like Shmuel Hyman."

"Amens" started to rumble through the audience, and Ken whispered to the Pastor to remind him that this was "just a wedding," and maybe it might be wise "to tone things down a bit."

But Pastor Burnham had one final salvo. "Ken's future knows no limits. I pray to the Lord Jesus that one day we will be here again to celebrate his election as governor of the great State of New York, and, who knows, as the next black president of these United States."

The pastor had to wait for the "amens" to die down before he got down to the final piece of business. "Kenneth Evers Williams and Betsy Bonita Brown, under the watchful eyes of our Lord Jesus, and JoJo Jones, and under my authority under the laws of the State of New York, I now pronounce you husband and wife."

Naturally, Ken had written a song for his wedding vows. After they kissed, and kissed, and kissed, he turned the mic on and sang it to Betsy, as the church organist accompanied him. It was not a country song. She tried her best—unsuccessfully—to keep from crying.

How I'll always love you
How I'll always care
Never need to fear dear
Always I'll be there

Now's the time to tell you
How our love just grew
Every time you said to me
That you love me too

No more when or whether
No more need to wait
Finally together
Time to celebrate

We're a lucky couple
With your magic flair
And with all my love for you
We're a perfect pair

What a special feeling
What more can I say
You make me so happy
On this our wedding day

As they kissed once more, three gun shots broke the silence. Betsy's screams resonated throughout the far reaches of the balcony as the blue suit was soaking up the pool of blood.

37

"Who was the lunatic?" asked Betsy as she and Ken were being driven back to the Police Commissioner's office.

"A former cop named Ciarán O'Reilly," answered Commissioner Donnelly.

"Hey, that was one of the cops who murdered the Dunne kid years ago," said Ken.

"That's the guy," the commissioner said. "After you ripped him apart in your deposition and got twelve million from the city for the kid's estate—and got him and the others fired from the force—he was hell-bent on revenge. We found all sorts of scary things in his apartment in Greenpoint. All sorts of bomb-making materials, manuals on how to make bombs, and lots of anti-black and anti-Semitic stuff. Even a bunch of swastikas on the wall over his bed. But you're safe now."

"But Aidan, how did you know with all those men in blue at that side exit that he was the one you had to shoot?" Ken asked.

"Very simple. I was sitting in the front row, not too far from that exit. There were four there. I had handpicked all the police in the place. He was not one of them, so I knew he must be there to cause trouble. Unfortunately I missed all the kissing while I kept my eyes on him. When he pulled out his gun, I shot him."

"But why three times?" asked Betsy.

"When police shoot, they must shoot to kill, and they are trained to fire three times. It's called triple tap."

"Well Aidan," said Ken. "I guess I owe you my life."

"Forget about it. Try to put it out of your mind and concentrate on becoming a great DA."

38

Ken took the commissioner's advice. Even though it was weeks before the general election and a few months before he expected he would be taking the formal oath, he started to make the transition from private to public life.

First, he decided to call Ty Cohen and ask him to have dinner with him at the Queen. After Ken introduced him to Franco, the two of them sat privately at Ken's table.

"I'm sure you're curious why I wanted to speak to you," began Ken.

"The thought did cross my mind," responded a surprised Tyrus Cohen.

"Look, Ty, you did a highly professional job in the way you handled the Jackson trial. We were all impressed. You are a skilled and ethical prosecutor. I would hope you will stay on during my administration."

"I'm flattered, Mr. Williams. I was just trying to do my job. I'm ashamed of the way it turned out. I had no idea that Racanelli would stoop so low. I've been thinking that the right thing for me to do is to submit my resignation even before you take office."

"Not so fast, Ty. I would like you to try the Shmuel Hyman case and to make you head of the new Sex Crimes Bureau I plan to establish."

"I'm flabbergasted, and honored," Cohen responded.

"I want you to meet Shmuel's daughter now, Ty, and try to make her feel safe in your hands. I'm going to call and ask her if she's up for visitors."

～

Deborah was happy to get Ken's call. "Come right over," she said.

When they got to her apartment there was coffee and chocolate chip cookies on the table.

"Homemade," she boasted, as they sat around the small dining table.

"They happen to be my favorite, Ms. Hyman," commented Ty. "If Mr. Williams doesn't take any soon I may be tempted to eat all of them."

Ken quickly changed the conversation. "How are you holding up Debbie?"

"I'm okay, Mr. Williams, I think I made the right decision, but it was hard. I don't know whether I could have done this without Dr. Feuerstein's counseling. I've got to repay you someday for all the money you must have paid her."

"Don't worry about it Debbie. It's the least I could have done what with everything you've been through. Now let's talk about something else. I've brought Mr. Cohen here. He's going to be prosecuting your father right after I officially become DA. I thought you should meet and get to know each other."

Debbie looked at Ty Cohen as he finished the last cookie. "I assume, Mr. Cohen, that Mr. Williams has told you everything."

Ty got serious in a hurry. "He had to, Ms. Hyman. I'm deeply sorry for everything that has happened, but I will try my best to make this as tolerable as possible, although it admittedly will be hard. Let's start by calling me Ty."

She seemed impressed by his kindness. "Well Ty, please feel free to call me Debbie."

"Thank you," he politely responded. "I see you have the same first name as the person who wrote that book on your coffee table. Besides your names, you and Deborah Feldman have a lot in common."

"We do, but she was never raped by her father. Have you really read her book?"

"Yes. Mr. Williams' wife gave it to me. As a Reform Jew, I wasn't all that familiar with the Hasidim. The book helped me learn about that world and gave me some insights into what you must have gone through."

"That book, my wonderful mother, and Dr. Feuerstein, all gave me the courage to leave my Hasidic roots and father and make a new life for myself."

As Ty Cohen stood to leave, he asked Debbie: "If it's alright with you, I'd like to come back and start talking to you about how I plan to handle the trial."

He paused for a moment, before adding: "I'll devote all my time to it. I have no domestic distractions."

She gave him a shy smile, but said boldy, "It's hard to believe a nice, good-looking Jewish man like you is not married."

Ty was not used to being at a loss for words, and his face reddened before he sheepishly responded. "I never thought of myself as good-looking, Debbie, but coming from an attractive Jewish girl like you, it's a very nice compliment."

Debbie was blushing as she walked Ken and Ty to the door, but she thanked them for coming and told Ty that she looked forward to "seeing him again soon."

"I'll look forward to it also," said Ty.

"And I'll have more chocolate chip cookies waiting," Debbie said, as she waved goodbye.

⌒

Ken caught up next with Gary, Betsy, Mickey, and Ron Kuby back at Kuby's office.

"Here's what I've been thinking, guys," began Ken. "Gary's coming with me as my chief assistant. Mickey will be my chief investigator.

Betsy can't be part of my team. It's just the price she's got to pay for being married to me. I'm going to have a no-nepotism policy."

"I read your mind before we all got together here, sweetheart. Someone has to take over the practice and keep you sane. I'll put together a new law office."

"Good, it's all set," said a smiling Ken.

"One more thing," interjected Gary. "Tina and I are planning to get married on Christmas in Greece and spend our honeymoon there. You'll all be invited to the wedding."

"That's hot-shit great news," said Mickey. "Let's all go. I'll bring Mouse."

"It's doable," said Ken. "The uncontested general election may be just a few weeks from now, but I don't take office until January 1st. It's perfect timing for one big fat Greek wedding. I'll have Ashanti check out the airfares. Are you going to be doing this in Athens?"

"Tina's got lots of relatives in Greece. They've booked a beautiful facility overlooking the Aegean Sea in a suburb about a half hour from the big city."

"We have lots to celebrate," said Betsy. "What a cool idea."

39

By the time the official results were tallied on election night, Ken Williams had become a celebrity. His picture was everywhere. The next day he was on *Good Morning America* being interviewed by its new hotshot anchorwoman, Nancy Bannister. In the evening he was interviewed by Kelsey Rose on PBS. Betsy had a hard time sorting out all the congratulatory e-mails. And the president of the United States even called to invite him and Betsy to the White House. It was all heady stuff.

James Neary couldn't wait to get out of town. He cleared out his office and rumor had it he was somewhere in the Bahamas. Ken made arrangements to do some modest redecorating of the DA's office, and he and Trish took title to and moved into JoJo's apartment.

With all the moving and the constant inundation by the media, Ken and Betsy were happy to board Delta flight 262 from JFK to Athens, Greece, a few days before Christmas for Gary and Tina's wedding—and their own belated honeymoon. Gary, Tina, Mickey, Mouse, Kuby, and Tina's mom flew with them.

The wedding would take place in front of a small Greek chapel overlooking the beautiful Aegean Sea. Tina had prepared Gary for the ceremony and warned him that it would be long.

They met with Father Goulandreis at his church the day before the wedding. He was the priest at the beautiful church in Agia Marina, a village near Glyfada. Since no Greek priest would marry someone who was not Greek, Gary had become Greek Orthodox, and Father Goulandreis told him the Greek name for Gary was Kiriako.

Gary was surprised to learn that the priest was married and had two children. Father Goulandreis was young and handsome—with his long black hair and close-cropped short black beard. He wore the traditional long black robe. It was trimmed with a deep red sash around the collar. He explained to Kiriako that unlike Roman Catholic priests, Greek Orthodox priests could be married.

Gary liked the sound of his Greek name and told Father Goulandreis that he thought it was a good idea for priests to be allowed to marry.

He asked rhetorically, "I don't suppose you have any Greek priests molesting little boys here?"

Father Goulandreis assured him there was no such thing. "Of course, we have monks, and they are not married," the priest said. "But they are salted away in monasteries and there are no boys there."

"What do they do there?" asked Gary.

"They are truly in love with God, Kiriako," answered Father Goulandreis. "They take care of their monasteries and pray the rest of the time."

⌐⌐

The wedding ceremony the next day was exactly as Tina had told Gary. The two of them asked Tina's two Greek cousins, Christo and Eleni, who lived in Athens, to be the *koumparo* and *koumpara*, the Greek equivalent for best man and maid of honor. Their principal role was to hold the *Stefania*—the crowns of marriage—over Tina and Gary's heads and walk with them and the priest, with the bride and groom's hands tied together, three times around a small table, which held the cross and Holy Bible. In fact, it seemed that everything was done in threes. In addition to the walk-arounds, rings were placed on and off the bride and grooms' ring-fingers on their right hands three times by the *koumparo*, they drank from a common cup of wine three times, and prayers and blessings were recited by the priest three times.

"No wonder the wedding is so goddamn long," Mickey whispered to Mouse, as they stood standing on a rise above the church ground taking it all in. "Can't they do it once and get this torture over with?"

Mouse shot him a dirty look. "Be respectful, Mickey, before He strikes you dead. There's obviously a good reason for it."

After the third circle, the priest gave a benediction before removing the crowns. He then separated the couple's joined hands, took a picture with the married couple, and had the bride, groom, *koumparo,* and *koumpara* sign a document signifying the marriage. With a radiant smile on his face, Father Goulandreis wished them—in English—a "long, happy, fruitful life" together.

After cheers from the onlookers, dinner was served. Gorgeous flowers were arranged on the tables. The American guests had never tasted such an array of mouth-watering Greek appetizers, let alone the succulent lamb on a spit. And the delicious Greek wine from the Peloponnese topped it all off.

Father Goulandreis could not have been more friendly. He stayed for dinner and since the entire service was in Greek, he sat with Mickey and Mouse to explain, in his perfect English, the meaning of what they had just experienced.

"Thanks, Father," said Mickey respectfully. "It's all a mystery to me. But why three times for everything?"

Father Goulandreis patiently explained. "Well three, of course, represents the Father, the Son, and the Holy Spirit. Actually, the service is divided into two parts. The first is the Service of Betrothal or Engagement, during which the rings are exchanged. The second is the Service of Marriage or Crowning, during which prayers are offered for the couple, the crowns of marriage are placed on their heads, the common wine cup is shared, and the ceremonial walks take place around the table."

"But why do they have to walk around three times?" asked Mickey impatiently.

Father Goulandreis knew the question would be asked and was pleased to give a detailed answer. "As the bride and groom are lead around, three significant hymns are sung by the priest. The first speaks of the indescribable joy that Isaiah the Prophet experienced when he envisioned the coming of the Messiah upon the earth."

"But Isaiah was Jewish," exclaimed Mickey.

"Of course," Father Goulandreis quickly responded. "It all sprang from the Old Testament and we honor our Jewish roots."

Mickey was startled. "Wait till I tell my buddy Abe Rosen that the Greeks are really a bunch of Jews."

Father Goulandreis continued undeterred. "The second reminds us of the martyrs of the Faith, who received their crowns of glory from God through the sacrifice of their lives, and reminds the newlyweds of the sacrificial love they must have for one another in their marriage. The third is an exaltation to the Holy Trinity."

Mouse had a question. "What about that wine cup they drank from three times, Father?"

The priest explained, "The common cup serves as a witness that from that moment on, the couple shall share everything in life, joy as well as sorrow, and that they will bear one another's burdens, the token of a life of harmony. Their joy will be doubled and their sorrows halved because they are shared. Whatever the cup of life has in store for them, they will share equally."

"I think the Jews do the same thing," said Mickey. "Looks like you stole everything from them."

Mouse shot him a dirty look, but Father Goulandreis just smiled and said, "I'm not so sure that the Jews did it first, but it doesn't matter. A good idea is a good idea wherever it comes from."

The priest had heard enough and politely excused himself.

Mouse glared at Mickey for what seemed like minutes before she spoke to him. "Mickey, I learned a few Greek words since I've been here and you are one big *malaka*."

"What the fuck does that mean, Mouse?"

"Look it up, jerk," she screamed, her voice rising on the word "jerk."

Soon the Greek band that Tina hired started to play Greek music, and everyone joined in a circle as Christo led the dancing and singing to the traditional *Orea Pou Einai E Nifi Mas*. Tina told Gary it meant "Our Beautiful Bride."

Not to be undone, Ken then sat down at the keyboard and played and sang the song he had written for the newlyweds the same day he had heard Tina's Greek cousins say *se agapame* to Gary.

> In Greece we say
> *Se agapame*
> It's what we sing
> On your wedding day
> But if you can't speak Greek
> Then English must do
> And you just say
> That we all love you

The melody was so catchy that the whole place sang it, louder and louder, over and over again.

After the wedding, they all split off and hit three of the 227 inhabited Greek islands. Gary and Tina went to Santorini, Ken and Betsy went to Mykonos, and Ron Kuby took Tina's mother, Mickey, and Mouse to Spetses—the birthplace and home of Bouboulina, the famous female revolutionary who spearheaded the successful revolt in 1821 against the Turks, who had occupied Greece for four centuries. She was one of Kuby's idols.

They were all back in Brooklyn by New Year's Day for the swearing in of the new district attorney.

40

It was a cold first day in January when Ken stood on the steps of Brooklyn Borough Hall ready to be sworn in as Brooklyn's thirty-fourth district attorney. Three rows of seats had been set up behind him for family, close friends, and an array of dignitaries. Rabbi Horowitz was sitting next to Commissioner Donnelly in the front row. Mickey somehow managed to get the seat on the other side of the police commissioner. Gary, Tina, Ezekial Thomas, and Franco sat in the second row. Trish and Troy were in the third row, next to Debbie Hyman and Ty Cohen who sat holding hands. Debbie's mother sat nearby. She looked pleased.

Pastor Burnham gave the invocation:

"May the Lord bless our new district attorney and give him the wisdom and judgment to do right by his people, and all the people. We all remember Deacon Jones, and we pray that his sacrifice and work on Earth will not have been in vain. I am sure that JoJo is looking down on us now with love in his heart and with pride in the great deeds that Kenneth Williams has accomplished and with confidence that great things lie in the future for this disciple of our Lord Jesus. Amen."

Betsy stood next to Ken holding the Bible as the governor administered the oath.

Ken kept his remarks simple.

"Today marks the beginning of a new era of justice for the people of this great borough. All religions, colors, and genders will truly be treated equally and with respect. My office will be open to all who may have grievances with any authority figure, regardless of their position or status. Thank you all for coming and sharing this special occasion with me. It's time to go to work."

The press was out in full force and had questions for Ken and the governor. The first was for Ken from the predator reporter. He knew it was coming.

"What are you going to do about the Jackson case, Mister DA? It's still technically alive. Your predecessor wouldn't move to dismiss it. He dumped it in your lap."

Ken glared at the reporter that everyone despised before answering.

"You obviously know my feelings about it, Mr. Margiotta, but since I represented Troy it's not going to be up to me. It would be an obvious conflict. I've asked the governor to appoint a special prosecutor to wrap it up. I'm confident that whoever is appointed will realize that it's time to put a formal end to the case and ask the judge to dismiss it."

Margiotta was not done.

"Who's it going to be, Governor? Some rubber stamp for our new DA?"

The governor was quick to respond. "It's the attorney general's call, but I've already asked him to appoint someone who is beyond reproach and is respected by the legal community and the public and who will do what's right. He'll review the entire case and make the final decision. But from what I've read in your paper, it seems as if a great miscarriage of justice has been done by the former DA in bringing that case to court, and I suspect that the quicker we put an end to it, the better for all."

The reporter for the *New York Times* also had a question for the governor.

"What do you plan to do about the former DA and his chief prosecutor, Mr. Racanelli?"

"Good question, Neil. The special prosecutor will also be tasked with investigating whether criminal charges should be brought against them."

The *Times* reporter had a follow-up question.

"'Mr. Governor, Brooklyn is not the only place in the state that has borne the brunt of corrupt public officials. By my calculation over thirty state public officials have been convicted of crimes while you have been governor, the most recent being the speakers of both the Senate and Assembly. Do you plan to do anything to stem the flood of corruption in your administration?"

"It's not a fair question," shot back a clearly agitated governor. "I didn't elect those people, and I've introduced a broad ethics bill this past year. But while we're here, I'll take the occasion to announce that I am going to form a blue ribbon commission to root out corruption in every corner of our great state and rid us of every corrupt politician it uncovers."

"That's a pretty tall order," came a voice from the middle of the reporter's scrum.

"Maybe so, but I'm confident that the head of the commission will make it a hallmark of my administration and see to it that those who have abused their public trust are prosecuted and sent to jail."

"And who might that special person be, Governor?" came another voice.

"He's standing right next to me," shot back the governor.

Ken tried to remain unfazed, but he had no idea this was coming.

⌥

Two days later, as he was hanging some pictures of himself and Betsy in Mykonos in his new office, Ken received a call from John Horan, the governor's general counsel, who told him the attorney general had appointed James Gleeson as the special prosecutor.

Ken knew Gleeson from the old days when they both were Assistant United States Attorneys. Gleeson had successfully prosecuted John Gotti—the "Teflon Don"—and had then been appointed by President Clinton to the federal bench and served with distinction as a United States District Judge for many years before he left the bench to return to private practice. He was so highly regarded that the attorney general thought he would be the perfect person to wrap up the Jackson case and also to determine whether criminal charges would be warranted against Neary and Racanelli.

Gleeson called Ken the next day to schedule an appointment.

"Looks like we've both come a long way from our days in the Office, Ken."

The reference to the "Office" hit a responsive chord. It was the buzzword for the Eastern District United States Attorney's Office and all those who had "the privilege" of being an EDNY AUSA there. Ken and Gleeson were bonded members of that "club."

"I'm glad you're going to be doing this, Jim. They couldn't have picked a better man. I would like to get this out of the way as soon as possible so I don't have to be distracted from all the things I have to do now to shape things up here—and purge Neary's taint."

Gleeson was understanding. "I'll get on it right away. But I have the responsibility to do my due diligence. I just can't sweep it under the rug. As soon as you get the files of the trial together, I'll send someone down to pick them up and get right to work. From what I've read about it, I imagine I will be able to turn it around pretty quickly."

Ken was confident that Gleeson would agree that the Jackson case should now be dismissed. "Thanks, Jim. That's all I can ask for. I'm sure you'll find it smells like hell."

⌁

It didn't take long. Two weeks later, Gleeson came to see Ken.

"I couldn't believe my eyes," he told Ken. "How could Racanelli stoop that low to get a phony conviction? I'm going to recommend that he be prosecuted. And I suspect that Neary will have to also stand charges for his misappropriation of public forfeiture funds. I'll be scheduling an appearance before Judge Cogan in the next day or so to move formally for the dismissal of the Jackson indictment."

"I'm pleased that you agree with me, Jim. The case against that poor Jackson kid was rotten to the core," said Ken.

Just then, Ashanti, who now was sitting comfortably in Naomi Moskowitz's old chair, buzzed Ken on the intercom to tell him that Gerald Shargel, the famous criminal defense lawyer, was waiting outside.

"Somehow he knew that you had an appointment with Mr. Gleeson and said that it was imperative that he speak to both of you."

Ken and Gleeson had a lot of respect for Shargel. He was also one of the boys from the old days at the Office.

"Alright, Ashanti, send him in," Ken said.

They greeted each other warmly, like old fraternity brothers.

"Good morning, Gerry," said Ken. "You're looking dapper as ever. Private practice has been good to you. That looks like a suit I couldn't afford."

"What can I say, guys. I've been representing some bad people with lots of bucks. Gleeson is going to be doing the same thing now with that big fancy firm that he joined. But I confess I'm a little jealous, Ken. There's no higher calling than the path you have chosen. You'll make a great DA."

"Thanks Gerry, but I suspect you're not here to make idle chatter. What brings you to town?"

"Actually, I wanted to talk to the special prosecutor. I called his office, but they told me he had an appointment to see you. I'm glad I caught the two of you together. I have a new client who contacted me yesterday, and he wants to cut a deal. As you will see, time is of the essence."

"Do you really think it's appropriate for you to barge in on us right now to discuss a cooperation agreement?" asked Ken, clearly upset.

"I would not be here otherwise."

"Who is this important new client? asked Gleeson, curiously.

"Rufus Kong, better known as King Kong. They found him in Puerto Rico and charged him with running the biggest drug business for the Columbian cartels in the last decade. He was the Brooklyn connection. A lot of the stuff was found in a stash house on Chess Street. He's prepared to testify that he saw Troy Jackson shoot Menachem Mendel Bernstein."

"He wouldn't be the first," shot back a furious DA. "We've already done that dance with Neary's cooperators. We don't need to go there again."

"Yes, you do. You are the DA now. You've taken the oath to do the right things. And anyway, the Jackson case is no longer yours. It's now in the hands of the special prosecutor."

Ken could not believe what was going on.

"Why is this not just another cooperator willing to say anything to save his neck? There's a big odor here already."

"I understand, Ken, but King Kong has what he likes to call a 'Get Out of Jail Video.' You can watch the whole thing in glowing Technicolor. Just how Wee Willie Wexler described it. The King's a video buff and a pretty shrewd guy. He never dirtied his hands directly. When a big drug deal went down, or any hit, he videoed it. It was his safety valve. If he ever got picked up, he figured he could easily cut a deal. The jury would not have to believe him. The video would say it all."

Ken Williams sunk in his chair. Three days later, Special Prosecutor James Gleeson appeared before Judge Cogan and asked him to set a date for the retrial of LaTroy Jackson.

Epilogue

The overarching story is, of course, the trials (literally) and tribulations of the protagonist Ken Williams. His character was fashioned after Ken Thompson, the African-American lawyer who came from nowhere in 2013 to improbably defeat the reigning longterm Brooklyn District Attorney Charles Hynes. In 2016 Ken sadly passed away from an unexpected illness at just fifty years old, leaving a wife and two young children. But during his regrettably brief time as Brooklyn's new DA he had instituted needed criminal justice reforms and earned the public's admiration. This book is dedicated to his memory.

Ken Thompson's successful campaign against Charles Hynes was fueled in large part by his relentless attacks against the former DA and two of his principal subordinates, Michael Vecchione and Louis Scarcella, for obtaining tainted murder convictions against blacks. This inspired the highly fictionalized characters of James Neary and Anthony Racanelli.

There were many tainted convictions. I have essentially told the true stories about a number of them. The principal one, of course, was the inspiration for JoJo Jones. In real life he is Jabbar Collins, who indeed was convicted for murdering a Hasidic rabbi and spent sixteen years in jail before being exonerated.

Vecchione's misdeeds, leading to Collins' exoneration at the habeas hearing, and Hynes' condonation of his chief prosecutor's behavior, are accurately reported in the decision I wrote denying the City's motion to dismiss Collins' civil lawsuit. As I explained, my colleague Judge Irizzary concluded at the hearing that Vecchione was indeed complicit in strong-arming the key witness to testify untruthfully at Collins' trial, and, moreover, he failed to inform Collins' lawyer that the witness had orally recanted his testimony—an omission in violation of his *Brady* obligations. This was shocking. Prosecutors just can't behave that way—it's against our Constitution. As for Hynes, Judge Irizarry noted that he would not acknowledge Vecchione's wrongdoings and she called his office's conduct "shameful" and "a tragedy."

Hynes publicly supported Vecchione and paid the price by being the first long-term Brooklyn DA in memory to go down to defeat in a Democratic primary. He left office under a cloud as a result of the report from the New York City Department of Investigations that he allegedly wrongfully used public forfeiture funds to help finance his campaign. In addition, his good friend, the chief administrative judge of the Brooklyn state courts, resigned when it was also disclosed in that report that the judge was taking an active part in the campaign, which is against the Judicial Code of Conduct. Subsequent to Thompson's election, the U.S. Attorney's office, after a full investigation, determined that no criminal charges would be brought against either Hynes or Vecchione. As for the former judge, who is a past president of the prestigious Federal Bar Council, he has returned to private practice and enjoys a fine professional reputation.

Hynes' fall from grace was a tragedy. Other than the regrettable misdeeds I have here recounted, he made notable contributions during his twenty-four-year tenure as Brooklyn's DA in addressing important criminal justice issues. For example, he initiated the Drug Treatment Alternative-to-Prison Program (DTAP) to help drug-addicted nonviolent felons return to society. He also created the ComALERT (Community and Law Enforcement Resources Together) public safety program which supports individuals on probation or parole as they re-enter their Brooklyn communities; the program was validated by a Harvard University study which found that it reduced recidivism by more than half. And he is credited with establishing one of the most comprehensive programs designed to specifically address domestic abuse as a criminal issue; moreover, with the collaboration of former Mayor Giuliani, he implemented a citywide program to monitor convicted domestic violence offenders.

While the guts of the Collins habeas case are true, I have taken literary license with how it unfolded before Judge Gonzales/Irizarry with the fictionalized testimony of Solomon Butler and the other trial witnesses, and the deep-sixing of Solomon's fictionalized letter. And everything else about the Hynes and Vecchione characters is also fictionalized, except in two respects: The reports of Hynes' currying political favor with the Hasidim has been reported in the press and, in particular, in a lengthy article by Rachel Aviv in *The New Yorker* recounting the Sam Kellner criminal investigation. And it is true that many other blacks who were convicted and imprisoned while Hynes was DA have been exonerated.

After Ken Thompson took office, he appointed a still-active blue-ribbon committee chaired by three distinguished attorneys, Gary Villanueva, Bernard Nussbaum, and Jennifer Rodgers, to review more than fifty allegedly improper convictions, resulting so far in an astounding twenty-one exonerations. Vecchione was only implicated in a few of these prosecutions; virtually all of them were reported to be the handiwork of former detective, Louis Scarcella, who did indeed use the same witness—the late Theresa Gomes—in at least three of his trials.

⁓

Ken Thompson had tried a case before me many years ago when he was an Assistant United States Attorney in the Brooklyn U.S. Attorney's office, and I was a pretty new judge. Neither of us knew then that years later the Collins case would be a cornerstone of his primary campaign, and that I would be the federal judge who wrote the decision in Collins' civil lawsuit, triggering a ten million dollar settlement of the case.

The essence of Collins' plight, in the personage of his namesake JoJo Jones, is therefore true, including his profound jailhouse lawyering. But otherwise JoJo's travails and testimony and behavior at the habeas hearing, as well as the aftermath, were the product of my imagination.

In addition to Thompson's political campaign against Hynes, the inspiration for the other key part of the book—Ken's representation of the Troy Jackson character—flowed from two trials before me of a twenty-two-year-old African American, who was accused as a member of a gang in one of the crime-infested Brooklyn projects of killing a rival drug dealer six years before. The first jury hung, but he was acquitted of the murder at the retrial. I was fascinated that this young man, who was then leading a law-abiding life, had to have his world uprooted and came so close to spending the rest of his life in jail. While the inspiration was real, the entire story about Troy and Trish Jackson, the post-incarceration criminal activities of the fictionalized Menachem Mendel Bernstein, and the surrounding cast of principal characters—the Chess Street Crew, Betsy, Gary, Ezekial, Rabbi Horowitz, Ashanti, Naomi Moskowitz, A. Cecil Leonard, the gang at Arturo's, the newsmen, TV hosts, Drs. Anagnostou, Gold, Feuerstein, and my wonderful personal doctor, the real Martin Post, and, of course, Mickey and Mouse—are all my creations.

I have peppered the book with lots of other true accounts that riveted me when they happened and advance the story. The Louima, Dunne, Diallo, and Plaza Hotel maid cases are largely true, but the names and portrayals of all the police officers, the Italian diplomat, the diplomat's lawyer, and the maid have been fictionalized, as well as the criminal exploits of Officer Ciarán O'Reilly. In real life Ciarán is the wonderful Artistic Director and cofounder with Charlotte Moore (our jury foreperson) of the Irish Repertory theater, which is one of the finest off-Broadway theaters in New York. Also true are the stories of those judges and the female prosecutor who were the victims of disgruntled revengeful litigants and the shock-jock radio commentator, including the death threat I received from Gaspipe Casso.

As for the police, while the Abner Louima episode did regrettably occur at the 70th precinct, there is no Officer Markham I know who works there; I simply borrowed the last name of the fiancé of one of my daughters.

And while I have accurately reported the ongoing stop-and-frisk dynamics, I have profound respect for the men in blue and the daily dangers they encounter in keeping New York safe.

My recounting of the Crown Heights trials is accurate. In that regard, the reader probably has correctly surmised that—in addition to writing the opinion in Collins' civil lawsuit—I was the Judge Felix Black who presided over Lemrick Nelson's last trial. However, Hynes' role as well as the introduction and development of the characters Lillian Bloom and the predator reporter Jimmy Margiotta are all made-up, except in one respect.

There was a reporter for the *Daily News*—John Marzulli—who, until recently, covered the Brooklyn federal court, and he had throughout the years taken whatever opportunities he could to paint "Judge Black" in an unfavorable light. It started when I was the front-page headline of his newspaper, and Marzulli wrote a story highly critical of my anti-death penalty comments during a murder trial where the government was seeking the ultimate penalty. I had questioned whether it might be a waste of time and taxpayer monies, since it was improbable that the jury would vote for death under the circumstances of the case.

I was right, but was taken to task by Marzulli for being so outspoken, and it earned me the appellation of "Judge Blockhead." Ever since, Marzulli was the veritable fox in the judge's henhouse. The most recent shot was his account of my grant of a suppression motion in a stop-and-frisk case, which led the *Post* to branding me a "lunatic judge." My comments about the case that I made from the bench are accurately reported and highlight the dangers to the independence of the judiciary when newspapers are more bent on entertaining their readers than responsibly reporting the challenges facing judges in the discharge of their oath to apply the rule of law.

Be that as it may, there is little a judge can do to take on the press, and surely if Marzulli reads this book, the "predator reporter" may say more nasty things about "Judge Blockhead." I hope, however, that he has a sense of humor and gets a kick out of my "revenge."

⌇

There are many more true parts. The conditions at Rikers and the SHU are accurate, as well as the suicides; but the names of the victims have been fictionalized out of respect to their families, and I've taken literary license with the time frames to fit the flow of the story.

Although today he is respected by many as a leading spokesperson for racial harmony, Al Sharpton's past is accurately reported from many reliable public accounts and is used as a counterpoint to the development of Ken Thompson's character. And the comments made by the public officials and the families of victims in the "Black Lives Matter" march in New York City are all accurate. So too is Ron Kuby's bio; however, I have taken liberty with his character to make him, with his consent, a fictionalized part of the book.

The account of Sam Kellner and the reaction of the Hasidim to his going public about their efforts to cover up the sexual misdeeds of a member of the Hasidic community, as reported in *The New Yorker* article, led to the made-up story of Shmuel Hyman and the plight of his wife and daughter, but the quotes from the anti-abortion proponents, even for rape, are accurate, as well as the story of Deborah Feldman and her book.

A word of caution about the Hasidim. Their history and lifestyle are accurate, especially their view of the role of their women, but by no means did I intend to denigrate them. They are a by-product of a brutal anti-Semitic history, and devote much of their lives to doing good deeds in our troubled world. They are a respected and revered part of the fabric of their communities.

And then there's Brooklyn. In a way, the book is a tribute to that wonderful borough, and the places where I have taken the reader, including the two restaurants, David's Brisket House and the Queen (with its wonderful maître d', Franco), and, in Manhattan, Arturo's, are all accurately depicted. So too is the recounting of *The Merchant of Venice* and the two religious rituals of the laying of *tefillin* at the Hasidic synagogue and the Greek Orthodox wedding. And so, too, is the extraordinary Christian Cultural Center; obviously Pastor A.R. Burnham is in real life the center's great spiritual leader A.R. Bernard.

Finally, a word or two about the names I have used. I have taken literary license to use the last names of many of my judicial colleagues, but there is no correlation between their characters and the truth. However, Judges Scheindlin's and Glasser's cases are correctly reported. And John Gleeson—Jim Gleeson in the book—was a distinguished colleague of mine before he recently returned to private practice; and he did successfully try the John Gotti case when he was an AUSA.

Notably, the judges of my court, which is the Eastern District of New York, collectively comprise an outstanding bench, of which I am proud to be a part.

I think I have parsed the principal reality and fictional parts of the book, except for one more thing: Ken Williams' musical chops are fashioned after my piano playing and song-writing hobbies. Yes, I did indeed write all the songs—and the charts are in the Songbook. Moreover, as I explained in the my note to the reader at the beginning of the book, they have been recorded and can be streamed through my website and all digital services. And, of course, if the book ever becomes a movie. . . .

Good Instead of Bad

Look What She's Costing Me Now

Lonesome Together With You

Everybody Wants to Go to Heaven

Country Western

Voice

Every-bo-dy wants _____ to go to Heaven But no-bo - dy wants to
So _____ if I e - - - ver get to Heaven I'm ne - ver go-nna tell a
I'm not sure _____ I'll go to Heaven Or the place _____ where the devil re-

die And an - y-one who tells you differ-ent-ly is ly-ing.
lie You'll ne - ver see me look-ing miser-ab-ly or cry-ing.
sides Whe-ther I'll end up an - ge-li-cally or fry-ing.

While I want e - ter-nal peace of mind I'm not read-y to leave this
When I'm in my fi - nal rest-ing place There'll _____ be a big smile up-
But on my judg-ment day, I'll say a - men And _____ say the same things to

world be - hind Cause no - bo-dy's seen _____ that big guy in the sky
on my face Cause here's what I'll tell _____ that big guy in the sky
both of them The de - vil him-self and the big guy in the sky

That's why I'll al-ways be _____ the lo-ving kind And I'm _____ not li-ving life
I al-ways was _____ the lo-ving kind _____ I ne-ver lived life
I'll say I'm glad I was _____ the lo-ving kind _____ I ne-ver lived my _____ life

wast-ing my time _____ I try to make _____ the most _____ of ev-e-ry day _____
wast-ing my time _____ I tried to make _____ the most _____ of ev-er-y day _____
wast-ing my time _____ I tried to make _____ the most _____ of e-ve-ry day _____

I drink good whi-skey, I have good friends I'm li - vin' and lov - in' 'til my
I drank good whi-skey, I had good friends I lived _____ and loved _____ 'til my
I drank good whi-skey, I had good friends And lived _____ and loved _____ 'til my

earth-ly end _____ Cause wait-ing for the next life ain't the na-tu-ral way
earth-ly end _____ Cause wait-ing for the next life wasn't the na-tu-ral way.
earth-ly end _____ Cause wait-ing for the next life ain't the na-tu-ral way

So if I Wait-ing for the next life Ain't the na-tu-ral way.
I'm not
'Cause

350

Like Father Like Son

High and Dry

How I'll Always Love You

1. How I'll al-ways love you
2. Now's the Time to tell you
3. We're a luck-y cou-ple

How I'll al-ways care
how our love just grew
With your ma-gic flair

Ne-ver need to fear dear
ev'r-y time you said to me
And with all my love for you

Al-ways I'll be there
that you love me too.
We're a per-fect pair

2. No more when or whe-ther
3. a spe-cial feel ing

No more need to wait
What more can I say

Fi-na-lly to-
You make me so

2X Go To Measure 17
ge-ther
ha-ppy

Time to ce-le-brate

D.C. al Coda   *Coda*

On this our we-dding day

Se Agapame

foxtrot

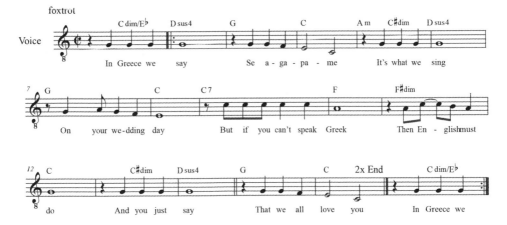

In Greece we say   Se a-ga-pa-me   It's what we sing

On your we-dding day   But if you can't speak Greek   Then En-glish must

do   And you just say   That we all love you   In Greece we

ACKNOWLEDGMENTS

In 2001, Kenzi Sugihara left a long and distinguished career in traditional publishing houses (lastly as a vice president and publisher at Random House) to create—together with his wife, Nancy, and their son, Kenichi—SelectBooks, Inc. From that date to the present, the Sugiharas have published over two hundred highly regarded fiction and nonfiction books. I am fortunate to have my book added to that number. One simply could not ask for a better publisher than SelectBooks, and I cherish the extraordinary personal support and care each Sugihara has given me: Kenzi, as the leader of the pack, selected *Race to Judgment* for publication; Kenichi took control of its marketing; Nancy took charge of the editing process and with her co-editor, Lara Asher, fastidiously attended to every detail to make the book as good as it could be.

There are many others to whom I want to express my gratitude. First, Steve Zissou and his wife, Sally, wined and dined me at their beautiful villa in Kia, Greece when I plotted out the story and appropriated their last name for my black Joe Pesci-ish private eye. And Joe Tessitore read the first draft and gave me great ideas on character development and the charm of "putting Brooklyn" in the book. He also introduced me to Jim Zebora who, early on, provided valuable editorial help.

Next—in no necessary order—I thank Ron Fischetti for bringing Joe to me, my cousin Leslie Chosed, for encouraging me to never give up, and my friends who read the book and made valuable edits and suggestions: Henry Miller, John Horan, Frank Velie, Gary Villanueva, Steve Hyman, Marshall Cohen, and Al Kellman, as well as my judicial colleagues, Brian Cogan, Ray Dearie, and Dora Irizarry.

And I thank my law clerks, Geoffrey Johnson, Nick Phillips, Daniel Horowitz, Gillian Kuhlman, Ty Cone, and Colleen Faherty for their invaluable research and suggestions in their extracurricular spare time; never once did they compromise their judicial responsibilities to lend a hand.

A special thanks to Doug Wigdor, Ken Thompson's ex-partner, for introducing me to the Christian Cultural Center and to Pastor Bernard—who gave the book his blessings—and to my court's Chief Marshal, Charles Dunne, for his firearms tutorial.

A special thanks also to Peter DiZossa for creating the music charts in the Songbook, to Steve Edwards for helping record my songs, to Zach Bloom for making them available to the reader through my website, to my conscientious and invaluable PR team, headed by Jane Wesman, and to Steve Kalafer and his wife, Suzanne, for their special entrepreneurial and promotional skills in their efforts to make the book a commercial (as well as literary) success.

Thanks also to my brother and Shakespeare scholar, Len, and my sister-in-law, Naomi, for their support, and last, but certainly not least, to my girls Debbie and Tina, and their mother Betsy, my wife. Without their love and constant encouragement this book would not have happened (and, of course, I would have had to make up different names for three of the main characters).

About the Author

FREDERIC BLOCK was appointed United States District Judge for the Eastern District of New York on September 29, 1994, and entered duty on October 31, 1994. He assumed senior status on September 1, 2005. He received a bachelor's degree from Indiana University in 1956 and an LL.B. Degree from Cornell Law School in 1959.

During his twenty-three years on the bench, Judge Block has presided over a number of high-profile cases, including the criminal trials of former Bear Stearns hedge fund managers Ralph Cioffi and Matthew Tannin, Kenneth "Supreme" McGriff, Peter Gotti, Lemrick Nelson, and nightclub magnate Peter Gatien. He regularly sits by designation on the Ninth Circuit Court of Appeals.

In 2012 Judge Block authored *Disrobed: An Inside Look at the Life and Work of a Federal Trial Judge*. He also coauthored the 1985 off-Broadway musical *Professionally Speaking* (music and lyrics). He has published articles on a variety of legal topics, including "Tales of an 'Active' Senior Judge," *ABA Litigation Journal*, Spring 2011; "Reflections on Guns and Jury Nullification and Judicial Nullification," *The Champion*, July 2009; "Senior Status: An 'Active' Senior Judge Corrects Some Common Misunderstandings," 92 *Cornell Law Review*. 533 (2007); and "Civil Liberties During National Emergencies: The Interactions Between the Three Branches of Government in Coping with Past and Current Threats to the Nation's Security," 29 *N.Y.U. Review of Law and Social Change* 459 (2005). He was also a contributing author for *Perspectives on 9/11* (Yassin El-Ayouty ed., 2004), and for the New York State Bar Association's textbook *Federal Civil Practice*. In 2007 he penned a *New York Times* op-ed addressing the financial burdens of death penalty prosecutions.